Quantum Women
by Tyree Campbell

Quantum Women
By Tyree Campbell

Cover illustration: "Quantum Women" copyright 2015 by Laura Givens
Cover design by Laura Givens

First printing October 2015

Nomadic Delirium Press
Aurora, Colorado
http://www.nomadicdeliriumpress.com

For Lorraine Pinelli Brown –
friend and supporter, writer, Delta reader . . . quantum
woman

Contents

Introduction to Quantum Women

A quantum is a self-contained unit—of energy, light, and so forth. It exists in and of itself, irrespective of its surroundings. But it can be, and usually is, part of a team.

A quantum woman, then, is a self-contained person, independent, yet willing to be part of a team if the right teammate comes along.

Quantum women aren't superheroines with superpowers, they're not "chicks in chain mail," although they might be, as Pamela Sargent wrote, "Women of Wonder." One or two of them might remind you of Jim C. Hines' characters, who challenged guys with a "do we look like we need rescuing?" For the most part, quantum women are everyday folks in a science fiction or fantasy setting. They might be home-makers or home-wreckers, homely or homey, but all of them are focused, determined, willful, and independent. To those who have men in their lives, they are partners and companions, equals and not subordinates.

And yet, like any of us, they find themselves in extraordinary situations where a bit of heroism can save the day. Here, on these pages, are the ones you'll encounter.

In "A Nice Girl like You," a freelance mercenary named Emer Bridget McClafferty acts on her own behalf to stop a corporation called Genetic Detailing, or GenTail, from developing DNA splices that would enable them to rule humanity. Assisting her in this project is Tsebieh, one of GenTail's victims, whose DNA is a mishmash of human, vegetable, and cheetah, among others. But Tsebieh has one talent that GenTail does not know about. The question is, will she use it to assist Emer?

"Vapors" was inspired by a line from "Trouble," an Indigo Girls song, in which "every girl can have a wife." Such relationships are easy to form on other worlds, where there are far more important matters to concern folks. But when a couple returns to Earth to find out why there is no more space exploration, they discover that Order has been imposed over the entire planet. No deviations permitted.

"Gallium Girl" was originally published under another title, but for this collection I decided that this was more appropriate. It's a coming-of-age lesbian werewolf tale that hopefully will become one day the first chapter in a novel.

A magazine called *Not One of Us* had the good sense to publish "Skellig" some years ago. The story title comes from the title of a Loreena McKennitt song, about the preservation of knowledge by monks during the dark ages—Skellig being an Irish monastery. The story takes place, however, on the coast of Oregon, where a supernatural being issues one final temptation to the last woman on Earth.

"Striations" is a tale of atonement, as seen through the eyes of an adolescent girl marooned on Ganymede.

In medieval China, storytellers used to inscribe their tales on stones in villages, and folks would come around to read them. "That I might sleep . . ." tells of what happens, in an alien society, when storystones are forbidden and one storyteller violates the restriction.

Every lake has a Lady. Some of them are teenagers, and maybe they don't care for their jobs. Duty calls in "Acorns"—but does it call loudly enough?

The early population of the Old West, and doubtless of other pioneer societies, was predominately male, which meant there was a need for wives. A booming business thus formed around mail order brides. "Home for Supper" tells of the problems encountered by one such mail order bride . . . on Mars.

"Devotional" was originally intended to present some of the back story of a character in a novel (*The Quinx Effect*). But it also stands by itself as a tale of pluck and determination in the face of very cruel adversity.

"Starlet" takes a common, humdrum occupation—customer service—and removes one of its more skillful practitioners to interview for the same sort of work, but with unusual benefits.

In some areas of India, widows were expected to throw themselves on the funeral pyres of their husbands. This act was called suttee, also spelled sati. "Suttee" deals with a situation among the Jovian moons, and a woman who has just lost her rebellious husband. She cannot go on without him, but her culture forbids her to kill herself. What then?

"Tree Hugger" was written for an alien vampire publication. Not all vampires go after blood, you know. This one is a dryad, and is addicted to tree sap. When she arrives on Earth, she discovers that the indigenous sentient population (that would be us) engages in tree abuse.

Equality between the genders comes in two forms: *de jure* and *de facto*. The argument as to whether there will ever be *de jure* equality in a male-dominated society can be made elsewhere. In space, the early settlements (will) consist of pioneer societies, where women and men are forced to work together to survive. Space, after all, is merciless and indiscriminate—it does not care whether you are a man or a woman when it kills you. In pioneer societies on other worlds, then, de facto equality obtains . . . at first. After survival is assured, and industry begins to make footholds, gender roles develop . . .

"The Martian Women," which closes this collection, is the tale of five generations of women on Mars, and takes you from pioneer society through industrial society to . . . a future where *everyone* has to work together to survive—for all time.

Come meet the quantum women.

Tyree Campbell
Colo, IA
August 2015

A Nice Girl Like You

"She just sat down at the corner table," said Big Gooey.

I braced myself with a slug of bootleg Jameson's before turning my head discreetly toward Tsebieh. "She looks human," I said, after he had wiped the counter around my drink with a flourish. The maneuver failed to repair the maculate condition of the faux hardwood.

"DNA splice," explained Big Gooey, as he probed his ear with the point of a tusk the size of my forearm. He looked strong enough to have removed it from the creature while it was still alive. His mustache bristled, the last twitch of a sepia burrowing animal that had crawled onto Gooey's lip only to succumb to his breath. "Experimental thing. She shoulda died."

I looked again. Tsebieh was not of that physical type which invites second glances. She was sitting on a bench at a window booth on this side of the Universe, at just enough angle for me to catch the tiny downward curls of the corners of her mouth while a stevedore from a galleon newly arrived at the Spaceport braced an arm on the table and broached his offer. Nobody ever fell in love here in the *Tarry A'Dea*, but now and then some of the patrons tumbled into lust. Anyone could see from the expression on her face that she was having none of it—anyone except the stevedore. As he leaned down, placing more weight on his arm, Tsebieh made a little move quicker than my eye could follow, and in the next instant the stevedore's chin cracked on the tabletop and the wrist of that arm was in her grasp just above the debris-cluttered floor. She had slender, pale fingers, delicate-looking in the shadows under the table, yet clearly she held his limb in a grip of iron. Her mouth moved, and words whistled just far enough to reach his ears and his alone. Then she released him, and he departed, rather more swiftly than he had arrived, blood welling through the gash in his chin and dripping onto his traveled gray pullover, where it added to an unsavory retinue of other stains.

"Does she ever say 'yes' to anyone?" I asked Big Gooey.

For an instant Gooey's eyes darkened to tangerine, and I knew I'd asked a borderline question. Everyone has a history. Those who don't want theirs probed sometimes migrate out here to Chthonia, living *ad hoc* lives, unable for a variety of reasons to return to their worlds of origin, and he was wondering whether I'd meant to violate the no-pry rule. Then the eyes reverted to their normal color, not quite lemon, not quite pus, and under the mustache his thick lips parted in what was, for him, a flicker of amusement.

"Depends on the question, Mac."

I'd seen no need to burden him with Emer Bridget McClafferty, which is what appeared in the natal records long ago and far away, or with any of the other names I'd adopted during the subsequent thirty seven Standard years. Big Gooey would presume an alias no matter what I gave him, and "Mac" was generic enough to render plausible, if necessary, a case of mistaken identity.

Nursing the first two drinks, I hadn't revealed what it was I wanted to ask Tsebieh, only that I had need of assistance from someone of her reputed talents. It was unnecessary to add a wink and a nudge. Big Gooey knew damn well what I was referring to, and he wanted in the worst way to ask me just how the hell I'd come to know about her, but he, too, had to maintain the no-pry protocols, although, being a bartender, he was permitted considerable leeway.

I scanned the rack of tins against the wall behind him. "Warm up a bowl of *gretel*, please. And side it with some of those crackers."

Big Gooey's eyebrows merged like rutting caterpillars as he fulfilled the request, setting the nuke to a proper 356 degrees Kelvin and the timer to twenty five seconds. I spread three small silver coins on the countertop, and as the nuke signaled the end of its programmed task they disappeared into Gooey's huge paw. Whatever his opinion of my imminent ploy, he would not interfere.

The uncovered stoneware tureen Gooey presented me on a saucer contained a viscous brick-red liquid full of pink and reseda vermiform chunks. Proper *gretel* resembles nothing so much as "entrail stew," and although this had come from a tin, it retained the pungent, distinctive odor of decomposition. Gingerly I carried the tureen and its steaming repast to her table, and noted the do-not-disturb frown with which she greeted me.

She had the rich voice of a cello, played with a taut steel bow. "I

11

ordered nothing."

"This is for me."

She arched one auburn eyebrow at me, her only response.

I remained standing. "I can't remember whether you mix the crackers into the *gretel*, or eat them separately. I was hoping you'd know."

She gave me a five-count. "It makes no difference."

"Thanks. I didn't want to insult the meal by—"

"Sit down."

I did so. After another pause, Tsebieh said, "*Gretel* probably won't do you any harm, but I doubt you'll like it."

"So you think I should just eat the crackers?"

"You've done your homework."

"Some of it. Not enough. Would you care for this, then?"

She gazed out into the moonless night, her pale eyes shadowed by the infinite black and by a past I could only guess at. You don't escape from GenTail's Abyss without killing someone. Even someone with her gifts would have to dispatch the field generator tech.

"It's not magic, what I do," Tsebieh said, still fixed on the blackness. Her words spilled onto my ears like spring rain, just before the flowers come up. If I hadn't remembered she possessed an alimentary canal capable of digesting *gretel*, I might have been entranced. "It's mathematical. That's why the field generator works. There are limitations. I can only go to places I've been, or seen, or have a clear vision of. And I must be in physical contact with the world of their location. And no, I don't read minds. They had developed the DNA splice for that, but upon further consideration realized that their own minds would become transparent as well. Possibly one day they'll develop a splice that will enable someone to block a mind probe..." Suddenly her eyes widened. Then, turning back to me, she said very softly, "No. Besides, all the data for the telepathy splice is on computer. No hard copies. And the computer is absolutely impenetrable. It's the ultimate no-hacking zone. There's even a dampening field surrounding it, a countermeasure against explosives."

Tsebieh was talking too much. I wondered how long she had

examined the possibilities from all angles, weighing this method of entry against that, measuring obstacles against her abilities, until futility set in. She'd begun life as a vegetable, and now, on Chthonia, she was regressing to that mental state.

Slowly, almost imperceptibly, the tureen of *gretel* slid across the tabletop to her...and vanished, as did she.   But she left me the crackers.

👁👁👁

Like taverns everywhere that cater to clandestine activities limited by various ill-conceived statutes, the *Tarry A'Dea* let rooms on its second level for various periods of time, some measured in minutes, some in years.   During prolonged absences from their normal surroundings, people become lonely or bored, and biological relief without the complications of emotional attachments can be had, like any other goods or services, for a price. (You pay someone to cut your hair, right?   Although you could cut it yourself, someone else, properly trained, makes a better job of it, right?) On the way to the stairs and up, I received no less than three come-hithers, including one from a young woman whose maculate attire and disheveled condition clearly bespoke a desperation for funds. Passing her by, I scrawled a mental note to have Big Gooey present her with a complimentary meal or two, and arrange for her to "find" a couple leafs of folded currency. As to the other offers, while I certainly appreciate a man who comes and goes, I was not in the mood. Tsebieh had vanished from the booth, but now that we had established contact, however tenuous, she might pop in at any time. And there are some activities that should not be popped-in upon.

I'd taken a room at the far end of the hallway, next to the emergency exit—events that constitute emergencies are not limited to fires, and in my line of work it's always prudent to have multiple escape routes.   The touchpad on the wall beside the doorjamb accepted the code Gooey had given me, and as the door slid open the traditional odors of old exhalations, stale love, and something edible left out too long whistled past me and down the hallway like liberated ghosts. A dim ceiling panel began to glow at a touch to the wall pad, yielding just enough light for me to see that the single room was unoccupied and that the bed was empty, covered, and too small for two—although, to be fair, couples in this room seldom slept far apart, if at all. The single window was closed, the heavy drapes pulled, and I doubted there was enough light to silhouette me to the casual viewer outside. In the shadows of a far corner stood a rack on which I might hang my clothing, and beside that a commode and a sink. If I wanted a shower, I'd have to use the common room.

The bed squeaked when I sat down, further dampening any nocturnal ambitions I might have had. There were places in the Universe where the rhythms of life were accompanied by cheers and applause, but not here, where yielding bedsprings announced the vulnerability of one or both of the participants to anyone who would do harm. Perforce celibate, I could only wait for developments, and doze cautiously in the meantime.

I reckoned more than half the night had passed by the time Tsebieh entered. She did not use the door. In one moment I was alone, in the next she was standing before me, and in the next I had the ancient military automatic pistol out and aimed at her gut.

She withdrew a pace. "What is *that*?"

I carry a pistol because most security detectors are keyed to plastic and energy cells, not to metal, and because firing it makes enough noise to startle an adversary, a useful advantage in the event the first bullet fails to find its mark. I did not tell her this.

"Next time, knock," I groused.

Long ago Tsebieh had been developed as an alien sentient species—they'd done good work on her. The light that shone from above and behind her cast her face in delicate grays and glows, the humanizing effect startling, and I averted my eyes, blinking away the entrancement.

"I'm not going back there."

"You don't have to," I said. "Just get me inside."

"You're insane."

And I thought, *Insane is what they did to you.*

Between the booth and now she'd changed to a rugged travel outfit of cammie jacket and denims, and sturdy black boots. Chthonia is not known for ease of terrain. She'd made up her mind to flee into

14

the hinterlands.

So why come to see me?

I patted the bed beside me. "Sit down, Tsebieh."

Given what usually took place in this room, her hesitation was understandable. But she obeyed, maintaining a discreet forearm-length of distance between us, pale eyes wary in the dim light. A hint of lilac mixed with the musk she emitted, the blend as effective as pheromones. In my research I had not considered how the spliced DNA might affect her sexuality, except to hypothesize that they would not want her to reproduce unless it was under their auspices. Now, in proximity, she became a liability to my personal and mission security.

"The firewall is impenetrable," Tsebieh said in a low voice, hands clasped between her knees as if to avoid gestures and, perhaps, physical contact. "Passwords comprise the respective DNA of those few who are authorized access. And GenTail will backtrace any attempt to access data, even to Chthonia." She turned her face toward me. Eyes the color of fresh rainwater sought answers from mine. Once again I felt as if I were a snake rising from the basket to the rhythm of her charms, gently swaying. "Surely you are aware of this. Yet you have a plan you must think will work, else why come here."

I forced myself to look away, to break the hypnotic hold. "If you are about to leave, this no longer matters to you."

"They will find me. They will trace me through you."

Light filled the room in that moment and haloed the dark figure who entered. A millisecond too late I recognized the destitute woman on the stairs—still disheveled, but now aiming an energy weapon. I did a tuck and roll and came up with my own weapon. And in the next instant Tsebieh was holding my pistol. Five times it bucked in her hand, the reports slamming off the walls as if we were inside a barrel, and the woman spilled back through the doorway.

Leaving me on one knee, on the floor, staring in disbelief at my own empty hand.

The tavern shook, and I knew it was Big Gooey, stomping along the hallway. At the door he paused over the body on the floor, then turned a face like a parboiled walrus on me.

15

Before he could vent his rage over the violation of his establishment, Tsebieh said, "She tried to protect me, Gooey. She had nothing to do with it. This is something else."

I rose and crept warily to the corpse—bodies, like weapons, are always presumed to be loaded unless you unload them yourself. This one had a crimson quincunx just under the sternum. You could have covered all five dots with a coaster.

On the floor under the woman, a puddle began to form. Its color matched that of the splatters and streaks down the fractured wall opposite the doorway.

"You use hollow points?" said Tsebieh, hushed, as she passed the pistol back to me.

I tucked it under my belt and pulled the jersey over it. "It's not a toy," I said. "And what I do is not a game."

"I think both of you should leave now," said Big Gooey.

☯ ☯ ☯

As soon as we left the *Tarry A 'Dea* it began to rain. Nevernow, the settlement of which the tavern was the centerpiece, consisted of rough dwellings and shops, small irregular gardens, and clusters of orchards managed by an expatriate populace that regarded strangers the way the Cyclops viewed sailors in distress. Shelter was unlikely.

Tsebieh nudged my arm, and gestured toward the distant escarpment southeast of the settlement, a forbidding dark mass whose broad shadow cast by Vanth almost reached us. Nyx, Chthonia's other moon, lurked just below the eastern horizon. When it rose, we would easily be visible, even in the storm, silhouetted against the night like paperboard targets. I was about to set off when I felt a brief but intense wave of dizziness. When I opened my eyes again (I did not recall having closed them), Tsebieh and I were standing inside a cavern. The burble of an underground stream replaced the hiss of rain. But I could still smell her lilacs.

"I'm impressed," I told her, regaining my equilibrium. Apparently she came here often—the cavern was lit by a charcoal brazier that stood in the middle of the uneven floor. But the air inside the cavern was cool and moist and old, and I began to feel chilled. "What's your range?"

Tsebieh turned away, and seemed to find something on the cavern wall worthy of fierce attention. Her chest heaved in the aftermath of the effort she had just made, and between breaths she gasped, "I'm not going back there."

"I *told* you—"

"You can't get there from here."

She folded her arms and straightened her spine, unyielding as the wall she stared at. Water dripped from my hair down my face and back, and I blinked as if it were tears. With a stark assertion she had dismissed me. Yet I was still here, even if shunned. What was it she wanted to hear from me?

Outside, lightning flashed, and I caught a glimpse of it through the narrow slit off to my left. A malnourished child might slip into the cavern easily enough, but Tsebieh was safe from adult intruders who lacked her teleportation skills. I squeegeed the rain from my hair and went to peer outside. Briefly the sky lit up, revealing massive banks of black cumulus. Grumbling shook the air seconds later.

It looked to be a long storm, and a long night.

Tsebieh had stowed some rations in a small plastic cooler near the brazier. I rummaged around inside it and finally extracted a stalk of something green, and began to munch on it, remotely wondering whether I was devouring one of her long-lost relatives. Suddenly that thought took solid form inside me—I might have violated her personal repository, and not a food bin.

Tsebieh whirled—she'd disclaimed telepathy, so perhaps I'd made a sound, of disgust, annoyance, apology. Across the cavern our eyes locked, and hers seemed to penetrate to the back of my skull. I felt like the marionette of an absent-minded puppeteer wondering what that wooden cross was doing in his hand. Then time resumed, and I could move the strings. Again Tsebieh turned away, and drifted to a rock ledge beside the underground stream, and sat down. Her demeanor issued an invitation for me to join her there. I did so. Ancient waterflow had worn the ledge smooth, with a shallow depression that fit my sitting contours comfortably. In the stream glinted the silver of quick, tiny fish. They flitted from one spot to another so swiftly that they might have employed the same method of movement as Tsebieh. Like stars they sparkled. And they had no eyes.

For a while we sat in silence, watching the little fish. They swam as if they possessed an innate sense of position relative to their environment, negotiating the channel with an economy of movement, darting hither and yon without collisions. The attraction they held for Tsebieh was perhaps subsensual. And there are many kinds of darkness, and only one of them involves the absence of light.

I was aware of her, sitting there, on many levels. Long ago, confronted by personal disaster, I too might have fled. But I'd received training in the operation of weaponry and the applications of force, and these I'd turned against those who had provoked me. The price on my head was far less than that on hers, but it was enough to warrant—

"She was after *me*," I said, blurting the realization as it arrived. The fish scattered briefly at the sound of my voice.

Tsebieh was trailing her fingers in the silver water, creating little eddies in which hopeful silver wraiths searched for food, her silver eyes now on me. The force of her persona came not from this world. Like some ancient queen, half leader, half temptress, she cast out her aura and netted me. Had I been encased in stone, I could not have been more immobilized. And she still smelled like lilacs.

The susurrus of her voice might have hypnotized a predator. "Not, perhaps, for what you think. You *are* the woman called Loba?"

My throat tightened. How could my purpose have been known in advance? "Among other things."

"May I know your true name?"

"Emer McClafferty."

"Emer, yes—the great love of Cuchulainn, faithful to the last, despite his many infidelities. Tell me, Emer, what are you faithful *to*?"

Of their own accord, my fists clenched to stone. A desiccating, pungent stench reached the nostrils of my memory—burnt hair and bones, lingering long after the event. Charred framework like skeletons. Leafless trees from an early Van Gogh sketch. With a mighty effort I turned that page.

"You want me to distill a philosophy of twenty words in ten seconds from three decades of experience. I won't even try."

"There are bad people out there," Tsebieh said quietly, succinctly. "And you kill them."

"That's one level of definition."

I thought I knew what was coming next: the tired, specious argument that a killer of killers was morally no better than those she killed. But history has amply demonstrated (though few have learned the lesson) that only dead "bad people" harm no one. Morality be damned, someone has to stop them from harming others. Why not me?

But recently I'd retired from contract work. Of late it had grown tedious, and so I'd opted for voluntary assignments—such as this one.

"And the corporations will not intervene," Tsebieh whispered. "No matter what the harm done, the corporations merely cluck and tisk and then find a way to profit by it." Abruptly she scrambled to her feet and strode away, toward the narrow opening, once again illuminated by the charged black clouds. The glow from outside swirled around her like a creek flowing past a boulder, and cast her in pale silver and shadow as she stood hugging herself, though the warmth from the brazier now filled the chamber.

We'd entered a time of darkness, the interruptive light dangerous. The storm raged as if against her universe, but within the chamber, inside her impregnable fortress, she was safe. She might retreat here from all save her conscience. I'd heard the undertones earlier, in her voice. To deprive GenTail of the ultimate toy...but could it be done?

I could not know Tsebieh's thoughts. Perhaps memories flashed before her, and she was reviewing them for inspiration, for guidance. Of a sentient species, she'd begun life as a reject: a clone no longer needed to provide vital organs to its primary. They'd allowed her to flatline in the repository, and stored her for general harvest, until GenTail purchased the rights to her DNA, as it had done at the commencement of so many other experiments. Revived in GenTail's own concept of image and likeness, they'd spliced into her selected characteristics of cheetah, Polychaeta, and spinach. And other things.

Given sunlight, she could never starve—the chlorophyll in her skin would activate if hunger grew extreme. She might adapt to cold by hibernating. And her feline quickness served her well in defense.

But the feline in her also rejected the docility GenTail required of her. Tsebieh came to brook no more experiments, no more alterations. No longer would she submit herself—*the* cardinal sin in the eyes of those who regarded themselves as in authority. The fates thrust the necessity of escape upon her, and she created the opportunity she needed, taking with her the genetic imprints for telekinesis. She was the only one of her kind, if GenTail was to be believed.

And I believed them in this instance. Tsebieh had been their prototype. Forgotten, unwanted, the GenTail technicians might do with her as they wished, and if the experiments ran awry, they might with impunity convert her to so much dust. But she had escaped before they'd conducted sufficient tests, and they were reluctant to alter another being until the test results confirmed their hypotheses.

I might confirm them: I'd witnessed the disappearance of the *gretel* and of herself. But nobody was going to ask me.

Reluctant, was GenTail...but not unwilling. The longer Tsebieh stayed away, the safer she was. There was no shortage of subjects on whom to conduct experiments, and sooner or later the testing would resume. Unless someone prevented that continuation.

Unless someone stopped them.

And there was only one way to do that.

In the shadows by the wall, to one side of the narrow entrance, Tsebieh turned back around. Eyes like freshly stamped coins gazed through mine to the back of my skull. *I don't read minds*, she had asserted in the booth, but I could feel her inside me, rummaging around. Again I asked myself: what was it she wanted to hear from me?

Across the floor of the cavern she drifted, slowing as she drew up to me. I'd not been aware of her height until this moment—her eyes, on a level with mine now, bored into me. I could see my reflection in them. And still I smelled the lilacs.

"If you should obtain this genetic program for telepathy," she asked, "this Teleos Splice, what do you propose to do with it?"

I shrugged one shoulder. "Destroy it somehow."

"Not sell it to the highest bidder? Not attempt to profit by your theft?"

"Is that what you think of me?"

Her hand grasped my arm. "Who are you working for? At least tell me that much."

"In this instance I am self-employed."

"Altruistic? A hardened killer with a soft spot? You, Loba?"

"Call me Emer," I told her. "I prefer that. I have my reasons."

Slowly she nodded, to herself, as if she had confirmed a suspicion. "I think I see. Your one good deed. Very well: what computer skills have you, that you might attempt entry?"

"None that are unusual."

Tsebieh threw up her hands in exasperation. "Then *how*—?"

I told her.

Her voice came out between a gasp and a hush. "I never thought of that."

👀👀👀

Although Tsebieh continued to hint at misgivings about the project, the subtle conception of my plan cheered her somewhat during the Track to Mendellia, the aptly-named planet on which the headquarters and laboratories of Genetic Detailing were located. Even so, it was a rough three hours. Confined inside my *Tisiphone*, she became a pacer stalking the gangway between bridge and galley, while I dozed. From time to time there came a clattering from the galley, a rattle of utensils and containers, after which she would emerge porting small plates heaped with crackers and spreads. She munched nervously and sloppily, brushing crumbs from her cammies, and spoke little until we had drawn to within half an hour of arrival.

"Tisiphone?" she said, finally alighting on the starboard captain's chair. "That sounds Greek. Not one of the Fates, surely." She shook her head once, as if debating with herself. With the movement, the overhead illuminative panels gave her short chestnut hair an iridescent sheen. "Furies, perhaps?"

Early in my career I'd succumbed to a maudlin impulse and so

21

christened my 'skip, a blatant advertisement of my occupation and my purpose in life. I'd even dubbed my 'skip's computer Alecto, and had thought of adopting Megaera as a professional name. But I had sobered, and the silly sentimental gestures passed deservedly by the wayside. I'd retained the 'skip's name because it was familiar. Because, in some ways, the 'skip herself was a familiar.

"She was the 'Avenger of Murder,'" I told Tsebieh.

She was silent for a moment. Then: "Someone was taken from you."

The ingenuous statement struck me like a mallet. I busied my hands with the intercom toggles, with a crease in my black denims, with a lock of loose hair. And all the while, Tsebieh allowed me my diversions, waiting patiently for her response.

After my two years at Corporate Security Academy and a year of the usual low-profile security and investigative assignments while I got my professional bearings, I'd taken a brief furlough back to the village of my youth. It wasn't there. They'd razed it. Killed the inhabitants, torched the buildings and the orchards and the fields, plowed everything under. Parents, friends, first loves, even the two stray dogs I'd fed nightly from the back porch despite Mom's admonitions. All gone. The land was scheduled for development...

I checked the virtual distance indicator. Ten minutes to deTrack, fifteen to destination. There was enough time to remember. *Damn Tsebieh, anyway.* But the malediction was unfair. The memories were hardly her fault...

And as I stood on the spot of the village square, I caught whiffs of what had happened. My hair had gotten too close to a campfire once, when I was a child. The stench surrounding me was like that, only a thousand times more powerful. A thousand villagers, counting the livestock. All gone. Because someone had the power to erase them. Because the land was scheduled for development.

My voice was just audible over the memories. "It was long ago and far away, Tsebieh."

"Now there are things wrong which must be put right, is that it?"

I felt a growl catch in my throat. "Is everything so goddamn simple for you? Kill bad people? Right wrongs?"

Tsebieh did not respond to the jab. Seven minutes to deTrack. The extreme port side of the instrumentation console houses several bits of non-standard instrumentation that would probably violate the 'skip's warranty, if discovered...if the *Tisiphone* had a warranty. I flipped a toggle and gave us a new transponder identity—one that would, I hoped, deflect suspicion from our arrival.

"I won't justify what I do with a platitude, Tsebieh," I said at last. "In the beginning, no, I was...enraged and outraged. I lashed out at the innocent and guilty alike, Tsebieh. Sometimes I had a contract...sometimes not. I wanted justice...I wanted balance for my loss. But Space denies us that expectation. The vast distances preclude effective law enforcement. Oh, maybe here and there local laws apply. But nobody was going to call the murderers of my village to account."

"So you held them accountable."

How could she know precisely which ghost to confront me with, *how*?

"I did nothing of the sort. I have no idea who destroyed Liffee— my village. In time, Agriculture Corporation built and operated banks of storage bins there—so it might have been AgCor Security who 'cleared' the land for this...or it might have been some other corporation. It hardly matters, now."

The *Tisiphone* shuddered briefly, and we deTracked. The stars returned. And 10,000 kilometers ahead hung the mottled blue-green and brown orb of Mendellia. We were visible to their sensors, to their security satellites.

"I changed nothing, Tsebieh," I continued, talking more now to relieve my tension. It occurred to me that I'd spoken more words with her than with any other person in the past ten years. Why the talking jag? Because she listened? "In fact, some of those killings created job openings desired and paid for by other corporate personnel. In fulfilling my contracts, I was doing them favors. I solved nothing. I changed nothing."

"You might have run away," Tsebieh pointed out. "If you can't change it, then get as far away as you can and hope they don't find you."

"What you did."

"But you found me."

I shrugged. "You made it easy. You stayed on Chthonia. You grew roots. That's one reason we might succeed here. Corporations are not mobile entities. They can be found."

She swiveled the chair to face me. "Why, Emer, is that a note of wistfulness I detect?"

"Go to hell." I made a face, at her and at the universe in general. "I can't afford the vulnerability of roots...but yes, if you must know, *yes*, I'd love to have at least a *pied a terre*. At least that."

"As would I," she whispered. "Roots...a place to return to."

"They tend to burn those. Or haven't you noticed?"

And her response was lost when the port communications monitor hissed and a red light on the console began to blink. Someone wanted to talk with us. I heard Tsebieh swallow hard. My own heart was a stone, sinking. I keyed the XMIT, and the hard, stern face of a young man appeared in the monitor.

"Identification and purpose?" Clearly he was a man of few words. He favored a bristle cut for his light brown hair, and his eyes, of the same color, lacked depth. The ideal employee—one day to be bred by GenTail, if the experiments on Tsebieh should prove successful.

"Captain Stahl of Corporate Security, aboard the *Sternweg*," I said. "My aide, Corporal Jensen. We're here for business and pleasure. I wish to see your commanding officer, Captain Bogaty, about...some security matters. Also, my aide and I wish to go fishing."

"Stand by, sir." The monitor blanked.

Tsebieh hissed. "Are you—?" she began, but obeyed the chop of my hand, cutting her off while I flipped the Mute toggle. "*Are you out of your mind?*"

"Probably. Tsebieh, I have several 'borrowed' transponder programs. I know Captain Stahl...enough to know that Bogaty has heard of her. You, I made up...nobody's going to check on the aide. It's the day shift down there; Bogaty will be busy with normal routines. We'll have a couple hours of *unsupervised* visit. Understand?"

"That may not be enough—"

"Hush," I snapped, as the monitor reactivated. The man of few words had a few more for us. The Captain would see us at the end of the duty day, in three hours. We had a room in the Bachelor Officers' Quarters, behind which we might downdock the *Sternweg*, and permission to fish the lake half a kilometer to the south. We'd have to provide our own tackle, and our own flatbottom, or fish from the shore.

"You are also instructed to avoid downdocking within half a kilometer of the galleon *Bremerhaven* while it discharges cargo," he said. End transmission.

I set the *Tisiphone* to autodock and pocked a knuckle on the point of Tsebieh's shoulder for attention. "I've cammie CorpSec uniforms stowed aft. We should change."

"We're not going fishing?" She got up and followed me to the stateroom. "The lake is closer to the GenTail R&D Labs."

"Low hatchway, watch your head." I ducked inside and made for a stack of bins set against the bulkhead next to the bunk berths, and drew open a drawer. "I'd prefer we remain close to the *Tisiphone*, if not aboard her," I said, tossing her a folded set of CorpSec cammies and a set of corporal's pips. "If we do have to be seen, I want us to blend."

Fortunately Tsebieh and I were almost of a size. She sat down on the lower berth and began to unlace her boots while I laid out a uniform for myself on the upper. It was impossible not to notice that she still smelled of lilacs, not to be aware that she was doffing her clothes. I had not prepared for the sheer impact of that awareness. I felt as if I'd just walked into a stanchion I'd not seen.

I backed away from the berths. Already she was naked save the undies, and was about to climb into the trousers. "Tsebieh..."

One leg in, one leg out, she looked up. Her "Oh" was barely audible. I watched her chest rise and fall, ever so slowly, with a time-weary sigh, not quite of exasperation, not quite of regret, as she straightened to face me, arms at her sides, defenseless. "It's the lilacs," she whispered. "I'm...sorry, I cannot turn them off. But...the attraction you feel for me is only physical. If that helps," she finished

25

lamely.

My throat felt parched, as if by desert air. "A lot of relationships begin that way."

A light impact trembled the *Tisiphone*, bringing her to ground and the two of us back to our purpose. We had arrived. Tsebieh turned away from me and resumed dressing, as did I, and we spoke of this no more.

❧ ❧ ❧

The GenTail R&D Labs were located not merely on the other side of the lake, but some eleven kilometers under it, encased in continental granite and virtually indestructible alloy. To physical, electronic, and energy field probes the Labs were opaque and impenetrable, but the encasement was as nothing to someone of Tsebieh's telekinetic abilities. But in the euphoria of having persuaded her to assist me on this self-imposed contract, I'd neglected to determine the parameters of her abilities. I'd supposed that distance was irrelevant—and then she had stipulated that her type of telekinesis needed to be performed from spot to spot on the same planet. That obstacle had been overcome with our arrival on Mendellia.

Mass imposed certain limitations of its own. I hadn't expected her to move an entire planet, or even a continent—merely myself, all 178 centimeters and seventy seven kilograms of me. It seemed simple enough.

But Tsebieh sat down on the lower berth, and shook her head. "You are hardly a bowl of *gretel*, Emer. Think of it this way: you exert your muscles in moving an object in standard gravity. The telekinetic neural module in the brain is not a muscle, of course, but the principle is similar. The more massive the object, the greater the strain, whether physical or telekinetic. Worse, if the object is sufficiently massive, you could strain a muscle, rupture a tendon, tear a ligament. The brain can suffer analogous injuries."

I stared at her. "You mean you *can't* do this, after all?"

"I do not mean to disappoint you, Emer. I have some idea of what this project means to you."

I turned away, walked to the bulkhead, and kicked it. A low

gong resonated throughout the *Tisiphone*. "Do you really? And what do you think that is?"

Her voice was just audible over the echo. "Redemption."

I barked a laugh. "For what?"

"Your life. Your career."

Her stab was accurate—only partly so, but enough to sting. It was an effort to face her, to meet her eyes with mine. "I regret nothing, Tsebieh, except the lost opportunities to do something positive, something constructive. My anger got in my way. But not this time."

"Tell me more," she urged.

"We haven't time for this right now, remember?"

"Tell me more."

I kicked the bulkhead again, and leaned against it, arms folded. My eyes felt hot now. I spoke in a voice not mine, of thoughts only partially assembled and forced prematurely into the light of analysis. "Very well. There are always people who fight back, who do not care for what they regard as senseless rules imposed upon them. Some of these people are malevolent, that's true enough. But others simply want to be left alone to live their lives, make their mistakes, indulge themselves as they choose, generally without harming others. You find them in many places, Tsebieh...on planets like Chthonia, and in places like the *Tarry A'Dea*. It's not easy, but even now anyone who truly wants to and is determined to do so can opt for freedom by escaping to the Fringes...to the regions where Corporate control is negligible at best. As the Corporations expand, so do the Fringes...and there will always be Fringes. There will always be a place for the likes of you and me to flee to, to live.

"Or so I had supposed. But the Teleos Splice, in time, can destroy the Fringes. It is the ultimate in social and economic control. It can be used to compel *everyone*, no matter how distant, to operate on the same frequency, so to speak. The Fringes will die of neglect; eventually no one will *want* to flee there. Everyone will be doing whatever they are told to do, *forever*. That is what the Teleos Splice makes possible, Tsebieh. We will all think the same thoughts, *forever*. We will think what they tell us to think, do what they tell us

27

to do, buy what they tell us to buy, love and hate what they tell us to love and hate. Those who are in charge, they've been doing that to us for millennia, in one way or another, but there was always somewhere else to go: new lands, new continents, the New World, the Solar planets—but now, once the Teleos Splice is perfected, they can *enforce* their uniformity of thought, of belief, of behavior. They can compel orthodoxy. I want no part of that society, of that universe. Now *please*, get me inside there and let me do what I came here to do."

Tsebieh did not move from the bed, nor did she lift her gaze from the floor. "So this is personal, for you," she said quietly. "It is not altruism which impels you. This is a selfish act."

I shrugged. "So it's a selfish act."

Tsebieh's voice dropped to a whisper, the eye of the storm. "Everything they did to me, they said it was for my own good."

"Tsebieh..."

Slowly she lifted her face. In the dim light of the stateroom her skin took on an odd reseda glow, powered as if by some internal source, and her eyes shone silver at me. She did not speak of the unimaginable horrors of having her thinking processes experimented upon, of undergoing compulsory alterations in the very core structure of her being, of her spirit, of her soul. She spoke only of the interior of the R&D lab. The lack of inflection in her voice emphasized her furious control over the lightning and thunder behind it.

"The only room of interest is the computer room itself," she said, and I strained to listen, to catch her words. "Security is less than you'd expect. Because unauthorized entry is impossible, no sensors are emplaced. However, I cannot know the effect of telekinetic penetration of the dampening field that surrounds the room. It is possible that porting you through it will raise an alarm. If that should happen, you will have from five to eight minutes to complete your task—the time it takes for an individual who is authorized entry to reach the entrance to the computer room, confirm his or her identity, and enable the doors open. It is also possible that your body might interrupt various signals. The computer is not hardwired in any way. Exchange of information is done through variable-frequency

28

microwaves—another reason why the computer is unhackable."

I strapped on my shoulder rig, and verified the full load in my pistol. "I'll use the commo tube to keep you advised of my progress," I told her. "You can transmit from the bridge comm."

Tsebieh shook her head. "The transmission might be detected, and certainly the dampening field will kill it."

"Then how—?"

Like this, Emer. They can't detect this, yet.

My knees buckled. "I thought you said you can't read minds."

Not can't. Don't.

"They experimented with the Teleos Splice on you, then?"

But they've no idea how successful it was.

I shoved aside a billion questions and instead drew a deep breath, as if preparing to dive under water. "I'm ready."

A wall of dizziness slugged me like a crashing wave in a storm, inundating me. Pressure on my chest inhibited my breathing. In its wake I was aware of a hard surface under my boots. I could barely stand. I braced my arms on top of something—a desk or table—and waited until the universe decided to hold still again. My pounding heart continued to flood adrenalin throughout my body. I was as ready for anything, including my own death, as I would ever be.

Balance returned, and in the darkness I switched on the pencil beam on my cap and scanned about. I was standing inside a cube approximately three meters on a side, beside another cube perhaps one meter on a side that rested on the floor—the computer. This face of its cowling was blank, so I walked around it until I came to the maintenance door Tsebieh had assured me would be there. It felt made of structural plastic, and slid open to the left at my touch. To a computer curious about my identity, I might have been a systems engineer.

"Tsebieh."

Right here, Emer.

Her "voice" sounded strained. "What's wrong?" I asked her.

Inside to the right is a small control panel. Look for Release, or Cowling Release, and enable it.

I scanned the interior of the main computer. I saw a mass of compact technology and heard some faint whirring. I saw nothing that might indicate a control panel.

Tsebieh's silence was long enough to make my heart begin to stutter. Something was not as she had expected, or had given me to expect...but what?

Look again. It has to be there.

"I don't see it."

Omigod. Oh, God...

My mind clenched like a fist—the effect of Tsebieh's panic. Instinctively my hand dipped to the weapon under my arm and grasped the butt. The cold metal comforted me only a little. If Tsebieh lost the telekinetic connection with me, I was trapped beyond rescue. With luck I might dispatch one security guard per round when they came for me, as inevitably they would. I felt reasonably certain that GenTail had far more security guards than I had bullets.

"Tsebieh!"

I can't...

"We're running out of time, Tsebieh."

But you promised me...you assured me...omigod...

"Tsebieh! What should I do?"

I thought I heard her scream, the shriek of an eagle mortally wounded. It might have been my imagination. Then a light puff of air buffeted my right side, and I caught a hint of lilacs. Her shoulder brushed mine as she leaned forward, bracing her arms on the cowling. She was making little sounds with each rapid respiration—*uh ugh uh ugh*—as if she were suffering from an acute coronary disturbance. In the light of the pencil beam she turned horror-filled silver eyes toward me. She looked on the verge of passing out. I tried to steady her, but she drew from a reservoir of strength and shrugged violently away.

Damn you, Emer.

"Tsebieh—"

"Don't talk!" she hissed. "Shut up shut up shut up."

"It's a blown mission," I said. "Let's just—"

The wrath of her "No!" reverberated in the small room like a thunderclap. Snatching my pencil beam, she peered into the opening, studying the layout, comparing what she saw with what she remembered, the way old friends do who've not seen each other for years. "You're right," she said dully. "It's not there." She aimed the beam at the floor and finally scuffed her boot at some object there. With a little whimper she sat down tailor-fashion on the floor, hunched over, mewling.

"Tsebieh?"

The beam trembled in her hand. She brought it to bear on a corner of the cowling, where it joined the floor.

"They've bolted it down," she whispered.

"Then we can't move it," I said. "We can't steal the whole fucking computer. The mission is a scrub. Let's—"

"Shut up. I can't think." Tsebieh pressed fists to her head as if to compel thought by the pressure of her terror, and began to rock back and forth the way autistic children do, listening to their own music. She was withdrawing into her own black depths, and there was nothing I might do for her.

On the other hand, I wasn't going anywhere without her. I knelt down and slipped an arm around her shoulders. She stiffened at the contact, but otherwise did not resist. The scent of lilacs was overpowering. "If we leave now," I said softly, "we can come back. If they come here and catch us, we lose that option."

Tsebieh continued to rock against me, making little mewling noises, as if the spirit of her no longer inhabited her body. I heard something squeak and scrape, and aimed the pencil beam in that general direction.

The bolt on the flange at the right corner of the cowling had emerged a full two centimeters from the floor, and ever so slowly was turning.

Another faint sound reached my ears, as if a small terrestrial creature were crawling through dry leaves—against the sleeves of my cammies the fine hairs on my forearms were coming erect. I stood as paralyzed as a bird before a snake, watching the dark magic unfold. The bolt twisted round and round, slowly, inexorably, emerging, another centimeter and another. Tsebieh was gasping for air. The light from the pencil beam reflected back at me from the perspiration on her pale forehead. Eyes squeezed shut, she was focusing all of her unique energies on the task at hand. Beads of water dripped from her nose, the point of her chin. And finally I heard a dull *clunk* as the bolt fell free.

Every evil thing they had done to her for her own good, she was turning against them.

"That's one," she whispered, breathless.

Behind me the next bolt protested its astral extraction. If one could summon the dead, they might make that sound as they emerged from the floor. I felt the urge to light a candle. But the pencil beam was sufficient unto the darkness.

A *clunk*, followed at a longer interval by another. Tsebieh was leaning against the cowling, her breathing shallow, her face chalky. She peered up at me through half-lidded eyes.

"Don't try to stop me, Emer..."

I knelt down again. "But you're dying."

Drained of her physical strength by the effort she had put forth, Tsebien pushed against me ineffectually. "One more, Emer. Then we can take this with us."

I stood up, and put my weight against the cowling, testing its resistance. "With only one to secure it, I should be able to snap the flange—"

"Not structural plastic. And don't speak, please."

Enfeebled and wan, Tsebieh returned to her task. Unable to assist, I found that I could not bear to watch her exertions and the effects they had on her. By the time I reached the far corner of the cowling, the bolt securing the flange was all but free. But at what cost? And what might we accomplish now?

"Tsebieh?"

"Your concept," she gasped. "My purpose."

I dashed around the corner, fearing the worst, but she had managed to pull herself erect, albeit on unsteady legs. I gave her a once-over with the pencil beam. Many in the past I had killed, or watched die, enough to recognize that she was on the verge. Her death was a consequence I could not permit. If someone was meant to die in this venture, it should be me. I had initiated it; I was

32

responsible.

But Tsebieh was having none of it. "Ready, Emer?"

"Damn it, Tsebieh, at least pause for breath!"

She shook her head once, emphatically, the only gesture she had the strength to make, and slumped over the top of the cowling. Before I could protest, darkness buffeted me, a sensation rather different from my telekinetic journey into the computer room. If she expired while I was in transit, would I be condemned to walk a night like Hamlet's father, but in a night that existed for myself alone? Would I ever catch the scent of lilacs again?

👁👁👁

I came to in a darkness that seemed to confirm the worst of my fears and expectations. The floor chilled me through the cammie fabric, and some massive object with canvas straps supported me. My fingers crept along them to the buckles. In my other hand I still grasped the pencil beam. I had to will myself to raise it and enable the light.

I was not aboard the *Tisiphone*.

Around me stood stacks of cargo crates, secured to the bulkheads as proof against zero-gee. The stencils indicated a wide range of disparate products, the sort of inventory one might find in a delivery craft. Scanning for Tsebieh, I gave them only token attention. Belatedly it occurred to me to hail her through my thoughts. But she did not respond. My heart sank.

Although the crates were secured, I was not, but the craft was still bound by the gravity of Mendellia. I climbed to my feet and waited until the waves of unsteadiness abated before panning the beam around the cargo bay. A lump in the shadows against the adjacent bulkhead looked dishearteningly familiar. I dashed to it, to the echoes of my footfalls on the deck, and fell to my knees beside her. She was barely conscious. I folded my legs under to create a lap, and cradled her head on it. Silver eyes shone up at me.

"You were the target, Emer," Tsebieh whispered hoarsely, "and not myself."

What the hell are you talking about? Aloud I added, "Huh?"

"GenTail must have suspected you had a purpose for me. You

33

had to be stopped. But of course they wanted me alive."

The woman who intruded on us in the Tarry A'Dea*?*

"They knew we might be coming here, Emer. But they did not expect...what we did."

And what did we do, Tsebieh? Where is the computer?

"I put it aboard the *Tisiphone*. I enabled the automatic pilot after 'creating' a few astrogational glitches. The course will accidentally take the cruiser into the Mendellian star, which it should be reaching...about now."

They're following it? GenTail is chasing it?

Tsebieh's head rocked in my lap. "No...monitoring only. It's all over for them...for now. We deprived them of much more than the Teleos Splice. Everything they had done, all their records of all their projects, were stored in that invulnerable and impregnable computer. They have decades of work to recreate, perhaps even a century of it. We hurt them beyond their ability to calculate. Fortunately for you, they'll believe you dead aboard the *Tisiphone*."

"*You* hurt them, Tsebieh," I said.

"Yes...yes, I did, didn't I?" The deck under us trembled gently, and I knew the cargo craft—the *Bremerhaven*, I remembered—was tracking into a position around Mendellia preparatory to departure for the next leg of its journey. Tsebieh seemed to be listening to other voices. "They've cleared us for departure," she said at last. I felt a momentary queasiness as zero gee took effect. "I rather thought they would. According to the captain, your next port of call will be Zlatka."

"*Our* next port of call, you mean."

"Someone like you can reach the Fringes easily enough from there."

"Tsebieh—"

"Don't talk. And do not weep."

I drew a wrist across my eyes. "I'm not crying. The air in here is dry."

"You'll have to disappear for a while, Emer."

"Tsebieh, no." I leaned over her, and embraced her, to hold her there. But I could not restrain the part of her that would leave.

34

"Emer..."

"Right here, Tsebieh."

"Aboard the *Tisiphone*...when we changed clothing. You would have kissed me?"

"More than kissed."

"Kiss me now."

Lips tasting of tears are always best for kissing. Despite her condition, her mouth was wet and inviting, and I longed to linger there forever. But the contact could not endure. And I felt a sharp pain in my lower lip—she had bitten me.

Confused and a little frightened, I drew my face from hers to stare down at her. Her lips were stained with my blood. "Tsebieh, what was that for?"

But the scent of lilacs had faded, and she was gone.

Five years passed before I dared return to Chthonia. The escarpment southeast of Nevernow had changed little, although the terrain in front of it was less than familiar. It had rained the night Tsebieh and I had fled to the safety of her cavern, and it had rained the night I buried her on the gentle slope in front of the entrance. It had still been raining when I slipped into the *Tarry A 'Dea* to arrange discreet transportation elsewhere.

The Chthonian sun shone brightly these days of late spring, but I was shaded where I sat reading meditative poetry on the grass under the tree that had grown so swiftly on the slope near the entrance to the cavern. A low tray beside me supported a tall glass of gin and tonic and a small bowl of nuts and dried fruit. From time to time I glanced at the tree, both in reverie and in awe. The trunk seemed sturdy enough . . .

The trunk seemed sturdy enough, but the elongated growth within it had now spread the bark almost to the bursting point. I turned a page, and put a finger to the scar on my lower lip, and wondered whether our daughter would have eyes of silver.

(Not that it matters, but this story was born on an evening spent reading, among other things, In the House of Sorrows, *by Poul Anderson, and listening to Indigo Girls'* "Trouble"*, especially one particular line, and wiring on a couple bottles of Grolsch. TC)*

Vapors

Earth had changed in the 144 years since the departure of the Eridania colonists from whom I descended. Around me the State of New Hudson sparkled, gleamed, shone forth. Where, then, the pollution and crime the historical texts complained of? And where the noise? Private polychrome conveyances passed along the street as if on rails and connected to one another, the hum of their power sources no more annoying than the song of a distant insect. Street vendors scouted for potential customers, their hawking muted to a courteous "May I help you find something?" People smiled, and made way when I inadvertently drifted into the oncoming flow of pedestrians. If this was truly New Hudson, what had happened to the slums and the ghettos and the "Psst! Step in here and gimme your money"? And everyone wore white surgical masks like the ones we had received without explanation and were instructed to don upon clearing Quarantine at Hudson External Port. Boys in drab uniforms had then aimed us and a group of schoolchildren on tour from the State of Bruxelles toward the lobby and the city immediately beyond, and we passed from one domed environment to the next. Directions were non-existent. Apparently we were to proceed to DOOPHUS along a pathway of trial-and-error.

Krysza, walking beside me, shrugged ignorance when I cocked an eyebrow at her.

Rarely did conditions Out There match expectations. That's what made it so interesting. But here? On Earth? This world of human genesis laid the foundation for our very existence Out There. We'd studied the videos and the documents and the photos in preparation for the inquiry we'd volunteered to make on behalf of Eridania. We knew Earth . . . didn't we? We were her children . . .

If Krysza and I were not who we thought we were, who the hell were we?

Krysza tucked a long stray lock of ochre hair over her ear. Under the mask, her nose twitched. "Air tastes funny," she said.

It had that desiccated flavor of the air in our 'skip, between stars. Ever eat a breadcrust while you mouth is dry? The memory of the flakes sticking to your gullet lingers long after you've swallowed. This was like that, only swallowing failed to ameliorate the condition. Krysza coughed, then sneezed. The sounds brought me back to the street. She was not alone in her distress. Tiny puffs from behind the masks of passers-by indicated a contagion of respiratory discomfort. But what in this surgery-room atmosphere could cause it?

At the first intersection we paused for the traffic flow indicators to change color, and garnered speculative appraisals from several young men—and from a young woman who averted her eyes quickly when hers met mine. Krysza elbowed me sharply in the ribs, a playful reminder that, while I might be permitted the occasional dalliance, it would be with someone of her choice. Several paces away, a woman clad in faux tweed and puce leggings that revealed an attractive bit of knee and nothing else tugged at a leash. The dog, if dog it was (cross a chihuahua with a cocker spaniel and dye the result electric pink), sniffed at a waypost, turned around, and lifted its right rear leg.

A ray of sunshine flashed from the waypost diagonally across the intersection from us, choking off the woman's "No!" I heard a sound not unlike that which you cause by inadvertently laying the screwdriver across the battery poles. The woman vanished. The leash fell limp to the walkway; the dog ran off, trailing it.

Stunned, I could only gasp, as did Krysza, who clutched at my hand.

A passing conveyance, its operator temporarily distracted by the incident, intruded into the intersection just as the indicators changed color from amber to crimson. Another ray of sunshine gleamed, and this time the *pop!* assaulted our ears.

The conveyance vanished, and its occupant.

My throat felt raw. "What kind of place *is* this?" I whispered.

"Order," said a young man—not one of the oglers. His was a hatchet face, the blade the nose and chin, tanned as old hide.

I nodded, eyes still on the waypost. About twenty meters high it stood, topped with a slotted bulb. I'd seen photos of bad weather sirens rather like this.

"I'm Laird," he said. He did not offer his hand.

My heart settled back into a decent rhythm. "Charlene Nash. This is my wife, Krysza."

He eased back a pace. Furtive eyes flicked from side to side. "Your . . . wife."

His tone alerted me to unknown dangers. "Is there a problem?"

Laird licked his lips. Something was awry . . . but what? "Have you two, uh . . . you know. Here. In this block, I mean."

"Have we two uh what here in this block?" Beside me Krysza stifled a giggle. "Oh! No." Not that it was any concern of his.

Visibly relieved, Laird looked at me again. Dark eyes absorbed my attire—a green jersey, a pair of old but still serviceable black jeans, and field boots—and Krysza's—similar, except her jersey was pale violet, like her eyes. With his inspection I became aware of our conspicuousness. His was what we call an outsuit, relatively form-fitting and quite utile. Underneath his body looked functional, though I was not inclined to test the theory.

"You are Externals," he said, as if that explained a question he had not asked.

Krysza sniffled, and cleared her throat. "We're from—"

" . . . outside New Hudson," I broke in. "We're looking for DOOPHUS." He frowned ignorance, and I added, "It will be an office of some sort, probably a large one. We are to report in person. We have an inquiry to make." Such were our orders.

His eyes—they were almost chocolate in the sunlight—betrayed his puzzlement. Still, he ticked a fingertip at a keyboard implant in his left palm, then keened his head, as if listening. Belatedly I spotted the nodule in the dark hair just above his right ear.

Finally he said, pointing to his left, "Two blocks from here. It is one of the older buildings, perhaps one of the Originals. You seek the second level below ground."

I remained uncertain. "Perhaps you might be kind enough to escort us?"

Laird shifted his weight from one leg to the other, and looked away. His countenance suggested he regretted having offered conversation.

"Krysza and I won't do any uh-what in your presence." I tucked a note of plea into my tone. I was unaccustomed to requesting assistance. On Eridania it was offered in advance of need. "Is that satisfactory?"

His voice grew sullen. "This way, then."

We followed him. He stayed just far enough ahead of us to make the casual observer doubt Krysza and I were in his company. After half a block I'd had enough, and snagged him by the shoulder, spinning him around. "Are we doing something wrong?"

Laird almost laughed. "No, of course not. How can you?" He made a face at us, inconvenienced by the need to explain the (to him) obvious. "There is no wrong. There is only Order . . . here, as it is in your State. What did you think, that we were different? Externals! You think everything is a new wonder. I assure you it is not. We are quite like you."

Already I'd begun to doubt that, but I let his delusion survive. "Order" meant . . . what *did* it mean? Who made the rules here?

Krysza's lovely brow furrowed. "You mean, if we cross against the light, we will be killed?"

Laird bade us onward. "Don't cross against the light," he said, as if it were that simple. Well, perhaps it was. But not on Eridania.

At the corner we crossed with the light. And with the next. Pedestrians and small shops formed a defilade through which we passed without hindrance. From the row of eateries athwart the middle of the block there should have emanated aromas to inspire appetites. Instead, to the accompaniment of the *whirr* of tiny fans embedded in the walls above the shop windows, we scented only sterility. Even Krysza's alluring lilac perfume had dulled, diluted to parts per trillion. Absent the touch of her hand, if I closed my eyes, I could not sense her . . . which seemed a waste of friendly proximity. Our reflections in a window recalled to me just how much we stood out in our attire . . . and made me aware of the eyes on us. Truly we were Externals.

But another pair of eyes, somewhere beyond the range of the reflection, weighed on me. I doubted the waypost had keened to Krysza and me, wary of potential infraction. This surveillance felt, not technological, but personal. Someone was interested in us.

Krysza felt it, too. Her lilac eyes swept around us as we drifted onward, but failed to light upon any particular person. For a moment we were back on Eridania, in the Thronx Forest, playing Hide-and-Seek. But that had been a game. Again I wondered who made the rules here.

The structure toward which Laird led us was indeed venerable, its pale brown blocks fragmented and pitted with age and by ancient skirmishes. A battle had once been fought near here, perhaps the *Intifada* of New York that I had read about, the uprising of immigrants uneasy with the ways of their adopted land. It was none of my concern. My eyes, and Krysza's, swept toward the future. Whatever was past, had already happened.

Doors slid open when we ascended the brief set of gray plastic steps, shallow depressions in them hinting that the interior of the building was at one time frequented. Under our masks Krysza and I coughed as the rush of freshly-dried air reached us. We stepped into the foyer, but Laird remained at the entrance, his duties completed. I beckoned him onward.

He turned and fled.

"This does not bode well," Krysza whispered.

Her soft voice echoed through the chamber and down dimly-lit corridors long abandoned. Around us tiny fans hummed, inhaling dust and odors, replacing them with unhydrated air. My throat clogged, and I coughed. The atmosphere of Eridania was similar to that of Earth . . . or was supposed to be. There is a constant newness, standing on the front patio of the cottage in the sunlight, beside your wife, taking in the morning's first breaths. For unfathomable reasons, New Hudson had chosen to befoul its air with dry molecules, and Krysza and I could only share spasms racked with coughs.

Which rather took the romance out of it. And the newness.

Krysza pointed.

A directory was affixed to the wall, its black field age-faded to grays, the white plastic letters stained as if by an explosion of coffee. Names of people and offices, numbers of rooms. Some of the letters were missing. Our destination was indeed on the second subterranean level. Another wall sign indicated the location of elevators. We followed the arrow and reached two sets of sliding doors. I pushed the button for Down, without effect.

"Stairs," said Krysza.

The excitement of impending completion spurred me onward. In that way, I suppose, accomplishing a task is rather like love-making. Krysza felt it, too. Her field boots *tock*ed the plastic steps ahead of me, and echoes thrummed me as I passed through her vacated space. Two flights of stairs we took, and arrived at B Level. Here the air seemed moister, or perhaps it was my imagination. But the emptiness remained.

The building was unoccupied.

We'd reached a long corridor lined on either side with doors at regular intervals. Some had signs or placards indicating the purposes within. A length of luminous tiles divided the ceiling as far as we could see. The first door we came to bore a three-digit number, the next two units higher. We turned and headed in the other direction.

Krysza removed her mask and drank deeply of the air, the inhalation singing past the glob of mucus that had formed in the back of her throat. She coughed once to clear it and breathed again, quieter. Under the jersey her breasts trembled with the effort. "I don't understand this at all," she sighed.

Aboard our spaceskip *Eclair de Lune* (I like DeBussy, Krysza loves pastries, as we've explained on too many occasions) we'd received our ANTIs, standard prophylactics against all manner of organisms and proteins. We were as immune to disease as the human body could be made. Whence then our distress?

An echo reached us, faint as old starlight.

We'd brought no weapons, despite the possibility of being accosted in an alley as the videos suggested—ours was a peaceful mission. But Krysza was trained in aikido, and she was tenacious.

Eyes and ears keened to stealthy approaches, we continued down the corridor, counting off the room numbers. The echo remained unrepeated. I recalled the line from Poe: Only this and nothing more.

Krysza tugged me to halt. I'd glanced at the door and been about to move on. Belatedly the number registered. Black block letters on the door just below the fogged window read: Domestic Organization for Off-Earth Population/Habitation, U.S.

We'd arrived.

And no one was home. I turned the door handle, anticipating resistance, and it yielded readily enough. Inside the room was dark and unoccupied. I felt for the wall switch and toggled it. In the ceiling, three of the ten tiles began to glow faintly. A fourth flickered and died, like a final hope. Had we come for nothing, then?

The room contained a desk of some dark hardwood that the little fans kept free of dust, and a captain's chair on casters behind it, and a sofa by the left wall, its wine upholstery faded now to blush rose in spots. There were no windows, of course, but set into the right wall was an aquarium scene, in three-dimension colors that shifted as the viewer moved through the room, so that the fish seemed lifelike. The movement was, perhaps, as illusory as our mission. Life had been here, and departed.

Krysza gave a little cry of dismay. She'd reached the same conclusion.

"All this way . . ."Her eyes were dry. The tears were in her voice.

A door in the far wall might open to answers. I tested it, but the lock was proof against unsolicited entry. The drawers of the desk were equally as secure. We might pry them open and rummage around inside, but to what end? We'd expected artstate technology, know-it-all computers, opulent resources. We'd found an abandoned room free of dust and of spirit. Fourteen light-years we had come, yet were no closer to making the inquiry. We might as well have remained on Eridania.

Krysza drifted to the sofa and flopped down, I beside her, to the hiss of cushions yielding. Bashing our heads against a blank wall had left us dazed. What now? Whither now? If a successor had been authorized to DOOPHUS, it lay beyond our ken. We might seek it out, if we knew whom to ask. The room was empty. The building was empty.

Presently I grew aware of Krysza, leaning against me. In desperate straits, love finds a way to expression. In a settlement of millions, we had stumbled into a spot of privacy. We required no encouragement to take advantage of it.

👀👀👀

There's panic, and there's resignation. One evening some years ago, when Matthew Carlson and I were getting to know one another quite well in the living room, my parents returned early from work. In the panic that followed, I wound up wearing Matt's denims and one of his boots. Our faces were flushed and hot, bodies wet. My parents said not a word, but smiled at us stumbling and bumbling around the sofa, and headed to their room and the shower they needed

I doubted Krysza and I could dress ourselves in the one point four seconds it took for the office door to open. We didn't try.

The man who entered was rotund and genial, his expression on the verge of befuddlement. He paused just inside the doorway, laced his fingers across his ample chest, and said, under his mask, "My my my."

He had the eyes of one who had seen the body of a woman and took pleasure in the viewing, but did not regard her nakedness as a forthright invitation to couple. After a moment, he turned away, without blushing. "Dear me. I'll only be a moment. Please forgive me for interrupting."

Krysza's jaw dropped. "Who are you?"

From somewhere in his tent of a shirt he fished a key, which he began inserting into one drawer after another in the desk. "My my my," he said, oblivious to the question. He had a coarse, rather high voice that addressed his surroundings but no one in particular. "I'll only be a moment. Yes yes yes. Now where did I put those . . . ?"

Gingerly Krysza and I finished untangling, and got dressed to the rhythm of his my-my-mys. Presently he uncovered the object of his search—a box of data cards—and eased himself around the corner of

43

the desk and made for the door. Befuddled he might be, but he had remembered to secure each drawer.

"Wait," I said.

"Hmm? Oh, dear me. No no no. Please, indulge yourself. I can review these files in another office, you know. Yes yes yes. Well, of course you don't know. My my my. Of course not." Chuckling at some private mirth, he opened the door and started to step through.

"Please wait. I think we came to see you."

"To see me? Oh, my dears, no no no. I assure you I have absolutely no interest in your—"

"About Eridania," said Krysza.

"Oh. Oh?" Relief washed over his face and sparkled his eyes. "Eridania, you say. My my my." He held aloft the box. Under the mask his bulbous nose quivered as he gave a tiny cough. "These are the referent project histories. A message was forwarded to me from an STS, after passing through so many offices, so many offices, yes yes yes. They're coming back, you know. Well, of course you don't know. No no no. How could you know? I must study—"

"We're here," said Krysza, on focus as always.

". . . them to refresh my . . . my dear, what did you say? You're here? Oh, my my my. That is precious, that is. Yes yes yes."

"We're come from Eridania," she went on. "We're to make an inquiry."

He slumped against the wall, to the accompaniment of a minor vibration. "Oh, my." His hand lowered, the box slipped from his fingers and fell to the floor, breaking to scatter six crimson cards on the floor. Krysza gave a little cry and scurried after them. One struck my ankle, and I rescued it.

"You're here," he repeated. "From Eridania. To make an inquiry? My my my." He accepted the five from Krysza. I got up and dumped the sixth into his massive palm. Large he was, and quite overweight, but I got the impression he was also immensely strong. And immensely gentle.

He filled the box and closed it, and set it on top of the desk, then removed his mask as if to honor his guests. "I am Doctor Flavian," he announced, in a tone that said we might direct our inquiry to him.

He looked at us, one and then the other, expectantly.

Proper formal address on Eridania required that Lady Charlene Nash and her Mistress Krystyna be introduced by a third party, but we were no longer on the planet, and in any case no one has used formal address for a century or so, except on rare and special occasions at the onset of lovemaking. I presented us as I had to Laird.

"Oh, dear me," he said. "My my my."

"You *are* in charge of DOOPHUS?" I pressed.

"Yes yes yes. Yes yes yes. That is, there is no one else. I am my own staff, you know. Well, of course you don't—"

"Doctor Flavian," said Krysza, her tone a knock of authority on his door. "Where are the colonists Earth promised to send? Why has Earth failed to maintain communications with Eridania? Why haven't people followed us out into the stars? Why have you forsaken us?"

"Oh, my dears," breathed Flavian. "Oh, my very dears."

I wanted to growl. "What!"

"You don't know? Well, of course you don't know, why would you? No no no. Oh, my dears, Earth no longer needs to found colonies elsewhere. We have Order now. Our population is stable and obedient. There is no longer any impetus for space exploration and settlement. No no no. This very office exists now only because it was established. What was established, must remain established, thus preserving Order. Someone must therefore staff it. Yes yes yes. That has been my privilege for . . . my my my, has it been that long? And my predecessor staffed alone as well." Flavian glanced over his shoulder. "They found him deceased in that same chair."

I was about to ask why anyone would bother to look for his predecessor if nobody cared about the office anymore.

"His personal wealth had accumulated in his account," Flavian went on, "and someone made an inquiry. Just as you are making now. Yes yes yes. They found Doctor Ashlon . . . rather mummified, so they said. My my my. He was almost completely desiccated."

"Like the air," I muttered.

"What's that, my dear? Oh, yes." He put a hand to his mouth and coughed behind it. "My my my. Quite."

I had to ask. "What is Order?"

An echo of footsteps in the corridor dopplered in. Someone was approaching at a run. One person, by the sound of it. Flavian's expression said he, too, was genuinely puzzled. As the sound grew nearer, Krysza tried to thrust me behind her, the better to protect me, but the Unknown is always best faced together, side by side. In the frosted door window a shadow loomed, with a pale face. Belatedly I thought of securing the door.

Into the office burst an unmasked woman who somewhat resembled Krysza. Flaxen hair swirled like an umbrella as she spun about. Wide blue eyes sought us and found us. "You're here," she breathed, and coughed. "Oh, you're here."

It was the young woman whose eyes briefly had met mine at the intersection.

"Did you two make love in here?" she cried. "Please tell me you haven't made love in here."

On Eridania there is considerable preamble before one asks such a personal question. Sometimes years of preamble. Krysza and I exchanged glances. "We have, in fact," I said.

She whimpered, and put her fists to her head. "Oh, no. Oh, no."

And then she screamed.

🌑🌑🌑

The door I'd been unable to open led to, among other things, a wash basin. While Doctor Flavian fetched a glass of water, Krysza and I sat the young woman on the sofa (her name, she'd mumbled, between sobs, was Hypasha) and took turns trying to calm and console her, with minimal success. Alternately she sipped and coughed, the sounds punctuated by Flavian's my-mys and oh-dears as he trudged around the room. From time to time he fluttered his fingers on his chest, a bureaucrat out of his bureau. I understood something of what he felt. A creature of routine, he'd encountered a development beyond his expectations. Krysza and I felt the same way toward Earth. So very little matched the information in our briefings.

At last Hypasha gasped, and nudged the glass away. Vacant blue eyes gaped around the room. "All gone now. I can't go. You can't take me with you."

46

I caught her chin and tilted her face toward mine. "Let's start at the beginning. I'm Char—"

"I know who you are," she snapped, and wrenched her chin from my grip. "I overheard you introduce yourselves to that boy. And I know exactly what you are. That's why I followed you. I thought . . . I thought . . ." She put her fists to her head, and for a moment I expected her to scream again. But she regained control of that primal urge, swallowed, and forced her words out. Focus returned to her eyes, and with it a clarity as cold as space. "I couldn't figure how you stayed alive this long. But when I looked up DOOPHUS in my PC, I knew. I *knew*. I was going to ask you . . . I came here to find you, to ask you . . . to *beg* you . . ." And then she broke down again. Tortuous sobs wracked her body, tears matted her hair.

PC, mouthed Krysza, to me.

My fingers went to Hypasha's right ear, and found the lump. "Palm computer," I said softly, to my wife. "They're wired here. Maybe linked to some central network. It must have something to do with Order."

"It has everything to do with Order," said Flavian, leaning now against the front of his desk. "Yes yes yes. Everything you say and do is recorded and evaluated." He jabbed a thick finger at the ceiling. What I had supposed to be air vents were apertures for sensors. The room was under constant surveillance. Audio and visual, probably even nosmic. "Should you perform an act that warrants your deletion," Flavian went on, as if from behind a podium in a lecture hall, "you will be deleted at the nearest intersection. This was explained to you at the beginning of your sixteenth year. There is a list of proscribed acts. Yes yes yes."

"I'm fourteen," protested Krysza. "Milady is fifteen."

"Earth years," I whispered.

Krysza rolled her eyes, chagrined.

"It doesn't matter," said Hypasha, despondent now. Her voice was a wood rasp on old knots. "You made love here. It was recorded. When you reach the next intersection, you will be deleted."

"That is insane," said Krysza.

"That is Order," said Flavian. "Yes yes yes. Order keeps us

secure. As we comport ourselves, so shall we live."

"Are you telling me that what Krysza and I did in here was *wrong?*"

Hypasha swung her head from side to side, slowly, sadly. "There is no wrong. There is no right. There is only Order. You may do what you wish. You are free to do so. But if you perform a proscribed act, you will be deleted."

Krysza repeated herself, a clear signal of her utter astonishment. "This is insane."

"Who makes up this list?" I asked. I wanted to have a word or two with him.

Flavian gave me a blank look. Hypasha said, "I don't think anyone remembers. It's been this way all my life. If I hadn't begun to realize what I was, I might never have given the matter anymore thought than anyone else does."

Flavian was still drawing a blank, but his mouth worked. "And what is it that you are, my dear?"

And almost immediately, he added, "Oh, I see. Yes yes yes. My my my."

Krysza hugged herself at the same time I felt a stone form in my stomach. "We can't leave this block?" she said. "We can't even approach an intersection?"

Hypasha looked away, her answer transparent. Krysza coughed again, and I'd had enough. "What the *hell* is wrong with the air here?" I yelled, to no one in particular.

Flavian's slate remained empty. "Nothing is wrong with the air. No no no. It's purified to ensure that nothing is wrong with it. No impurities allowed. No no no. We are quite healthy here, my dears, I assure you. On Eridania you might experience respiratory difficulties, but not here, not on Earth."

"They pass ordinary air through an intersection," Krysza whispered bitterly. "And it comes out breathable."

The stone in my belly became a boulder. I rushed from the sofa and grabbed Flavian by the throat. "*What have you people done?*"

The Universe's gentlest hands tugged at my arm. A damp cheek nuzzled my shoulder—Krysza was weeping. "Let it go, beloved," she said. A sweep of her nose across my sleeve removed a couple teardrops. "It's too late. There will come no more. Eridania must survive on its own, as it has these years."

Flavian, for all his bulk, seemed to cower before me, and I released him. He'd done me no harm . . . probably his bureaucratic ancestors had meant no harm, either. They'd sought only Order, and they'd gotten what they wished for.

We had to tell Eridania: Make no more inquiries.

As for those who had other, divergent wishes—

Krysza knew my mind before I'd reached the decision. She gave me a little nod and a kiss, before I returned my attention to the sofa and to Hypasha, still despondent.

"You have to tell them," I said, and gave her the operating instructions for the *Eclair de Lune*. These were in fact quite simple. An order of "Return to Eridania" was required, nothing more. Hypasha's face radiated lambent joy, then sorrow, as the full implications of my instructions sank in. I shook my head once, firmly, to end her lament before she made it. Krysza was right: we had no choice.

I glanced at Flavian. "Take him with you," I said. "His function here is at an end.Let him breathe some air."

"My my my," said Flavian.

Hypasha hesitated. Now that the moment of decision was upon her, she was experiencing the perfectly normal momentary faintness of heart.

"You said yourself it was what you wanted," I reminded her. "Take it. Explore, live, fall in love. And remember us to Eridania."

Hypasha stood up, her expression sufficiently eloquent. "Yes, of course."

They left. No tearful goodbyes, no my-dears, for which Krysza and I were grateful. Flavian continued to appear numbed by sudden events. But he was a Doctor of something, and that would prove useful on Eridania. Perhaps, in time, he could explain to the colony why they were now, and of right ought to be, independent.

"What now?" whispered my wife.

"We can't live here, beloved. Not our way."

She looked at the sofa, and then at me . . .

The Unknown is always best faced together, side by side. In the morning, we decided to cross against the light.

Gallium Girl

The dreadful sounds coming from the area of the cooler in the rear of the store invested Lybbie with more than the usual apprehensions about her job: a woman, alone, late night, convenience store. She always labored with those four strikes against her—five, counting her real name—and she'd hardly been up to bat. But the sounds were something else entirely.

Lybbie had only just become aware of them, because they had been so strange that she'd had no point of reference for them, and therefore they could not be. But the snuffling and smacking were insistent, and she realized that they had been going on for some time. Minutes, perhaps. Standing on the slightly elevated floor behind the register, she listened with growing trepidation. She sought to place the noises in a familiar context, something in her experience. An image coalesced in her mind, of a frustrated plumber using a plunger to unclog a toilet that had been stuffed with marshmallows. The image explained the growling and the *thucks* and the *snarfs*. But there was no plumber in the store. There was, in fact, as far as she knew, no one else in the store.

Maybe someone came in while I was stocking the chips. Yes, that could be. It's just a late-night customer, grousing.

Only this, she recalled, from Poe, *and nothing more.*

He could not have entered through the back door. She had locked it just after seven, three hours ago. *Didn't I lock it? Oh, God . . .*

As the uncertainty shredded her nerves, she glanced up at the security mirrors. The aisles were empty. The mirror that reflected the back of the store was still out of alignment—Carson had promised to have it reset, but the store manager did not have to work the late shift, hence the procrastination—but Lybbie caught a glimpse of a reflection in the glass doors of the cooler. Something dark hunched near the sour cream. What the hell . . . ?

Her heart felt like a cooked turkey giblet, lodged in her throat. It gave her contralto a tremulous note. "Everything OK back there?" she called.

The darkness seemed to shift. It's not a shadow, she thought. The notion entered her mind then that Bigfoot had migrated to southeastern Arizona and was now scavenging for party dip. This was impossible, of course, but there was a costume rental here in Sierra Vista, and perhaps he was on the way to a party somewhere. Lybbie herself had once toyed with the idea of attending a Halloween party dressed as Mary Marvel, the superhero wife of Captain Marvel. If she stopped slouching, her figure could handle the red tights, but her hair was straw-yellow and long and straight, not golden and curly, not suitably superheroish, and her eyes were not cornflower blue but a sort of not-quite-jade-not-quite-serpentine. Instead, not a party person, she had opted for a nightshirt and bed. Now she wished Bigfoot would follow her lead.

Something solid yet soft thudded to the floor, like a glob of dough. The frozen biscuits were in that area. Had he opened a tube of them? If so, why? As she stepped down from behind the register a tiny internal voice told her to call the police, but the mystery had already hooked her, like a scab that just had to be worried loose to see if the wound had healed. Most times, a little dot of blood formed, because the scab had been removed too soon. But that never stopped you from worrying the next one loose.

"Hello?"

The sounds stopped momentarily, then resumed with vigor. "Insignificance becomes me," Lybbie muttered. She crept closer to the end of the aisle, but as she prepared to turn left, to confront the customer, something flew past her into the canned soups next to her and tumbled to the floor. Lybbie stifled a yelp, and looked down at the remains of an oblong, waxed cardpaper carton. The end had been shredded, and marked by what appeared to be tooth prints, as if the customer had been desperate to get at the goodies inside. To get at Luanne's Extra Firm Tofu.

Lybbie stood up, rounded the end of the aisle, and yelled, "What's going on here?" quite before she recognized what she was confronting. A dark shape rose up on hind legs, freezing her in her tracks. A *werewolf*? No . . . a man in a werewolf costume. The muzzle of his mask was smeared with tofu. It dripped from his fangs and his paws, and tiny globs of it festooned his chest fur.

Knowing a confrontation was imminent, Lybbie felt her heart race. She was on the verge of pointing out to the festive customer that he was going to have to pay for all the tofu he had consumed on the premises when he lowered his head slightly, and looked directly into her eyes.

Wrong again, she realized. It *is* a werewolf.

It charged her. Petrified, she could only scream. Paws thrust at her blouse, tearing it open. Instantly the creature released her and emitted a long, mournful howl—and dashed away, leaving her to spill onto the floor like a pudding. Packages of bread and hot dog buns cushioned her as she slumped helplessly against the shelves.

After a while Lybbie began to hear moans, little clusters of *uh-uh-uh*s, over and over. She became aware of movement, of someone rocking back and forth, and of other sounds as the movement disturbed the clear plastic wrappers of the hot dog buns. Presently she came to accept that she herself was the one moving, and moaning. But neither stopped.

She sat on the linoleum, her left leg straight, right bent at the knee, ankle under her left knee. Something cold pressed against the bare skin of her right thigh: the empty tofu container, caught under her skirt. She pried it out and held it up to the light for examination. It seemed quite ordinary. But what was it doing out of the cooler?

And then she remembered: Oh.

The moaning stopped. She was not conscious of having stopped it. I should call the cops, she thought. I should report this. The decision taking shape, she thought about what she was going to say.

. . . The store out on Highway 90, that's right, just before you get to Moson Road . . . yes, a werewolf, that's what I said. It broke into the cooler and ate all the tofu . . . no, tofu . . . that's right . . . yes, a werewolf ate the tofu. And then it attacked me and tore my blouse, and ran away . . .

"OK," she muttered. "OK, I can't call the cops. I can't leave this mess for the midnight relief. Who's relieving me? Eldridge, right. I can't leave this for him. And I can't explain it to Carson, he'll fire me.

53

So I have to clean it up, and hope they don't notice the loss during inventory week."

Slowly, like an accordion opening, she got to her feet. *Story of my life.*

🐱🐱🐱

Swing shift, Lybbie told herself, wasn't all that bad. You got to sleep at night, and you had a few hours of daylight to enjoy before you went to work. It was better than having to sleep during the day and be up all night like a vampire.

Like a werewolf.

She slouched in front of the mirror in the bathroom of her efficiency apartment in the southern part of town. Except for the cross pendant, she was naked. In her recent memory she did not see herself driving home after Eldridge had relieved her, or climbing the stairs to the second floor of the apartment complex, or unlocking her door. Vaguely she remembered stripping off her clothes, because the light rustle of fabric across her nipples as she shrugged out of her blouse had given her the first sensation she could recall since she had stood and begun to clean up the mess around the cooler. She had also stepped out of her red plaid skirt and her undies.

So why are you in front of the mirror?

"I don't know," she answered herself, without enthusiasm. "Maybe because I'm the only one who wants to look at me." In the mirror she saw the bed behind her, and on it the teddy bear body pillow with one eye missing. In the light from overhead, the other eye seemed to be winking. "Except you, Claire," she said, seeking to reassure the teddy. Briefly the winking continued. For an instant she saw another shape there, and whirled around, mouth open for a scream. The teddy reformed, oblivious to its temporary transformation.

"No nightmares," she pleaded with it.

🐱🐱🐱

Stepping into a steam-filled shower stall always gave Lybbie the feeling that she was a ghost, a spectral entity hidden—no, *trapped*—within her own contrived misty aura. Here she was safe, the outside universe reduced to vague images that broke through the steam here and there but never lingered long enough to reclaim her. The steam

54

muted her senses. She was aware of the heat of the water without feeling it. The only sounds that reached her ears were consistent with the shower.

As for touch . . .

The experimentation had begun at fourteen, not long after her first period, and quite by accident. Touch had felt good, and more touch had felt even better, and the more thorough the touch, the more exquisite the sensation. The very first time, at the moment of peak sensation, she had started to scream, then choked it off, hoping her mother had not heard. After her breathing had slowed, and with her body still dripping lather and water, she had whispered, "Wow." Lately she had come to see that all of her wows had been marvels of solitary engineering. There had been several boys, but none with anything close to the skills that she herself had developed over the years. She had remained safe, clean, and alone.

For now, she forced herself to be content with allowing the shower to cleanse her of the day she had just passed. In the desert, water was expensive, and she did not earn enough to indulge too frequently. Where water was rationed, she had to ration herself. The caress of steam vapors would have to suffice.

Not until Lybbie had finished drying herself did the realization break through the wall her subconscious was trying to erect: *I saw a fucking werewolf tonight.*

Still naked and somewhat damp, Lybbie sat down on her bed, clasped her hands, and clamped them between her knees. Hunched over, she stared down at the small throw rug that cushioned her feet against the bare concrete floor. It had a design like a Native American talisman in turquoise and tangerine, but it could not defend her from the events of the evening. What did it mean, to see a werewolf? She had supposed the Dark Side to be something the entertainment industry invented, its creatures designed to chill and thrill, nothing more. Even now a part of her refused to credit what she had seen. Yet something had ripped her blouse. What, if not the creature?

She reached for the garment, which lay at the foot of the bed where she had cast it while disrobing. The top button was missing, and there were several tears on either side below the collar that rendered the blouse unusable, at least for work. She might wear it to putter around the apartment. It had cost her twenty five dollars, and she had worn it perhaps half a dozen times. She could not charge a replacement to the convenience store.

Finally she stretched out on top of the bedcovers and reached for the teddy bear body pillow, drawing it close alongside her. She wrapped her arms around it, and draped her right leg over it. With her face pressed against the furry neck, she began to weep softly.

❧❧❧

Morning arrived uninvited. Lybbie threw an arm over her eyes to blot out the sunlight and rolled over, one leg draped over Claire. Dream sleep had not quite left her, and for a moment she experienced an erotic chill, as if she had not slept alone, after all. She murmured something unintelligible even to herself, and blinked rapidly, awakening at last.

"Gmorn, Claire," Lybbie sighed, and disengaged herself from the body pillow. She sat up, dropping her feet to the rug. Scraggly straw-yellow hair spilled over her shoulders and breasts, giving her something of a Godiva look. *I'll bet*, she thought, getting to her feet, *I could ride a fucking horse through this town, dressed like this, and nobody would notice.* Cobwebs of sleep vaporized in the morning sunlight . . .

. . . and a dark shape flashed across her mind, a creature bristling with hair and teeth, ripping into her memory before it, too, vaporized.

"Jesus God!" cried Lybbie. Eyes wide and wild, she looked around. Saw nothing to alarm her. Her arms felt strange. She raised her left, examining the forearm. The skin was covered with goosebumps, and all the fine pale hairs had come erect. "Jesus God," she whispered.

In a crisis, she thought, do something, anything. She moved to the old armoire in the corner by the window and rifled through it for panties, denim cutoffs, and a turquoise tee two sizes too large. Quickly she dressed, throwing on a pair of open-toed sandals for good measure, and went to the dinette for breakfast. The last of a box of muesli went into a bowl, followed by milk from the cooler, which, when she poured, emerged from the mouth of the bottle in clots.

56

Exasperated, Lybbie poured the remains of the outdated milk down the kitchen sink, then stared out the window at the street alongside the apartment complex. As yet no one was stirring. Saturday, she remembered. *I am so not going to have a day like this*, she told herself firmly. She tucked a five into a front pocket of her denims and headed out for breakfast at the McDonald's down at the intersection.

👀👀👀

Service was relatively quick at the McDonald's, Lybbie being at the moment the only patron. She carried the tray with its two breakfast burritos, cake of hash browns, and cup of coffee to a table for two across the aisle from the bank of condiments, and sat down. In the background she heard a glass door open and close several times, but she did not look until she became aware of a dark shape in her periphery. She glanced up, and swallowed a scream.

The man standing just inside the side entrance might have just emerged from her waking nightmare. On any other previous day she would have readily dismissed him as a bag man, but not today, not now. Lybbie kept very still. He had not seen her yet. His narrow, pinched face and deep-set, bloodshot eyes were all but obscured by a thick mane of graying black hair. *Hasn't the man heard of razors*, she thought, and then banished the question from her mind before, as if he could hear her thoughts, he went off in search of one. *No sharp objects for him*, please!

Abruptly the man turned toward the rest rooms. Lybbie stifled a hiccup of humor. *Do werewolves shave?*

A discussion slightly louder than the usual order-placement at the counter snagged Lybbie's attention. Remonstrating with the cashier was a young woman attired in rags. Dumpster-diving-day for the bag people at McDonald's, Lybbie thought. This one was wearing denim cut-offs rather like hers, but with the seams open all the way up to the beltline, revealing that she was either naked underneath or wearing a thong. A length of green and white bungee cord, tied in a bow in front, served as a belt. Above that, a tattered yellow tee covered the essentials of her upper body. It too was open along the sides, the hem tied in knots on either side. Her feet were shod by a

57

pair of shower clogs, the left clearly larger than the right, and the strap of the right one had popped loose, so that she had to crimp her toes to keep it on.

"There's nothing I can sell you for a quarter," the cashier repeated. "And you aren't dressed for . . ."

The woman indicated her feet and upper body. "Shoes plus shirt equals service," she said brightly.

The cashier defaulted to the primary objection. "But you have no money."

As the woman turned to leave, Lybbie's eyes locked with hers. Face suddenly hot, as if she had been caught snooping in someone else's closet, Lybbie averted her gaze, but before the moment could pass into oblivion, she looked at the woman once more, and on impulse made a little gesture toward the chair across the table. Without hesitation the woman accepted the offer. As she seated herself Lybbie took a moment's smug satisfaction from seeing the cashier frown.

"Lybbie," she said, extending her hand, and withdrawing it after a brief clasping during which she imprinted the woman's face in her mind. A shock of uncombed shoulder-length hair the exact color of freshly-sheared copper framed a heart-shaped, almost anime-like face dominated by wide, deep violet eyes. On that face, the snub nose seemed diminished. The anime similarity ended at the mouth, though. Instead of full-lipped, round and pouty it was wide and thin, the lower lip cracked here and there by the desert heat. Despite the ever-present Arizona sun her pale skin was unburned, albeit seriously freckled. All in all, concluded Lybbie, as she withdrew her hand, it was not a beautiful face, but a face not to be forgotten.

"Short for Elizabeth?" asked the woman. Dryness lent a touch of smoke to her contralto.

Lybbie cringed. "You wouldn't believe me even if I showed you my birth certificate."

"Perhaps not. But I wouldn't laugh, either. Oh, and I'm Claire."

The coffee cup in Lybbie's hand paused halfway to her mouth. "Oh, but that's who I sleep with," she blurted, and almost dropped the cup on the tray. "Oh, jeez, I didn't mean to say that."

Claire brushed aside the *faux pas*. "That doesn't sound to me as if you're referring to your boyfriend."

"I don't have . . . I mean, no, that's my teddy bear body pillow."

Shut up, Lybbie. Shut up shut up shut up.

"I really don't need both these breakfast burritos," Lybbie added quickly, fleeing the scene she had inadvertently created. "Impulsive of me, but I thought . . ."

Claire smiled. Heretofore Lybbie had thought a smile capable of lighting up a room to be a Hollywood figment, but the table did brighten, as did her spirit. "I could make do with that, or half that slab of hash browns," said Claire.

Lybbie slid the tray to the middle of the table. After sniffing the burrito Claire took a big bite of it, hardly stopping to chew before she forced more into her mouth.

"I actually have money," said Claire, before swallowing. Her tongue flicked over her front teeth, scouring fragments of egg free. "I just neglected to . . . well, it's in my other clothes, along with my key. I have to call the landlord to let me in, and he won't be available until—what's wrong?"

"He's back," Lybbie whispered hoarsely. "Jeez, he's back."

"He who?" Claire glanced at the counter, and turned back. "Oh. What about him?"

Feeling a chill, Lybbie rubbed her bare arms, but said nothing.

"He scares you," said Claire. "He scared you?"

Lybbie fought the urge to scramble to her feet and dash away. From the man, yes, but also from Claire, and from the embarrassment of having disclosed personal information, and from . . .

Mentally Lybbie shook herself as a dog just out of the bath. From *herself,* she had been about to think. To flee from herself.

And from the knowing way Claire was looking at her. Lybbie had no frame of reference for describing it, no one having quite looked at her in that way before.

What way?

Well . . .

As if Claire were a gardener and she were a freshly bloomed rose under her protection.

Lybbie made a little sound of exasperation, and took a sip of coffee. *That sounds so*, she told herself, and stopped, unable to complete the thought.

"Lybbie," Claire said softly.

Lybbie blinked. "Sorry. Drifting."

The redhead grinned. "I've been known to do that."

"Yes," said Lybbie. "He frightens me."

"Have you seen him somewhere before?"

Lybbie hesitated. "I'm not sure . . ."

"Ah! He reminds you of someone that frightened you. Or—or some*thing*." Claire glanced at the man again. "Maybe you had a nightmare about werewolves or something. I can see how he might remind you of that."

Lybbie just stared at her.

Suddenly there came the sound of impact, and Lybbie started, with a little whimpered scream. The man had struck the counter for emphasis. "No, no *meat*!" he fairly shouted. "Just the green pepper. I can't have meat. I'm vegan."

"Looks more like he's from Arcturus," whispered Claire slyly. Lybbie resumed her stare. "Hello?" added Claire, snapping her fingers. "That was a joke. You know. Joke?"

Exasperated, the man threw up his hands. "No! *Forget it*!" he yelled, and strode angrily out the exit.

"I don't think he means you any harm," said Claire. Her eyes went to the clock in the wall above the counter. "Oh, hey, I gotta make a phone call. Oh, wait, it's thirty five cents. Damn!"

"We can go to my apartment," blurted Lybbie.

Did I just say that?

Claire flashed a grin, then shook her head. "Not on the first date."

Lybbie sputtered. "What? *Oh!* No, *no*, I'm not a—"

Before she could complete the clarifying protest, all thought came to a screeching halt. She had always supposed that to be a figure of speech, but now it seemed to her, as she listened to herself as if from a distance, that her brain was indeed grinding down, like a train pulling into the station. Metal wheels no longer rolled on metal rails, sliding now instead. The conductor in her frontal lobe set the handbrake. She was parked on a siding now. In a moment she could proceed, going back the way she had come, or . . .

Or.

The Universe had passed by on the main track, and now she was free to go. The brain fired up again, and its first act of cognition was

Oh

My

God

In slow motion, as if she were unaware of the act, Lybbie set her coffee cup down on the table. Her eyes stared through Claire, through the great glass window that divided the eating bay from the playground outside, through the plastic Ronald, and the parking lot beyond, and beyond that the Superstitions and the Dutchman's yellow gold and on out to the farthest quasar.

Is that possible? How would I know? Whom can I ask?

Something hot and abrasive seized her wrist. Like a long telescope suddenly closing, she withdrew from the quasar, the Ronald, the window, *snap!*

"—all right?" Claire was pleading. "Hello?"

Lybbie felt her irises focus.

Claire released her wrist and blew a sigh of relief. "*There* you are. For a moment there I thought you were someone else."

"Someone else," whispered Lybbie. "Yes. Maybe . . ." She dragged weary fingers through her hair. "Oh, hell. I meant you could make a call from my place. It's not far."

"It's OK," Claire said gently. "I accept."

Lybbie had expected Claire to follow her into the apartment, and was somewhat puzzled to turn around and find her still standing in the open doorway. During the ten-minute walk from the restaurant to her place, they had touched upon careers: Lybbie had some interest in history and geology, which dovetailed rather nicely with Claire's background in anthropology and a fondness for spelunking and rockhounding, though neither woman had gone further than her junior year of college. By the time they reached the entrance to the apartment complex, they had touched upon current prospects, at which point Claire had become pensive. Now, at the top of the stairs, she had grown reluctant.

Lybbie spread her arms in an unspoken question.

Claire's smile flickered. "I just recalled thinking that you had become someone else," she said carefully. "And now I'm on the verge of entering your . . . lair, as it were."

"I was just . . . thinking, is all. Please. Come in."

Claire stepped into the room and closed the door behind her. "It must have been something I said, then."

Lybbie's response was an absent whisper. "Yeah." She snagged the phone from its charging base and handed it to Claire. "I'm light on food, but I can probably find something more for you to eat."

"Doubtless," Claire said blithely. Punching out a number, she declined the offer with a shake of her head.

When she began speaking to her landlord, Lybbie went to the dinette, to the window that looked onto the alley one floor below, and stood with arms braced against the sill, staring out in the general direction of the green dumpster. A part of her wondered what the hell she thought she was doing. Another part of her—

She knows the answers to your questions.

"But I don't know what to ask," Lybbie muttered.

"A glass of water would be—" Claire called.

The abrupt end to the sentence made Lybbie turn around. Claire had dropped the phone onto the bed and was doubled over, hugging herself.

"Bathroom!" she managed.

Lybbie pointed, and Claire staggered in that direction. "No, the *other* door," said Lybbie. "That's the closet. Are you OK?"

Presently from the bathroom came the sounds of retching. These passed. Lybbie remained where she stood, as if nailed to the floor. The toilet flushed. Water ran in the sink. She heard spitting, and a sound not unlike that made when drinking water from a cupped hand. A brief silence followed, during which Lybbie rather imagined that a towel was drying the redhead's face, mouth.

Mouth, thought Lybbie.

She started when Claire emerged from the bathroom, pale and drawn. Dark streaks down the front of her ragged tee suggested water, not partially digested food.

"Sorry," Claire said weakly. "It must have been the sausage."

"I feel fine," said Lybbie.

"Sausage prefers blondes," said Claire. "Um, the landlord will meet me in twenty minutes."

"Twenty minutes?" Lybbie repeated, still a bit numb.

"Not enough time, sadly." She glanced around the room: at the unmade bed, at the armoire with the second drawer still open, at the dinette with a few dirty dishes on the counter. "Cozy place," she allowed.

"Not enough time for what?" Lybbie asked.

"So that's Claire," said Claire.

Lybbie moved to the bed and started to sit down, then thought better of it, as if something was lurking behind her, concealed within its own shadow, guiding her actions without explanation.

"So was it something I said?" pressed Claire.

"Grandma Moses," said Lybbie. "Cornelius Vanderbilt."

In the dim light from the window Claire's eyes glistened with mirth like sparks from an amethyst crystal. She barked a laugh. "What?"

Lybbie began to rearrange the two pillows at the head of the bed, making an inverted L with the Claire teddy. "Late bloomers," she explained. "Grandma Moses didn't realize she was an artist until she was like eighty. Vanderbilt didn't earn his first million until he was almost seventy."

"I see. So you think there's someone else inside you, trying to get out?"

"I don't think it's trying very hard," said Lybbie, straightening the top sheet and the comforter.

"If you live in the dark, you do tend to blink at the first contact with light. Discovery is like that."

The simple statement shocked Lybbie with its clarity. She stopped fiddling with the bed covers, but would not look at Claire. "You know what I'm talking about," she said, very softly.

Claire's tone contained a desultory shrug. "Life is discovery. Of who you could be. Whether that's also who you are, or who you become, is rather up to you. We all have potential."

Lybbie nodded. "So what would you do if you thought you were on the verge of discovery?"

"Me? I'd run with it."

Lybbie stood up, and looked at her at last. "Is that what you did?"

Claire grinned. "I'm Popeye. I yam what I yam. Hmm, or is that Descartes?" She jerked a thumb at the door and began edging toward it. "Anyway, speaking of running, I must. Landlord, remember? Thanks for the . . . thanks for sharing."

"Wait---"

"Gotta go."

And she was gone.

☯ ☯ ☯

All air left Lybbie. She felt invertebrate as she collapsed, sitting, onto the bed, jostling the Claire pillow hard enough to make it almost sit up. Had she the strength, she would have wept. Instead, she clasped her hands and held them tightly between her knees, and hunched forward, fighting for breath. *Haugh, haugh, haugh.*

God what did I do?

What do I do?

Lybbie slowly sat up.

She seemed interested in me as a person. As a friend. She knows I don't know where she lives. She knows where I live. If she is sincere, she will return.

"And what do I do then?" she asked the pillow.

The single eye merely winked at her, a reflection from the overhead light.

Her forearm, laid across her upper thigh, touched something crinkly, something hard. She slipped her hand into the pocket and found a dollar bill and a quarter and a dime and two pennies, the change from breakfast.

The coins should have been a quarter and three pennies. *There must have been a dime in the penny well,* she thought. *All lucky breaks appreciated.*

A dime I could have given her for her phone call, and not invited her back here.

Lybbie got to her feet and made for the dinette. "You're over-analyzing," she scolded herself. On the counter dirty dishes beckoned, and she dropped them one by one into the sink, the silverware last. After the forks landed she heard another metallic sound, and realized belatedly that it had come from the alley below. She peered out the window. The hairy man from McDonald's had thrown open the lid to the dumpster and was rummaging inside it.

Lybbie's heart raced. Had he followed her home? Did he know she lived here? Even as those questions formed, he looked up at the windows, as if searching for something, and she ducked back before he spotted her. She wished she had curtains to draw, but there was no help for it, not now. She dashed to the door and closed the bolt and set the security chain. If the man changed into a werewolf, she doubted the measures would keep him out of her apartment, but he was not a werewolf yet.

Another *clang* reached her ears and she cringed. Perhaps he was frustrated by the poor pickings in the dumpster and had slammed the lid. What would he do next? Go door to door, checking for unlocked ones?

Lybbie ran back to the dinette window and risked a peek. The man was not in the alley. She leaned closer to the window, to increase her angle of vision. Nothing. The alley was empty, save the dumpster and assorted detritus. Nothing moved. He was not there.

Oh God . . .

She could call the police. She could tell them . . . what? That a hairy homeless man was going through the dumpster in the alley behind her apartment? Oh, yes, they'd come right out for that.

Lybbie growled in frustration. What to do?

She took a breath. She took several. She leaned on the counter and stared out at the alley and tried to relax. To think.

I could hit him with my Claire pillow.

Claire, she thought. She would know what to do.

No . . . she would expect me to know what to do. That's the kind of girl she wants.

65

She ran back to the door. Listened. Undid the chain and threw open the bolt. Cracked the door. Listened again. Nothing.

Wait. A knock? It came from downstairs. She heard voices. A man's voice, gruff and . . .

Girl she wants?

"Shhh!" said Lybbie, listening carefully.

You said "girl she wants."

"Yes I did. Now be quiet. I'm busy."

A door banged shut. Presently she heard knocking again.

He was indeed going door to door, as she feared.

Lybbie re-secured the door and returned to the bed to consider her options. The simplest was not to answer the door if he knocked. But if she did not answer, perhaps he would think that no one was home, that he might break in with impunity. As an alternative she might leave the apartment; if he broke in, he could do no harm to her.

"Lair," Claire had called her apartment.

Would she want a girl who would not defend her lair?

"Oh, she doesn't want me," said Lybbie, with an air of finality. "Passing ships in the night. Or at McDonald's. What is that quote? Longfellow?" She thought for a moment. "'Only a look and a voice; then darkness again and silence.'"

It was the silence, she thought, that was the killer. The hairy man in the hallway below was as nothing compared to that silence. She'd had her look, bestowed upon her by the vivid Claire, and the voice as well, the little words and hints. She understood that now. The way Claire had looked at her. *What did she see that I cannot see?* The remark about first dates. Claire's sly retort at being offered something to eat. And . . . and that bit about there not being enough time. That *had* to mean—

"Omigod," whispered Lybbie.

Claire had departed, hurriedly, and darkness had indeed returned, and silence.

Lybbie closed her eyes. What would it be like? Touching her body the way she touched herself. Being touched the way she touched herself. But there would be so much more. Her mouth on mine, and on me. My mouth on her . . .

66

Lybbie shivered, and rubbed fresh goosebumps on her arms.

"But how do I know that's what she wants? What if she was just being sassy?"

She had no answer for herself. She thought she caught a glimpse of something lucent in the back of her mind, but the knock at her door dispelled it. She swallowed a scream. *The kind of girl she wants would defend her lair.* So be it.

In the utility drawer next to the utensil drawer there was a small ball peen hammer she used for driving tacks into the wall, to hang pictures and calendars. Silently she drifted across the floor, opened the drawer, and withdrew the tool. The knock came again, more insistently this time. She waited, hammer raised and ready, without responding.

The doorknob jiggled. Again Lybbie stifled a scream. Her knuckles whitened around the hammer's handle. She waited. She hoped to hear muffled sounds, of the man moving off down the hallway to the next apartment. Ears keened, she listened for knocking. Perhaps there was a series of fuzzy thumps; she could not be certain.

Lybbie held her breath.

She kept very still, hammer aloft, eyes transfixing the door. Minutes took hours to pass. No more sounds reached her. Had the man left? She could not determine this unless she opened the door, and that entailed risk, a risk she did not have to take. Gradually the hammer descended. Her arm was growing weary, and the threat no longer felt imminent. Her lips parted to issue a sigh of relief. It was over, at least for the moment.

The hammer began to slip from her hand. She caught at it, and tossed it onto the old stuffed chair she had salvaged from a yard sale. Now it looked different, somehow: solitary, alone. *Single occupancy*, she realized. *I have a chair because I don't need a couch.*

She screamed at the peremptory knock at her door. In fright she forgot the hammer, but there was no time to remember it because as soon as her scream died she heard a voice in the hallway.

"*Lybbie!* Are you OK? *Let me in!*"

Lybbie dashed to the door, threw the bolt and chain and yanked it open. The shape of Claire seemed to materialize right there in the hallway. It was all Lybbie needed to see. She glommed onto the redhead, throwing arms and legs around her. At first Claire staggered under the unexpected weight. Then she gathered herself and stepped into the apartment and kicked the door shut behind her, while Lybbie cried into the side of her neck.

Gradually Lybbie's feet lowered to the floor, but her arms remained in place, thrust around Claire's neck. She tried to stop crying, and gave up. She felt as if a fortress had surrounded her, the effect of Claire's embrace. With Claire in no apparent rush to disengage, Lybbie stood there with her. Soon her respiration calmed.

. . . girl she wants.

Lybbie took a step back. For a moment she closed her eyes, and opened them again, and nibbled at her lower lip. Claire shot her a puzzled look.

"The hairy man," said Lybbie. She did not bother to dry her face. "He was here."

Claire's expression faded to neutral. "That's not why you withdrew from me."

Lybbie hesitated. "I was frightened."

"Without fear, you would not possess the courage to overcome it," said Claire. She glanced at the hammer on the stuffed chair and added, "Besides, I think you can take care of yourself."

The redhead had changed clothes. Now she was attired in a short, green plaid skirt and a white jersey, and she had found a pair of tan sandals for her feet. She had also combed her hair and, probably, bathed. The faintest hint of Lady Stetson wafted from her. Belatedly Lybbie realized that she had recognized Claire by her eyes, her anime face. It astonished Lybbie to see that the brief but intense physical contact had hardened Claire's nipples. It astonished her even more to realize that she had in fact noticed this—and most of all, to realize that her own were in a similar state.

Jeez.

A smile toyed with the corners of Lybbie's mouth. "Girl she wants."

"What?"

Face suddenly warm, Lybbie shook her head quickly. "Nothing. You came back."

"I *had* to leave. But I didn't think we were finished."

"We?"

"You and I," Claire explained. "But I like 'we' better."

"Saves syllables, does it?"

After a stunned silence they both laughed. Then Claire said, the words blunt and direct, "That's not why you withdrew from me. The hairy man isn't here to be afraid of. You're afraid of the pronoun."

Lybbie whispered, "Yes."

"Stand up straight."

"What?"

Claire began to broadcast orders in staccato. "And square those shoulders. Look me in the eye. Look the Universe in the eye. Say hello, Universe."

Lybbie grinned, despite herself. "Hello, Universe."

"You slouch because your boyfriends have mostly been your height or shorter," said Claire. "I've seen it before. It's so unnecessary. Be you: if that's not good enough, neither are they. Sit down on the bed."

Lybbie obeyed. "I don't know—"

"Who you are," Claire finished for her. "Yes, I saw that. Your moment of discovery. Your eureka. I told you what I would do."

"Run—run with it?"

"You want to know. You want to find out. I don't know why it has taken you all these years to discover yourself. A late bloomer, you said. So am I. I understand." Claire lowered her eyes to Lybbie's tee. "I think you know your truth now. But it's only part of the truth. It's why I came back. May I sit down? There, beside you?"

Lybbie's heart pounded. She braved a "Yes."

Claire plopped down on the edge of the bed, to Lybbie's right, and twisted slightly to face her. She started to reach out, to take Lybbie's hands, then thought better of it. "You showed compassion for a stranger in need," she said softly. "Your mind is stimulating, your intellect challenging. Despite struggling to make do, you have not given up. You have . . . sorry, what was that?"

"I asked you how you knew that," Lybbie repeated.

"That you haven't given up?" Lybbie nodded, and Claire went on, "The books in that bookcase. No cookie-cutter romances for you, nuh-uh. No, I see: histories. Orwell's *Down and Out in Paris and London*. A geology text—"

Lybbie waved her hand dismissively. "I haven't read three-quarters of them."

"So you've read a quarter, then. Don't look at what you haven't done. Everyone has stacks and scads of stuff they haven't done. Look at what you've done, and then do more. Look at what you're going to do."

"What am I going to do?" Lybbie wanted to know.

Claire paused. She gazed briefly down at the floor. "You said you had no boyfriends," she said quietly. "No lovers."

Lybbie shook her head. "I never said that. I started to—but didn't quite."

"And the reason why not?"

Lybbie fell silent for a moment. "They don't wow me," she said at last. "I suppose you're going to tell me that I haven't met the right wowwer yet."

"I don't have to. You just did."

"Oh, that is so fucking profound," snapped Lybbie. She scrambled to her feet and moved away, and began to pace the floor in front of the armoire. Her voice grew louder as she vented. "You know so much about me. You know so much, period. So wise, you are. And I know what you are. I 'got' that bit about self-discovery. So yes, you had your big moment. But it's not that easy for others. For me. And how *can* you know so much? You're my age, right? How can you know all this about me and I don't even know it?"

"I'm twenty four."

Lybbie threw up her hands in disgust. "That's even worse. I'm three years older. What did I miss? What have I missed?"

"In some ways, I'm quite older," said Claire, still calm.

"More experienced, you mean."

"Yes, if you wish. Lybbie—"

Lybbie whirled on her. "Then where are *your* lovers? You have all this knowledge, all this experience. Where *are* they?"

Claire's eyes darkened, moist with regret. "They found out what I was, and left."

"That doesn't make any sense at all!"

"Lybbie—"

"*What?*" Instantly she was contrite. "What is it?" she asked, her voice softer.

"You're still afraid of the pronoun. You are not truly vexed. You are reacting from fear."

Lybbie sighed. "Yes. I am. And behaving badly. I'm sorry."

Claire patted the spot on the bed that Lybbie had vacated. Lybbie sat down, and folded her hands in her lap, and gazed down at the floor, and waited. For several seconds there was only the sound of their breathing. Dimly she was aware of the increase in body heat, and suspected that it stemmed from proximity rather than passion. The recent physical contact with Claire had been the result of fear and relief; sex had had nothing to do with it.

Even so, the contact had also brought her to the verge of arousal, and Claire as well. Their thin cotton shirts had been insufficient to conceal this fact. If that signified desire in Claire, then surely it signified the same for herself. More, when she had thrust her face against Claire's neck, there had been a momentary urge to kiss her there. From that point, it would have been a simple matter to shift her face around to Claire's, to touch lips with hers, and then to . . .

Lybbie's chest heaved, and she shuddered with sparks that cascaded from her neck and shoulders and disappeared down her spine. Her groin stirred.

Oh dear God . . . I do . . . I am . . .

Lybbie lifted her gaze to Claire. Neither spoke. Where before Claire had been bold and confident with her knowledge, now she looked placid, benign. She was waiting for something. Her distinctly non-anime mouth bore just a trace of a smile, the lips moist now and reflecting light from the overhead. Presently Lybbie leaned closer, and almost lost her balance. To support herself she threw her right arm across Claire's shoulders, and scooted herself over the comforter. Claire's hands, clasped in her own lap, did not move. Seconds passed, and the gap narrowed between their faces as Lybbie drew herself ever closer . . .

Can you hear my heart now?

—and closer. Warmth became heat. Lybbie's nervousness refused to abate, so she ignored it. It was just as well, for in that moment their lips touched, and then there was only heat and heartbeats.

Lybbie thought: *It's . . . different. It's like kissing—me, but not me.*

Then Claire's lips parted slightly, and Lybbie stopped thinking altogether.

Scant seconds passed, and there came a moment when Lybbie completely surrendered. She thrust herself against Claire, into Claire, her tongue a living thing now, Claire's darting past hers, then withdrawing, only to caress Lybbie's and to suck on it, to draw it further into her mouth. Lybbie lost her balance and slipped inadvertently from the bed to the floor.

And sat there gasping for breath.

Wow.

She felt Claire's hands on her arms, lifting, and a moment later she was back on the bed. Claire's eyes shone. Lybbie rather imagined that her own did as well. She tried to find her voice, failed, and cleared her throat to try again.

"It might be well to take your necklace off," suggested Claire. "We don't want to tangle our hair." She dipped her fingers under her own jersey and fished out a fine golden chain with an amber cabochon pendant set in gold, and drew it over her head, clearing her hair. Lybbie did the same with hers, and spilled it onto the night table. After Claire passed her the golden chain, the weight of it took her by surprise. She paused to examine it, hefting it in her hand.

"This," said Lybbie, her voice husky now, "this is real gold."

"I know. I had it made."

"But—but this weighs . . . it must be a thousand dollars in gold."

Claire shrugged. "A bit more, I think."

"But—"

"I told you I had money, Lybbie."

"But *this*—"

"Belongs on the night table," Claire said firmly, "next to yours."

"Yes. Yes, of course. There."

Claire spread her hand against Lybbie's chest and gave her a gentle shove, sprawling her onto the bed on her back. While Lybbie arranged her head on a pillow, Claire clambered further onto the bed and stretched out beside her, head resting on her left hand aprop her elbow. Her right index finger began to trace little designs on Lybbie's jersey, just over her sternum.

"You snogged me," said Claire.

"Sorry. Won't happen again."

Claire pouted, and Lybbie added, "Or will."

Lybbie felt Claire's fingertip expand its tracing to include the inner swells of her breasts.

"So what is Lybbie short for?" asked Claire.

"My Dad was a high school chemistry teacher," said Lybbie. "And very eccentric."

Claire began tracking her finger down now, toward Lybbie's navel. In sprawling onto the bed, the tee had ridden up, and Lybbie expelled a puff of air at the contact with her bare skin. Tiny muscles fluttered on her abdomen, as if a flock of butterflies had landed there.

"So?" prodded Claire.

"Molybdena," said Lybbie. "Female form of molybdenum. Or so he supposed."

Lybbie felt Claire's finger—fingers, now—pass over the front of her cutoffs, and down the top of her right thigh. For a moment she was in her shower, lathered up. But it was not quite the same. This was not her own practiced touch, but the touch of—another woman.

What am I doing?

"Molybdena," repeated Claire, savoring each syllable. "Oh, I quite like that. Hmm. Very high melting point, molybdenum. Let's see if that's true." She withdrew her hand. "Close your eyes."

Lybbie obeyed. "What are you going to do?"

"What do you want me to do?"

"Oh, that's not fair! I don't know—"

"Close your eyes."

73

" . . . I don't know anything about . . . I don't know how . . ."

"Shh! We're women. We aren't built for invasive, penetrating love-making. We aren't takers. We aren't built for taking what we want. We're givers. I give to you, you give to me. I make you wow, and you make me wow. We give to each other. That's how it works best. Touch is our guide. We respond to it. The response tells us we're doing something right. You touch yourself, right?"

"Well . . . yes."

"Keep your eyes closed. You wow yourself?"

"It's the only—"

"Shh. I understand. It's OK. But given a choice, wouldn't you prefer that I did that for you? That I gave that to you?"

"But you aren't even touching me now—" And she gasped, a prolonged expulsion of air, as Claire's fingertip unexpectedly passed with a feather's caress across her left nipple. It came erect instantly, and in the same moment Lybbie arched her back. The gasp finished, she collapsed back onto the bed.

Presently Lybbie opened her eyes. The sensation of unexpected contact had left her bereft of thought. If Claire had placed two paddles against her body and yelled, "Clear!" she could not have elicited a greater response.

"Never," she sighed, not quite speechless.

"It's not something you could do to yourself," Claire pointed out. "You always know where your hand is."

"I can do without the analysis of technique."

Claire laughed. "Sorry. Just one more observation: you were named for the wrong element. I believe gallium melts at room temperature."

Lybbie was inclined to agree, but said nothing as Claire's hand resumed its tracing, its journey. Once more she closed her eyes, and set her senses adrift. To relax utterly she spread-eagled herself, her arms crossing the T of her body. Her left hand smacked against the top of the night stand, jostling the necklaces. The impact distracted her from Claire's touch.

My tee completely conceals my necklace. How did you know I was wearing one?

"Are you all right?" asked Claire. "For a moment there, you tensed."

"I hit my hand."

Claire leaned across Lybbie and drew the injured hand to her lips, kissing it gently before setting it back down. "Better?"

With Claire's breast pressed over her mouth, Lybbie could only mumble a response. The contact itself was stunning, and Lybbie's right hand twitched as she stifled the urge to slide it under Claire's jersey.

As if reading Lybbie's thoughts, Claire sat back on her haunches, grasped the hem of her jersey with both hands, and drew it up over her head, casting it to the foot of the bed. Her tan suggested she had worn a loose tank top on occasion, but only rarely a bra. Her breasts, like Lybbie's, were not much larger than average oranges; she scarcely required any support.

"Your turn," said Claire.

Lybbie hesitated. "I'm not sure I'm . . . ready to . . . to . . ."

"Take your top off? It's just like the showers in high school gym class, right?"

"That's . . . that was different."

"True." Claire laid back down and propped her head on her hand again. "I'm sorry. It's new to you. You've never been naked and sexual with another woman. You want to be . . . but at your own speed, your own time."

"I'm sorry. I'm . . . just not ready to take my clothes off."

"Well . . . I had hoped to assist you with that. Don't want you doing all the work."

Lybbie laughed, despite herself.

"And don't be sorry," added Claire. "At least you haven't asked me to leave."

"I would never—" began Lybbie, and froze. She had reached for Claire to reassure her, and instead palmed her breast, almost cupping it, her fingers slipping between Claire's flank and arm. Before she could withdraw from contact, Claire pressed her upper arm against Lybbie's hand, securing it there.

"If you do not wish to touch me," said Claire, "I'll release you."

Lybbie swallowed. "All right. I mean, no, it's OK." On impulse she took a chance, moved her thumb, brushed it across the nipple, which was pebbly now. Claire drew a breath and leaned into Lybbie's palm, and made a tiny sound, half-growl, half-yum.

It was almost, but not quite, the same sound Claire had made while eating the burrito. Which had not stayed down. She had blamed the sausage.

But mine was OK.

Lybbie pulled her hand away.

Claire's eyes widened. "What is it? What's wrong?"

The possibility that had just flown through Lybbie's mind vanished before she could hold it down for examination.

That doesn't make any sense at all!

I said that earlier. Because Claire had said her lovers had found out who she was.

But wouldn't they have already known?

The hard knock at the door startled them both. Claire's hand moved with dazzling quickness to cover Lybbie's mouth, while Lybbie went rigid with fear.

"Shh," hissed Claire, the sound just audible.

Lybbie nodded, and Claire removed her hand. It's him, Lybbie mouthed.

The doorknob rattled, but remained locked. They turned their heads to stare at it. Claire sat up, then pulled Lybbie up.

"You didn't do the chain!" Lybbie whispered hoarsely. "Or the bolt!"

Claire twisted off the bed and knelt on the floor, dragging Lybbie to her knees to face her. Hands vised Lybbie's arms, and she almost cried out.

"Listen to me," said Claire, her lips moving against Lybbie's ear, her voice fierce. "I will never, ever harm you. Understand?"

"N-no . . ."

"*Ever!* And I will never let anyone harm you. Believe that."

Lybbie did not move.

"Please, Lybbie." She sounded almost in tears. "*Believe* me. *Trust* me. I do not want another lover to leave me. I do *not* want to lose *you*."

Something thumped against the door. Lybbie heard a splintering sound. She stiffened in fear. "Claire," she breathed. "It's the hairy man. He's a werewolf."

"No," said Claire. She stood up, and took a few steps back. "He's not."

At the next impact, the door began to give, but Lybbie now paid no attention to it. Before her eyes, Claire's hair grew and darkened, her face elongated and her mouth filled with a carnivore's teeth. Her body changed, darkened, the breasts atrophied to nothing more than nipples, the elastic band that secured the green plaid skirt expanded almost to breaking, the sides of the sandals split open and their straps tore apart.

Frozen on her knees on the floor, Lybbie screamed. The door yielded. The hairy man burst into the apartment. His eyes found the armoire immediately, then grew huge as Claire stepped into his view. He started to flee, and was snared by a pair of massive paws. Claire thrust him against the wall, and kicked the door shut.

It shocked Lybbie to learn that Claire had a voice in this form. She spoke carefully, deliberately, in one of those deep artificial voices Lybbie had heard on scifi shows. "If you ever return, if you ever tell anyone what you saw here, *I will hunt you down and rip you apart.* Do *not* nod your head at me. I do not require your understanding, only your departure." She threw the door open again. "Go! *Now!*"

The man dashed down the hallway. The echoes of his footsteps faded.

Lybbie wanted to scream again, but could not make a sound. She knelt on the floor by the bed, gaping like a beached trout. She felt like a pudding. She hadn't the strength or the will to climb back onto the bed, or to prevent herself from spilling onto the floor.

At the sound of impact Claire dropped to all fours, tail protruding from her skirt, and padded over to Lybbie, where she whimpered, and licked her face. White showed all around Lybbie's jade irises. She wanted to withdraw from Claire's ministrations, yet dared not move.

"I promised you," whispered the werewolf.

"Goway!"

Tears formed in eyes still purple. "All right."

Claire loped away, to the floor in front of the armoire, and laid down. Presently her body shrank, the hair withdrew into the body, the nails into the wolf toes and the wolf toes became human toes and fingers. The head shortened and broadened, the hair lightened once more to copper. At the end, only the eyes remained unchanged.

With a huge effort Claire stood up, kicked the burst sandals from her feet, and retrieved the jersey from the bed, while Lybbie shrank back from her, and finally collected herself enough to crawl onto the bed, never taking her eyes off Claire.

The werewolf tilted her head, as if considering what to say and whether to say it. Cautiously she approached Lybbie, and dropped to her knees beside the bed, and leaned her upper body onto the comforter as if in supplication. She did not touch Lybbie.

"For me," she said gently, almost pleading, "It has always begun with a bit of lust. Love takes longer. It means learning to accept flaws, it means learning to trust . . . it means caring. Last night, in your store, I found you attractive as well as brave. That was the lust. I was going to . . . well, to lick you. Then I saw . . ." Her eyes went to the chain on the night stand. With great care to avoid contact with Lybbie's she retrieved the golden one and draped it around her neck.

"Silver," whispered Lybbie.

"I'm very sensitive to it."

"I shouldn't wonder," Lybbie muttered.

"So I start with lust," Claire continued. "It's never lasted long enough to transform into love. I've begged and pleaded, but no one could . . . stand me, not after they saw . . . what else I was. It's funny. You understood the concept of being 'someone else,' so I wondered whether you knew, or at least suspected. But you never said definitely."

"I thought you were talking about . . . your orientation."

"I realize that, now. Lybbie . . . you've only just discovered yourself. The hardest part is *allowing* yourself to learn. With me, I hope. With me. Like I said, previously it's never lasted long enough. But I truly think, in time, *this* time . . . Lybbie, I could love you."

"Me and a vegan werewolf," muttered Lybbie.

"I was vegan before the change. You keep your attitudes, your gender, your . . . orientation."

"How did . . . ?"

"Short version? I was rockhounding in the Superstitions. I found a fissure in the rocks, and slipped inside to investigate. I was attacked. When I came to, I found myself among all these rotting burlap sacks of nuggets and dust."

Lybbie sat up straight. "You found *The Dutchman's Lost Mine?*"

"I didn't see his name anywhere. But yes, I suppose so. I have to be careful, not to spend too much at one time, but . . . but it doesn't matter right now. I'm sorry to have frightened you, Lybbie. But I meant every word I said to you."

Claire pushed herself up, and stood.

"Where are you going?" Lybbie asked.

"Where do you want me to go?"

Lybbie sat looking up at her for a long time. If asked, she could not have said what or whether she was thinking. Glimpses of flashbacks passed in review in her mind, without drawing comment from her. She felt, rather than saw. There was a lot of fear, most of it fear of the unknown. As the flashbacks came to an end, she wondered whether she was afraid of the werewolf or of the love. It was easy to say both. But it was just as easy to say neither.

"Nowhere," answered Lybbie.

Claire inclined her head in acknowledgement. It seemed to Lybbie that her expression was one of immeasurable relief.

"We have some things to work out," said Lybbie. "Where we live—"

"Your place," said Claire. "Mine's a dump."

"And where we work—"

"Quit your job," said Claire. "We'll travel, explore."

"And discuss things before making decisions," said Lybbie, with some asperity.

"Sorry. It's a big change, for both of us," said Claire. "We have time."

"And find you some sort of elastic wardrobe."

"Not spandex. It tends to fly apart like a grenade."

"But first—"

"First, if you don't mind, I'm going to take a shower," said Claire. "Right after a transformation, I usually smell like a wet dog."

"I was just going to suggest," allowed Lybbie.

As steam began to filter out of the bathroom, Lybbie assembled from her closet some clothing she thought might fit Claire, at least until she could retrieve her own from her "dump." Lybbie's head filled with odd thoughts, about dietary changes and adjustments, about going back to college, about where to cache spare clothing. Gradually it occurred to her that she was avoiding the one subject she truly ought to be thinking about.

Cautiously, almost timidly, she went into the bathroom. Wraiths of steam gathered around her, the territory familiar to her, and she relaxed. On the other side of the frosted doors she saw a pixellated pink-tan silhouette splotched here and there with globs of soapsuds. She cleared her throat for attention. "I could scrub your back," she offered.

"Won't that mean you have to take your clothes off?"

It did.

Skellig

Text 1

How did they cope with solitude, those sainted recluses of yesteryear? Francis, Jerome, Columba. Even Luther in his monk's cell (though no saint he). Of the sounds of night what spectres did their solitary minds fashion? What phantasms did the daylight bring them? What did they see?

I must know. Because . . . how does one distinguish between an hallucination and the Devil?

The circumstances of Jerome are perhaps the more relevant for me. In Chalcis his tongue was a Latin teardrop in a sea of Greek and Syriac. Effectively he was incommunicado, as am I now. In the desert—surely analogous to the fine white sand of this beach upon which I sit alongside my diabolical hallucination—Jerome's linguistic isolation was moot. Temptation came to him there in his own language. This he resisted (he asserted) with prayer and fasting. It is easy for one to be abstemious in the desert—or on the beach. My empty stomach yearns, churns, aches like rock against raw bone. But my mirage—if mirage she be—refuses to get herself hence.

Why would the Devil appear before me in the form of a *woman*? Were I a man, I might applaud the choice. But I have never succumbed to a temptress.

Does Satan know something about me that I do not myself know?

Who am I writing this to? For?

I am so *alone*!

How did they cope?

She pats my hand: it's okay. Her touch feels real. A woman's . . . no, a human touch. The touch of one of my own kind. How can I be one with her flesh if she is Satan?

I don't even know how to look that up.

Text 2

Her name is Nicole. So she announced, striding out of the water onto the shore, naked as a morning star. In another time and place the Devil was known as Old Nick. Old Nicole? But she is somewhere between late teens and late twenties, I should think. I lost the ability to estimate ages of youth as I approached forty. I may be forty now. I have neglected to count the days. Some chronicler I am.

The water dripping from her body was real enough. Two pages of manuscript now have splash marks where the salt has faded the paper, black smears where the ink ran. If I have time, I shall copy them. I doubt I shall have time. ". . . having writ, moves on."

"Why?" she asked.

I felt the impact as she dropped to the sand. Do hallucinations possess the quality of substance? I needed no amplification of her question. Many times I asked it of myself, until at last I took pen in hand and began to compose a chronicle of my days. If no one is there to record it, does anything happen? But I am here. I am still here. That is my curse.

It has been said that history is written by the winners. What then have I won? Because I am the last one left. Just me and my mirage.

"*Perscribo in tabulas,*" I answered. "*Ergo sum.*"

A smile toyed with the corners of her mouth, and died. "The Cartesian prison."

"You've studied."

"There was no need," Nicole said archly.

"Get thee away from me, Satan."

"You are not a believer."

"No?"

"Shall I tell you what you are, Jasmine?" I shrugged, and she went on, "You believe that the Prime Mover created this existence for ineffable reasons and then abandoned it, as a child would a toy. All that has come to pass since the moment of creation is the result of existence flowing in harmony with natural laws. This moment, then, was inevitable."

"That inevitability does not follow."

"I skipped several trillion steps of logic." Nicole grinned, then sobered. "I assure you the events that occurred and the choices that were made have led inexorably to this moment in . . . the event horizon of Creation, if you wish."

"You are suggesting it was inevitable that we destroy ourselves."

"I am suggesting that the choices that were made had foreseeable consequences. If you choose to stand in front of a speeding truck, you will be smashed flat. You chose to ignore the truck, believing in the invulnerability of your ignorance, when you might easily have averted catastrophe. Do you know how you came to be in this place at this time?"

"I walked here."

Text 3

Around the turn of the millennium most of the planets aligned themselves in syzygy, a periodic if infrequent event. Numerologists predicted great changes and strangeness. Nothing much happened. But an alignment of conditions, events, and circumstances occurred a couple decades or so later. Unseasonal weather reduced agricultural productivity. Droughts in overpopulated regions led to famine. The moths that pollenate moonflowers vanished, along with other supposedly insignificant species. Warmer weather invited tropical maladies further north. And hundreds of other factors all came to fruition within a short span of time.

And one morning I awoke to find myself utterly alone.

No smells of coffee or exhaust fumes.

No hum of machinery, no car horns, no hustle and bustle of people on their way to work.

No students at the community college where I taught Western Civ.

No bodies.

Everything had come to the proverbial screeching halt.

Battery-powered radios received static. Dial tones on telephones hummed promisingly, then yielded bleak silences after the first pressed digit. A back-up generator at a hospital provided enough juice for me to send e-mails, but quit a few days later, with the queries unanswered. So I wandered. I roamed. I found cities, dams, bridges, tunnels, roads, lead weights for balancing tires, discarded plastic soda bottles, all the signs that we had been here. But no more we, only I.

Natural sounds continued unabated. A cardinal, joyous upon discovering a supply of rose hips on a wild bush. The susurrus of a zephyr through silver maple leaves. The mournful cry of a family dog, as alone as I. And rain . . .

My God, *rain*!

How it rained!

I walked. I searched. In the rain. Drenched. I shivered, and searched, and walked. From the coast to the Cascades, and back to the coast. The Willamette flooded all the way to the Columbia, carrying with it the detritus of Corvallis and Salem—the libraries and laboratory equipment and fishbowls and castered swivel chairs. The coastal rivers from the Nehalem to the Yaquina became raging torrents. Everywhere in the littoral I walked, it squished. And I shivered, howling like the family dog left on its own.

And one day—it might have been August—the rain stopped. The sun shone. I returned to Corvallis, scavenging, and came to grasp the reason I had been spared: I was meant to tell my story, to record it in a journal. But the location was wrong—to fulfill this destiny I required the music of the waves, the sun-heated sand under my bare feet. The Dunes invited me. Abandoned grocery stores sustained me, unattended mini-malls provided for my every physical need . . . *almost* every physical need.

The line of my life had straightened.

And each day I watched the sun set in the ocean.

Text 4

Letter after letter, line after line. Perhaps in this ultimate of Dark Ages I am more fortunate than my occupational forebears. Believing their transcriptions honored their God, the Benedictines and their scrivener brethren paid homage with their perfections. Each parchment became an act of worship, each calligraphic blackletter an obeisance to canon, each gilded illumination an adoration of the Most High. I have no such aspirations, only a supply of Bics and reams of Southworth parchment paper, courtesy of an office supply store.

"This is futile," said Nicole one day, emerging from the waves after her morning dip. While I continued to scrawl with weary hand, with cramped muscles, her Nordic features percolated with vitality. She made a joyful pirouette, her flaxen hair casting droplets over my work. I uttered no maledictions. If Satan she was, then accursed was she also, far beyond the power of my feeble epithets.

She toweled off the bulk of the droplets and sprawled, still glistening, onto the beach blanket, folding her arms for a pillow. "For whom are you writing these lamentations?"

A tissue blotted the shower she'd given my work. I slipped another sheet of parchment paper onto the clipboard and began to copy the damaged paragraphs. "For others who may yet live."

"There are no others."

"I have only the word of the Great Deceiver for that."

Nicole grinned up at me, pale gray eyes sparkling with humor. "For an atheist you possess quite an armament of theological terms."

"I told you—"

"Yes, yes, you told me you were an apathist. You don't care whether God exists or not." She rolled onto her right side, elbow propped, head resting on her hand, a flow of dark wet gold over her shoulders and breasts, the smile more in her eyes now. "You admit to the possibility I might be Satan. Why, then, might I not be God?"

"I wish you'd wear some clothes, Nicole."

"If you are the last human, why do *you* wear them?"

My hand slipped. A word misspelled for posterity, as the monks had miscopied on occasion . . . or perhaps the future would wonder what we ancients knew that they do not.

"Day after day," muttered Nicole. "Scribble, scribble, scribble."

Having finished transcribing the damaged paragraphs, I resumed the story of my life. "I am running out of time. I don't know how much is left."

She slapped sand with a flat hand and barked a laugh. "And I'm

85

distracting you."

"Not at all. I like men."

"There are no men left."

"So you say."

But I pressed the pen too hard, and tore the paper.

Text 5

How did they cope with their monumental task, those scrivener monks?

They had quills and ink. I have my ballpoints. There we are on equal footing. They had candlelight in their solitary cells. I have sunlight on a beach. Advantage, me. They had inventories of scrolls and parchments to copy. I have . . .

I have perishable paper and a memory which, over time, will mislead me. Advantage Benedict.

In addition to my journal for a posterity which might or might not exist, I had vowed to preserve human literature. Books, I decided, might be preserved in freezer bags. I rescued several wheelbarrow-loads of salvageable works from a ruined bookstore, and rifled a convenience store for the bags. Conducting the literary triage, I decided to save the classics first: *The Iliad* and *A Farewell to Arms*, among others. Reference and non-fiction next. Genre works could wait. As for the Harlequin romances, self-actualization books, and the collected works of Danielle Steel . . . they may be doomed.

I wonder if the Benedictines felt the same toward their preservations.

I've adopted their regimen. From dawn till dusk I write in my journal, with an hour here and there cadged from the schedule to allow me to tend a small garden, to exercise, to meditate. Nicole helps with the gardening. I have not observed her eating regularly, although she and I share a can of mini-raviolis now and then. I do not know who . . . or what . . . she is.

I know who I am. I will preserve as much as I can of the record of human endeavor, in the hope that, should the population begin to reconstitute itself, it will not have to re-learn everything. Did the monks hold to that same hope? Or were their efforts focused solely on praising their God? What were they thinking, in their dank windowless chambers in the monasteries on the Irish isles or high on the hills of France and Italy? I sit here on this beach, armed with Bic and clipboard and paper against a slowly descending night.

She peers over my shoulder, regarding my efforts. Her hair brushes my shoulders. "You had a fairly normal adolescence," she says. Her slender pale fingers are surprisingly powerful as she massages the knots in my neck and back. "When did you acquire your stubborn streak?"

Text 6

I dumped an armload of boxes of freezer bags onto the beach blanket. Nicole barely moved. She might have felt in the sand the footfalls of my approach, but the sun was in the west, casting shadows behind me, and in any case the impacts of my steps could not have foretold of the burden I carried or of my intent to unload it onto the blanket. Yet she had barely moved. How had she known she would be safe?

"As long as you're going to devour my foodstocks," I said, massaging my aching hands, "you can help."

Sunlight illuminated half her face as she looked up at me. "You admit you need my help. The help of Satan. Or of God."

"Either way, you earn your keep. Or go on a diet." I fetched the wheelbarrow from the sidewalk above the sand line, rolling it unsteadily across the sand to her. It was full of books I'd found in a flooded used bookstore. Some were still damp, but the Sun would dry them soon enough.

"I can't fit those art books into these," Nicole complained.

"You can fit *Henry V.*"

She gave me an arch look. "Shakespeare lives in paperback. But who will play the roles? Oh, that's right, you still believe others are alive. What if they are all on the island of New Guinea? What if they only speak Gimi? *Much Ado About Nothing* in Gimi, played by pygmies with metacarpals stuck through their noses." She shook her head, sweeping golden tresses over her sunburnt shoulders. "How far civilization has fallen. Just you and me and a couple hundred New Guinea headhunters." She held up one of Thor Heyerdahl's books. "I know! This will instruct them on how to build a boat sturdy enough to reach Oregon."

"The *Kon-Tiki* traveled westward, Nicole."

She picked at a flap of peeling skin. "A trifle."

I kicked a box of quart bags toward her. "Get busy."

"My, but you're bitchy today. Is it that time of the month? No more tampons at the mall?" She opened a bag, slid a book into it, sealed the bag, and frisbeed it onto my blanket. "What *is* the expiration date of a tampon, anyway?"

"Do not mock me, Satan."

Nicole paused in the middle of inserting a book—a reissue of a Heinlein novel. "It's not PMS, is it? You've finally reached the conclusion that you cannot record every single detail of your life as an example to nonexistent others. You're hoping to save books in sealed bags, to show what your species was like." She made a pretense of thinking about that, to the accompaniment of little movements of her free hand—rubbing the side of her nose, massaging her chin. "That might extend their life considerably. But not long enough, I think, for the squirrels to evolve into intelligent life forms."

I resumed my journal. "There *are* others, Nicole."

"What if you're wrong? What if there aren't?"

"There *are.*"

"Then humor me. What can it hurt to speculate?"

Bravely I tossed the words out. "If there are no others, then the human species dies with me, and I'm leaving behind the legacy of our civilization for any extraterrestrials who happen by."

"How ethnocentric of you, to assume that they will be able to read . . . or to recognize that these books and your journals contain information meant to be read."

I don't know why I threw the pen and clipboard at her. Perhaps frustration had been accumulating without my awareness of it. "*Then what's the point?*" I yelled. "If we can leave nothing behind, then why do *anything?*"

"The only thing humans ever leave behind is a part of themselves."

"Oh, that is so *fucking* profound, Nicole."

"'Nicole'? Not Satan?"

I scrambled to my feet, spilling sheets of paper onto the blanket, and walked away on unsteady legs. "Satan, Nicole, Lucifer, what does it matter?"

Her voice reached me like feather touches. "I think you know exactly what I meant, Jasmine."

I turned back around. Nicole had not moved from the blanket. The clipboard had skipped over her body and lay paper-side-down on the sand. The Bic had somehow gotten stuck point-first in her hair, just above the right ear. Her smile was a trembling thing, inspired no doubt by some maudlin prime-time Fox Television drama—just before the commercial break, the woman about to be rejected tries to invite affection with her vulnerability. "Don't you want me, Derek?" the woman might have asked, plaintively.

I was hardly Derek, but I understood the direction of her prod, all too well. I stalked off.

I can feel her eyes on my back. Are they red now? Has she perhaps metamorphosed, grown horns and a tail? I dare not look around. I long for touch, any touch, the touch of mine own kind. Touch is the leitmotif of human intercourse. Nicole looks human . . . but how can she be? And for his temptations the Devil has been known to assume human form.

So, for that matter, has God. But does God issue temptations?

Text 7

The sun is further south—I have begun to take measurements, correlating these with information in some of the books I have salvaged, and I believe my estimate of August to have been accurate. Given that, it is now late November . . . but the temperature reached eighty degrees around two o'clock by the Sandial—the broomstick

89

gnomon accurate only to the nearest half-hour, by my estimate. Earth has warmed. I don't know how quickly the icecaps will melt, but perhaps I should consider a move inland.

At the outset of this catastrophe I traveled as far east as the Cascades. I still cannot believe that no one is left in Manitoba, Vermont, Martinique, Iceland, Nepal. There is no reason for Nicole to have lied. There is no reason for her to have told the truth, either. Am I truly the last?

I think I must assume so. And so, *quo vadis, Iasmina?*

Whither goest thou?

The salvage of books has progressed well. I write for a while each day, and then I stuff books into freezer bags, and copy again. And so it goes. But I shall have to move inland. The sea level surely will rise. I must protect the books. I've considered a site in the Cascades, but they are of recent volcanic origin, and could erupt at any time. Somewhere in the Dakotas or southern Canada might be geologically safer . . . but it would take years for me to move everything there by wheelbarrow.

There is still gas at the pumps. A motorcycle with a sidecar would be easier on fuel than an SUV, and with so many roads and bridges washed out, a motorcycle would be more practical. It could be done . . . it's a contingency plan.

But I cannot draw my eyes away from the beach blanket, empty these several days now.

Text 8

"An angel of the Lord declared unto Mary, and she conceived of the Holy Ghost."

That's how I learned it. Later it became Holy Spirit. A God by any other name . . .

And Mary bore a son, clearly the issue of a union between male and female. Had parthenogenesis occurred, the offspring would have been female. Canon holds that only God can create; Satan can only copy.

If one believes such things.

I have been pondering this—not as an act of faith, for I have none, but as a practical matter of the survival of the species. Nicole has returned, radiant as the Morning Star. She has spoken to me of duty and responsibility, matters of which Satan possesses not a whit of moral authority to discuss. Yet I find her credible, persuasive . . .

While I wrote, I felt her presence behind me, as if she had not been there and then was there. My fingers ached like bone against bone. How long have I been writing? Months . . . and to what end? Inside a monastery, ensconced within my scrivener's cell, I might have dreaded the invasions of the Goths, Vandals, Avars, Huns, Saracens, and lamented in advance the wanton destruction of all that I had preserved and illuminated. Here, on the beach, the encroachment of the sea would surely prove as deadly to my work as the incinerations of the Romans in the Library of Alexandria.

What was it all for?

But despair was the tool of Satan, to induce vulnerability to his wiles.

Her wiles.

She touched my shoulder, and knelt beside me, her breast soft against my bare arm. The contact jarred my pen, and I miswrote. Gently she slipped the pen from my fingers, took my hand in hers, and massaged each digit, easing the ache. Satan cannot heal. But he can deceive with illusions, deceptions.

At length she pulled back, legs doubled under, hands folded in her lap, looking as demure as it is possible for a naked lissome young blonde to look. She held her head inclined slightly forward, hair flowing onto her shoulders and breasts as she gazed absently at the sand in front of her knees, as if she were waiting for me to speak.

"It's still no, Nicole," I said.

Her voice was the sound of froth dissipating in the wet sand after the wave departs. "May I ask—if I were human, and demonstrably the only other human, would you then yield?"

I retrieved the pen, and continued the interrupted account. "A question which implies that you are not in fact human."

"A question which you pointedly avoid answering."

"Very well. Given the circumstances you suggest, my honest

answer is: I do not know."

"An honest answer. Jasmine, I have taken—"

I held up my hand for pause. "I am busy, Nicole."

"Writing for whom? Preserving for *whom*? There are no others, Jasmine. I have taken them."

In that instant of revelation I felt drawn to her. Her words rang true. But how were they significant? What was their relevance to me now? I set the pen down, turned the clipboard over to protect the paper and placed it carefully on the blanket, and turned to look at her. She was not human. But what did that leave?

"I have taken them to my Realm," she went on, answering my unspoken questions. "They had become an evolutionary dead-end. I will not bore you with the litany of human failures, Jasmine . . . *my* Jasmine. The Universe might have been theirs to explore . . . but they preferred the mire they had created here on this world. Of all of them, I chose you . . . just as, long ago, another progenitor was chosen."

"Not chosen by you."

"My Adversary took a chance, and failed. Now it is my turn."

"You lie!"

"If I am Satan, that is possible. If I am God, it is not. Either way, you are the last one left, and you are my Jasmine. Where is the difference?"

I scrambled to my feet and ran toward the ocean. Roaring filled my ears and my head, blinding me. Dry sand yielded, then wet sand supported my footfalls, and at last I was in water up to my knees, my waist. I had no idea where I thought I was going. A wave parted around me and collapsed onto the beach, its momentum pulling me with it. Salt water stung a cut on my arm I had forgotten about. I strode forward, toward the sun.

And slowed. And stopped.

Text 9

It is dark. The stars are born again on indigo. Nicole has built a small fire under a windswept tree. I did not see how she ignited it—

perhaps with a match, or simply by pointing her finger. But I am chilled in my clothes still damp, and the fire is warm.

Firelight dances on her pale skin as she stands before me, not a pace away, arms at her sides, as are mine. I am thirteen again, at my first dance. Do I wait to be asked? A bulb of dry seaweed pops, a small comet arcs toward the ocean. My heart leaps like a colt in its first meadow.

She reaches out and clasps her hands behind my neck. She is at once as young as that colt and as old as the Appalachians. Firelight flickers in her pale eyes . . . or Hellfire. It ceased to matter which when I came to a stop in the ocean.

One by one she opens the buttons of my damp shirt and shucks it from my body. Then she drops to one knee, uncinches my jeans, peels down my Hanes, and I step out of the circle of chill fabric at my feet. She rises, and her arms go around my neck once again, while mine remain at my sides, uncommitted.

I am sixteen momentarily, in my bedroom while my parents are at work, and nervous. I have done this before, twice, in a back seat and in a barn, but this time it has meaning. Alex loves me. He has told me so. And I will give him what I can. Whatever I can. So he stands before me, and undresses me, and in a moment we will tumble onto my bed, to the aromas of cinnamon incense and fresh sheets and our own musk. That is how I feel.

But none of this happens.

I am standing on sparse grass under a ragged tree near a fire at the edge of a beach on the coast of Oregon, before a naked young woman who does nothing more than clasp her hands around my neck and hold me at arm's length. I am not ignorant; I know how women make love to one another. It is not something that holds an allurement for me. Despite this, I am prepared to involve myself—but nothing is happening.

"My Jasmine," she whispers at last. The fire is beginning to wane, and soon we shall be illuminated only by the stars and the luminescent froth of the waves. "Mine, because I spared you for this. To start over. To begin anew. In time Earth will heal itself. Rivers will run clean, fish and birds and butterflies will thrive, the air will not smell like rust and sewage."

Her words were soft to my ear, and I was listening to my body. Too long had I gone without touch, any touch, the touch of mine own kind. Satan Nicole might be, or perhaps God, but she was in this moment human. The need to give, and to receive, began to consume me, and overwhelm her words.

"If it matters not whether God exists, the same is true of the existence of Satan. What then is left, Jasmine?"

I felt my lips move. "You. Me. This beach."

"And if I should touch you, so that you will give birth . . . ?"

The question brought me blinking back to the moment. "The child will possess something of you," I answered, "and of me. If it is a male child, you will have been God. If a female, you may have been Satan. You will have birthed a population of men and women, or perhaps of women only. Nicole?"

"Yes, Jasmine?"

"Must we think of such things in this moment?"

"Shall I touch you then?"

I reached for her. "Touch me. Yes, for the love of God, *touch me*."

"I have touched you. You will give birth."

My heart stuttered, as did I. "That's it? That's all?"

"Whether I am Satan or God, you have yielded to me by choice."

My tongue licked my lips of its own accord. I spoke thickly, still gravid with anticipation. "I was hoping for a little more than . . . this."

"That is neither the way of Satan nor the way of God. Only if I were human might I indulge with you."

Like an old tire, I lost air. Everything drooped: hair, jaw, breasts. "So what am I to do now?"

"Whatever you think best. Your will is free. It is not encumbered by duty to me, whoever you believe me to be."

The anchor of her arms around my neck eased abruptly, and before my eyes she vanished. I sank to my knees on the sparse grass beside the fire that was now no more than embers, and called her name, the way a dove calls to its lost mate. Nicole did not answer. It did not matter whether she answered or not. Either I was with child, or I was not. My life would continue to unfold as it would.

In the dark I reached for the beach blanket and drew it around me, and curled up in its folds and fell to sleep.

Text 10

The unfulfilled anticipation of the act of love had left me as exhausted as the act itself might have done. Sunlight awoke me. I shook myself free of sand and grass, and hung my clothes on the lower tree limbs to dry in the sun. In the sand around me I saw only my footprints, and no indentations at all where Nicole had been standing.

God is known for tribulations, Satan for temptations. Both amount to the same thing: the need for choices.

I can move inland, or not. I can continue to record my life and my thoughts, if I wish, or simply to preserve books in freezer bags . . . or abandon the attempt to salvage anything of this cycle, as I have come to think of it. *My Adversary took a chance, and failed*, Nicole had said. *Now it is my turn.*

Of a certainty I am with child. Regardless of its heritage, this child will possess something of the powers of its . . . progenitor. Therefore, it is not the only child I will birth. Now it is Nicole's turn, and one day I am determined we shall try again to reach the stars.

Of the past cycle of beliefs, I retain my apathy. If we are to be guided, we shall be guided—over that, we have no control. But whether by God or by Satan, I cannot say.

Perhaps if I close my eyes to both, I will not know the difference.

Striations

Space is the sister of the sea. It is an unfathomable mistress who can turn on you without warning, who yields her love and her bounty grudgingly, whose shores are rocky graves for the unwary and the incautious. Space, like the sea, can hurl you into a forever darkness . . . or cast you in the glow of an unforgettable sunset.

Red sky in morning, sailor take warning.
Red sky at night, sailor's delight.
But when the sky is *blood* red . . .

I don't know what hit us. An asteroid, a shard of olivine. It doesn't matter. People were sucked out through the jagged hole in the sleeping quarters, just aft of the galley, so I learned later. Mother, Father. Reynolds Hall, the geologist and amateur magician. With nothing to balance the internal pressure in their bodies, they exploded. A thin layer of frozen blood dust coated the Visor of the *Achaea*. Through it I could see Ganymede, vaguely magenta now through the blood, looming, growing larger by the second.

Red sky in morning . . .

Unable to sleep, I'd snuck out of my berth and crept to the bridge. The *Achaea* was on autopilot, and the PlayPal-ROM I wanted to try out was hardly going to interfere with ship operations. The collision occurred just after I booted up "Sargasso"—not the adult version, but the one where you get points for killing kelp. All sealable compartments automatic-ally closed off from one another in order to contain the damage. The *Achaea* might have survived, had she not been knocked off course . . . had we not been passing by Ganymede en route to the Jupiter slingshot that would boost us back in to Ceres Station, where we were to live and work for the next twelve years . . . had someone more experienced than a thirteen-year-old girl been available to wrest the helm from the AP.

Scannar continued to operate. It began to sweep the approximate impact area as calculated and updated by the NaviCom, and finally settled on Croton Crater, in the twilight zone between Ganymede's dark and Jupiter halves. The destination stabilized and confirmed, a warning siren shrieked throughout the bridge, and a red light began to flash on the instrumentation console.

I must have strapped myself into the captain's chair. And commoed for my parents and for Doctor Hall. And keyed the transponder to signal distress.

I must have done . . .

❦❦❦

I awoke to pain all over and to the acrid arid stench of electrical fires, and cried out. Mom. Dad. Murma. Doctor Hall. I'd come to rest on my left side, in the almost-dark. Above me through the jagged wound in *Achaea's* hull the margin of Jupiter glowed pastel colors, like a sad Christmas ornament. Something nearby popped at me like a startled viper . . . an electrical cable, objecting to the eviction from its comfortable port. I rolled away while it continued to spit protests to anyone who would listen. Power was still up, somewhere.

My eyes grew accustomed to the dark and to the irregular glow of naked electricity. I sat up. Everything hurt, but I could move okay. I felt a bead of liquid trickle down my right side, along the ribs. It's funny about wounds—you want to know how bad it is, but you can't look. My finger found a shallow, jagged, slippery gash that nauseated me when I touched it, and a corresponding tear in my jersey. Neither required immediate repair.

Little of the *Achaea* had survived intact. I was still on the bridge, what was left of it, and I had a fractured hull over me, and a few fragments of this and that strewn about, including the captain's chair into which I'd strapped myself, now rooted into the bare rock of the moon like a stubborn, windswept shrub. How I'd freed myself from it, I could not remember. The Visor was gone. The hatch aft of the bridge had sprung; a dark Ganymede lay beyond.

I should have suffocated. Or frozen solid. Or both.

Ganymede has a thin atmosphere, though I could not recall the exact constituents, and its surface temperature makes that around Station #6 on Beardmore Glacier in Antarctica, where my parents and I had been posted to acclimate ourselves to cold and danger and deprivation, seem balmy. I was glad I wasn't dead. But why wasn't I?

Things are supposed to freeze on Ganymede. Water, carbon dioxide. Argon. Siberian huskies. Yet I couldn't even see my own breath.

A momentary dizziness staggered me as I got to my feet, and I fell back onto a pile of rubble. A hand was sticking out of it, the wrist to the elbow. Dead, alive? I couldn't tell. I tore at the plastic shards, scattering them around me, discarding colorful electrical wires in clumps like some mad Italian dinner. In the light gravity they almost floated, soaring in gentle arcs back to the ground. I cleared the arm, the shoulder, part of the torso—a woman.

Mom?

But she had not packed outsuits, intending to buy some at the Ceres Base Exchange. In Space, you travel light.

A sheet of console bulkhead covered her head. I could not lift it—lighter gravity does not negate inertia and mass, as Doctor Hall kept drilling into me while we acclimated on Beardmore in preparation for Ceres—but I did manage to slide it from her face.

Definitely not my mother.

The left side of her face was scarred, and her short dark hair had been trimmed badly with dull scissors. She wore neither jewelry nor cosmetics. She had a strong jawline—like mine, I think, when Mom says I'm being obstinate—but her face was slack now. She was unconscious. The arm I'd exposed was limp and unresponsive. I tried as best I could to check for neck and spinal injuries, but dared not move her.

The electric viper was still hissing at me. If the ship's computer had survived the impact, and I could cadge some power for it, I might transmit a *m'aidez*. In the pile of debris I found an emergency torch, and flicked it on. The beam of light ruined my dark vision, but I was able to locate several fragments of the *Achaea*'s instrumentation console. Although wholistically enabled, most functions were discrete and compartmentalized—one application might operate, even if the others did not. Unfortunately, none of the fragments I found were related to communications.

I returned to the woman and knelt down beside her. Rescue would require her active involvement . . . whoever she was. To pry her loose from unconsciousness, I gave her a gentle nudge—

. . . and she grabbed my ankle.

I fell back, reopening the gash in my side. Fresh blood trickled.

"You're just a damn kid," said the woman, and sat up. With a long steady effort she dragged her legs one by one from under the rubble, then got to her feet and surveyed the damage around her. She combed fingers through her hair, dislodging other fragments, then fluffed it, the way my mother did whenever she was exasperated and needed to try a fresh approach to a problem. But she was not my mother.

"Who are you?" I asked.

"Shut up. Go away. I don't want you here."

"Don't be insane. Where can I go—"

As soon as I voiced the protest, she spun around and rushed at me. I was too stunned to flee. Her hands squeezed my throat as she lifted me to her eye level. Her face was a mad, twisted thing, like a Picasso on a controlled substance. The scarring stood out like veins. Her eyes were pale as ice, hollow and unseeing. She shook me, just once. It hurt, from my neck to my toes, and flooded the space behind my eyes with sparks. Then, ever so gently, she set me back down on Ganymede. Her hands brushed my clothing, removing unwanted particles, as if I were about to go outside and play with the Hampton twins. I expected her to turn me around, give me a swat on the ass, and send me on my way with a caution not to beat up Billy again.

"You should not have come here."

"Oh, like I had a choice?"

She hissed annoyance, rather like the electrical cable, and made a dismissive gesture.

"Where is here?" I drifted after her, careful not to approach too closely. "What is this place?"

Something along the crater wall had snared her attention. I peered into the shadows—the Sun's reflected light from Jupiter's gases cast everything in grayscale—and saw nothing of particular interest. Without realizing it, I drew up beside her. She turned her head abruptly, and I skittered away.

The look she gave me was pained, as if something I'd said or done had raked a nerve . . . perhaps jarred a memory loose. Then her eyes paled again, and I edged further away, arms out before me the way

Master Yun had taught me.

The woman stepped into the dark grays, toward the rim of the crater and the wall of ice there. Stars shone in the dome above without twinkling, their colors more distinct than when observed from Earth. Betelgeuse truly is red. But there was something else, something with a faint gloss to it, interposed between us and the infinite sea of stars. It reminded me of a desert mirage, slightly shimmering, ephemeral, non-existent.

On Earth the dry-cleaners send the good clothes back to us encased in clear plastic wrappers to keep the dust off. The wrappers usually have words printed on them. Danger of Suffocation. Keep Away From Children.

Between me and the stars was the same sort of plastic wrapper. A gazillion times stronger, a gazillion times more capacious.

"You *live* here?" I gasped.

Her response was a fragile thing, a soap bubble floating toward me that I might *poik* with a fingertip.

"Live? No . . . "

I ran after her. "But this *is* a biodome, right? You have facilities, right?" My heart leaped like a trout just hooked. "You *can* commo for help, right?"

She came to a stop in the middle of the sheltered crater, still as Lot's wife, but without having looked back. For just a moment, she inclined her head, as if in prayer or sorrow. But the moment passed, and once again she was the hateful creature of inexplicable emotions, who might explode or caress without provocation for either. I braked, wary. Any person is capable of extremes, but one usually sees warning signs. She embodied both violence and tenderness in simultaneous responses, as if they grew from the same source within her.

Her voice carried to me, old as light from the farthest star. "No one will come here."

"Why not?"

She remained so still, she might have been carved there by some ancient sculptor. I crept closer. I remembered the pigeons around Rome's *Fontana di Trevi*, eyeing first the little seeds I spilled on the ground, then me, as if I meant to snag the birds as they fed. The pigeons had been brave enough . . .

I plucked at the sleeve of her outsuit, and withdrew apace, rather like Wiley Coyote in the classic Roadrunner Cartoons, wondering why the catapult had not fired. Again I touched her, and dodged back.

"I am Harper," she whispered.

And in that moment I knew that I would never escape from Ganymede. I knew that I was dead.

For seven years Doctor Hall and his staff had trained me as if I were an adult, so that I might accompany my parents on their posting to Ceres Station. My Spaceways knowledge was almost equal to theirs, lacking the experience of living in order to flesh it out. From the components strewn about in the bridge of the *Achaea* I should have been able to cobble together a distress beacon. That part of me, the part that finds a way to stay alive despite the odds, was functioning.

The rest of me was . . . destabilizing.

Harper.

I sat on the ground in tailor fashion, trying to solve a Rubik's Cube of electronic debris. At first the various parts remained uncoordinated, but then a power jack fit a port in a commo module, so I plugged it in. An amber light glowed on the small keypad. I might derive a signal from the power, but I still needed something to boost it with, or it would be too weak to be distinguished from the quantum hiss of the Universe.

Harper was a part of history recent enough for me to have heard the name. I recalled a headline or two from around the time I'd begun Schematics with Doctor Scott (the dream class of every eight-year-old girl, right?), but news was Earth-generated, and I had no intention of remaining on Earth. Whatever befell that planet after I left was not going to be a part of me. Words in black block font across the front page flashed past in reference to the woman whose biodome I now shared, however unwillingly. Scientist. Astronaut. *Mad* Scientist.

Mother.

Someone had decided for society that the execution of criminals was uncivilized. Chuck a nerve gas canister into a day-care center (as in Philadelphia)? Derail a shipment of nuclear waste (as in western Iowa)? That's a mere three decades of free room and board at taxpayers' expense, with time off for good behavior. Not even Harper's abomination could reactivate the lethal injection chamber.

A storage bin from the *Achaea* had been thrown clear and survived with but a dent and a few scratches. I'd hoped it contained a battery pack, but all I found was a spare palm recorder and a sampler bag of M&Ms, neither item particularly useful for communicating between planets. My logical self took refuge once again in my cloud of fears and anxieties.

I knew of Harper's whispered history because she had been admitted to the NASA/ESA Developmental Unit not three years before my parents and I were selected, although she was gone from the program by the time we arrived. It was the sort of thing you learned about, like sex, only when your parents weren't around.

And who knew how much of it was true? How *could* it be true? How could she—?

"We're losing air," said Harper, beside me.

I yelped, spilled the components, and crabbed away from her until I had room to stand up.

She proffered an open tin of field rations, and I clasped my hands behind my back. "Think I'll just stay skinny."

The pain I'd seen earlier in her pale eyes flashed briefly, and faded. She slipped a strap from her shoulder and extended the canteen to me.

I waved it off. "You said we were losing air."

"The biodome self-seals in the event of a puncture, even a ship-sized one. The bottom edge is—"

" . . . held in place along the contours of the terrain by sealant. Let me guess: the force of the puncture by the *Achaea* pulled it loose at some point."

"So NASA trains the children, too, now," Harper said softly, and lowered the canteen to the ground between us.

"What do you care?"

Her right hand was a rigid claw that raked the air. She hissed like a puma. And again the moment passed . . . only this time the outburst seemed to have weakened her. She sank to her knees on the thawed rubble of the crater floor, and sat back on her haunches, and closed her eyes.

I took a gulp of recike water—water is supposed to be a tasteless liquid, but this had no taste at all—and snapped the lid back on the canteen. "So dig out the sealant tubes and get to work. I'll even help."

"I have no sealant."

That news panicked me worse than her identity. "You have to have. It's compulsory issue with field equipment."

"What is your name, child?"

"Quinx Terwilliger."

"The law said I could not be executed, Quinx. But I could be allowed to die. Out of sight, out of mind, you know. So I was exiled here. It was not expected that I live. You understand?"

But she was seeking sympathy for her plight, not an understanding of it, and she had no right to be anything but unforgiven, so I said, "You killed your children. You were going to cook them."

For a moment she went rigid as stone. Glacier eyes froze me in this frozen place. Then the inner demon relaxed its grip. Her voice came dull as a lead bell. "It's likely we'll die from lack of oxygen before I'm that hungry. A year ago I might have welcomed death, any death. But not now, not after what I found . . . "

Her voice trailed off. She'd fallen into some psychotic reverie that might make her even more dangerous when she pulled out of it. I had no idea what she might have found that could make her want to live. Peace of mind? How could anyone reconcile an inner light with the horror of . . .

Though I had not eaten in hours, I had to swallow my gorge. Acid stung the back of my throat. Suddenly I could not bear to be near her.

"No," I said, and started walking toward the crater wall that had attracted her earlier. "I have to do something."

The crunch of rubble said that she was following, and I quickened my pace. "A solution might be possible," she said. "One of us has to go outside."

I stopped, and turned around. In that moment her eyes flashed a final madness, then faded to rainwater, and she too stopped, five paces away, as if she respected my wish for distance of separation.

"One of us?"

"And you would make a smaller hole."

"I knew you would say that."

"But I'll go. Did you know I would say that?"

Harper detoured to my left, to the shelter tent that had been her residence for the past six years or so, and soon emerged encased in a white Lifesuit. The heavy boots kicked up gray Ganymede dust as she approached me, and for a mad moment I thought she was modeling it. But a sweeping gesture followed by a jab invited me to check the security of her airline.

I did so, from a distance, and signaled approval. In the enormous left mitten she carried a short-range commo unit, which she held out for me to take. I keyed it, and we went through the standard "read me read you" tests. Her utility belt bore the usual gizmos, none of which was useful in resealing a contour hem. But she would not need them. I had an idea of what she was planning to do. If it succeeded, she might have to remain outside. I was not so naive as to believe she meant to sacrifice herself for me to atone for her sins. But the ulterior motive eluded me.

Perhaps Harper meant to pitch me outside at the last moment. There I'd freeze, and be available for harvest . . . a forearm today, a calf muscle tomorrow. It was not an unreasonable possibility. In receipt of the signal from the emergency transponder, Ceres Station probably had already dispatched a shuttle or two to check for survivors. It would arrive in a day or so. Harper's story would be plausible—all passengers lost to space through the gash in the hull. They would believe her, and why not? Who would bear witness against her? And when they were gone, she would supplement her field rations.

But regardless of her ulterior motive, the biodome could not long tolerate the loss of air. For one thing, air pressure helped maintain its flexible rigidity. Below approximately 8 psi, it might well collapse. For another, we were soon to have trouble breathing without assistance. We had to take measures to staunch the outflow of air. And I saw a way to adapt her plan so that it placed neither of us at more than minimal risk.

"Do you have a blanket?" I asked her. "Or some lengths of rope. Even an outsuit you want to spare."

Harper just stared at me without comprehension. I resumed my spacewalker's shuffle toward the perimeter of the biodome. I had scant idea of the leak's exact location, but she had been headed in this general direction. As I drew near, I thought I could hear it, the most frightening sound there is to a space traveler: the hiss of escaping air.

It was leaking at a point just in front of the glacier that had overlain that section of the crater wall. In some places the ice poised above the crater basin, and in others it reached all the way to the bottom. In the extreme cold, the glacier was a pale blue network of fractures, some severe enough to be regarded as crevices, others merely lines on the face of it. Behind it, the upthrust crust of wounded Ganymede loomed, as if the glacier were all that stood in the way of the wall's collapse. Doomed to cold, we were also protected by cold.

"Like Antarctica?" asked Harper through the pocket com, carrying the blanket I'd requested.

I glanced at her over my shoulder. The pale mad look of her eyes had faded to a polished serpentine. She looked quite ordinary. "This is much colder," I said. "And starker. I was going to say it looks like the face of the Moon."

She moved to stand beside me. "Look closer," she urged, and for a weird moment all I could think of was Hansel and Gretel being invited to peer into the oven. At any second she might pitch me outside . . . on the other hand, she did not have to signal her presence and her proximity by speaking with me at all. Demented she was, but neither half of her was devious. "You've been trained, Quinx. Show off a little. Tell me what you see."

"It's something disguised as ice?"

"No doubt your instructors loved having you in class."

"Probably this glacier originated from ice melted by the impact which formed the crater, splashed here, and refrozen. A glacier is made of compressed ice. This wall is what, half a kilometer high? I suppose that might be sufficient to cause compression, although I see no signs that this ice was ever in a plastic condition. No warping or folding, for example. But it is ice, crystallized water, with crystalline properties."

"Your instructors loved you," said Harper. "What about the striations?"

The question lost me. "Striations are lines on the surface of a crystal that reflect the internal arrangement of molecules. They're especially prominent on iron sulfide, for example—fool's gold. Ice is visibly unstriated. I don't know why. Maybe it's because ice expands when it freezes, rather than contracts. That might distend the surface enough to smooth the striations, especially as it freezes from the outside in, while crystals of amethyst, say, grow from the inside out. Perhaps you mean fractures? Those are usually irregular, as the result of internal distress or plasticity. Impacts, such as by a hammer, might cause a conchoidal fracture or two."

"You received full marks in class, I see. Suppose I told you I had found some striated ice."

"Striations also indicate inner flaws. I'd have to conclude something is disturbing the internal arrangement of molecules in the crystal."

"Just so." She turned me slightly by the shoulders before I could protest the touch, and pointed to a spot at my eye level on the other side of the biodome plastic. The lines there were as prominent as those on pyrite.

"Omigod," I whispered.

Harper nodded. "My word, exactly."

"But . . . what is it? And how did it come to be here?" But she could not answer. "Have you taken any readings?" I went on. "For radioactive decay, atomic decomposition?"

"With what?"

"Oh. Right."

"You asked for this blanket," she said, unslinging it from her shoulder.

A small pile of boulders and rocks, strategically emplaced, would reduce the outflow of air to a mere gasp, if that. This would secure the biodome at least until the arrival of the shuttles. If I read Harper correctly, she planned to remain outside the dome for that period. What she might do if they denied her the necessary tubes of sealant, I had no idea.

"When you lift the plastic hem to slip outside," I explained, "lay the blanket under it, half in, half out. Pile as many boulders as you can on top of the blanket. Come back inside. If we yank the blanket through the gap hard enough, we ought to be able to spill enough rocks onto the hem to effectively if incompletely seal it."

"You split that infinitive," said Harper.

I don't know why I took that as a compliment for the idea, but I smiled . . . rather, I felt the corners of my mouth tug against my will. Perhaps I was more frightened than I thought, about the air loss. Harper's eyes took on that mad pale cast again, the smile no doubt triggering the memory of some long-repressed image. I took a precautionary step backwards.

Harper gave me a grim, hard look, then ducked down under the hem and crawled through the gap already opened by the force of the *Achaea*'s puncture, and she was outside. For perhaps three seconds, air rushed past me in one direction, cold in the other, and met in a swirling haze of frozen particles all around me. Through it I could see her spread the blanket as I'd suggested. I began to have doubts. The seal had broken for a two-meter stretch, and the blanket was not that wide. Surely she could not arrange a dispersal of boulders sufficient to reseal the plastic hem. There was no danger that any of the boulders might punch a hole through the plastic . . . but we might be able to push our hands against the plastic from inside, and thus arrange the boulders more efficiently. But if not, if not . . .

I did not see what happened to Harper. In one moment she was standing before me on the other side of the biodome plastic, holding a boulder the size of a good pumpkin. In the next, she was lying under a pile of them. Something had collapsed out there.

My memory of the next few minutes, the next few hours, is nebulous, but some details fly past, like visions wafting in and out of a closet. I rushed to her shelter tent and foraged all her clothes . . . a nightgown, a pair of shirts and denims, and three outsuits. An extra pair of Lifesuit mittens. I could only wear one pair of boots, but I drew on all the socks I could find, dirty and clean. On the wood-and-canvas cot she had spread one of those arctic-issue sleeping bags, plump with down. I slung that and all four remaining blankets over my shoulder, and humped them to the repair site. Harper was still down. Alive or dead, I could not tell, but she did not respond to commo. I memorized the scene, searing it into my mind, gauging distances and positions. I closed my eyes briefly, opened them, and took a final look at the scene while I drew a series of successively deeper breaths. My heart pounded. In my mind I went over precisely what I would do, in the order I had to do it. One, two, three. Like that.

In SCUBA training off the Bahamas I'd been able to hold my breath for four minutes, but here I did not have the luxury of time. I estimated thirty seconds were all the Fates would allow. I drew a final, huge breath, let half of it out as they'd taught me, and then coiled blanket after blanket around my head and shoulders, arranging them by feel and touch after the first one. Finally I threw the sleeping bag over my head like a great hooded cape, and drew it around me.

The plastic hem caught briefly at the sleeping bag before I thrust myself forward on hands and knees, breaking that hold. Quick turn to the right. Boulder, boulder, and a much larger mass that yielded slightly to the touch. The right leg, said my memory. I got both mittened hands around it and slogged backwards. One knee, a third of a meter, another knee, another third. The blankets surrendered to the cold. My forehead and nose no longer felt the roughness of wool. My eyes were closed, but were too numb to blink. I tugged at her leg, and lost air with the effort, and tugged again. I dared not scream. My left foot probed the unsealed portion of the hem and pushed through. Harper's hand struck the top of the sleeping bag, startling me. My arms and legs were numb now, and I was having difficulty controlling their movements. Everything began to go numb. I could not even exhale. No longer could I move, although I had the vague impression of movement. Blackness set in . . .

☯☯☯

I dreamed I was drowning. Vast hard pain awoke me, and I discovered that I was submerged in water, naked. Not a bathtub, but a metal basin large enough to hold most of me. A gnome in the back of my mind whispered that it was the *Achaea*'s shower stall. My lower body was twisted to one side, so that my legs might bend, and thus fit. Above me hovered Harper, her hand spread on my chest, holding me down. Her other hand was massaging my legs. My mouth and nose remained above water, nothing else.

I did not want her touching me. I tried to scream. It came out a hoarse whisper.

The water was lukewarm. The gnome wanted to know who "luke" was. I laughed, and it came out a hoarse whisper. Gradually it occurred to me that I could feel the water and its temperature. But my body still ached. Sometimes I'll sleep wrong, and an arm will fall asleep, and recover with tingles that hurt. This was like that, but all over.

I tried to protest. It came out a hoarse whisper.

"Don't try to talk," said Harper.

I could move my arms. I tried to push her hand from my chest, and failed from weakness. But she let me up, just a little.

"Try not to splash," she said. "This is almost all the water I have."

I heard myself moan.

"The pain will pass."

I pushed her hand from my chest, and crossed my arms. "You say my lie."

Harper handed me a towel I had missed earlier, and bade me stand up and dry myself. "I thought you would let me die," she said, wistfully, as if she wished I had let her.

Dried, I began to shiver. Harper aimed me toward the sleeping bag, now back on the cot, and zipped me after I climbed inside. I had no body heat to collect within the down cocoon. Suddenly I was very cold.

Harper knelt down beside the cot, her face a scant half meter from mine. I could see my reflection in her serpentine eyes. "The maddest, bravest thing I've ever heard of," she said, still wistful. From somewhere she produced a small teddy bear.

"Murma!" I snaked an arm out of the cocoon to receive it. "Oh, Murma . . . Harper, you *found* her . . . "

Harper's smile was a flickering thing, like a candle in an open window.

"Such courage they need, out here." Her voice was quiet, as if she were reading me a bedtime story. "You belong here, Quinx. My dream, once upon a time."

I just looked at her.

She sat down on the crater floor, folding her legs under. "My dream," she said quietly. "Since I was much younger than you, Quinx.Everything I did was directed toward that dream. Piano is not nearly as excruciating as analytic geometry."

I laughed, despite myself.

"I see you know that, too. Well, I took all the courses, and extra ones, and trained in college, and had three years in the Marines, and completed all the prerequisites. Maybe you know about the sleepless nights, too? No? Staying up to solve one more equation, or analyze the last bioscan results? Ah, so you know. Perhaps you do feel the pull of Space as strongly as I once did.

"Not obsessed, just determined. But I wanted it all. I fell in love, married, had children. He knew my dream . . . he understood it, he said. He said. And I worked, and lost sleep, and cared for . . . our children, and drove myself, and stole moments to study and to practice. And they sent me to Antarctica, as they did you, to train. And to Samoa, and Iceland, and places that were similar to the terrains I would encounter one day. And each time, before I left and after I returned, there was a fight . . . "

My voice was returning. "I don't need to know this. I don't want to know this."

"It is the life you have chosen, Quinx. It has recognized who you are and who you were meant to be."

"It took my parents."

"Yes, and it let you live. Why?"

"I didn't ask."

"Quinx: no weaknesses. And what would you do if, on the very morning of your triumph, of your acceptance on a mission, you were—"

"*I wouldn't try to eat my kids!*"

Her eyes remained serpentine, as if her crime was no longer relevant. "If you have a breaking point, Space will find it and test you."

"You failed your test."

Her eyes emptied of color and feeling. Resignation husked her voice. "He stood in the front doorway and told me I was not leaving . . . that I was staying home to raise his children. His children. I missed the shuttle. I missed the launch. My status was revoked. I was unstable in my domestic life. I was unfit for the program.

"I cried for weeks . . . months. I . . . did things to myself. I hurt me, for having failed me. For having failed the dream I was given. I don't know who I was. I don't know who I am. I deserved to be in Space. Now I am in Space, but I don't deserve it. That's the worst punishment . . . I wish they had killed me. I wish you had left me out there."

"C-c-cold."

She put her hand on my forehead, the way my mother tested my temperature. "I should put you back in the water."

"No. Hurts."

Feeling had returned, in full force. The cold radiated outward from my spine, chilling everything in its path. The skin on my wrists and ankles was on fire. I began to quake. My teeth chattered.

Harper unzipped the sleeping bag and climbed in beside me. I was in too much pain to protest, or to fear her. She wrapped her arms around me and drew me as close as she could, and resealed the bag. I wanted to run away. But some part of me was drawn to her warmth. I did not understand it. And after a while, I did not care.

When I awoke, perhaps hours later, Harper was asleep, the arms that encircled me limp and unresisting, the body from which I had drawn the sustenance of warmth now cooled by mine. The scarred side of her face lay open before me like harsh terrain. She might have done that with a cheese grater. Or he might have done it to her. I did not want to know. Now her face was flawed, like her inner spirit.

And in the light of the glowstick that dangled from the center pole of the shelter I saw the tracks down her cheeks that said she had cried herself to sleep. And I knew this was not the first time for that.

I nestled Murma against her, and got up to find my clothes.

The squawk from the radio made me jump. I followed the sounds back to a corner of her shelter. They'd left her a short-range PRC, probably to tease and torment her. I adjusted the gain and keyed the mike.

"This is *Achaea*, go ahead."

A man's voice. "This is the shuttle team *Dione 37* and *Dione 43*. We have your wreckage on the scanner. Please identify yourselves."

A shadow fell over me. Harper had awakened. She was clutching Murma like an infant . . . and she was weeping.

"*Dione 37*, this is Quinx Terwilliger . . ." I glanced back at Harper. "Or would you rather speak with my Mom?"

"Is anyone else with you?"

"We're all that survived. We seem to be inside some sort of biodome. There was a scientist here, I think, working on some project. We found her body in the *Achaea*'s rubble. Is that who you mean?"

"We'll downdock just outside your airlock. Please be in plain sight when we arrive. Out."

Harper waited until I had closed the mike. "Are you insane?"

"They might recognize you by that scar. We have to do something about that, to buy time enough to get you onto one of those shuttles. You *can* pilot one, right?"

"Quinx, they'll kill me. They'll think they have to, to protect you. Just tell them . . . what we found."

"What *you* found." My mind had gone off on its own and taken control of my mouth. I forced it back to focus. Her scar would get her killed . . . but there was something Doctor Hall said he used to use, when he did magic shows on stage.

I rummaged through containers. "They left you rations, right? We'll need . . . let's see . . . syrup for those inedible pancakes."

"Syrup!"

"Please, just find it. We only have a few minutes."

Still clutching Murma, she opened a fresh container and withdrew several of those little packets we used to step on as kids, on the sidewalk, just because the mess drove our parents crazy.

"And ketchup. And one of those tins with the crackers and peanut butter."

She piled them onto a small field table, and began opening the tin. "What in the world are you thinking?"

"Stage blood."

She paused in her opening. "What?"

"Doctor Hall used to . . . never mind. He was aboard the *Achaea* when we got hit. He'd done stage acting at a rec and theater center. Small town." I took the tin from her and began mixing the concoction. "He told me about stuff they improvised for props. Syrup has the consistency, and you add red food coloring to it. I hope ketchup works. And for the clotting effect you use peanut butter. Presto, stage blood! Hold still."

With one of those little plastic knives that come with the kits I spread the goo over her scars. A flaw over a flaw, I thought. Perhaps the one negates the other. I do not know. I do know she saved my life. And I know she might have harmed me, and did not.

Within minutes the stuff had coagulated. A bandage might have aroused suspicion, so we kept the fake wound uncovered. In the dim light of Jupiter and the glowsticks, she might pass what my Dad used to call "muster." Like the blanket, it was the only chance we had. She had.

☯☯☯

The four crewmen from the two *Dione* shuttles were kind enough to insist on examining Harper's grave, located under the boulders piled over the leak. By this time "Mom" had put on Harper's

113

Lifesuit. They even addressed her as Doctor Terwilliger. She maintained a discreet distance behind us while we approached the burial site.

"And there's something else," I told them, before they could slip outside and unpile the rocks. I pointed to the dark shape embedded in the ancient ice. "Run a scan on that. Is it what I think it is?"

The mission team leader aimed his scanner at it. Seconds later, he ran a second scan. Then he stared at the ice. His voice was hushed, reverent. "My God . . . "

I glanced over my shoulder. Harper gave me a long look, then slipped the helmet on and secured it.

"And what do you think this is?" the team leader asked me. I had their undivided attention now. Or rather, it did.

"It's a dark shape embedded in the glacier." I peered at the readings, having trained in Antarctica on that particular model. "If that scanner is calibrated, it's emitting slow but controlled bursts of electrons and neutrons. That means it is artificial. Someone made it. And I don't think their Zip Code is in this Solar System."

Behind us the *Dione 37* lifted off.

"Hey!"

They ran a few paces, and stopped, perhaps having grasped the futility of pursuit. Finally the team leader turned back around and glared at me. "Do you have any idea what you've just done?"

I hung my head contritely. "She said she would kill me if I told. And I was afraid she would kill you, too." I'd rehearsed the words, but even so, they sounded lame. I added a timid, "I'm sorry," and hoped I was not overdoing it.

But they had already returned their attention to the thing in the ice.

❧ ❧ ❧

So I made it to Ceres Station (obviously). I'll be staying on here, working, learning, growing up. They keep asking, but I don't know why I did what I did. Given another chance under the same circumstances, maybe I wouldn't do it. I mean, there is no way for society to forgive her.

The stars look different here on Ceres. You can almost smell them, they're so clean. I've been assigned to radio astronomy, but now and then they let me scan with the optical units. They think they're giving me a thrill, but I prefer to dream with the naked eye. It's so black out there, with those tiny points of light. I understand why the ancients played connect-the-dots with them. It gave their lives meaning . . . perhaps it gave their dreams substance. I don't know . . .

I do know that sometimes I can connect the dots against the vast black backdrop, and I can see her face. It's not scarred anymore.

That I might sleep...

The boulder of white feldspar in the center of the Shavrrna village square was empty of meaning. Neither pictographs nor ideographs did it bear, nor any marks or inscriptions that might serve to convey information. Not ten seasons of rain ago had I visited Shavrrna to leave my own marks. These, too, were gone.

Obliterated? If so, why? To what possible end?

Or had some dark magic swept them away. But again, why?

The sense of foreboding was a lizard scurrying up my spine, its tiny claws raking my scales. I shrugged it off. Things happen for a reason. Even dark magic does not act of its own accord, but is directed, purposeful. The erasure of the feldspar had not been a random, senseless event. Someone had willed it so.

Passing adult Shavarrsh scarcely acknowledged me with a glance, but the young gazed fixedly, their inquisitive vermilion eyes remaining on me until their parents tugged at their tails, urging them away. The season of sun had fallen upon Shavrrna in full force, tanning their wintry olive drab hides to a vivid verdant green, and all around me hung the ripe, intoxicating aroma of old cabbage. The harvest of the season's first crops had begun, the vegetables and fruits and berries not eaten prepared for storage during the season of the chills, and after long days in the fields and over the hearths, surely the Shavarrsh still had need of quiet moments around the storystone.

I sat on the grass at the base of the feldspar, in the shade of the massive *kerka*, waiting, but no one stopped to hear my tales or to watch while I recorded them. A light breeze bade the fresh green leaves above speak to me, their rustling reminding me of a tale I had once told, long long ago. From a pouch at my side I withdrew a *plume* and a welljar of *tinte* and prepared to inscribe the parable of *The Tulip and the Chainsaw* onto the white face of rock worn smooth by the abrasive they had used to eradicate the earlier inscriptions. I remained alone in my task, so I thought, but when I neared the end of the parable, and began to inscribe the explicit lesson—that regardless of the damage inflicted on a flower by those of a mindless, destructive bent, a flower will bloom again the following year—I was startled to hear the tiny, plaintive voice behind me.

"Why are you smearing paint onto that stone?"

I turned around, almost spilling the *tinte*. The question had been asked of me by a young female Shavarrsh, surely no more than seven or eight seasons of rain on this land. Could she not interpret the ideograms I had so carefully scriven onto the stone? Had the adults not taught her?

I started to respond, but her female parent appeared, tugging at her to draw her from my work. Voices faded as they departed in the direction of the dwellings.

"But *mahr*, I just want to know why she—"

"I've told you time and time again to stay away from..."

It occurred to me, hearing these fragments, that there is nothing so desolate as a storyteller without an audience, nor so plaintive as a tale which reaches no other ears. I felt as if I had carried this boulder on my shoulders, from village to village, for a century of seasons. For reasons not evident, the adults in Shavrrna had stopped listening, and had neglected to teach their young that there was something to be listened to.

What could have happened here?

My stomach began to rumble.

During visits past, the Shavarrsh had brought in the middle of the day and just before dark tureens and ewers and amphora containing nourishment of which I and those gathered around me might partake. Aromas tantalized me, but nothing was brought. If I desired sustenance, I would have to rummage through the *kibikopila* at my side. I touched the drawstring looped over my shoulder, and thought better. Food might wait, and it is ever useful to assert control over one's internal functions.

So I sat once more, and waited once more. The leaves above continued to sing. In a sea of movement, of living, I was alone. I recalled some lines lilted to me by my own *mahr*, further back in years than I cared to remember:

Be not alarmed when troubles come
And you find that I am alone

117

Please only rock me quietly
That I might sleep until this passes

With another color of *tinte* I began to inscribe this fragment onto the feldspar. From behind, someone approached. I could hear the blades of grass double and snap under their weight, and feel the vibrations of their footfalls. Finished, I put away the tools of my life, and turned around, my heart beginning to skip like a child on the first day of the season of sun.

Seeing the two adult males, my heart thudded into the pit of my first stomach. Already I knew that nothing good could come of this.

The closest one said, "You are being detained. Come with us. Do not resist."

Armed with only a *kibikopila* of dried fruit and vegetable matter and some scrivener's tools, I had scant means of resistance. At least, I thought, as they led me away, I might in time learn the facts as they pertained to the erasure of the storystone.

☙☙☙

But they told me nothing helpful. Thrust into a dank cavern in the north face of a limestone cliff, and secured within by a portcullis whose counterweight was a boulder of approximately my size, I was reduced to simple meditations upon the tales I told and to waiting for someone to explain the need for my incarceration. The orientation of the entrance denied me direct sunlight in which I might warm myself for the coming cool night, but I found that, late in the day, I might capture the energy I needed in a sliver of light from the west.

Unfortunately, that spot had already been taken.

Her name, she said, was Mashrrv, and she had been in this cell since the onset of the season of chills—a circumstance which moved me to allow her first turn in the warmth, what there was of it. I did not think her so old, but after a speculative tilting of her head, an appraisal of eyes pale yellow in this dim light, she concluded that she remembered me.

"I was but a nestling at the time, Storyteller," she told me, "only recently come from the egg, clumsy and without guile. My *mahr* brought me to the storystone the night before your arrival, to await

118

your coming. There were fresh berries from the mountain shrubs, and tubers from the soil moistened by the last of the seasonal rains, and much gaiety. We had gathered in circles, the shorter of stature in front the better so as to see and hear you...and oh, as the disk of light arose from the horizon you came, on foot, as if you had just emerged from that disk. Did you intend that effect, I wonder? I've always wondered that."

"It is customary for the storyteller to approach from the east at the birth of the day," I said. "I do not know the origin or purpose of the custom."

"You are the only storyteller I have ever seen," said Mashrrv. "No others have come after you."

I could scarcely credit the sounds which reached my *timpana*. "Oh, surely not! What about Glembethth? And Orrthag? And I know Ffazgl spent a full season of sun in this region."

Mashrrv's tailtip fluttered in distress. "None of them, Storyteller, oh, none know I. Nor have I heard these names. None has visited since you."

"And why have they placed you in here, Mashrrv?"

Her green skin paled to chartreuse, and she averted her eyes. Again her tailtip tattooed the dirt. "I invoked the parable of *The Tulip and the Chainsaw* to demonstrate the futility of fighting," she confided.

I wondered whether we were being overheard. Though I saw not so much as a shadow outside, I began to suspect as much when Mashrrv led me to the cool rear of the cavern, and I kept my voice low. "Which fighting is this you speak of?"

"Many villages have we fought, Storyteller, in these few seasons. Urtha's Ford at the great bend of the Savernon. And as far away as Windscape, at the edge of the great Cornukibi plains. Even tiny Uthrrvna at the first cataract up the Savernon—"

I was unable to contain my horror. "In the name of the Light of the First Day, *why?*" Mashrrv withdrew a pace; I had frightened her. I slipped my tail over and under hers, reassuring with coils. "Forgive me, young one. I meant no trembling."

"No one asks why," she replied. "No one dares. But I know

119

why."

"You must tell me."

Mashrrv gave me a sidelong, upward glance. Now her eyes were darker than the tartfruit which flourishes along the banks of the Savernon. Her voice dropped. "It is said that at Urtha's Ford it is possible to impede the flow of water. It is said that the Urthash could do this." And she cast her eyes about furtively, fearing ears in the limestone.

"It is said?"

"It is what is heard."

Scant light of day remained. In our sliver of warmth our shadows had lengthened to the east wall of the cavern, and now they were dying, as was the day. I felt a chill, but there was nothing to be done about it. Mashrrv trudged to the west wall and curled into a ball there, to preserve what warmth she might until indirect light of the next sun roused her. I might have followed her example, for surely she knew the caveways.

But *she knew* the caveways. She had accepted her incarceration. This I could not do, for two reasons. First, to accept my circumstance without question gave my imprisoners sanction, for I would then have been placed here by my own permission. And second...

Second came my duty as a Storyteller. I had now an audience—a captive one, true, but an audience nevertheless.

On most rock the dark colors of *tinte* show best. With light, they would show on the limestone. But light and warmth were denied me. I selected a broad *plume* and a fresh welljar of *tinte* and a vial of pulverized *vozvor*, a difficult substance to work with because it will burn through scales on contact. Carefully I tapped three measures of *vozvor* into the *tinte*, capped it tightly, and shook it quickly. In the confined space, and without sufficient air, the burning soon ceased. The welljar felt warm in my hand.

In the now-almost-dark I cautiously approached the back wall of the cavern, and began to inscribe my tale. Alive with *vozvor*, the pictographs and ideographs glowed, and gave me just enough illumination to finish my task.

At the next light Mashrrv clapped her hands together and crowed, at first in pleasure, then in dismay. "They will see it," she cried, with furtive glances over her shoulder. "You must remove it. Quickly!"

I began putting away the tools of my craft. "No such thing will I do."

She continued to fret. "For this defiance they will not feed us."

"And should we dwindle our days here, eating?" But my presumption was improper: alone, I might protest in my manner, accepting consequences. But Mashrrv had neither been informed of my choices, nor had she acquiesced in them.

"Forgive me," I said, and prepared an erasive solution which reeked faintly in the cave.

Her hand on mine stayed me. "Perhaps you are correct, Storyteller. The village would speak with one voice, muting ours in here. About that, we can do nothing. But we need not be silent for our own sakes. Leave the story, please."

I led Mashrrv toward the opening of the cave, there to absorb as much warmth as possible. When we were comfortable, I said, "Tell me of your sight of the parable. How came you to be here for it?"

Mashrrv flicked her tongue, uncomfortable with our possible proximity to the ears of others. I nuzzled her with my nose, a reminder that our voices would not be stilled. "The interpretation upon which I drew is standard," she said slowly, thinking her way through it. "Destroying the flower over and over again will not diminish it, for it returns each season. Accommodation, with the flower here and you there, allows both to thrive."

"Such a lesson we impart to the young."

"But it was said the parable warns that we cannot defeat our enemies," she continued. "In this, it opposed the wishes of our village."

"Of the leaders of the village."

"Yes."

"Leaders change."

"But if the young do not learn of the storyways, how will the leaders themselves grow differently?" Her tail thumped against the wall of the cave, and she made a gurgling sound of mirth. "So I asked them if they were at war with flowers," she said. "And after some consternation, they confined me within. Storyteller...I'm hungry."

I shared my morsels with Mashrrv, while the light brightened, and faded, and died. We drew what warmth we could, and curled up together, still hungry. Our captors had seen the glowing inscription on the wall, perhaps, and had condemned us to silence, condemning our words as well. I touched my hand to Mashrrv's neck and felt the life coursing, but slower than it should have coursed. The strength of her voice had concealed her true weakness. Deprived of warmth, of light, and now of food, she was falling into that ultimate torpidity. Long ago our ancestors had survived the seasons of chills through such torpor, but they had done so on bodies filled with nutrients in preparation for that deep slumber. For us, our hunger remained, the ache of stone on raw bone.

She would not awaken, come the next light.

Two lights have passed and Mashrrv remains still, her life coursing so feebly that this time I scarcely could find it. When I touched her neck, I thought to hear a sound from her, but perhaps it was the settling of the stone around us, no more.

And so I resumed my task. *Tinte* remains, and ought to be used. I have inscribed on these walls the Tale of Mashrrv and the Storyteller, the lines of words coming to a close on the wall above where I sit holding Mashrrv, sharing with her what little warmth remains. Presently my hand will move, and inscribe a final word, and will then fall to my side as I curl around her and sigh the very last of my words with the very last of my strength. One day, perhaps, the Tale will be found, and perhaps read, so that the readers will know that we clung to our ways and our truth—and perhaps the power of our truth will give them strength in their own times of troubles...for leaders cannot lead when no one will follow.

"Oh, Mashrrv," I will whisper, and, gently rocking her, lay my face across her body, and bring my last story to an end.

Acorns

The tableau unfolded for Vianna in slow-motion. From across the street she saw the girl pass by the alley, saw the hand reach for her from the darkness and yank her within. A scant second later she heard the scream, but it was not the girl's. Vianna reached the scene in a trice, in the way of her kind, but the fight was already over. Down the alley fled the owner of the hand, now *hors de combat*, and it was in her nature not to take the life of one who was departing from the field of honor, however dishonorable had been his intentions. In the dark he seemed slightly bent over, as if he were clutching something to him, and she could smell battlefield blood, sweet and coppery in the damp night air.

Beside the dumpster, the girl straightened. A flick of her wrist closed the butterfly knife, which she tucked into a front pocket of her dungarees. In the indirect, hazy light from the street lamp her hair was not quite yellow, not quite brown, long and somewhat disheveled. Her eyes, Vianna saw, were pale, like her own.

The girl gave Vianna a "What?" look. Then she squinted at her. "You've been following me."

Vianna did not bother to deny the charge. She shrugged, and drew the long sepia cloak around her bare shoulders, covering the simple white gown. Already the encounter had taken a bad turn. The girl was too wary now. In her haste to assure herself of the girl's safety, Vianna had jeopardized the establishment of trust. She would have to find another approach.

The girl was older than Vianna had first thought, probably on the verge of twenty, and filled with what was these dark days called attitude. Perhaps she was already lost. Vianna tightened the cloak against the cool September night and moved away, her footsteps whisper-silent on the broken concrete of the sidewalk.

"Wait."

The girl's voice had lost just a trace of its street edge. It was enough to cause Vianna to turn back around.

"I have seen you," said the girl, stepping closer. "In the shadows, the past couple days, maybe a week. I know I have."

Vianna tried deflection. "Southaven is not so large."

"You have all of Memphis to skulk around in." For a moment the girl gazed across the street and into the night. Neon signs in need of repair blinked in red and green. A vertical post of orange letters affixed to a corner of a building advertised a HOTE. All these colors were reflected on the girl's face.

She turned back to Vianna. "I'm called Garnet."

"That is not your true name," said Vianna.

Garnet's eyes widened. "How would you--? All right, no, I took that name because I'm usually up to my eyeballs in schist." She paused, and when Vianna did not respond, she added, "It's a mineralogy joke. You know? Mineralogy?"

"Do you know mineralogy?" asked Vianna.

Garnet's expression soured. "Maybe I should thank you for coming to my rescue," she said, her voice gravelly with irritation. "But I didn't need your help. I don't know why you're following me around, but I don't need any help to deal with you, either." With a final look that Vianna was unable to read, she turned away and vanished into the darkness of the alley.

👁👁👁

It was easy enough for Vianna to drift unnoticed with the wind along the street, and the idle passer-by might have seen a flutter of something dark and undefinable, nothing more than that. A concentrated, closer look by one of her kind would have discovered a tallish, slender woman with dark hair and eyebrows, a straight but obscure nose, a pale slash of a mouth. The wind sculpted the cloak around her long legs, and revealed something even more out of place than the woman herself: something long and rigid down her left side that dangled from the thick leather belt tight around her, just above the hips. Two pouches also hung from this belt, both over her right hip. One of the pouches jingled softly as she took irregular paces on the broken sidewalk.

At the corner Vianna paused, and glanced back over her shoulder. At this point an observer might have caught a glimpse of a shadow, might have gotten the impression of someone standing there. She herself saw everything, except the one person she wished to see.

And yet--was that a whisper of Garnet that she heard on the wind? After a moment she shook her head; she could not be certain.

Nearby a bottle tinkled, and rolled into the gutter. She turned to look, knowing already what she would find.

Salvation Army had given the man his garb--the drab and threadbare overcoat, the pair of farm boots with the left heel worn down as if by someone with a deformity, the work glove with the fingers cut out on his right hand. The wall of the check-cashing and payday-loan kiosk, its windows long boarded up, now gave him support as he sat on the sidewalk, straddling a crack, legs extended-- and Vianna realized she must have passed over them during her reverie. He was looking up at her now with the eyes of one who was too drunk to be fooled by wisps and shadows, and she saw that she was real to him, not a flutter on the wind.

She blinked. She had seen it before, too many times. She would see it again.

Help him.

Nimue's voice, her conscience from the old ways.

Vianna keened to her inner ear. There were guidelines by which her kind abided. Compassion for the weak. Comfort for the injured. *Coup de grâce* for the battlefield dying. And, from time to time, providing a weapon with which to combat the forces of evil.

An incipient smile tickled the corners of Vianna's mouth and lightened her eyes as she gazed down at the man. "You are drunk," she said, without sharpness, though her lips did not move and no one could have heard with their ears the voice in which she spoke.

"Strue," muttered the man on the sidewalk. His head rocked back and forth. "Strue."

"Have you a job?"

The man hoisted a soggy paper bag, out of the bottom of which the empty bottle had slipped. "Swhy Yi drink. No work."

"But you can buy wine."

"Stolit."

Vianna's expression still retained the almost-smile. "You can drink or you can work. Choose."

"Sno work aywhere."

125

"Choose, please."

Bleary eyes rose to meet hers. It was impossible to say whether they lifted because he wanted them to, or because she had commanded it. "Wanna job."

Vianna gave a little nod. "First, you will sleep. In an hour, when you awaken, you will walk across the street to the hotel. The man there will give you a key. Go to the room, and bathe. You will find there clothing suitable for work. Get some sleep. In the morning, go to the wholesale book and magazine warehouse five blocks down the street and ask for a job. You will be given work in the warehouse, filling orders, and you will be trained in the operation of a forklift. It is up to you, whether you keep this job. Do you understand?"

The eyes remained bleary, but she thought she saw in them a stirring. "Unnerstan'," said the man.

"Sleep now."

After his eyes closed, Vianna again peered along the street, again in vain. Either Garnet was incurious, or she was despite her youth adept at concealment in the manner of their kind. Even so, if the girl was there, she should have seen her, sensed her. She was not there. On Vianna's eyelids weighed a sadness that sleep could not relieve . . .

She became aware that she had drifted to a small park, dark at this hour. A car passed, the light from its low beams brushing past her cloak and revealing a wooden bench in disrepair, its paint flaking. Above her hovered the branches of an old poplar, misshapen by the city air and the need to trim it from the power lines. Voices she heard, of men in low, slurred conversation. She moved away from them, toward the grass on the other side of the bench, hoping to avoid attention, but it was not to be.

"Hey, lady, where ya going?"

Vianna's shoulders slumped. Weary, she turned around. There were four of them, more than she had thought. Perhaps a bar had just closed somewhere nearby. The alcohol they had consumed made her visible to them. One man carried an aluminum baseball bat, though she had no idea why he might have needed such an implement in the bar. Another carried a bottle of beer by the neck; it appeared to be almost empty.

126

"Whatcha doin' out so late?" asked Beerbottle.

Baseball Bat added, "This a dangerous neighborhood, lady. We oughta walk you home."

Under the cloak Vianna's fingers closed around the hilt. "Believe me when I tell you that this cannot end well for you," she said quietly.

A third man, of average height and wiry, fished a hand into his front pocket. "You bet it'll end well," he snickered, and looked to his companions for approval as he withdrew a knife and flicked it open. "Ain't that right?"

Eyes glinting in the starlight, Vianna produced a broadsword from under her cloak and held it at ready. The sight of the long blade gave the men pause, but only for a moment and only because it was unexpected. Then Baseball Bat stalked forward. A backhanded swing passed the end of the bat within a foot of her face, but she did not draw back or raise the sword defensively. Her complaisance seemed to embolden the men, and they moved to surround her.

"It's not even real," declared Beerbottle.

Vianna steeled her heart. She had given them more warning than they deserved. It would not do to kill them--too many questions would be asked and, more importantly, too many official eyes might watch the streets of Southaven and make her task with Garnet more difficult. Lightly wound them to discourage them, then.

Again the bat flew toward her face, and this time she caught it against the *forte*, corkscrewed, and tapped the edge of the blade gently against the man's hand. Blood appeared immediately even as he yelped, and streamed over his fingers as he dropped the bat. It clattered on the sidewalk, and with the sound Vianna swept the broadsword flat into the beer bottle, shattering it. Again blood flowed, this time from glass cuts. The swing turned her to confront the opponent with the switchblade, but as she did so, a throaty roar and the squeal of brakes brought the tableau to a halt.

An ancient and battered black GMC pickup had arrived. Two men and one woman, attired in medieval garb, rushed from the cab and bed, all brandishing edged weaponry of various designs. One Vianna recognized as, of all things, a cutlass. As she prepared to meet this new threat, the woman yelled at her, "Get in the back! Hurry!"

The four men backed away into the deep shadows under the poplar, two nursing bloody but superficial wounds. Vianna ignored them now, her heavy dark brows knit. The woman was addressing *her*?

"Don't just stand there!" said the man who had been riding in the truck bed. Though he reeked of ale, he appeared to be steady enough as he beckoned urgently to her. "Let's get outta here before the cops come!"

To Vianna's utter astonishment the woman grabbed her by the arm and began to usher her toward the pickup. "C'mon, honey, no telling who's calling the cops right now. We don't want any trouble."

"Who are---?"

The man who had beckoned jumped into the pickup bed and held his arm out to Vianna, while the woman nudged her forward. Vianna lowered her defenses and sheathed her broadsword. Whoever these people were, they meant her no harm, and thought they were helping. Boosted by the second man, she climbed aboard. Almost immediately there was a squeal of tires, and Vianna was thrown onto the bed. The woman caught her and broke her fall.

"Easy, honey. Jacob's always a bit heavy on the foot."

Vianna read the woman's name tag. "You are Lady Godiva?" she asked, puzzled.

"That's my Ren name. What's yours?

"I am named Vianna," she said, and drew the cloak around her.

"You must have lost your name tag in the fight," said Godiva. She leaned with the truck as it rounded a corner and sped off into the night. "Love your sword, though."

"*Domina Pergamus.*"

"Oh, your Ren name," said the man. His name tag identified him as Marco Polo. He took a drink from his beer can. "Latin something."

"It is the name of my sword," said Vianna.

The man hefted his cutlass. "I haven't named mine," he said, and put it away. "Lucky we came along when we did. The SCA and the cops have a kind of understanding when there's a Ren Fair in town, but it doesn't extend to actual swordfights on public streets."

"SCA?" asked Vianna.

Polo stared at her. "You're not . . . one of us? Society for Creative Anachronism?"

An apologetic look came into Vianna's pale eyes. She shook her head.

Polo's eyes remained wide. "That's . . . that's a *real* sword?" he gulped, pale now. "You were really fighting with a *real* sword?"

Vianna smiled faintly. "It might be best if I left you at this point," she said.

Polo rapped the back window of the cab. "Pull 'er over, Jake. She wants out here."

"You sure about this, honey?" asked Godiva, as the pickup stopped by the curb. "There's no street lights, and this is not the best neighborhood . . . "

"I will be quite safe," said Vianna, standing up to climb over the side. "Thank you for your kindness."

Her long legs swept her to the broken sidewalk, where she stood until the pickup vanished into the night. For a brief moment she had felt a chill, a recognition that some people still appreciated the old ways and even practiced them after their fashion. It gave her a spark of hope, but only a spark, for there remained the difficulty with Garnet.

👁👁👁

Cloak tight, Vianna found a doorway with steps in an alley beside a store and sat down, slumping against the jamb. The cloak served to cushion her, in the way of her kind, so that she slept comfortably. She dreamt of water, pining for it. Despite the abuse humanity had heaped into the lakes, the substance of water itself was pure, nourishing the spirit and the soul, a proper medium for the purity of the magic she wielded. In her dream she submerged herself into it, glowing with the vitality it bestowed, dark hair floating all around her, the thin white gown she wore under the cloak now clinging to her. Water enhanced her beauty. Motionless, she might have been marble worked by Michelangelo, the curves of her body tenderly buffed by the Master's gentle hands, the eyes always seeming to watch those who watched her, the eyelashes like snowflakes, the mouth half-open, sensuous and inviting. In the water she remained still, waiting to be called, waiting to be summoned. To almost anyone passing by the doorway she was a shimmering, a trick of the night or of the dawn.

These were the worst moments for her: tucked inside the cloak, alone, out of water and out of light. Thousands of light-years from her world, her forests, her lakes, her waters. Trying to nudge in the optimal direction a people that did not wish to be nudged, that had no ears for her, no eyes for her and for the promise inherent in her being. Pearls, she thought, closing her eyes, before swine. In these dark moments it was easy to sink into a bleak oblivion, even if just for the night. It was easy to forget that every now and then, oh so heart-wrenchingly rarely, she saw a spark in someone's eyes, something to which she might add her own light and thereby alter, just a little, the race of this people toward oblivion. Inside the cloak, where she had to hide--it was the way of her kind--where she was alone in the dark.

Time counted, the way it does, before and forever, and the dark became gray for Vianna once more.

The face appeared before her as one peering from above into the pond in which she was immersed. Through half-lidded eyes she saw the girl's face, an Impressionist's portrait against the backdrop of the Sun about to return to a sky now the color of mourning doves. The girl's lips moved, but the words failed to penetrate the water. Vianna blinked, and swam to shore.

"Where is your cloak, child?"

"I'm hardly a---," began Garnet, and stopped abruptly, transfixed by the stern gaze from Vianna. She dropped her eyes. "I . . . pawned it. I sold it to a pawn shop." Then, defiantly: "How did you know I had a cloak?"

"The same way I know that your real name is Ruiselle, child."

The girl drew away. "Stop calling me that."

Vianna began to walk, with the expectation that the girl would accompany her. As yet she had no destination in mind, but the two of them together were more visible. Mobile, they might attract less attention. "Why are you here . . . Garnet?" asked Vianna. "Why did you come here?"

130

"Here? To you?"

Vianna hesitated. Had Garnet's demeanor been less pricklish, she might have expanded the question to include "here, to this world." But Garnet had sought her out, for some reason. No bond had been established, but it was open to possibility now. She had to tread gingerly.

"You did find me," Vianna said gently. "Do you drink coffee?"

"Only because it is too early for ale."

Up the street a diner had opened, catering to early risers. Vianna grasped Garnet by the elbow to lead her on, but the girl pulled back. "I can't go in there," she protested. "They . . . know me in there."

Vianna's hand did not yield. "There will be no difficulty. Come."

"You don't understand---"

"But I *do* understand, Ruiselle. And I tell you that you will not be accosted. You possess the power to assure yourself of this, though we would prefer that you refrain from using it to your own advantage."

"I have no idea what you're talking about," said Garnet. At the entrance to the diner they paused, and she looked away as if to flee. A shadow clouded her, not quite guilt and not quite shame, and visible only to Vianna. There was no place for her to run; small stores lined both sides of the street except for a small gap across the way, where stood an old oak as gnarled as a carpenter's hands, its roots poorly sheltered by sparse, unkempt grass. A bench near the intersection marked a bus stop, the bare wood and concrete flaked here and there with the remains of a coat of red paint. A page from a newspaper fluttered along the sidewalk, eyed by a nervous squirrel.

Garnet relented, and allowed Vianna to escort her into the diner. They sat in a booth by the window, facing each other. The waitress arrived with a pot of coffee and two mugs, giving Garnet the excuse to break eye contact. She seemed as nervous as the squirrel, now scrambling across the back of the bench. The waitress poised for their order, Vianna said, "We shan't require anything but coffee, thank you."

"Very well, ma'am."

When she was out of earshot, Garnet said, "What did you do to her?"

Vianna did not answer. She poured coffee for both of them, added a packet of sugar and half a thimble of milk to hers. Absently she stirred, the spoon clanking against cheap porcelain from time to time. Her pale eyes seemed intent on the table top, the floor beneath that and the Earth, and the Universe. Garnet's voice reached her as a pleasant static, a sound that she might adjust out of existence if she so chose.

Finally Garnet heaved a weighted sigh and, gazing out the window, muttered, "Stupid squirrel."

Vianna spoke as if she had not been lost in reverie. "Why do you say that?"

"Burying an acorn there by the tree," she grumbled, and stirred her own coffee, though she had added nothing to it. "Every year at this time it does that, every year. As have squirrels before it, year after year, decade after decade. Every year at this time since the glaciers melted, they've been burying acorns."

"Probably not under that tree, I wouldn't think."

Garnet chuckled, then frowned, as if betrayed by her own sense of amusement. "It's all they do," she continued. "All they've ever done, all they ever will do."

"Perhaps that's so," Vianna agreed. She tested her coffee, found it just too hot. "Or perhaps one day, thousands or tens of thousands of years from now, a squirrel will notice that a sapling has sprouted where the previous autumn it buried an acorn, and it will try a different location the ensuing autumn. After another thousand years, squirrels will deliberately plant acorns where the trees will afford them the best protection from predators, or where they will be certain of a rich harvest of acorns. Or perhaps not. Who can say?"

Garnet was silent for a long moment. Then: "Are we still talking about squirrels?"

"How is your coffee?"

The girl made a face. "I don't like it."

"It's too early for . . . "

A young man had entered the diner, and was speaking in urgent, hushed tones to the waitress. His right hand was jammed into a pocket of his dark blue windbreaker, the hood of which obscured much of his face.

" . . . ale," finished Vianna, and stood up. "I suppose your sword went the way of your cloak."

"I needed the money."

For what possible purpose? thought Vianna, but held her tongue. "Very well. Remain here, please," she instructed, and moved toward the counter, hands and forearms visible outside the cloak.

The waitress was now standing at the cash register, a stricken look on her face. She turned fearful dark eyes at Vianna, approaching. The young man turned also, his hand still in the windbreaker pocket. He might have a weapon, or not. Vianna could not be certain. Anger narrowed his eyes, but there was a tension behind them: he was angry because he was afraid.

As she drew into sword range, he seemed to aim the bulging pocket in her direction. His expression conveyed a dark intensity, but the higher pitch of his voice betrayed him. "Stay where you are," he said. "And you, hurry up with that money."

The register drawer popped opened. Before he could reach across the counter, Vianna said, softly, "Your mother keeps your room ready, in case you need a place to stay. Go home. Think about what you want to do, what you need to do."

The waitress stared at her in open disbelief. The young man drew back. "You . . . ," he began, and licked his lips, uncertain.

"This is not what you want to do," Vianna continued, in the same tone. "This is not you. Please, go home."

He looked at the few bills in the drawer, then back to Vianna. Plainly he wanted to reach for them. "I-I told her I could make it. I said . . . "

"You said you did not need her," Vianna finished for him. "You and I both know you did not mean that. She knows it, too. She does not want this for you. Let her care for you, just a little longer. She needs that just as much as you do."

The young man withdrew his hand from his pocket. It was empty. He pointed at her, for a moment, and lowered his arm. "How can you know . . . ? You *can't* know . . . "

Vianna looked at the waitress. "There is no need for the silent alarm. Nothing has happened here, and no harm has been done. He is going home."

He nodded. "Yes. Going home. I'm . . . " Unable to complete the thought, he turned and departed from the diner, certain of his destination, if not his reason.

The waitress closed the drawer, and stared at Vianna. Finally she said, "How did you do that?" she asked.

Vianna smiled faintly. "Did you see me do something?"

"You hypnotized him."

"Perhaps."

Vianna drifted back to the booth, where Garnet was sipping from a glass of water. Impossible to read the girl's face, though she had witnessed the tableau. She said, with some asperity, "You might have been killed."

"He had no weapon," said Vianna, "as you saw."

"Was it worth it?"

"Oh, my dear child. It is not given to us to know the effect we may have." She opened one of the pouches dangling from her belt and took three coins from it, placing them on the booth table. "We plant many acorns. We cannot determine in advance whether they will grow."

The girl stood up, abandoning her beverage. "So we do what we do because that is what we do? We're freaking squirrels?"

"Is that not enough?"

"No!"

"Come."

🐛🐛🐛

The sun had come up, the cerise and salmon stain that preceded it now almost gone. Shadows fell long on the sidewalk as the pair made westerly. Vianna tightened her cloak; early morning passersby would see only the girl. People were filtering onto the sidewalk: early-shift crews for the fast-food restaurants, women hurrying to daycare before work, a few high school students, men in grubbies off to the sanitation services. For Vianna the only difference between this and any other day was the company of the girl. She wondered

134

whether Garnet had taken notice of the heartbeat of this suburb. These people, these squirrels.

At a store window she paused, and Garnet paused with her. The human traffic had thickened, and they had been headed upstream. The window gave them respite. Beside them, a young woman was remonstrating with her son, whose hand was pressed against the glass. She tugged at him, and berated him, and ordered him to "forget that stuff, and come on! I'm going to be late."

Vianna looked. The window gave onto a small hobby shop. In the display was a plastic model of a space shuttle, the object of the boy's desire. Suddenly Garnet dropped to one knee beside the boy. "It's okay," she said softly. "Someday you can have a real one."

"What are you doing?" the woman demanded. "Leave him alone. Come on, Matthew!"

The boy went with his mother, but kept looking over his shoulder at Garnet, who winked at him and stood up.

Vianna shot her a quizzical look, and the girl shrugged. Finally Vianna nudged her into the doorway and out of the flow of traffic. A flip of a hem tossed the cloak around them both. Garnet frowned, but said nothing. In a trice, in the way of her kind, Vianna whisked them to another part of the suburb.

Reaching a grassy slope, Garnet stumbled, and fought for balance. Then recognition set in, and she spilled onto the grass. Vianna drew up beside her and offered her hand, but Garnet merely glared up at her.

Vianna looked around. There were dwellings in the area, but only a few people about, and none who would be disturbed by their presence. "You recognize this place," she said.

"You knew I would," growled Garnet. "Why did you bring me here?"

"You were sent here. This is where you are to be."

Garnet gazed out at the lake. It was small, and stained here and there with algae, and marred here and there by refuse--a candy wrapper, an empty bag of corn chips, a plastic soda bottle. She kicked at a fragment of paper on the grass, and it fluttered away in the breeze.

"I would like to know," said Vianna. "Why did you speak to that boy?"

The girl made a face. "I don't know," she said at last. "It seemed . . . I don't know."

"Go on."

Garnet grabbed her hair in her fists. Her face twisted in frustration. "I don't know. I don't *know*. I shouldn't have, it's not me, it isn't me."

Vianna hid a smile. The strength of the girl's denial gave a clear view of her inner conflict. Accustomed to waiting, she kept her counsel and waited.

Presently Garnet spoke again. "I hate this lake. The water is filthy. I think they used to rake it out, once, but no more. The concrete border is slimy with algae. There are dead koi rotting on the bottom. Drunks pee in it . . . and other things."

"It cannot touch us, Ruiselle."

The girl gave her hair a final twist, and leaned back aprop her elbows. "Oh, I know, I know. The purity of the water, right? It is the substance of the water that touches us, nothing else. When we emerge from the lakes, we come clear of the water and of whatever is in the water." Ruiselle paused, and pointed. "Once I saw a little girl come to the water's edge, just over there. She saw me. But for my face she saw her own reflection. I wonder if she saw herself all slimed with algae and potato chips and . . . "

Vianna knelt, and touched the girl's shoulder. "It is not given to us to know the effect we may have," she said. Her voice was the touch of a dandelion flower on bare skin. "Like the squirrel, we plant many acorns."

"But these people need water to live. How can they treat it so?"

"Ruiselle."

"I know, I know." The girl sighed. "I've . . . misbehaved, haven't I?"

"Had you not spoken so to that little boy, I might worry."

"So: we are what we are, and we do what we do. Is that enough?"

"It can be," said Vianna. "We hope it is."

"I suppose," said Ruiselle, "I had better go back in."

"Not until you are properly attired, young Lady."

Very early the next morning, in one part of the city, a pawnbroker wore a puzzled frown as he tried to fathom how someone had robbed him without disturbing the alarms.

And in another part of the city, just before sunrise, a little boy dreamed.

Home for Supper

ONE

A skimmer from Central Biosphere brought her out, a Michelin woman resplendent in metallic white, with the great tinted fishbowl over her head to keep the UV out and the O in. Everything was ready at the site, but with no one to greet her she seemed to hesitate. It wasn't what she had been led to expect.

But there was no help for it, not now.

She brushed a thick layer of orange dust from one of the hermetically sealed olive drab plastic shipping crates on one of the olive drab plastic pallets, off-loaded two of her years ago in preparation, and sat down to wait. The tinted fishbowl reflected the panorama as she looked around, at the rocks and gullies and the distant crater wall--and the red-orange dust devils that a wandering zephyr kicked up, the only things other than herself moving that she could see. Later, in mad moments, she would give them names, but for now she was indecisive as to a course of action.

But there really was no other choice but to begin, and she soon saw that, and commenced unpacking the crates, slowly and methodically at first, waiting for help to arrive, looking up from her labors now and then in anticipation, then methodically when it began to occur to her that help might not be forthcoming.

The tarp base was laid out first, on the flat of terrain William had obviously prepared for it, and she was careful to smooth out the creases in the virtually impenetrable 100-mil plastic, ironing some of them out with her massive white boots. Then came the prefab walls, one by one, interlocked in place, including the airlock at the entrance, and finally the snap-tight roof.

By this time the Sun had begun its descent. Inside the protective outsuit she had already begun to perspire--in the light gravity maneuvering the parts of the house was relatively easy, but overcoming the initial inertia still required muscular effort. On Earth she would have looked forward to soaking in a hot bath after her labors, but here water was gold. A thermal well had been sunk nearby to promote water from the frozen underground reservoir--at least he had done that much, she sighed--but surface water was only available during the seasonal polar cap melting, not due for another month.

Another Earth month, she remembered. The local calendar remained undeveloped. Another chore for her.

The crate containing the airlock operation mechanism was the most massive, and it took her the better part of two hours to maneuver it into place, to set the power jacks in the ports according to the schematic, to affix and seal the air hose, to fit the compressor in its housing. She could not test the system's operation, not yet, nor dared she open the valve to the nitrox tank. One more chore, more vital than all the others together, yet awaited her.

She opened the crate filled with tubes of sealant. Each prefab section was self-sealing--the manufacturer had to allow for the stray meteoric fragment--but the joints themselves required a manually-emplaced seal. Step by step, with the persistence of a metronome, she sealed every nook and cranny of the Individual BioDwelling, as it was identified in stenciled black block lettering on the crates, the IBD wherein, once it was erected and inflated, she might doff the outsuit and live a more or less normal day.

The final tests completed, she doffed the protective suit and breathed filtered, soulless air.

Only then did she notice the note on one of the remaining unopened crates. She was not so long from Earth that the feel of real paper on her fingertips made her keen for her ancestral home--that would come much later--but the simple words assuaged her anxieties.

Out prospecting. Home for supper. We'll put it up together.

She sat down on the crate. Ain't that just like a man, she thought.

She dug into a pocket of her lavender leisure suit for the scrap of paper that had brought her here, a form from the Sears Catalog, completed in William's sprawling print. *Wife needed. Long hours, hard work, few rewards, shared dangers. Looks unimportant. Must meet NASA weight requirements. Respond William Grady, Mars Central.*

He sounded like a man who wanted forthrightness and honesty, qualities she readily attributed to herself, so she had sent him a photo and mentally crossed her fingers. Within two months she had a NASA flight ticket, a certification that she weighed 132 pounds (twenty eight under the limit for women), and a notarized statement that she had no financial or medical encumbrances that might prevent the arrangement she sought.

She looked out the window beside the airlock. No sign yet of William.

She shrugged. He'll be home for supper.

Several crates remained unopened, and she glanced over the stenciled lettering for inspiration. A plastic folding table. Folding plastic chairs. Pellets of freeze-dried nourishment, enough to last for decades. A futon for two. Packets of seeds.

Seeds?

Corn, beans, tomatoes. And foil envelopes of soil-prep bacteria. And instructions. And small hand-tools, and a collapsible shovel.

She scoffed, and pitched the packets back into the crate. William would be home soon, and he could brief her regarding the household chores and maintenance. And . . . other things. Nuptials, for one.

One of the crates contained clothing. Black denims (he'd gotten the size right) and simple jerseys for indoor wear, protective suits for outside. Some frilly things, also the right size, although at her size she scarcely required much support. And . . .

She held up the black negligee against her body, assessing the fit, blushing all the while.

She poked around in the clothing crate, careful not to disturb those items obviously meant for him, and found a more practical sleeping garment, a knee-length shirt. She wondered which William would prefer. In their correspondence they had not broached the topic of intimacies. Well, he would be home soon, and they could discuss them after supper.

The skies were clear. There would be stars. That would be nice and romantic.

William had been here for four years. Probably, she thought, he needed little encouragement to be romantic.

140

She blushed again.

In a corner she spread the futon, testing the padding and comfort, and arranged two pillows side by side. Once more she checked the window. He would be home soon. What would he think if the first thing he saw was her arranging the bedding?

Supper . . . she set up the folding table by the front window and arranged the chairs just so. Pity there wasn't a candle or two; the glowstix would have to suffice. No plates or cups or utensils, but some of the packing was styrofoam, and she selected two small blocks of it and scooped them out to fashion bowls. And for supper . . . *let me see.* She picked through the packets of pellets, discarding idea after idea. This evening, of all evenings, the meal ought to be perfect. Sirloin steak . . . yes. She placed two pea-sized pellets in her bowl, and four in his, for he would be hungry after a hard day prospecting and she was his wife and he was her husband and she ought to see to his well-being. Sirloin. Potatoes, of course, with gravy, lots of gravy (she gave him an additional pellet of this). Vegetables. Oh, he probably didn't like those, and she would have to find ways of getting him to eat them. Broccoli . . . no, not broccoli, not tonight. If only there were a salad pellet.

She settled on carrots and celery, one orange pellet and one chartreuse pellet for each of them.

And for dessert . . .

She glanced at the futon, and blushed.

Supper was ready. William ought to be home soon.

Dusk did not stay for long in the thin atmosphere. She glanced out the window and it was still daylight, and when she glanced out again it was dark. Supper was ready. She sat down at the table. In their correspondence he had seemed a kind and loving man, simple and hard-working. He might be late on occasion. He would not want her to go hungry. He would want her to eat, yes, he would.

So she ate. The sirloin first, washing this down with a sip of tasteless water from one of the canteens. The potatoes and gravy. The colorful veggie pellets. She chewed slowly, meticulously, pausing now and then to keen an ear to the airlock. Was he home yet?

Nothing.

141

She would have to remind him to call next time he was going to be late. He did not seem the kind of man who would deliberately give her cause to worry.

The night was really dark, darker than ever it had been in Arkansas. She peered up through the window at the stars. They were specks of light, slightly warped by the reinforced clear plastic of the window. The constellations would be the same here, she thought, and the Zodiac. She wondered what her horoscope had to say about this.

She sat with elbows aprop the table, chin cupped in hands, thinking about her horoscope. It would have to be different here. Two months for each sign, at least. Cusps would last a whole week.

Well, it was something to think about.

William must have been delayed by something at the mine. Yes, that was it. Couldn't be helped. He would bring her flowers, perhaps in the morning. He'd be happy and surprised, seeing all his wife had gotten done, waiting for her husband.

She turned her bowl over to remove food particles, and drank the last of her water--mustn't waste it--and . . .

We really need a cupboard in here, William.

For now, she left the bowl and canteen cup on the table, and hoped he wouldn't think her messy.

She turned the glowstix down to nightlight level, undressed, climbed into her sleeping shirt, and stretched out on the futon. William would be home for supper tomorrow. That must have been what he meant in the note. In the meantime, she would have to see to the house. She would need her sleep.

In the night outside the window she thought she saw lights, like aurorae, though these were unlikely here. The lights on some sort of terrain vehicle, perhaps. William was coming home. Dinner still waited for him. She sat up.

I'll be home for supper.

And the lights faded.

She thought he said good night.

After a while she went back to sleep, on her right side, legs slightly drawn up, hands clasped between her knees, lonely for a man she had never met.

❧❧❧

Sunlight awoke her to two cold facts. One, she had slept alone on her wedding night. It was not what she had expected. She would forgive William, of course--so many relationships failed because one or the other harbored a grudge about something from early on--because he loved her enough to have sent for her, sight relatively unseen, not that she was or ever had been a sight, a primary reason for her having accepted the proposal in the first place.

And two, it seemed she had arranged the futon in the northwest corner, not a location conducive to sleeping in in the morning, with the sun shining through from the southeast.

On the other hand, the sun served her as an alarm clock. She got up, stretched, performed her ablutions--taking care to send the wastewater back into the recyke--and sat down at the table, serving herself breakfast. This consisted of a granola pellet, a granule of coffee, and a pelletized orange, all washed down with a cup of water. At least the orange had a citric taste to it, and she salivated, downing it.

She had envisioned morning conversation before he went to work and she set herself to the household chores. William had failed to show for breakfast, but that, she decided, was no reason to deny herself the interaction. Practice made perfect, and between now and William's arrival she thought to hone her conversational skills as a means of keeping him . . . well, interested.

"I hope the orange wasn't too tart," she said. "Sometimes, when they freeze-dry them before they're fully ripened, you can get one that will sting your tongue."

She rather thought William would nod his head at this while he continued to gnaw on the granola pellet.

But was he paying attention to her? "I really think Thomas would be a good name for a baby," she said. "That was my grandfather's name, you know." She had mentioned this and much more about her family tree in correspondence, though she doubted he had studied for her quiz. "Or Meredith, if it's a girl." She had become

143

infatuated with the name after hearing it on one of her beloved soaps. "What do you think, William?"

Yes, dear.

Well, that seemed plain enough. She had hoped they would not fight over the choice of names. But you could tell, just by looking at his photo, he was not a hard man, not that way. The face might be rough, the mouth a little too austere, but he had kind eyes. The windows to his soul were kind.

Breakfast finished, she cleaned the table, then set about the dwelling in a nesting mood. Little remained for her to do, however, and her major contribution to the furniture arrangement was an overturned crate that became a bench under the back (south) window, where she was afforded a view of the eroded nullarbor that stretched to a cluster of small craters--the remains, possibly, of an ancient comet. She wished there were trees, and recalled that some plants might be possible to grow.

She spent the morning and the early part of the afternoon reading instructions, dressing for outdoor activity, and planning proper sites for her gardens.

The polar cap melts in another month. Best to wait.

"You're right, William," she said, chagrined. Suddenly she brightened. "But I can dig irrigation ditches in advance, and isolate the patches for cultivation. And some of these empty crates can store water." She nodded to herself as she drew on the outsuit. "I'll grow a nice garden for us, you'll see."

🙂🙂🙂

By mid-day she was perspiring inside the outsuit. At one point she had actually straightened from her labors to wipe her brow, and instead whacked the trowel against the tinted visor. Embarrassed, she glanced around to see if William had noticed. But he said nothing-- perhaps he himself had made similar instinctive movements while prospecting . . . or perhaps he was too much a gentleman to ridicule his beloved. Yes, that was it, that must be it. Inside the outsuit she warmed--how he loved her. Once more she leaned forward on her hands and knees and continued to excavate a shallow ditch that she hoped would carry meltwater to the plants she hoped one day would

144

provide them with a more familiar sustenance . . .

TWO

The visitor was attired in a white outsuit that conformed much more closely to his body than the bulky garment in which she had arrived. She watched through the front window while he trod uneasily on the pathways between the garden plots, as if he were struggling under a load of puzzlement. He had not come alone--at the controls of the bright blue skimmer docked some thirty meters away sat another individual, also in white, lounging almost insolently, as if he had no other purpose but to accompany the visitor to this site. Safety in pairs, she thought. Brow furrowed, she watched him for a few minutes, studying his face inside the clear fishbowl helmet. Now and then his lips moved, and she realized that the black rectangle of nanocircuitry in the top of the fishbowl included a communications system. He was reporting to his headquarters. She wondered what he had expected to find.

Finally she climbed into the outsuit she had arrived in and passed outside through the airlock. Surprised when the outer hatch opened, the man took several steps back and almost stumbled into an irrigation ditch. She envied him the far less cumbersome outsuit. By comparison her own felt like a deepsea diving suit.

She raised her hand for attention, then held up three fingers, two, and four, and pointed to her helmet. Seconds later his voice drifted into her helmet like a respiratory mist.

"I didn't expect . . . ," he began. "You are . . . Grady's, ah . . . ?"

"I'm Mrs. Grady. Please don't step on our beans."

The man regained his footing. "Yes, of course. Sorry. Mrs, ah, Grady, we weren't aware that anyone was living out here until satellite telemetry indicated the regular shapes of your, ah, gardens. And of course the IBD," he added, with a desultory gesture. His gaze swept over the gardens. "You've, ah, done something quite remarkable out here, you know that?"

She nodded proudly. "Built us a home."

"Ah, yes. Yes, of course. I doubt there'll be any problem with the claim, as you are Grady's widow. But our gardens have produced only a few pitiful, stressed crops, and frankly, we'd like to know---"

"I'm sorry," she said. "What did you say your name was?"

The man blinked. "I'm Assistant Superintendent Brinkman, Ma'am."

"Please pardon my manners, Mr. Brinkman," she said. "We haven't had many visitors out here." She grasped the hatch handle. "Would you care to come inside and set a spell? I could make a pot of tea."

"Ah, no, thanks, Mrs. Grady. But I would like to invite you to come back with me and tell us about how you made these gardens produce."

She shook her head. "Oh, I couldn't do that, Mr---" A pair of orange dust devils frolicked through the bean garden. "Thomas! Meredith Jane! You two stop that. I've told you and told you not to play in the gardens. You just wait till your father gets home and hears about this."

She smiled apologetically, then remembered that the visitor was unable to see her. "As I was saying, Mr. Brinkman, my William will be home for supper, and I have to get it ready for him, and finish up the housework."

Brinkman seemed to hesitate. He gnawed briefly on his lower lip. "Ma'am . . . Mrs. Grady, I'm sorry, but William Grady was caught in a sandstorm and killed over six years ago--the day you arrived, in fact."

"But I do have a lappie," she went on. "I would be happy to send you copies of my notes. Just give me your upload link."

Brinkman gave it to her. "Mrs. Grady, do you understand what I've been saying to you?"

"Yes, sir, I do," she replied. "And I surely hope the information I send you helps you in your endeavors. And now, if you'll excuse me, there's still some dusting to do, and I do need to steam the veggies. Good day to you, sir."

And she climbed back through the hatch, leaving him in the hot sun.

That night William did not come home for supper. She did so

wish he would call her when he was going to be late from the claimsite. But that was his way. The day done, she drew on her sleeping shirt and stretched out on the futon. Just before she drifted off to sleep she thought she saw lights in the night outside the window, rather like aurorae. The lights on some sort of terrain vehicle, perhaps. William was driving by to check on her. Then the lights faded, and she thought he said good night.

Good night, William.

❧ ❧ ❧

Communications with Superintendent Brinkman at Central Biosphere proved more frequent than she had anticipated. With the perseverance of a metronome she negotiated the trade of her notes for a less cumbersome outsuit--a pale azure garment that complimented her eyes--and some plastic tools useful in the cultivation of a kitchen garden. She also acquired some packets of seeds, accompanied by a request from Central that she keep notes regarding the application of her techniques.

There was no secret to her methods, she explained repeatedly to an incredulous Brinkman. The packets of bacteria thrived well enough in what passed for soil on the desolate orange world, but she had learned gardening from her father, who knew well what soil required.

"I still find it hard to believe that your gardens are successful because you pee on the plants," said Brinkman one day, still amazed.

She frowned at the transceiver. "That's not how I would say it, Mr. Brinkman."

"No, of course not," he said hastily. "We've been mixing the urinary recyke with the soils here, and I believe we're going to obtain results similar to yours. So far, at least, the plants look much healthier . . . thanks to you, Mrs. Grady."

She fell silent for so long that, when she finally spoke, she interrupted a query from Brinkman. "Do you ever come out here at night, Mr. Brinkman?"

"No, of course not. Night travel can be hazardous, unless an emergency justifies the risk." He paused briefly. "Why do you ask, Mrs. Grady?"

147

Her voice was pregnant with hesitation. "Does Mars have aurorae, Mr. Brinkman?"

"Well, I'm not sure . . ."

The topic broached, she went on quickly, "Because I see lights at night. Sometimes it's my William, of course, driving by on one errand or another for our claim. But most often I think there are others with him, and I wondered whether he . . . well, silly me, of course that makes no sense. I mean, how could he ride an aurora? I'm sorry to trouble you, Mr. Brinkman, and we'll just forget I mentioned this. I'll have some more notes for you first thing in the morning."

"Mrs. Grady?"

"Yes, sir?"

"We have received reports of lights, now and then, around some of the outlying settlements," said Brinkman, uncertainly. "In some psychological evaluations. When you're alone out here, sometimes the mind---"

"But I'm not alone, Mr. Brinkman. I have my William, and Thomas and Meredith."

"Ah . . . yes. Yes, of course. It's also possible for certain minerals to exhibit nocturnal fluorescence. For that matter, certain fungi and bacteria also exhibit this. We don't know of any on Mars, but they could exist here. Or I suppose you could attribute those lights to the spirits of those who have gone before."

"You mean died, Mr. Brinkman?"

"I'm not serious, Mrs. Grady. I don't believe in ghosts. But that explanation has cropped up here, in those evaluations I mentioned. And of course there's *The Cremation Of Sam McGee.*"

"The what, Mr. Brinkman?"

"It's a poem, Mrs. Grady, by Robert Service. One of the lines reads, I believe, 'the northern lights have seen queer sights, but the queerest they ever did see'." Perhaps that applies to Mars, Ma'am. This is a strange planet to humans, and sometimes we see things that we can only interpret from our own point of reference."

"So you're saying I'm not actually seeing these lights?"

"I don't know what you're seeing, Mrs. Grady. But I wouldn't worry about it. If they're real, they're harmless, and if they're not, they're a normal human reaction to . . . well, to solitude, Mrs. Grady."

"If ever I'm alone, I shall bear that in mind, sir. Until tomorrow, then."

👀👀👀

In the fullness of time she expanded the gardens so that they produced a surplus, and these she traded for other goods brought to her from Central Biosphere, including some new frilly things to replace those already worn out, and new outsuits for the children-- my, how they had grown! Why, Thomas was already a fine young man, and Meredith would surely be the belle of the ball one day. She scolded them when they tracked in orange dust, and chided them for their occasional lapse of language. And she saw to her chores, for her William deserved a clean place to come home to for supper.

She no longer sent gardening notes to Central. They were superfluous. Crops grew well in soil prepared with bacteria and fixed with nitrogen. Now and then some of the younger agri-labor technicians at Central seemed dumbstruck when talking with her, as if she were far above their station for what she had done, and she laughed quietly after the communications closed and they could no longer hear her. Such a simple obvious thing, she wondered that the techies had failed to consider it. Peeing on the plants, as Mr. Brinkman thought of it. Well, peeing on the soil. Now, of course, they imported nitrogen fertilizer--something with ammonia, she reckoned--and it seemed to work well enough.

The Martian colonies had proved themselves viable. When she thought about that, she decided that she and William had done their parts.

One evening, rather earlier than usual, she spotted the lights outside. This time, instead of passing by the IBD, they paused, poised, and her heart leaped.

William, she thought.

And not too late for supper.

Or other things . . .

Quickly she threw on the old black negligee, heart pounding, and she patted her chest like a schoolgirl, rather embarrassed by her anticipation. William was home for supper. Nothing else mattered,

149

not now. She gathered herself, adjusted a hem here, tugged at a strap there. Supper could wait.

Oh, William . . .

She opened the airlock to let him in.

Devotional

The last flake of old primer slipped from the window sill and onto the gritty pine floor to mingle with the others that had fallen over the years. Emily crossed her forearms along the rough bare wood and leaned through the opening. Moonlight the exact color of the little fish in the creek behind the house cast her freckled face in pure white and pious shadow and brightened her eyes to the blue of Rigel on a cold winter's night. Something dark moved in the clearing that separated the house from the forest--a nightbird, or perhaps a bat. It flitted down behind the irregular row of slabs of rotting wood and pitted granite that marked the cemetery, vectoring in on some insect fluttering among the family ghosts. Emily shivered. Something was always dying out there.

She knew the names on the markers by force of paternal rote. Pa had beaten them into her, branding her like a steer with the hot iron of vengeful memory. Her ancestors had moved here from eastern Kentucky just after the turn of the century. Ages varied, and causes of death. Smallpox, influenza, malnutrition. And gunshot, lots of gunshot. She counted the headstones to twenty seven, without seeing them. *These are your kin.* She always knew they were there. Sunlight glinted past them into her window in the morning, sharping her eyes. In the afternoon, the shadow of the house, a massive sundial gnomon, reached to the chipped granite stone over Orville Harper to tell her the time had come to prepare dinner with Ma. And at night the ghosts stirred to remind her of where she had come from and where she was going.

Emily had no need to look forward.

A wasp of wood stung her bare arm and broke off, and she pinched it free with her fingernails. The windowsill had started rotting two years ago, around the time the tornado scoured the ramshackle farms of Appalachian Tennessee, taking with it the chicken coop half a mile down the dirt road on Lee Mahon's patch of ground. Emily could repair the sill, given wood and tools. If they'd let her.

Noise from the living room caught her ear, and she turned

around, eyes a little wider in the dark. Were they coming for her? A guffaw, a thump. Someone had stumbled. Vance, likely. At fifteen, a year her senior, he'd yet to take three gulps from a mason jar without losing his equilibrium. He frightened Emily. There were always little jabs and jests, but she sensed he meant his. That one night he would sneak into her bedroom.

Her brothers hated her for that bedroom. She was the only girl of seven children. She had to have her own room, especially now that she was "nubbin' up." It's only right, Pa'd said. But he'd looked at her when he said it like she'd leaked a glob of spittle from the side of her mouth.

Emily plucked the sweaty cotton fabric of the checkered dress from her chest and prayed for even the lightest of breezes to waft through the window. She was more than nubbing. She hoped she wouldn't have to suffer indignities. Polly Johnson'd had to wear a wool blanket to school under her thin hand-me-down dress, not able to afford unmentionables. And when the blanket had started to stain that day...

Emily glanced at the mattress on the floor. Something scurried past the folded blanket toward a dark corner to avoid her eyes--one of the field mice who'd taken up residence in the pile of logs outside the bedroom wall, she reckoned. She called them all Gus. There were fewer of them these days, now that the snakes had emerged from hibernation. Gus could have the blanket, unless she needed it for school. When the beans came in next month, she could hustle a few baskets down to the stalls just outside Murphysboro, perhaps sell enough to buy some more underthings from the Goodwill on Oak Street. Maybe she'd even find some aluminum cans or intact bottles alongside the road. If she could cash them in without Pa finding out about them, she might even have enough left over to buy a little bottle of metallic blue.

The living room fell conspiratorially quiet. Pa was not yet home from work down at Dale's Repair Shop, where he was waiting for a tractor part from UPS, and Ma was still quilting over at the Tanners. Emily shivered, and slipped to the mattress, lifting a corner to touch the security of the loose boards. During the past two years she had excavated a hidey-hole large enough to accommodate her and her dream. The silence frightened her. At any moment Vance or Jacob might stagger through her doorway, drooling and leering and steeped in sour mash. Practice had enabled her to conceal herself within ten seconds. But if she was not quick enough...if they learned of her excavation and of the secret it contained... No, she dared not risk that, not now.

Outside her door a board creaked, and she dropped the mattress and rose swiftly to her feet, stepping away just as Vance pushed the door open. In the shadows his face became a besotted caricature of itself, and his twisted smirk revealed the broken upper incisor.

"Get out of here," hissed Emily.

Vance slumped against the doorjamb, weight on his left leg. The belt of his jeans had come loose but not yet unbuckled. His shirt was open, two buttons missing. "Lessee um," he muttered. "I wanna see 'um."

"No."

Vance lurched toward the mattress and, stumbling, kicked it askew. As he stepped on one of the loose boards, it popped up. Emily held her breath. But Vance simply twisted his legs and flopped down onto the mattress, the impact jarring a rubber doll's head and a green pewter airplane next to the wall. He stretched out on his left side, crooked an elbow and brought his face to rest on his hand. Ready for the show.

"Lessee 'um," he commanded, momentarily sober. "Undo them buttons."

Refusal might lead to a physical conflict, and he would learn that he could force her compliance. Better to control the surrender, Emily reached back behind her and undid two buttons. It occurred to her that her deliberation merely heightened Vance's eagerness, and made him more determined. Feeling nauseous, she shrugged slightly, easing the dress top forward from her thin shoulders, but held the fabric strategically in place.

Abruptly Vance scrambled to his feet, and stood unsteadily. His finger shook as he pointed at her. "Take it off."

If she did, thought Emily, and let him see, he might leave. He might leave her alone this time. But he would come back, again and again, until... She keened an ear toward the doorway. "That's a door slam," she said quickly. "Pa's home. Get out of here now."

"I din't hear nuthin'."

"You know what Pa'll do he finds you here. He opens that front door, I scream."

Vance trudged toward the door like a dog who'd peed the floor and wanted to get away before the puddle was discovered. Emily waited until the door had closed, then rushed to the mattress, lifted the loose boards, and scuttled into her hidey-hole. As soon as Vance learned that Pa had not in fact returned home, he'd come back...and assume she had fled through the window. She crouched down in the darkness, drawing ragged breaths and fighting the raspy sounds they made. *If they heard, oh, God...* Her fingers located by touch the fragment of candle and the book of matches. Late at night when she worked on her dream, she dared light it, but not now, not now. In the dark, with Vance drunk and no one to protect her, she could only wait.

After a while she snaked a hand out and felt for her dream. Plastic that should have been cold felt warm, as if it had somehow come alive to her touch. Her fingers recognized the saucer, and read the tiny indented windows like Braille, and she took solace in the raw power of the engine pods. One day, if only.

Outcast at home by her gender, Emily was also outcast at school. Math and science were too easy for her--in elementary school she had been put forward two grades--and still she shamed the boys with her swift and accurate responses, in class and on exams. Though she did not flaunt her scores, the girls eyed her with suspicion. What was she up to? Why was she interested in such things? Emily could have given them no clear answer. The daytime view from her window afforded her all she knew about life--that it began and ended violently or in sickness. But the view at night fed something within her that she was unable to define in words. And one day, in a store in Murphysboro, she chanced upon the symbol of that hunger. For three months, from November to February, she bought no lunch at school, hoarding her precious nickels and dimes. For three long months she added a ferocious plea to the compulsory nightly prayers: please don't let anyone else buy it. *Please let it be there.* Then, in early spring, while her parents and brothers were otherwise occupied, she ran three miles to the town and to the store and purchased a dream.

By this time the hidey-hole was large enough for her to fit into--not so much a shelter from abuse, though occasionally it did serve that purpose while Pa sobered or his anger waned, but as a refuge...a place to flee *to.* There, cowering in the dark, she might think and ponder and wish. The dream gave her meditations a form, a structure. This, she knew, was what was possible to her. One day, if only.

Above her she heard a scuffling. Vance or Jacob, perhaps both, had entered the bedroom in search of her. Though she had threatened Vance with exposure, in truth she dared not tell Pa about what he'd demanded of her. It was *her* fault she would have a woman's body, *her* fault that she tempted her brothers. Nor could she confide in Ma--whenever Pa administered punishment, Ma kept silent. She had no defender.

Her fingers closed around the plastic. Almost completed, it was. She needed only to cement a few more pieces together, then paint the finished starship the colors on the box. The starship *Voyager.* She'd heard of the show, and caught glimpses of episodes on some of the rare occasions when they visited someone who owned a television. Without the context of continuity, the episodes meant nothing to her. But the ship itself symbolized travel beyond dreams. Travel from here.

Escape from here.

Above her the scuffling stopped, and someone cursed in a low voice. Her door slammed shut. From somewhere far away she heard Pa's voice. She was safe for another day. She might emerge from the cocoon, and watch morning come to kill the stars.

The sun pierced the upper treeline to find Emily studying it through a smoked shard of glass. Mr. Hobbs was right, she thought, counting to three the sunspots. They might have been shadows of planets, so round they were. Mercury and Venus...she might go there one day, or to the moons of Jupiter. There were programs that might accept her. One day, if only. To Mars and Jupiter, and perhaps to infinity. But for now the smoky fragment was not large enough to shield both her eyes, and after a few minutes she had to pause and wipe away the tears that had formed, and with them the last crusts of sleep.

Behind her a board creaked, and she turned, but too late. Vance pinned her back against the window jamb and forced his hands under her blouse. A jagged fingernail caught at her flesh and tore it. In desperation she slashed at him with the smoked glass and opened a shallow gash in his left cheek, and blood welled.

Vance backed away and put a hand over the wound. "God*damn* you! You *cut* me, you little---"

"What's going on in here?" roared Pa, glaring at Emily. Under those terrible eyes she flinched, and dropped the incriminating shard.

"She *cut* me, Pa," cried Vance, pointing to it on the floor. "I din't do nuthin' and she *cut* me."

Pa unfastened his belt, and bent it double. "Turn around, girl."

"Pa, no," whimpered Emily, but she knew better than to hesitate or disobey. The leather strap whistled through the air and cut at her skin under the blouse, once, twice, and she bit her lip to keep from crying out. The third and last blow landed on a half-healed welt. A spark of pain exploded behind her eyes and buckled her knees, and she dropped to the floor, in too much agony to cry out. The welt was a souvenir of the striping she'd received four days earlier for, as the note from school said, "causing a ruckus." Dinosaurs *were* millions of years old, no matter what the textbooks said, but she resolved to keep her peace in class after that. Whippings were educational in that regard.

One day, if only.

"Bus be here in half an hour," Pa said, finessing the belt through the loops in his old jeans. His rough skin was dark with anger and last night's beard. "You hie yourself out there on time, girl."

Emily forced the words out. He had to hear them clearly, or he'd hit her again and again until he did. "Yes, Pa."

Left alone, Emily climbed back to her feet and trudged to the window. The smoked fragment had broken in two with the impact, and was now useless for her observations. Her eyes drifted downward, to the grave markers. There was plenty of room for more, in that field. One day they would all rest there--she, Ma and Pa, her brothers, and other kin. She wondered where they would place her marker...or whether they would give her a marker at all. Aunt Jackie once told her that her great grandmother and her aunt were buried out there, but no one knew where anymore. And there were low mounds, almost imperceptible and overgrown with grass, where girls were laid who had fallen to influenza or measles or a pox. They were spoken of in whispered memory...

One day, thought Emily, if only. Aunt Jackie had gotten out, moved to New Mexico after the Army and gone to college. If she could, Emily could...couldn't she? Like the fallen girls, Aunt Jackie was spoken of only in whispers, as if she had done something unspeakable . . . something to do with sex, Emily thought, though no one would ever say. To Emily she was a voice on the phone, tolerated only during the holidays. Emily had to let her dreams grow where she could hide them.

The door was closed, the front rooms quiet. She drifted to the hidey-hole and opened it, and lifted *Voyager* out into the light, where she might see it...where it belonged. Her heart lifted as she set the trap door back in place and drew the mattress back over it. One day she might travel to the stars in such a craft. It was possible, she told herself, showing *Voyager* the sunlight through the window. *Do you see where you belong?* she asked the craft. It could happen. She could make it happen. For now, though, the plastic spaceship needed a coat of enamel, and she needed to gain an education without appearing to do so. She reckoned the enamel harder to come by.

"Schoolbus, Emily," Ma called, and with the memory of Pa's belt on her old bruise, she hid her dream back in the dark and then hied herself to the bus stop.

👁👁👁

For Emily lunch was the highlight of the school day because she did not go to it, pocketing instead the three quarters and one dime the government gave her to buy food in the cafeteria. Her stomach muttered unpleasantly but bore up well enough as she sat on a bench on the perimeter of the schoolyard, where she might absorb the sunlight she so loved. In her lap a textbook fell open, an introductory to solid geometry for students two grades higher, and she absorbed that information as easily as her skin took to the sunlight. Other students passed by--boys, by the sound of their voices--and she ignored their caustic advice that a cookbook would prove of more use to her. Though she was accustomed to the jibes, they irritated her. She expected no approval from the ignorant, but surely there was someone in the school with whom she might talk about classwork.

An impact shook the bench--Amity Goodkind had just sat down beside her, dressed in a light floral print dress that fairly glistened in the sunlight and covered her chastely while allowing hints of the woman-to-be. Emily glanced at her once for identification, and withheld a greeting, for it was Amity whose protesting argument in science class had led to the note which had garnered Emily a striping. She held her finger on a figure in the geometry book and tried to focus, hoping that Amity would go away.

But Amity Goodkind was not that intuitive. "You were wrong the other day," she said, in a low, pleasant voice. "Those bones are Satan's tricks, to deceive us and lead us from the true years of the Good Book."

Emily said nothing.

"I feared you would mislead the other students," Amity went on, emboldened by Emily's silence and by a righteousness which wormed its way into her tone. "I feared your words would lead them to stray from the true path. I stood up for God. He created the Earth six thousand years ago. The years of those bones are false."

Emily's finger moved to another figure in silence.

"I wanted you to know that," said Amity.

Emily squeezed her eyes shut. *Don't say it. Don't . . .* "What makes you think I want to know that?" she asked, her lips tight and bloodless as she swore silently at herself for giving in.

The question seemed to startle Amity, and for long seconds she did not speak. Finally she whispered, "What did you say?"

"What makes you think---?"

Amity shot to her feet, and leaned slightly forward, pale eyes aflame as she faced Emily. Strands of yellow hair caught on her lips, but she ignored them. "Your *soul* is in mortal *danger* of the fires of eternal *damnation*, Emily Harper. I am *trying to save* you from that. Don't you *want*---?

"Go away."

Amity gasped. "*What?*"

At last Emily lifted her eyes from the geometric figures on the page. Amity Goodkind was actually perspiring with the effort of her imposed salvation. Her vacant gaze passed through Emily without effect. "Go. Away," Emily said again, and Amity's head jerked back as if Emily had poked a knife at it.

Amity took a step backwards, and another. Several students had paused to gawk, and she raised her voice clearly for their benefit. "Oh, I am gonna *tell!* I am *so* gonna tell..."

But Emily had already returned her attention to the book. Dimly she heard the slaps of Amity's shoes on the concrete sidewalk as she ran toward the school office, the sounds fading as the secants and cotangents reiterated their precise parables for Emily to solve. But presently her concentration flickered, and faded. Amity Goodkind *was* "gonna tell." In the hopes of forestalling another striping, Emily got up and headed for the Student Advisor's Office.

Emily felt eyes on her as she followed the sidewalk and the directional signs posted on the corner of the Admin Building. Already word had spread: she had rejected Amity Goodkind, she had rejected salvation. And dismissing Amity so peremptorily had not even been satisfying. She should have kept her peace and endured. As she passed the front office, she spied Amity remonstrating with Mr. Crocker, the Assistant Principal, but neither of them noticed her. At the door to the Student Advisor's Office Emily rapped sharply on the jamb and waited, hoping he was in and not out to lunch. The "Come in" afforded her a measure of relief.

Paul Archer sat at his desk with a "working lunch" of two bologna and cheese sandwiches and a can of Coke. The heat of the late spring day had rumpled his white shirt, and perspiration darkened his armpits. He finished swallowing and straightened his tie before he spoke. "Ah, Emily. I was just about to send for you from your history class. Please, sit down."

Emily did so, fresh spiders of worry scuttling up her spine. "To send for me, Mr. Archer?"

"It's about your proposed schedule for this fall, Emily," he said, sifting through stacks of papers on his desk. A graduate in Education Administration just three years before, he had accepted the position of Advisor at Redemption Public High School because no other positions were open, and he had become chronically overwhelmed by blank and half-completed forms. His face brightened when he found the one he sought. "Ah, yes, here we are." He placed the paper carefully on his desk blotter and read it once more, although Emily was fairly certain he had memorized it.

"Is there a problem with it, Mr. Archer?"

Archer sat back, and pushed the paper away. "Well," he began, and stopped. His pale brown eyebrows merged briefly, then parted. "Well," he said again, and closed his eyes as if in a silent search for words.

"I will take English Comp and History of Christianity in summer school," Emily pointed out. "With those required courses out of the way, I'll have room for another elective."

Archer cleared his throat. "Yes. Yes, of course. But...Chemistry?"

"Yes, sir."

"Emily...you haven't taken Home Economics yet."

Emily looked down at her feet. The sole at the toe of her left shoe was coming loose, and if she stepped into a puddle her sock would be sodden. "I'm not going to take Home Economics, Mr. Archer," she said quietly. "I'm going to take Chemistry."

"Emily, you can't graduate unless you take Home Economics."

"It's an elective course, Mr. Archer."

"Well, yes, it is, but---"

"Daniel Piersall and Isaac Sutton graduated, and they didn't take Home Economics."

Archer waved a dismissive hand. "Oh, but that's different. They're---" And he leaned forward slowly and folded his arms across the blotter and stared at Emily. "It doesn't sound to me as if you have

160

a cooperative attitude toward your class scheduling, young lady," he said sternly. "It doesn't sound that way at all. It sounds to me as if some bad influences have begun to disrupt your thinking. Now, there are reasons for the district's school requirements, good reasons, and you cannot simply flaunt them just because you---"

"It's 'flout,' Mr. Archer."

"I beg your pardon?"

"The word you want is 'flout,' which means to show contempt for. I don't flaunt my attitude, Mr. Archer. I don't put on airs with it--at least, I hope I don't, and if I do, then I surely apologize for that. But I intend to go to college, Mr. Archer, and I don't think Home Economics will help me do that."

Archer reached for a stack of papers and began tamping it onto his blotter to straighten them into a neater stack. "Yes, well...we'll see, Miss Harper. Why don't you think about this over the weekend, and perhaps on Sunday you can pray to the Lord for guidance. You do attend services, don't you? You do pray?"

What does that have to do with Chemistry? thought Emily. Aloud, she said, "Yes, sir."

"Very well, then. I'll see you again on Monday, after you've had time to pray, and have thought this over. Ah, and that's the class bell."

Emily stood up. "I'll need a Tardy Note, Mr. Archer."

Archer found a blank sheet of paper, scribbled a note on it, and scrawled his name below, then passed it to Emily.

Only after she opened her textbook in history class did she recall her original reason for seeing Archer. But there was no help for it, not now, and she pushed her fears to the perimeter of her mind while she dealt with the day's lecture.

👀👀👀

The scuttling spiders grew more active on Emily's spine as the bus approached her stop. Had the principal called? Did one of the boys bring a note home? But Ma was tending the stewpot and said Pa would be staying late at Dale's Repair Shop in Murphysboro, changing the spark plugs on Ben Farley's tractor and fighting with the timing. Emily hastened to her room and closed the door and stood still, leaning against it, heart racing, arms wrapped around her schoolbooks, pressing them to her breast as if they were the only things keeping her afloat.

It had been idiotic to respond to Amity Goodkind in any way, she saw that so clearly now. She might have withheld her question, might have kept her peace. Amity Goodkind was not relevant to her dreams. And to complicate matters further by challenging Mr. Archer on the relevance of Home Economics, well . . .

"Dumb, dumb, dumb," she muttered.

Of course, she hadn't actually said anything to Mr. Archer that would give Pa cause to stripe her, but a note home about it would surely upset him . . . and when the note about Amity Goodkind arrived on top of that . . .Emily shuddered. The welts on her back were beginning to itch, now that the healing had begun. She closed her eyes, and for a moment almost allowed herself to slump down the door to the floor. But that would mean surrender.

"No," she whispered savagely, and set the books on a small rickety table by her mattress. From an old military foot locker against a side wall next to the mattress she withdrew a worn and faded pair of blue jeans with one knee ripped open and the other almost worn through from kneeling while gardening, and put them on after removing her dress. Then she fished out a pale blue jersey and drew it on, and bound her hair with a rubber band, the chestnut pony tail dangling just to the nape of her neck. The entire outfit was her only defense. The fabric was thicker than that of the dress, and might better cushion the blows from Pa's belt, if it came to that. And although the jersey afforded her scant protection against the clumsy groping of Vance and Jacob, the jeans might thwart them long enough for her to find a way to escape.

Thus armored, Emily went into the kitchen, where Ma was still stirring the stew. "I'm going out to look for wild onions, Ma," she announced, and when Ma signified that she had heard, Emily walked out the front door, around to the back of the house, and quietly climbed into her bedroom through the unglassed window. Ten seconds later she was huddling in her hidey-hole, about to touch a candle to flame.

162

Illuminated, Emily felt secure: daylight in the bedroom above overwhelmed what little candlelight seeped through the cracks in the floorboards around the mattress. Only at night was firing a candle risky. Something light scrabbled over the left leg of her jeans, and she opened a cylindrical container and poured several seeds from it onto the dirt beside her leg. "Hello, Gus," she whispered, as the brown and gray mouse crept forward to investigate the snack.

After he had filled his cheek pouches and scurried off to tell his relatives of the trove, Emily turned her attention not to the model spacecraft resting on a sheet of cardboard on a ledge to her right, but to the underside of the floorboards above her. There ought to be stars there, she thought. She had no fluorescent paint, but she did have a bright red enamel nail polish she had never used, a Christmas gift from a distant aunt. Pa had called it "Jezebel paint" and had thrown it away, but Emily had retrieved it that night and secreted it in her hidey-hole. Yes, Jezebel paint for the stars. Amity Goodkind had spoken of eternal damnation--so be it. Hell for the stars was a fair trade, and she began to dab little red dots on the boards above, for Mars and Jupiter and the Red Spot, then for Betelgeuse and Arcturus and Antares, and all the other red stars she could think of.

Gus returned, and she set down more seeds for him. Grain from the skies, she supposed he thought. Gus did not question their origin or their purpose. The seeds were there--somehow--for him, and he made of them the best use that he could. *And the stars are for me. I don't know where they came from, or why they are there...but they are mine for the taking.* Her hand drifted out to the uncompleted starship, her touch the link between the dreams it represented and the dreams in her head. One day, if only. From a small box on the floor of the hidey-hole she withdrew a tube of cement with a sewing needle stuck through the end of it to keep the hole open. The clear viscous liquid within adhered to the needle as she drew it out, and carefully she touched it to each end of a strut and, following the guide, placed it carefully against the hull, holding it firmly there until the cement had dried.

"There, Gus," she said, when he or one of his relatives returned for more grain, "only seven more pieces and it's finished. What color should we paint it, do you think? Blue, like the example on the box? Or perhaps black, like space, with little twinkles like the stars all over the hull? What do you think, Gus?"

But Gus thought it was time to stuff his oral pouches and carry the loot back to his relatives.

"Maybe you have an Aunt Jackie," said Emily. "Maybe she knows what color it should be."

Aunt Jackie in New Mexico. She was far away...but not as far as the stars. If Emily could reach the stars, she could reach her. One day, if only. And in New Mexico she could bring *Voyager* into the sunlight and the starlight, where it belonged. Unexpectedly tempted by that vision, she nudged the floorboards upwards just a crack, just enough to see that the bedroom was unoccupied and the door was shut. Then, with a swift practiced move, she swept upward into the room, the hidey-hole door falling shut behind her and the mattress back into place, and she swept into the sky, into the stars, the starship in her right hand, arm extended as she danced, pirouetted, whirled around the room, her heart soaring just for a moment . . .

Only for a moment.

At the window she came to a halt, her eyes on the grave markers. Ashes to ashes, not stars to stars. And as if to remind her of that cold reality, the door to her room burst open. Emily whirled around, concealing the starship behind her. Pa had entered, brandishing a pair of notes. Behind him stood Jacob, smirking, for he had brought them home. Behind Jacob stood Ma, fretting.

"You just can't get yourself right, can you, girl?" snarled Pa, shaking the notes at her. His eyes smoldered like an open-hearth furnace. "That Goodkind girl says you rejected salvation, is that right?"

Emily lowered her eyes. "No, Pa."

Pa took a step closer, and yelled, "*Is that right?*"

"No, Pa, I didn't . . . I was just---"

"What's that you got behind you, girl?"

"Pa . . ."

"Let's see it, girl, and I mean *now.*"

"Pa, don't---"

But he grabbed her roughly by the shoulder and spun her around, and the starship flew from her hands and broke in two on the floor, the saucer section skittering across the wood until it struck her mattress. At the door, Jacob peered into the room, not daring to risk diverting Pa's wrath, but curious about the forbidden object, and behind him Ma fretted but made no move to defend her, and Emily saw all this as Pa spun her again and slammed her against the back wall of the bedroom, the impact jarring dust loose from the jambs of the unglassed window.

"It's the work of Satan!" roared Pa, and he stomped first one piece and then the other, and fragments of gray plastic flew in all directions while Emily's eyes went wide and she covered her mouth with both hands and tried not to cry out, though her eyes already were betraying her, and while she was staring in horror at the fragments Pa stripped off his belt and began to swing it with a fury Emily had never felt before.

"The work of Satan," and the leather strap tore at the back of her jersey and reopened the previous welts, and she refused to cry out, dropping to her hands and knees on the dirty wooden floor.

"I won't have it in my house," and the leather strap stung like lye like acid like a thousand hornets on the skin of her back, and Emily bit her lip to keep from crying out, and drops of blood as red as the stars she had dabbed in her hidey-hole began to splatter in the grit on the floor.

And then the blows fell in a deluge as Pa's yelling slipped to incoherence, spewing disjointed fragments about souls and Lords and Hells and sins. The blows rained on her arms, her shoulders, her back, her head, on old wounds and new ones, and she tried to scrabble away and to keep her penned he stepped too close to her and struck her with his fist instead of the belt, and the buckle cut into her back just above her right hip, and all the stars in the Universe exploded in the front of her skull, and she was in too much pain to cry out. She sprawled face down onto the floor, too weak to ward off the blows with her hands.

And the leather strap continued to tear at her jersey and her skin and her flesh, until her back was wet with blood and her ribs froze and she could not draw a breath, and her mouth left bloody smears in the grit on the floor.

And then it was over. Far away she felt footstomps, and heard a door slam. Her fingers clutched at the wood, tearing her nails, but she was in too much agony to feel any more pain. Her body began to tremble with the effort of revived respiration, and she made little sounds of, "Uhn-uh-uh, uhn-uh-uh," over and over and over.

Time telescoped, drawing out the pain. She might have lain there for an hour, a day, a year, as feeling returned to shriek at her, and she wanted nothing more than to lie still and die. She began to withdraw inside herself, away from the pain. If she could pull far enough inside, the pain could not reach her. But it pursued, as far inside as she fled. Wherever she went inside, the thunderhead of pain followed, waiting to burst open upon her when it caught her. And when she could withdraw no further, could only stand at the center of her life, it caught her, over and over again . . .

. . . and the room grew dim with the sinking of the sun, and shadows fell over her, turning the red to black. She was still alive. Her fingers twitched, and found a shard of plastic. She wanted to cry, and could not, she was in too much agony. She tried to breathe, and could not, her ribs ached and refused to obey her, but air whistled into her lungs and out, all the same. A splinter had lodged in her lip, but she lacked the strength to move her hand, to pinch it free. Gradually a numbness set in, dulling her mind though her body continued to shriek at her, and she bent a leg and pushed, and crooked an arm and pushed, and once more she was on her hands and knees on the floor, pony tail askew over her left shoulder and matted with blood from her back, rags of pale blue and dark red jersey hanging from her torso, and narrow crimson ribbons trickling down her bare arms.

Emily poised, gasping for breath. Her fingers closed around the plastic shard and a sharp edge of it bit into her palm, and she refused to cry out. Off to her left loomed the mattress. It promised a better cushion than the floor. Beside it lay pieces of the starship's saucer, and she began to weep softly. Tears mixed with blood on the floor below her face. With the deliberation of a sloth she moved a hand, a knee, dragging herself toward the mattress, collecting pieces of plastic along the way, ripping off her jersey to fashion from it a totebag, for there were far too many pieces of *Voyager* for her to carry them in her hands. She needed her hands for crawling. When finally the crown of her head butted the mattress, she felt surprised to have reached it. It was a simple matter, now, to pull herself on top of it and collapse. How she longed to do just that. If only.

But she was still alive.

Instead she fished a fresh jersey, this one lavender, from the foot locker and, gritting her teeth against the stinging of flesh torn again, drew it on. For a few moments she sat back on her haunches, rocking gently back and forth, trying to shut down her mind so that the pain could not get in. She wanted to think, and could not. But she could still see. She could envision what had to be done now.

And when she had brought the pain under control, she nudged the mattress aside, and opened the trap door to the hidey-hole and allowed herself to spill down into it. She landed in a heap on her shoulder and on her injured hip, and again bit her lip to keep from crying out. Her right hand clutched the totebag containing the fragments of her dream, and she drew it to her bosom to protect it while she squatted in the abyss. Her upper body rocked back and forth once more while she shut down her mind.

After Emily had gathered strength for one more vast effort, she stood up in the hidey-hole and tugged the mattress into position and let fall the hatch. Darkness enveloped her. And in that darkness she crouched, gasping for breath from the effort she had just made, the walls of the hidey-hole her support while she let her mind go numb and extend that numbness throughout her body. If she did not move now, she would be all right. She could breathe, and that was enough. The rest of her need only be numb, and she would be all right.

Later--and Emily did not know how much time had passed, though she was still crouching--boards creaked: someone had entered her room. Not Pa; the steps were too light, and uncertain. Ma, then. The light came on, and dim rays of it reached her in the hidey-hole. But the cracks in the floor were too narrow to allow her to see who had entered. More steps, toward the mattress, then to the back of the room and the window into the night. And someone else entered, heavier of foot. Pa? Emily heard words in a low and weak voice. Ma was speaking, and she keened her ears to hear. What was Ma saying?

But it was Pa's voice that she heard. ". . . git a flashlight and find her, drag her back here."

And then Ma said, "Let her be . . . she'll come back. She knows where she belongs."

Pa's growled reply was incoherent, but Emily heard more footsteps. And the door to her room slammed again.

Emily discovered that she had been holding her breath during the intrusion. Slowly she let it out, and held her body still while pain became a dull but terrible ache throughout her body. Thought required a deliberate effort, but she could think. Movement demanded the same effort, but she could move. If she could move, she could reach the stars and she could reach New Mexico and Aunt Jackie and be shunned and damned and whispered about with her, whatever it took, to reach the stars. If she could move . . .

Her hand could move to the candle, and she lit it. Her hands could move to the totebag, and she drew it open. Then to the tube with the sewing needle stopper.

And in the dim light of the candle she began to cement the fragments of the starship back together, one by one.

Starlet

By September she had come around to accepting that the leaves were beginning to turn in her years. Russet was the color of her life now, a little bit red, a little bit brown, not too brittle just yet. She was not uncomely. True, a hair here and there had lost its color, although there was something to be said for just a touch of gray, and she had acquired a wrinkle or two, just there, at the corners of the eyes. She kept in reasonable shape and wore sensible clothing that nevertheless, if someone were watching, might as she climbed out of her Mazda expose a stretch of alluring and tanned inner thigh. But no one was watching.

In her cubicle at work--she was a customer service representative for a leasing corporation--a bit of dust often collected in the lower corners of the engraved nameplate that sat atop her desk in bitter confirmation of her anonymity. Seventeen years she had worked there, yet she needed a nameplate to identify her? As if to reaffirm her identity she had begun of late a weekly ritual. Every Monday, taking a tissue from her purse, she carefully dusted each and every letter of her name, white block letters engraved on a woodgrain brown background: L-O-U-I-S-E G-O-O-D-R-I-C-H. It was a sensible name, abbreviated quite readily to Lou, and indeed there were several in the office who had shortened it, not from a sense of familiarity, but for ease of dialogue. In a world in which Acronym was a primal scream, Lou saved a precious syllable.

On the third Monday of that September the alarm did not sound on the nightstand beside Lou's bed. The crimson digits raced right on past 5:20, oblivious to the failure of Lou's hand to swat the snooze button and thereby secure ten more minutes of REM sleep. Darkness still shadowed the window, although just a hint of dawn lent a horizon to the eastern sky. The curtains had not been drawn. The bedcovers had not been pulled down, and the bed had not been slept in. On the night of the Sunday before the third Monday of that September, Lou Goodrich had fallen asleep on the folding chaise lounge on the brick patio outside, bracketed by a spindly *Dracaena* and an avocado tree, both in sturdy 12-inch clay pots.

The head third of the recliner had been locked at a forty-five degree angle to support Lou's upper body. She lay/sat there, sleeping, dreaming, the barest hint of a smile toying with the corners of her mouth, while the stars gradually winked out in the deep lavender wash that preceded dawn. She was still attired in the old gray short-sleeved jersey with the faded chocolate pudding and mustard stains and the proclamation that the contents of the jersey belonged to the Slippery Rock football team, and the faded denim shorts that had once been jeans, cut off halfway up the thighs because the knees had worn through during her gardening. Her sneakers, kicked off around midnight, had come to rest on the patio at the foot of the recliner to form a drunken T. On her lap rested a pair of binoculars, the black lens caps like discarded coasters on the round white patio table beside the avocado tree. Her hands grasped the binoculars in such a way that if she suddenly awoke and wanted to look at something, all she had to do was bring the eyepieces to her eyes and, perhaps, adjust the focus.

Inside the cottage, in the bedroom, the digital clock sped right on by 5:40, the very latest that she might rise and perform her ablutions and apply make-up and dress and wolf down a bagel with cream cheese and a cup of coffee and still make it to work on time. Outside the cottage, dawn hinted with increasing vigor, and gradually the stars faded against the lightening backdrop. All but one.

The imminent sunrise failed to overwhelm this star, as it overwhelmed Sirius and Procyon, Venus and Jupiter. Not that the star grew brighter; it simply was, and maintained the same intensity. Moments later, dawn brought Lou to a slow wakefulness. One pale gray eye and then the other blinked away the sleep, though her vision remained bleary. She yawned, and thumbed the sleep sand from the corners of her eyes, and saw the one remaining point of light. It shone in a part of the sky where, according to her star logs, nothing anywhere near that bright was scheduled to appear. It burned white, a type B star that had no business being there.

She sat up, thinking: supernova!

She temporized. Surely the professional observatories had already discovered it, named it, taken spectrographs of it, realigned the HST to drink in its entire electromagnetic spectrum and spew out data by the yottabyte. It would be new for no one's eyes but hers. Her fingers fumbled for the binoculars, and she paused, considering.

No bright star was supposed to be there. The odds of a supernova appearing at those particular celestial coordinates at this particular moment were . . . well, astronomical (she chuckled lightly at this). What else, then, could it be?

Well, an airplane, perhaps, or a helicopter. Never mind that most had lights that blinked. If it were an aircraft of some kind, why wasn't it moving?

Because it's coming straight at you!

Apprehensive, Lou now stared at the point of light. She had awakened from a dream whose details she could not recall, and perhaps that dream continued to influence her perceptions in some way. Because this could not be a star, or a supernova, or an airplane headed directly toward her.

She peered up at the point of light with the power of her uncertainty. There was something . . . odd about it. She couldn't quite put her finger on it. It was almost as if . . . nooo. She shook her head. No.

Still . . .

She reached up and swatted her hand at it . . . and knocked it across the patio and into the *Dracaena*.

Louise Goodrich was now fully awake, and gasping for breath. She told herself that she had merely smacked a firefly, but in her heart and mind she knew this not to be the case. Whatever this was, it was indeed new for no one's eyes but hers. And she had just bashed it into a potted plant.

She knelt down beside the *Dracaena* and separated the long and thin variegated leaves, peering into the heart of the plant. The glow located the star for her, there by the main stem of the plant, caught against a leaf. It was a queer little thing, still a point of bright white light, but without accompanying warmth. There seemed to be no solid object within that gave off the glow; rather, the light was self-generating, as a flame without a candle. A starlet, as she now thought of it.

Tentatively she put a fingertip to it.

She felt no contact, nothing to indicate solidity, but her arm seemed to stretch . . . and then it was indeed stretching, elongating, no longer her right arm but a tentacle, stretching into the starlet, which was pulling her in . . . *my God!* She cried out, caught in the luminous trap like a small animal. Help, she whimpered, bracing against the lip of the clay pot with her free hand, to no avail. Her shoulder looked as if it were coming apart, though she felt no pain, did not even feel her limb stretching. Ligaments and tendons remained unyielding, yet there she was, her hand already inside the starlet, and half her forearm. To the elbow, and she whimpered again, looking around wild-eyed for succor from anyone, a neighbor, a squirrel, *anything.*

Her shoulder now brushed against fronds. Her arm was almost gone now, somehow, into that tiny point of light. Still she struggled, her left hand clamped onto the clay pot like a vise, but now her torso leaned into the plant, into the starlet, stretching visually but not physically. In the back of her mind loomed incredulity. What could not possibly be happening to her, was happening. Questions formed, but she had no time for them. Her head . . . she had a Pinocchio nose! With her left eye she could see her right eye, distended from its socket. Her lips extended like a duckbill. Her hair now had a windswept look, tresses already into the fronds, and all she could see now was the starlet, the point of cold white light into which her right arm and shoulder and face and torso were vanishing. The light was brighter inside. Her left hand slipped, released its hold on the rim of the clay pot, and she fairly flew into the starlet.

Light blinded her now, so intense it was.

Holy, she thought, shit.

Lou poured, spilled, emerged into an office. The starlet popped soundlessly out of existence. She blinked.

She thought of it as an office because there was very definitely a double pedestal office desk, with a chair behind it that looked as if it were meant to accommodate a human being. The desk appeared to be made of dark hardwood, varnished and polished to a high gloss. The chair, of similar wood, was of the straightback frame variety, with cushioned seat, back, and armrests. It rested on the thick carpet that covered the entire floor.

No . . . the four legs hovered approximately an inch *above* the thick carpet. The desk, however, was firmly planted on the floor. There were no other articles of furniture in the office.

Despite her thundering heart and the hard lump in her throat, she said, bravely and to no one in particular, "So this isn't Kansas, then?"

The office was illuminated by a line of glowing squares, each perhaps a foot on a side, that bisected the ceiling. Lou saw no air vents, but the temperature was comfortable--much more so than in her cubicle, situated directly under an air vent, where the air was either much too cold or much too hot. This air had a flavor to it: fresh, oxygenic.

The desk stood opposite a wall with a rectangular seam in it, evidently a door. She walked up to it and pushed on it, to no avail. She tried clapping her hands. She tried snapping her fingers. The door did not budge. She said, "Open." She said, "Open, Sesame." Neither command achieved the desired result.

"So I'm staying here, then?" she said. She did not expect a response, and would have leaped out of her sneakers had she received one and had she been wearing sneakers.

The carpet was soft enough to soothe her unshod feet, and briefly Lou scrunched her toes in it. The chair behind the desk beckoned, and she walked over to it and sat down, tentatively, carefully, for it was literally floating in the air. She expected the chair to drop under her weight, but it remained afloat. The momentum of her body made the chair glide backward until it struck the wall, at which point it bounced forward again. She put a stop to the movement by pressing against the floor with her feet and by grasping the desk, holding her butt and thighs in place and in that manner securing the chair, which continued to hover.

Stationary now, Lou relaxed in the chair, hands on the padded arms, fingers curled over the ends. On the ends of both arms she encountered ridges. She leaned forward to examine them. The ridges formed ovals around flat areas evidently meant to be pushed by fingertips. She pushed the left one, and the chair descended to the floor. She pushed the right one, and the chair rose back to its

173

previous height. Holding onto the desk again, she gently wiggled her butt and moved the chair from side to side.

Better than casters, she thought.

After a spot of practice Lou was able to maneuver the chair just into the desk well, where she lowered it to the floor. Thus seated, she began an examination of the desk. The top was flat and glossy, but whether veneer or solid wood she could not say. It was also empty. She could not recall ever having seen an empty desk. It seemed almost a perversion of the natural order of things. She ran her palms over the wood, and discovered several imperfections in the surface, not quite ridges. Closer study revealed several small rectangles etched onto the desk top, rather like the lines in the wall that formed the door that refused to open.

Next she tried the drawers. Each pedestal was cut by four horizontal lines, suggesting three drawers, but try as she might, she was unable to pry them open. The wider drawer over the desk well also refused admittance, but at the final attempt to open it her hand slipped upwards and knocked open a long and narrow section of the top of the desk just over the drawer. This revealed two horizontal rows of ridged ovals like those on the chair arms, five ovals in each row.

Like buttons, thought Lou. How irresistible. But they were unlabeled. What, if anything, did they control?

She decided that it was intended that she test them, because otherwise surely those who had brought her to this place would have arranged to prevent her from doing what she was about to do.

She put a fingertip to the upper left oval. Immediately a tocsin sounded, like those aboard naval vessels, an impossibly loud series of rising tones. She shoved back against the chair, forgetting that it was no longer floating, and spilled backwards, tumbling from the chair onto hands and knees. The alarm continued, annoying and abrasive. Worse, what did it signify? She expected at any moment that armed insectoids would rush into the room and shoot ray guns at anything that did not belong, i.e., at her. She covered her ears with her hands, which muffled the noise somewhat but failed to address the problem. She did not know how to shut it off. She crawled into the desk well, hands still over her ears, and drew her legs up.

The alarm continued with the disheartening persistence of a metronome. She yelled at it. She cursed it. She attributed to it an improbable ancestry and mating habits. Finally, in exasperation, after she realized that no one had come to investigate, she scrambled furiously from the desk well, stood up, snarled at the universe in general, and pressed her finger hard against the lower left oval.

The alarm shut down.

Heart racing, Lou leaned over the desk, arms braced on it and elbows locked, and fought to catch her breath. She reminded herself that no harm had been done, and no one had come to investigate. Gradually her calm returned. She maneuvered the chair back to the desk well and sat down once more, taking time to examine the two rows of ovals--of keys, as she had now come to think of them. Clearly the console served as a keyboard of sorts, each with a specific command or function. Already she had learned the functions of two of the keys, and perhaps even something about the alignment of the rows. The upper row enabled, perhaps, while the lower disabled. It was a starting point.

She held her breath and touched a fingertip to the oval in the far upper right. A faint whirring sound from within spoke of activity. One of the smaller rectangles on top of the desk opened, startling her, and two cylinders emerged, each about half a foot long. The right cylinder was slotted horizontally, the left vertically. Lou scarcely had time for a frown of puzzlement before one of the cylinders began to emit sounds. Someone or something was speaking.

" . . . *zlutchen ix furthlenst gloodis teak moklagnug dichon tragtag grunnerhar bunk dirach---*"

The speaking--if speaking it was--stopped when Lou touched a fingertip to the far lower right oval, and the two cylinders retracted, to be covered again by the rectangle in the desk.

What, thought Lou, was *that* all about?

She tried the second upper oval from the right, gingerly, uncertain. The desktop did not change, but a voice--definitely a woman's voice--began to speak, emitting the sound from somewhere within the desk.

" . . . *turglamoguglala mogu. Shenihama tularana, shenya tularana. Pour parler et écouter en français, dites français.* To speak and listen in English, say English. *Shtoby govoreet ee---*"

"Wait," cried Lou. "Go back!"

" . . . *slooshat poroos---*"

"No, English. *English!*"

"Thank you for activating the universal translator function," said the woman, without changing inflection. "You may now proceed in English."

Lou's mind hit pause briefly. "Proceed to do what?" she asked.

There was no response.

"Hello?"

Well, it was easier than having to press 1 for English, press 2 for Spanish. But it was effectively the same thing, Lou suddenly realized. She had just pressed 1.

She returned her attention to the upper right oval. At her touch the cylinders extruded once more. " . . . what you people think you are doing with my account," said the same voice she had heard earlier. It spoke rapidly and in a high pitch with a hint of accent, as if the owner were an irritated member of a tech support unit in New Delhi. "What is this bill for and why is it so much, I don't have to pay the added-value tax, how can you people do this---"

Having leaned closer to the cylinders and verified that the voice came from the horizontally-slotted one, Lou tried to pick up the other one. It did not budge. Evidently she was merely to speak to it. The problem sounded exactly like the sort she had been solving for seventeen years: a simple matter of locating the account and identifying the discrepancy.

But how?

The voice continued to spew forth. Lou tried to think. She wished the man would shut up until she could formulate an approach, a plan of action. It never occurred to some people, calling customer service, that if they would simply shut the hell up and let the reps talk them through the problems, they might get their problems solved a lot faster. Lou sighed; no matter where you go in the Universe . . .At least she had experience. And patience. At work her supervisors had always commended her for her calm and patience, even as they reproved her for not dealing more quickly with phone calls, as if the number of calls she answered was more important than solving the problems presented to her.

Patiently and calmly Lou reviewed what she already knew about the keyboard, and decided that if the second oval from the upper right provided for language selection, the one below it just might provide for instructions, or at least allow her to ask questions. She pressed it.

The same woman answered, her voice just audible over the complaining man. "How may I be of assistance?"

That, thought Lou, was more like it.

"You may be of assistance," said the man, thinking himself addressed, "by removing those late charges from my account, as they were based on non-payment of the value-added tax, which I was not supposed to pay in the first---"

Lou shut him up by retracting the cylinders. "How do I locate accounts?" she asked.

"The top center toke enables a display, keyed to the language you have selected," answered the woman. "The bottom retracts it. The account holder states the name of the account, and the relevant information will appear on the display."

Lou pursed her lips and nodded. That sounded simple enough. She raised the display, reactivated the communication device, and interrupted the caller's monologue. "Sir, if you will state the name of the account in question, I may be able to resolve this issue."

"What? Who is this? Who are you?"

She found her pleasant business voice and gave it to him. "My name is Lou. If you will identify your account, I may be able to help you."

The man paused for a moment, and said something that sounded like "Golenod Snorgle Fecar."

Instantly data appeared on the display, in English, although it did not explain what a *golenod* was. Lou quickly scanned the account information, and said, "I have your account here, Mr. Fecar. Now, what seems to be the problem?"

Mr. Fecar began by speaking in a very slow and clear voice, as if he were addressing a child. He explained that his last three billing statements had inexplicably held him liable for value-added tax for the importation of golenod, and that his company did not import them, it exported them. Oddly, by the time he finished his explanation, he was speaking in a conversational tone. Crossing mental fingers for luck, Lou tried the simplest solution first, and to her great relief it worked--apparently the display responded to oral instructions. She credited the account with the value-added tax already paid, disabled the VAT function so that it no longer figured in the calculations for the periodic statements, and informed Mr. Fecar that his next statement would reflect these credits. Could she help him with anything else? He declined, but thanked her effusively.

Lou closed the communications and sat back in the chair. Another problem solved. She looked at the desk. "Is that it? You brought me halfway across the Universe for *that*?" The question revealed a notion she had not yet given voice to in her mind: that not only was she nowhere near Kansas, she might not be in the same galaxy as Kansas. Earlier she had assumed that creatures on the order of armed arthropods patrolled the corridor outside the office, but had not devoted much thought to what, in fact, *was* outside the office, largely because she had no means of leaving the office. The thought occurred to her that the woman might be able to assist her in that regard.

Instead, still curious, she opted to raise communications again. The querulous voice of a young man came through. " . . . not what we ordered. It was supposed to be double *sheviche* with extra *mirreth*, and no *kraakmul*. I can't stand *kraakmul*. I don't know anyone who likes it. How did this---?"

Lou retracted the device and took stock. The complaint almost surely had something to do with food. Had she been back on Earth, she might have thought the young man was talking about a pizza. What kind of customer service center was this, where they dealt with *golenod* and whatever came with double *sheviche* and extra *mirreth*? The company certainly had its fingers in a lot of pies.

She talked the young man through the checklist on the display and informed him that she was very sorry for the error, and that a fresh *zyvilla* with the specified toppings would be delivered to him at no extra charge. As she completed the transaction by retracting the display and communications, someone knocked on the wall: three raps, followed quickly by two more.

Lou's eyes widened until they ached. The knocks came again, and she started. Well, do *something*, she said to herself. If they want in, you can't keep them out.

I hope they're not too grotesque.

"Er, come in," she called.

"In a moment. Please relax."

Lou could scarcely believe her ears. The voice was that of a human male--a man--who sounded like he might be close to her own age. It was most unexpected. She had traveled--she had no idea how far, but surely it was a vast distance--all this way, only to encounter another human being? She loved the stars, and enjoyed good science fiction, but this, really, was too much.

"What do you want, then?"

"You've completed your interview."

That stumped her. Of all the words she had expected to hear, those four were the lowest on her list. "We've come to eat you," or "You're to be sacrificed to the volcano god," would not have surprised her unduly, but to find out that she had completed an interview when she had not even known she was interviewing, was . . . well, whatever it was, it definitely was. She had come a long way from the brick patio and the binoculars and the chaise lounge.

That was it, Lou thought suddenly. It's a dream. I'm dreaming this. I'm dreaming that I woke up, and a mysterious starlet transported me to another world, where I was still working in customer service. Now it all makes sense.

And now there's a man outside my door. It's been a long time since there was a man at my door. But the man is the proof. If this is a dream, he'll look like Brad Pitt. If it's real, he'll look like Garver in Accounting.

"What interview?"

"I'm coming in. I'll explain it all to you."

"Wait!"

The man laughed. "You *didn't* take off your clothes in there, surely."

Lou tugged the hem of her jersey down. "Can't you just check your surveillance cameras, or whatever you use here?"

"I could. I wouldn't. What's the problem?"

About to encounter an alien, even a human-sounding alien, Lou was getting cold feet. This whole business, she had to admit, was interesting. Not the problem-solving bits, those were her job, as if "her job" was only a small part of what and who she was, even though it occupied half her waking hours. The interesting bits, now, were the travel, the starlet, the unfamiliar workplace on the far side of Andromeda, the chair that floated while awaiting adjustments. For a few shining moments, however much within a dream state, she had been there and done that. She had been to the stars: a childhood dream come true. It might, if she awoke, have to be enough. But she knew, too, that now it could never be enough, and that if she did not awaken, it would not end.

Lou closed her eyes and crossed her forearms on the desk top and laid her head on them, facing away from the door. If she had to awaken, this would have to suffice for her snooze alarm. "Come in, then."

She did not hear the door open, nor did she hear him approach. She was aware, at the limits of her senses, of a warmth nearby, of respiration, of someone who was sitting across the desk from her. She forced herself not to look at him.

"I think I understand," he said.

The voice was real enough. It was much like her professional voice, even-toned and pleasant, with the just proper hint of competence. But Lou also detected a note of compassion . . . or perhaps she wished she detected it, and in her dream wishes could come true.

"You grasped your new circumstances readily enough, and without panicking," the man continued. "That was very---"

"Do you have a name?"

"Cooley. David Cooley."

Lou chuckled, despite herself. "Not Fulrshgard Nokthin?"

180

"And not Luke Skywalker, either. Did you suppose you were the only human who has been offered a position with us?"

"I hadn't thought of it at all. You were saying?"

"Exactly so! You remain calm, you stay on message, as it were. Your observers are very impressed with your self-control under these circumstances."

"I might react differently if I looked out the window and saw a blue sun or three moons."

"The sun is orange," said Cooley. "There are two moons, one the size of Earth's, the other a tenth that size. You can see them from your bungalow."

Lou blinked, and almost succumbed to the urge to lift her head and look at Cooley. "I have a bungalow?"

"Outside the city, where it is easier to see the stars at night. There's a brick patio in back. You can shop for plants and clay pots to put them in." Cooley paused, and added, "We want you to retain as many of your normal daily routines as possible, Lou. I'm sorry. May I call you Lou?"

Head still recumbent on the desk top, Lou nodded.

"What we want from you, Lou, is the sort of work, the quality of work, that you performed on Earth. We will of course pay you for it. The benefits, you'll find, are excellent."

"When you say 'we' . . ."

"Oh, yes, of course. Galactic Customer Service. 'No problem too big, no problem too small.' It's necessary to ensure the continuous smooth operation of commerce throughout the galaxy."

Lou nodded to herself. "When you say 'galaxy' . . ."

"The Milky Way. You haven't actually traveled all that far. Only a couple thousand light years."

"But you don't operate on Earth."

"No . . . Earth is one of our training grounds. For all sorts of businesses, in fact. All sorts of positions, from mechanic to merchant, from entomologist to etymologist. Have you ever noticed, one day someone doesn't show up for work ever again? Rumors slowly begin, about how the employee found a better job, or her husband had to move, or his wife wanted to be nearer her family. And you never hear about him or her again. Perhaps that's us. Not always, not even most of the time. But it *could* be us. Aren't you going to look at me, Lou?"

Lou shook her head. If this was a dream, it was becoming too rational, too plausible. It actually made sense, the way Cooley explained it. Seldom were dreams so well-organized. She began to feel apprehensive. It was one thing to look up at the stars from a great distance and dream, however hopelessly, of one day going *out there*. It was quite another to be transported to one of them, however improbably, and asked to consider employment.

"Why do you look at the stars at night, Lou?" asked Cooley, interrupting her thoughts.

Lou started. The question implied more than a random search for information. "You've been watching me?"

"Think of it as a part of the job interview."

"I'm not real fond of invasions of privacy."

"We are interested only in your ability to perform your duties."

"None of which, apparently, are related to my use of binoculars," countered Lou. Her reluctant sigh signaled acquiescence. "When I was a little girl, I thought we, humanity, would go to the stars one day. I wanted to be among those who went. After I grew a little older, I realized that the journey would occur, but not in my lifetime. I wasn't going, but at least others were. And now . . . so I sit in my chair in the evenings and look . . . and still dream."

Lou paused, and again almost looked at Cooley. "I suppose that fits some kind of profile for you."

"Your pay and benefits include discounts, should you wish to travel to other worlds during your vacations," said Cooley.

Lou felt her heart skip a beat. Cooley's statement pressured her in a way that she was unable to counter. In Customer Service, she had rules and contracts and--if necessary--a corporate legal staff to support her decisions, so that it was virtually impossible for a customer to impose his or her wishes on her. Cooley, however, was unregulated; rather, he was bound only by whatever regulations those he worked for chose to enforce. She had no defense against him, except . . .

"That's a very subtle high-pressure pitch," she said. "You don't want me to return to Earth, do you, Dave? Oh, I'm sorry. May I call you Dave?"

"You still haven't looked at me."

Directly Lou heard the words, she stood up and turned toward him. He was dressed in medium office garb--slacks and shirt, open at the collar--and he looked a little like Garver in Accounting. Maybe a little less pudgy. Less need for a comb-over. A couple inches taller than her five-eight.

It occurred to Lou that most of her confrontations were telephonic. The possibility of going nose-to-nose with a difficult customer disconcerted her. His eyes, as blue as the Pacific and certainly unaccountant-like, had much the same effect, which she reflected was probably why corporations preferred to interpose a switchboard between the customer and the customer service personnel.

"I have now looked at you," Lou said crisply. "Am I free to return to Earth?"

"Is that truly what you wish?"

Lou met his gaze and question evenly. "If I am not free to return to Earth, then I am not free here, either."

"You are of course free---"

"Then I wish to return to Earth."

The interruption seemed to take Cooley aback. "May I . . . be heard on this matter?"

A stalling tactic, thought Lou, while he marshaled his regulation-laden argument. He was treating her as a . . . nooo.

"If I say no?"

"Then . . . you may return to Earth immediately." Cooley held up a small device. "Is that your wish, then?"

The implicit surrender softened Lou. "What did you want to say?"

For the first time Cooley's smile appeared. His tone conveyed concern tempered with assurance. "Studies have shown that over sixty four percent of those who return to Earth for one last look choose to remain on Earth and decline our offer. Psychological evaluations tell us that this is due to a fear of the dream becoming the reality. Dreams are safe; living them, frightens humans. Those evaluations also tell us that, faced with the stark and abrupt reality of living under strange and unfamiliar conditions, humans prefer to remain with the familiar, with what they know."

"You're speaking of humans in the third person," Lou pointed out.

"I've been doing this job for some years now."

"Have you ever returned to Earth?"

"Not yet."

"When you say not yet . . . "

"I will when I am able to regard Earth as a place to visit, to take a tour of."

"Afraid of meeting your relatives?"

Cooley's smiled drooped. "One of the criteria for our personnel is that they have few . . . encumbrances. Your ex-husband and in-laws are of no concern to us, and your marriage was without issue. Your last immediate relative, your mother, passed away some three years ago. My condolences."

Lou hesitated for a moment, then dismissed his sympathy with a gentle wave of her hand. "Who actually selected me?" she wanted to know. "You?"

"No. Is that important to you . . . oh, I see." His smile warmed. "No, I'm happily married, wife and two kids. They're here with me. No, I'm . . . think of me as a headhunter, if you wish. A recruiter."

"When you say here . . ."

"This world is known as The Caz," said Cooley. "Short for---"

"Cazbah?"

" . . . Camdotaz. Our sun is called Serah. You will receive a full orientation, you know. It would be counterproductive to bring you here, then leave you to fend for yourself . . . although there will be some immersion."

"Are there other humans here?" asked Lou.

"Enough for you to develop a social life, if that is what you wish."

"I could be offended by that implication."

"And the way you phrased that says you are not. Nor should you be. I meant only that there is a human community on The Caz. In fact, we hold periodic get-togethers . . ." She made a little sound of annoyance, and he added, "What's wrong?"

"When something sounds too good to be true," said Lou.

"I see."

"I wish to return to Earth."

"Very well."

Cooley seemed to aim the device at the floor between them. There appeared a starlet, hovering a couple feet above the floor. The immediacy of the event stunned Lou.

"You know how it works," said Cooley. He stepped to the door, and it opened for him, closing as soon as he passed through the doorway.

"Hello and goodbye," whispered Lou, a little disappointed by the abrupt dismissal. She took a final look around the office, then put her hand to the starlet.

Again light blinded her, so intense it was.

Lou poured, spilled, emerged onto her patio, sprawling beside the *Dracaena*. The starlet popped soundlessly out of existence. She blinked. Plant fronds tickled her cheek, and she brushed them away irritably. She had fallen out of the recliner. She had been dreaming. An annoying, pulsating sound reached her ears--the alarm in her bedroom. How long had it been going off? She scrambled to her feet, almost stepping on the binoculars, and dashed into the kitchen to look at the clock on the stove. She hated to be late for work, hated it so much that in all the years of her employment she had been late twice, both times because of the weather.

The clock read 5:22. The alarm had been sounding for two minutes, and was probably what had awakened her. That, and her long-term habit of waking at that time in the morning, imprinted forever in her internal clock. Lou sighed in relief. She had plenty of time to get to work.

Strange dream, though.

☯☯☯

All day at work Lou held the dream ready for examination, pulling it out whenever there fell a quiet moment between customer complaints. She asked a few what-ifs, injected a couple of supposes, spent pensive moments during her breaks and lunch period, yet attended her duties with uncharacteristic tenacity, as if to negate the nocturnal fantasy lurking in the back of her mind. At one point she caught herself speaking too brusquely, and softened her voice in apology.

The last call of the day took Lou well past quitting time to resolve. Almost half an hour late for her evening routines, she stopped for take-out Mexican on the way home, and went straight to the patio after she arrived. The sun would not set for another two hours, and until the astral objects revealed themselves once more, there was little for her to do but munch burritos, sip a soda, and let her thoughts drift where they would.

The Brad Pitt dream test had failed her when Garver from Accounting showed up. How long did REM sleep last? The alarm had spent a futile two minutes sounding, and no more. Yet she distinctly remembered that it had been much later in the morning when she had encountered the starlet in dreamstate. The events of her dream had surely lasted longer than two minutes, if they were real.

But if the people of the galaxy could manufacture a conveyance like the starlet, surely they were capable of the temporal adjustments necessary to prevent her from reporting late to work. On the other hand, if they were so advanced, why would they have so many commercial problems that they would need a customer service department to solve them?

Lou growled, and kicked her heel on the foot of the recliner in frustration. The what-ifs and supposes were getting to her. How long until dark? Another hour? She dangled her hand over the side of the recliner. Her fingertips brushed the binoculars. She recovered the instrument and set the eyepieces to her eyes, bringing into focus a flower across the yard against the fence. A perennial, it had bloomed there every year for the past six years. It was blooming now. It would continue to bloom at this time of year each year for the rest of its life, however long that might be.

What if, thought Lou, the flower had a choice? Would it choose to move to an unfamiliar plot, or to remain where it was, with nice, nutritious dirt around its roots, water when it was thirsty, and nothing to do but bloom when it was supposed to bloom. Would it choose to remain a flower?

The question was too metaphysical for Lou. She thought that if she thought about it any more, her brain would ache. She dealt with--was used to dealing with--clear questions that had clear if occasionally complicated answers. That was who she was.

But she was also . . . she could be . . .

She could also have been . . . nooo.

Just the same, if it had only been a dream, the starlet would not return for her in the morning.

Suttee

you'll come and find the place where I am lying
and kneel and say an Ave *there for me . . .*

. . . and you will bend and tell me that you love me
and I will sleep in peace until you come to me

"Danny Boy" by Frederick Weatherly

Sweeney deftly negotiated the pullropes along the passageway toward *Da Cosimo*, intent on a drink or several now that she had been paid for the contraband she had just delivered. Vesta's artificial gravity invested her with a weight of just under fifty kilograms, or eighty percent Earth-standard, a reminder to her muscles of her planet of origin. Superfluous, gravity was just one of the exasperations on Vesta, albeit the least dangerous. As Sweeney drew herself into the tavern, the three men seated at a table in the far corner jogged her recollection of others.

In another place they might have worn uniforms, and even here in the neutral territory of *Da Cosimo* they had points of commonality, from the erect posture and squared shoulders to the hair shorn so close to the scalp that they seemed to be wearing sprayed-on berets, to the severity of countenance and bleakness of expression that marked them as very focused predators.

Sweeney, heart rumbling, had no doubts regarding the identity of their prey. But it was too late to turn around and make for her spaceskip *aDhainéal* at the Vesta Port Authority docks. In that moment of recognition she turned and aimed for a table at the opposite corner, seating herself with her back to the corner to protect herself on two flanks. Unless one wanted to take on Cosmo and his two bouncers, one behaved in this place with civility and decorum. An assault on her was almost, but not quite, unthinkable: officers of Port Authority, if in pursuit of orders, might violate that neutrality. Sweeney's security measures—the corner seat, the automatic pistol tucked under her belt and concealed by her gray sweatshirt—helped to augment her defenses against the "almost."

With two fingers she signaled her preference to the bartender. Moments later a serving girl arrived with a nippled plastic bottle containing two shots of chilled Laphroaig that would cost Sweeney five percent of the illicit fee she had just earned. In the dim light of the tavern the girl's legs, bare from mid-thigh, fairly glowed with vitality, and Sweeney briefly cast envious gray eyes at her before withdrawing into her defenses. The girl, at least, had purpose without the excitement of uncertainty.

Sweeney sighed, and sucked at her drink. In the back of her mind a familiar face smiled at her. *A fine pair we made*, she thought, in the voice and lilt of her native tongue. The smile dimmed, a warning that brought her back to the immediate moment. Of their own volition her fingers slipped under the sweatshirt and wrapped themselves around the butt of the old Army automatic pistol and the magazine of seven .45-cal rounds on-call inside it. There was no need for her to jack the slide back to chamber a round—she always carried an eighth in the pipe whenever she made rockfall.

The man from the far corner was approaching warily, eyes fixed on her left arm as if it were a snake. His tongue flicked against his lips once, a lizard's stretching exercise as it prepared to take on the insect. He reached the back of the chair across the table from her but did not sit down.

Sweeney inclined her head solemnly. "Snyder."

"Evening, Nollaig. You'll notice I did not say 'Good.' May I sit down?"

"As long as your hands remain empty, and flat on the table."

Snyder tipped the chair back slightly on the hinges that affixed it to the deck, then folded himself into it and leaned forward. Sweeney's left hand remained under the table, but he knew better than to object. "You docked at the wrong bay at the PA," he said, almost conversationally.

Sweeney's lips tugged at the nipple, and a stream of peat-smoked single-malt spilled into her mouth. "As soon as I noticed the error, I took corrective action."

189

"It's the seventeen minutes between your arrival at the wrong bay and the corrective action you spoke of that are of interest," said Snyder. His official tone added, "Of interest to Port Authority Imports Division."

"I was in the loo," said Sweeney. "Which you know, having hacked my L-chip."

Snyder's expression told her nothing. She always assumed someone was monitoring the signal from her implant. Even in the asteroid belt artstate technology made surveillance of individuals a routine matter. Given the ID codes and the associated L-chip frequency, anyone's location and itinerary could be traced, for as long as desired.

"For seventeen minutes?" pressed Snyder.

Sweeney shrugged. "I sometimes forget: never eat cafeteria food."

"And the cafeteria in question?"

"On Tally."

"Tally's not on your official trip ticket."

Again she shrugged, and hoisted the nippled bottle. "I'm just here for a quiet drink, Snyder," she said, prodding him to get to the point.

"You picked up four containers on Tally."

"Did not."

"I'll amend that. Four shipping containers were loaded onto your 'skip while you were in the cafeteria on Tally. What was in them?"

"Hypothetically speaking? I wouldn't have asked."

"Incurious? Or discreet?"

"I wouldn't have been interested." She drained the bottle. "I assume you found no trace of these hypothetical containers on the *aDhainéal* when you illegally searched him."

Snyder ignored the goad. "If we had, this conversation would be held at PAID."

Sweeney stood up, her left hand still under the pullover. "See you around, Snyder."

"Nollaig?"

She paused, and countered his presumption of familiarity with formal address. "Yes, Inspector?"

"It's one thing to smuggle foodstuffs and agricultural items past the Port Authorities to avoid paying the tariffs and local *ad valorem*," said Snyder. His voice straddled the boundary between official and amiable. "The PA's haven't the time or resources to track down all you 'indies,' L-chips or no. It's quite another to supply militant dissidents with the chemicals for manufacturing explosives. Don't go bearding the lion, Nollaig."

👁👁👁

Aboard the *aDhainéal* Sweeney collapsed onto the starboard captain's chair and allowed her mind to drift like a cloud, seeking its own level of relaxation. She had escaped for the moment, but Snyder had been right: transporting the components for pemex had been a venture of far greater risk than that to which she was accustomed. Worse, it had gotten her noticed. She drew scant comfort from having known the extra attention would accrue to her. It had been time—it *was* time—for her to move in that direction. The memories demanded it of her.

Once again she closed her eyes and gazed into the face in the back of her mind, the face of a spirit as stout as her own, but innocent still. Now a shock of hair even more golden than her own short locks had spilled over his left eye, and she could see the familiar and endearing sweep of his hand, nudging it back in place. He wore it long for her, only for her, because she liked to run her fingers through it, and to grab hold of it with both hands while they . . .

Abruptly she pulled back from her reverie, angry with herself for indulging in a moment of weakness. The pleasure of revisiting such a memory had to be *earned*. Not yet, she whispered fiercely. *Not yet.* Swiftly she initialized the 'skip for departure, not caring whether Port Authority granted permission, not even bothering to enTrack from orbit around Vesta. A terse go-code from her sent the *aDhainéal* directly from the docking bay into null-Space, and she was temporarily immune from the predations of Snyder, Port Authorities, militant dissidents, and black holes. She would catch hell and certainly a stiff fine when/if she returned to Vesta for not following departure protocols. It was unseemly simply to *poof* out of existence

191

even within the privacy of your own bay. Neighbors, Sweeney supposed, would natter.

With the 'skip safely in null-Space, Sweeney unbuckled the harness that held her in the captain's chair and drifted to the bridge's aft bulkhead. On the other side of the sliding door there was the loo in question, and she sat down, not to relieve herself, but to press a latch hidden behind the sanitary paper dispenser. The deck parted at her feet to reveal a compartment between the power housing and the cargo bay. On the 'skip's schematics the compartment did not exist; rather, the bay abutted the bulkhead that separated it from the power housing.

During the two dozen or so times the *aDhainéal* had been searched, it had not occurred to anyone that the cargo bay was two meters shorter than indicated on the schematics.

Sweeney peered down. The hermetically sealed plastic refrigeration unit that served as a casket, secured by straps to the deck, had not shifted or been disturbed during the Port Authority intrusion. She pulled herself forward so that her body lay stretched out on top of it. A tear formed, but she would not weep, not yet. "Rest easy, *mo chroi*," she whispered. The plastic was hard against her body, and pressed against bone here and there, but she slept.

👀👀👀

In her dream Sweeney was carried along in a current of the colors of death. Grays twisted and merged with pastels of turquoise and tangerine, and the terrain far below—she had entered the dream flying—seemed awash with writhing. Hell is filled with snakes, she thought, although she could not have said where this notion had come from. Doubtless, like the flying, it was a condition of her existence in the dream.

There was also a voice, and it was not hers. The words oscillated, soft and loud and soft again, in cadence with the swirling all about her, but she had heard the words before and now in her dream she could wash herself in the sound of his voice. He had been about to depart on an assignment when they had fought, and his tone was not kind, but it was *his* tone, *his* voice, and in the dream she clung to that like a child with a favorite blanket. Everyone dies, he had said, was saying, and it is better to die a death for something you believe in.

"Death is still dead," she cried, had cried. Then, ever so softly, "The only thing I believe in is you, *mo ghra*."

The swirls swallowed her then. There was more, but when she awoke, she could not recall what it was, only that he had been there, inside her, one more time.

Content atop the casket, she went back to sleep.

Static hiss awoke her. With deliberate movements she descended from the casket and resealed the hidden compartment and shuffled forward to the bridge. She was barely conscious. Somewhere in time a memory had been lost, and in a spot just behind her eyes she tried to retrieve it, but it would not reveal itself, it was not there. *Mo ghra*, she whispered. My love. The whisper was enough for now.

"Sweeney," she grumbled into the mike.

Unsurprisingly she did not recognize the man's voice, but he spoke the right Irish words. *"Ar mhaith leat deoch?"*

Yes, she thought, I actually *would* like a drink. *"Ba mhaith,"* she agreed, the code signifying that she was free to talk. In an aside, she muttered, *"Níl an dara suí sa bhuaile agam."*

"What? Yes, you *do* have a choice," the man snapped, countering her muted complaint. "It was understood that you had made yours."

"It was made *for* me," said Sweeney, with some asperity. "What do you want, . . . ?"

"If I must have an identity, call me Liam," the man continued. "Your drink is ready for you, if you are ready, when next you make rockfall."

Sweeney's heart thudded. "So soon?"

"Strike while the iron is hot," said Liam. After a brief silence, he went on, "You know, I never understood that saying. You're supposed to press your shirt, not beat it."

"It's a smithing term," muttered Sweeney.

"A what? It's a what?"

She shook her head, although Liam could not see her through the mike. *"Is cuma.* It doesn't matter." She closed commo before Liam could respond, then instructed Niamh, the *aDhainéal's* computer, to calculate and impose the next leg of her journey. Finally she climbed out of the chair and made for her stateroom.

The vanity in her stateroom was itself a vanity. She did not need it. The drawers and bins set into the bulkhead served much the same purpose. But the vanity came with a mirror, and he liked to stand behind her and watch her while she touched a light powder to her cheeks or brushed a gloss over her lips, he liked to stand with his hands on her bare shoulders and slowly slip them down over the upper swells of her breasts, and he laughed when, aroused, she slipped with the gloss brush or the powder pad. She remembered trembling . . .

And now she sat down in front of the vanity with only the memory of the dead behind her. She sat very still, staring at her reflection like a shrike eyeing prey. She had looked forward to the commo from Liam and the announcement that the components she had brought to Vesta had been assembled, that the explosive device was ready for delivery, but now that it had come she found herself strangely hesitant. It was not the anticipation of the pain about to come, that was nothing, it was as nothing compared to the loss she had suffered already. The hesitation stemmed from the utter irrevocability of what she was about to do.

"'And how can man die better,'" she whispered, her heart unexpectedly calm now, "'than facing fearful odds / for the ashes of his fathers / and the temples of his Gods?'"

He had said that to her, quoting from Macaulay's *Horatius*, just before leaving her for the last time.

With thoughts only of *him*, with ears keen to the echoes of his words and his love-words, Sweeney broke free of her hesitation. From one of the top drawers she withdrew a thick gauze anti-bacterial bandage, a roll of surgical tape, and a filleting knife. From the roll she cut four approximately equal lengths, then opened the bandage and pressed a length of tape along each edge of the bandage.

She did not look at it, nor did she contemplate what the bandage portended.

Crossing her arms, Sweeney grasped the hem of her sweatshirt, and drew it over her head, casting it aside with a desultory motion.

Her right hand swept up the filleting knife. She leaned forward, so that in the mirror she could see the back of her bare right shoulder. With the fingers of her left hand she probed and prodded, until finally the pressures produced the nodule: there, just there, deep in the muscle above the scapula, where it was next to impossible to get at. A surgeon could find it, but surgeons were registered with the Beltway Ports Authority and it was mandatory to report even a request to remove the L-chip. In theory it could be removed if one didn't care how much damage was inflicted during removal—and surely someone had removed it, else why the law that declared a person without one subject to immediate execution? Liam perhaps knew such people, but he could not trust her, not yet. Smuggling contraband was one thing. She had to prove herself beyond all doubt before they would allow her to deliver the device.

Níl neart air. So be it.

With a swift hard slash she cut the skin, the muscle there, and blood spurted. Again she slashed, deeper this time, and heard and felt the grate of metal blade on metal and plastic nodule. There was no pain because she was already in agony. The sensation of pain—the tearing of skin and flesh—hovered in the dim reaches of her mind. She knew it was there, poised to burst through her defenses, but she held it at bay by not caring. The fingers of her left hand pried the flesh apart, now slippery with blood. She drew her right hand up over her shoulder, seeking. The unnatural articulation of the shoulder joint would have made her cry out if she had allowed herself not to feel the agony of loss. *A Dhainéal,* she cried silently. *Oh, Danny . . .*

Growling against pain, Sweeney forced herself to dig her fingers into the incision and pry loose the nodule, tearing at flesh and muscle and nerve there. Finally she freed the nodule as one might pop a pea from its pod. Drenched in her blood, it rolled over her shoulder and onto the top of the vanity and stuck in a red puddle there.

In relief Sweeney screamed, and put her face down to the top of the vanity, and fought for breath: *haugh, haugh, haugh.* Blood spilled onto the vanity top, and mingled with her hair there. In her shoulder pain sizzled like a live electrical wire pulled loose from its mooring. She gave a little shrug, testing: the joint and muscles still functioned—not that it mattered now. Warm blood reached her cheek, her eyelashes caught in it when she blinked. One more thing had to be done before she continued to the next phase.

Sweeney sat up. More blood spilled from the incision and down her back. She pulled open the door to a small cabinet atop the vanity and got out a green bottle. The label identified it as Jameson whiskey. The bottle was not quite full, as if it had been opened only for a special occasion. Sweeney opened it again and took a quick swig, and toasted his reflection in the mirror. "For you, *mo ghra*," she said. Then, without allowing herself even an instant to think about what she had to do, she tilted the neck of the bottle across her shoulder and poured whiskey into the incision, disinfecting it, cauterizing it.

And she screamed.

The scream and the searing pain left Sweeney breathless. Again she fought the urge to pause for rest, to recover, and allowed the momentum of what she had done propel her toward what remained to be done. Quickly she scooped up the bandage and slapped it over the wound, pressing the tape to her skin as best she could, given the awkward position. Her shoulder joint protested this fresh abuse, and she snarled it back into submission. With the bandage fixed, she got up and went to the 'fresher for one of the folded bath towels. This she draped over her shoulder before she laid down on her bunk, adjusting her position to allow as much of her body weight as possible to press against the towel.

Settled, she spoke in a voice made hoarse by effort. "Wake me in an hour, Niamh." She then closed her mind to the past few minutes, and allowed exhaustion to take its toll.

The bleeding had all but stopped by the time Sweeney awoke to the gentle pulse from Niamh. Very carefully she rolled her feet to the deck and stood up, clutching a stanchion for support until the wave of dizziness passed. The red-stained towel slipped from her shoulder, revealing an equally stained bandage. She returned to the vanity and sat down once more, and prepared several small lengths of adhesive tape and another bandage. It were best done without thinking, she thought. She drew a huge breath, then ripped the old bandage from her shoulder. Fresh blood beaded along the incision, but it did not open. It looked to be approximately six centimeters long, and clean, for the filleting knife had been razor sharp. One by one she pressed the adhesive strips across the incision, the makeshift butterfly bandaids meant to keep the incision closed. Finally she placed the fresh bandage directly over the wound, and pressed it into place.

The L-chip—lens-shaped and the size of a lima bean—still lay in a puddle of her blood, almost dried now. The sight of it aroused in Sweeney a flood of nausea, of loathing. Nothing she had done before—carrying the stiffened corpse of her man to the refrigeration unit, or mutilating her shoulder, or reaching deep within herself to rip free the detested object—none of this had prepared her for the necessity now of touching the hated L-chip. With steeled will, because she was not finished yet, she pried it free with a fingernail and held it up for inspection. As a smuggler, she understood the Port Authority's desire to monitor her travels and activities. But even those who were constitutionally incapable of deviant behavior had security implants, victims of an administration's quest to achieve a perfect society. Space, she thought, was supposed to be free.

Was that freedom worth dying for? *He* had thought so. At the time, she had not understood this. Now she did. What had changed?

I could have accepted a life of subservience to the Port Authorities, could I but have lived it with you. But you chose to live your way, to live free, and in dying you chose for me as well. Because alive or dead, it is together that we are meant to be. I see that now.

I miss you, *mo Dhainéal*, she whispered. My Danny.

For a fleeting moment she thought she heard his voice, made husky by desire. *Ta me anseo.* I am here. She stared into the mirror, seeking she knew not what. His face and hands and body, behind her like before? If she closed her eyes, she could feel him, feel his hands on her oh *God!* With a mighty effort she struggled free from that memory. Almost, she thought, but not yet. There's still something left to do.

The face in the mirror stared back at her impassively, as yet unimpressed. My nose, she thought, my face . . . my freckles. She remembered his fingertip drifting across her face, playing connect-

197

the-dots with her freckles. Epona, the horse. Aoife the witch. A bunny. Then his lips replaced the fingertip, and he would ever so slowly outline other shapes, on her face—on her neck her shoulders her breasts her stomach until she grabbed his hair and wrapped her limbs around him and screamed at him for God's sake just *drill* me!

Sweeney sat back from the mirror, gasping for breath. *Don't do this to yourself.*

A trickle of blood began to seep from under the bandage.

Once more she looked into the mirror, and saw there this time a face at peace. Perhaps there was just a line or two of pain, just there, beside the eyes, but they would fade in time, and reunion would ease the pain of separation as if to nothing at all, as if it were not now, nor had it ever been.

Sweeney retrieved the sweatshirt and drew it on, then swept up the L-chip as she might have brushed a crumb from the table, and stalked off to the loo, to the latch that opened the secret compartment. After easing herself onto the lower deck, she leaned briefly on the cover of the refrigeration unit. Already the *aDhainéal*s transponder lay within. If she lifted the lid, she might catch a glimpse of him as she dropped the L-chip inside. Sweeney fought that urge, as ferociously as a wolf defending her cubs, a widow defending a memory. If she saw him, even for an instant . . .

It was not the thought of seeing his injuries that unnerved her, for they were not extensive, merely fatal. Nor was it the pale, cold, bloodless skin that put her off, for she expected as much—he was dead, after all. It was the contrast. She knew he was dead, but that fact had yet to reach her memories. As long as he remained alive in her living memory . . .

She cracked the cover and flicked the chip inside. My blood, she whispered, with yours, *mo ghra*. My love.

Eyes dry, she pulled herself erect. "It's time," she told him and the Universe, and withdrew from the hidden compartment.

❧❧❧

An hour later Sweeney returned to Vesta, knowing they were watching her, were aware of her. She could feel their distant eyes on her. The intensified surveillance was to be expected—Snyder as

198

much had warned her of this—but now she sought to use it to her advantage. With a practiced, gentle hand she brought the *aDhainéal* to rest beside the low wall of a small crater some fifty kilometers from the Vesta Docks and main settlement.

Immediately the countdown began. She had, she reckoned, half an hour, seventy five minutes at most, before someone from Port Authority arrived to investigate. In preparation for EVA she had donned her outsuit. Hydraulics opened the bulkhead that separated the hidden compartment from the rest of the cargo bay, and lowered the bay door to rest on the surface of the asteroid. In the minimal gravity she broke the inertia of the refrigeration unit and thrust it out of the cargo bay and onto the surface, guiding it manually toward a crevasse that perhaps had been opened by the impact that had caused the crater.

All the while, Sweeney wept. The sacrilege of abandoning the body of her man in this remote and soulless world raked her soul like raptor's talons. Her heart ached like bone against bone. She paused once, twice, to clutch at her chest under the outsuit, so hard it hurt.

Then it was done, without thought, without memory. The end of the unit dipped as it reached the crevasse, and its momentum carried it into the fissure. In slow-motion it dropped: three meters, five, and stopped. In her mind's eye Sweeney had already foreseen the next step, and had begun to implement it, carrying boulders and rocks to the fissure to conceal the unit, the casket, her man. It was done.

Sweeney continued to weep.

As if burdened by Vesta itself Sweeney trudged back to the 'skip and boarded. Prolonged minutes later, divested of her outsuit, Sweeney allowed her fingers, her digital memory, to program for departure, while she sat in the captain's chair and stared blankly through the viewscreen. At last, with the lift-off of the *aDhainéal*, a palpable weight left her shoulders. Now she was free. They were blind to her. They would not find her unless she wanted to be found.

The rendezvous point lay on the other side of Vesta, as far as one could get from the main settlement and still remain on the asteroid. Sweeney did not know who would meet her there, nor did she care. Nothing mattered but the device, the bomb they had assembled from the components they had off-loaded while she was in the loo. The risk was theirs now. She was free.

Sweeney made rockfall in the center of a crater, which offered little concealment but allowed such a field of vision that no one could take her unawares. There she waited, cargo hatch open to receive. She had, she calculated, another twenty minutes before Port Authority discovered that she and the *aDhainéal* were not at their electronically confirmed location. An all-out search would commence at that point. Whether PA would think to search the far side of Vesta, she could not say.

Despite the calm she had forced on herself, her heart began to pound. If only her contacts would hurry . . .

Through the viewscreen she saw them, at last. Two figures in white, transporting between them on a slideskid a dark object perhaps half the size of the refrigeration unit. For a moment Sweeney hated them. Of a certainty they had had their L-chips removed, and by a competent medic. She, however, could not be trusted, unless she removed her own chip herself. She did not concern herself now with their trust. Their cause was not hers, no matter what they assumed.

The *aDhainéal* shifted slightly as the two individuals boarded with the explosive device. Radio silence paramount, Sweeney remained unsummoned. Presently the two figures appeared before her again, each with a hand raised. In salute? In farewell? Though she doubted they could see her through the tinted viewscreen, Sweeney waved in reply, and enabled the 'skip into Track. What remained to be done, after all that she had been through, was a cakewalk.

👁👁👁

Seated at a table in *Da Cosimo* with her back to a corner, Sweeney sucked from a plastic bottle containing a double slug of Laphroaig. She had expected to be accosted upon entry, but no one from Port Authority was lying in wait for her. The L-chip, she recalled dimly. Of course they would not know where she was. But they would watch for her at her usual haunts.

Briefly she glanced around the tavern for the "eye" that was certain to be there. Several men were speaking into commo cameos, and it was impossible for her to determine whether any of them were reporting on her whereabouts. She downed another long pull of whiskey and let her mind float like a feather in the light gravity of Vesta, float to the dusty surface of the asteroid and come to rest there. All sounds save those of entry into the tavern she dismissed from her mind, and waited. They would send Snyder, she thought. Thinking she had betrayed him, he would demand this assignment.

It was not unthinkable that Snyder would mete out punishment in *Da Cosimo*, but once he spotted her, if he took the time to look at her, he would hesitate, pause, wait. He knew her Army history, and knew what she was capable of. He would talk. That was all she wanted.

Any moment now, she thought. It had to be.

Under the table she freed the old Army automatic from its clip and held it in her left hand. Carefully she thumbed the hammer back, breaking it out of its half-cock safety. In the noise of the tavern no one recognized the sound, although the metallic *click* echoed in her own ears.

Shadows and light moved near the entrance, and Sweeney held her breath. Into the tavern stepped Snyder, followed by the two security personnel who had accompanied him the last time she had visited *Da Cosimo*. Snyder turned toward her as if he had known exactly where she would be. Across five meters their eyes met and locked, and Sweeney shook her head once, a hard signal of warning. Snyder's hand arrested the arm of the man to his right, who had been about to draw his handweapon. At a sharp order from Snyder that Sweeney could not hear, both of his companions held their empty hands in front of them. Together they approached her table, the two companions flanking Snyder. At the back of the chair opposite her, Snyder halted.

"Sit down, Inspector," said Sweeney. Her tone did not make it a request.

"Sir," began one of the companions, "the law clearly states—"

"Belay that, Corporal," ordered Snyder, and sat down, very carefully and placing his hands palm-up on top of the table. Sweeney waited patiently while Snyder inspected her, knowing that he saw the same face she had seen in the mirror scant hours ago. "The corporal is correct," he said softly. "We have the authority *and the duty* to shoot you on sight. With your weapon drawn," here he lowered his eyes to the table, as if gazing through the plastic top to her lap, where she held the pistol, "perhaps you think you can take the three of us. Even so, others will come for you."

Something between them had changed, Sweeney thought. Previously they had been friendly adversaries—she a smuggler, he duty-bound to catch her in the act. For just a moment she felt a pang of regret. She had taken a small pleasure in the game between them. Now the game was over, and clearly he believed she had lost.

"I don't know whether I'm glad it's to be you, or not," said Sweeney. She took another pull of whiskey. "Incidentally, how did I do?"

In the space of half a minute Sweeney had deTracked from null-space inside a large conference room at Port Authority, on the level just above the security computer that contained all the tracking data for all L-chips in the asteroid belt, had off-loaded the pemex device, and enTracked back into null-space, scant seconds before the explosion.

"Damn you, Sweeney."

Not Nollaig, she thought. The game *is* over.

"Port Authority has lost all tracking capability," said Snyder. His voice was low and calm, yet Sweeney sensed the anger behind it, cold and palpable. "We have no idea where anyone is. The data cannot be recovered. We'll have to recreate the database from scratch. Happy?"

Sweeney shrugged. "It seemed well to 'beard the lion' while I was at it."

"While you were at it! What does that mean, while you were at it?"

"Here's what I want—"

The Corporal let out a gasp. "Inspector, you *can't* negotiate—!"

Snyder did not look at him. "One more, Corporal, and I will dismiss you. Go ahead, Sweeney."

The faint smile that crossed her face was a gift to herself. "You did not find me or the *aDhainéal* when you tracked his transponder," she said. "I want to be taken to that location. I want a few moments there, nothing more."

"If I refuse?"

Sweeney sat back, her face contemplative. "Maybe I can take the three of you," she said. "Maybe not. But I will get off all eight rounds. Some of them might strike people who had nothing to do with any of this." She paused, drumming the fingers of her free hand on the table top. "I'll want your word, Inspector."

"I accept your conditions," said Snyder. "You have my word."

Carefully Sweeney raised her left hand and passed the pistol across the table to Snyder.

❧❧❧

By the time they reached the far side of Vesta the sun, a point of starlight not quite a disk, had risen. While Sweeney remained under guard, Snyder and the corporal went EVA. After some ten minutes had passed, during which Sweeney wondered whether Snyder was reneging on his word, she was sent for.

Port Authority had discovered her ruse. The rocks had been removed from the fissure, and the refrigeration unit had been opened. Through the tinted visor of her helmet Sweeney saw that the lid had been left open, exposing the corpse of her man to space—or perhaps it had just now been opened. She had supposed that depth of understanding to be beyond Snyder. On the other hand, it was convenient if not prescient.

She did not look at them as she knelt down on the surface of Vesta, beside the fissure, peering down into it. Inside the helmet her lips moved. "*Ave, Maria, gratia plena, Dominus tecum. Benedicta tu in mulieribus . . .* "

"Sweeney," said Snyder, after she had fallen silent.

Sweeney stood up. Still gazing into the fissure, she whispered, "I love you." Then she straightened.

"We will recover," insisted Snyder. "All this damage you did, and for what? Do you truly imagine that you have furthered your cause by all this?"

Sweeney smiled indulgently, though he could not see her through the visor. "What I did was not about the cause, Snyder. It was never about the cause."

She turned slightly to face him, steeling herself for one final act, imprinting it on her mind so that even in death she would know what to do. She had nothing more to say, now. Through the visor she saw Snyder raise his right arm, so that her pistol was aimed at her head. He seemed to hesitate, as if he were waiting for a final word from her, or were trying to muster some words to say to her.

At last she saw a flash of light and felt simultaneously a terrible crimson impact. There was the sound of air escaping and the sensation of blackness shrouding the image she had implanted of her final act.

Fading, Sweeney twisted and spilled into the fissure, and as cold darkness won out she landed on top of her man.

Tree Hugger

Gone . . . her kith and companions, all gone. Their passing was not unexpected. They had known the damage done to this world by the Others was irreversible. Still, this past winter had taken most of them unawares, killed them while they stood, dormant and helpless, the precious, life-giving light from the two suns blocked by clouds and particulates. Only she, Pagan the youngling, had survived, and that barely.

As the winter faded into summer the sunlight returned, too late to save her kin. If only there were one other left, just one. Pagan dreaded what was to come, what had to be done. Like her ancestors, she would have to move on, to find another world suitable for her survival. To do that she needed to soak up every last ray of sunlight, for light was scarce during interstellar journeys. Her ancestral memories spoke of those who had been lost while traveling to this world of a double sun. Pagan hugged herself, shivering. This past winter the darkness and shadows had proved relentless and remorseless, leaving only husks that stood on the bluffs, stark skeletons against a blued steel sky. With the arrival of spring one sun bravely shone through the unnatural haze, and hope stirred within her when she saw an opening in the distant clouds. Soon the other sun would join in, and replenish her. Then, and only then, could her journey begin.

Exhausted, Pagan stood as one rooted to the ground while she awaited the arrival of sunrise. What a strange world she had reached--only one sun, and that weak and yellow. Here she would have only half a life, the other half spent in darkness. But she could have traveled no further. She was barely alive. Everything drooped.

Still, she had managed to place herself among potential colleagues. As soon as she had accumulated enough energy, she would introduce herself. Meanwhile, there were sounds to consider and evaluate: high-pitched squeaks and warbles from the flying things, and rustlings in the lower vegetation where some creatures agitated the fronds with their passing. Aside from indicating the existence of other living forms, the sounds meant nothing to her. But something else did: the metallic purr of a motor.

Pagan drooped further. *Did Others pollute this world as well?*

She keened her hearing to the sound, listening carefully. Something, someone, was approaching. She stood very still, watching, as a container rolled on wheels in her general direction, unnatural light spilling from two orbs set into its front side. Almost within reach of her it stopped.

The creature that emerged from the conveyance--for clearly such it was--resembled her sunlight self in many ways. Four limbs it had, two for locomotion, its carriage upright. The top of its body terminated in a large, bulbous growth containing sensory organs, just like hers, and perhaps that was where the central nervous system housed all of its processes. Though the night air was reasonably warm, Pagan felt a chill. In her ancestral memories, creatures of such shapes were capable of great thought and great deeds--and of great destruction.

Some day, she thought, *I will reach a world where there will be just us.*

The creature dragged another, similar creature from the conveyance, and spilled it onto the grass. It lay there, pale and flaccid, and Pagan caught just a whiff of a pungent nitrogen compound. Its limbs writhed, and it emitted sounds that Pagan recognized as speech. She listened carefully.

"What are you going to do, Montclair?" Its hairless head gleamed in the light from the orbs. "Are you insane?"

Syntax, thought Pagan. *The standing creature is called Montclair. The one on the ground seems angry and afraid.*

Montclair reached into its skin and withdrew a metal object that glistened in the light from the conveyance, whose motor still purred. "If the law won't help us, we have to help ourselves, Mister Wolfe. You'll be our statement."

The sounds emitted by Mister Wolfe increased in pitch and intensity as it tried to push itself away. "Stop and think, man. Killing me isn't going to help your cause."

"We'll see," said Montclair.

206

Instantly there was a flash of light from the object in Montclair's limb, accompanied by a sound unlike any Pagan had ever heard. More than a thunderclap, and yet of much shorter duration. A spot appeared in the center of Mister Wolfe's trunk--in the shadows it appeared to be black--and it settled onto the grass and did not move again.

For a moment Montclair stood looking down at Mister Wolfe. Then it tucked the metal object back under its skin. A remote memory registered in Pagan's mind. Not skin. Montclair covered most of its body with plant and animal tissue. Mister Wolfe did not. Which was the proper form of presenting oneself? She had to know, in order to blend in. For now, she had half a chance of being right.

Suddenly Montclair twisted in the light from the conveyance, confronting Pagan, its limb thrust back under its skin, seeking the metal object. Pagan kept very still, resisting even the light breeze that had come up. Presently Montclair straightened, and emitted a slow burst of air, and returned to the conveyance. Soon the purr of the motor faded into the night.

With nothing to do save wait for the sun to appear, Pagan reviewed the event that had just transpired, gleaning information for analysis. She remembered the sounds the creatures had made, though few made sense to her yet. Evidently Mister Wolfe was a male, if its physiological resemblance to the Others on the world she had left was any indication, and perhaps Montclair was as well. Montclair was clearly the dominant of the two creatures, and he covered most of his skin. Pagan concluded that a search for suitable covering would be necessary if she were to blend in.

A light appeared without warning, some distance away. It was square, and illuminated a large, white box that was capable of rolling in the same manner as Montclair's conveyance. Pagan noted several unnatural objects near the box, including a vine that led from the box to a very old tree. Hanging from the vine in the breeze fluttered several pieces of covering similar in shape to those on Montclair. One problem solved, thought Pagan, as soon as I can move.

A shadow passed in front of the light, and then the light went out. Pagan watched the sky in that direction. Already the horizon was graying. Soon . . . soon.

꩜꩜꩜

With the sunlight came warmth and energy, and Pagan absorbed it hungrily. Finally, with half of her nutritional requirements satisfied, she drifted off into the woods, studying the large, white box from this angle and that. Evidently some creature dwelt within, although she detected no one about. The shapes of the pieces of covering that hung on the vine clearly delineated the parts of the body they were intended to cover. Moving like an apparition, she snared a black piece for her lower body and a piece with red and black lines and squares for her upper, and donned them.

Deeming herself presentable to this new world, Pagan thought to sate another hunger. The selection was vast indeed, and it rather surprised her that no others of her kind dwelt here to accommodate and nourish themselves. Where were they? Surely they were not afraid of her, a kindred if alien spirit. It appalled Pagan to imagine that she was alone on this world too. Her spirit faded as she cast herself about, drifting from this tree to that, searching, seeking. Not one other like herself, not one. Alone she had passed through the void, and at times only the thought of companionship waiting for her had kept her going. In her weakened state, in the darkness between stars, with just the flicker of starlight to feed upon, a palpable despair had set in that only the arrival on this new world had dissolved. Now it hovered once more on her horizon. After all this time, all this distance, she remained the last of her kind. In the corners of her eyes tiny globules formed, and she touched a finger to them, collecting them, and then sucked the sweetness from her fingertip.

Do not weep for me, Thaxis, her oldest friend and her sap-father, had begged her, desiccating and dying. The nectar in her mouth reminded her of him.

Again she drifted, caressing this tree and that with her fingertips, feeling the life flowing within. At length she selected an older tree, with a trunk as big around as her thigh. Yes, this would do. All of her senses keened to the life force within. She opened her mouth wide, revealing long, sharp teeth in the corners of her upper and lower jaws. These she sank into the tree where the bark was thinnest,

208

and penetrated the phloem.

Immediately her mouth was flooded by viscous sap. She sucked hungrily, feeling the ecstasy build within her. Her body pressed against the trunk as if to join with it, and she rubbed against it in the manner of dayself mating. She felt her own fluids flow faster, overwhelming her thoughts, her being. If only there were one of her kind to mate with, or even one of the Others. Sap oozed from her mouth, and her tongue became a living thing, catching the droplets before they could spill to the ground. Sweetness filled her senses and drove her blindly onward. The trunk, rigid against her, incited her to rub it harder. She needed to join with it, to feel the hardness inside her, to feel it fill her with the sap of new life. She wrapped her legs around the tree, thrusting at it, thrashing at it. Never before had she known such an urgency. Youngling that she had been, there was no one to guide her. She needed . . . she needed . . .

Pagan moaned. *I need I need I need . . .*

Gasping for breath, Pagan eased back from the tree. The part of the lower body covering that had prevented her from true melding with the trunk was moist, sticky. Gingerly she touched herself. Sap that she had issued in her throes clung to her fingers, and she licked them clean, one by one. The sweetness evoked the very recent memory of the excitement of her senses, and of the need to share her sap with someone.

And there was no one.

In sudden alarm she stiffened, and pressed herself against the tree in an entirely different manner, seeking concealment and protection. Sounds she had just heard, though not nearby. She located the large white box, and spotted a covered creature walking in the direction of the spot where she had spent the night following her arrival. What did it mean?

If the creature was there, then the box might be empty. Pagan drifted carefully toward it, eyeing her surroundings all the while for the appearance of more creatures. Dew laced her bare feet and oozed between her toes. She recalled that Montclair had covered his feet, but there had been nothing hanging on the vine that resembled the coverings he had worn. Senses keened, Pagan continued her approach. An opening in one side of the box seemed to beckon. Swift as the wind she darted inside the box.

An array of smells assaulted her. Flesh had been burned; something had soured; musty spores floated; and all around she tasted the unnatural fragrance of a flower. The source of this last was a vial on a table top. Pagan sniffed at it, detecting no flower, only the fragrance.

Deeper inside this lair she heard faint voices. Following the sounds along a narrow passageway, she soon came upon a small box in a corner, on top of a shelf. Inside the box were two small creatures yammering at one another. A few of the sounds they made reminded Pagan of those that Montclair had made. In front of the box stood an apparatus that suggested it was made for sitting on. A shaft of sunlight through a square opening in the roof pooled directly onto the apparatus, and there Pagan sat down, basking in the warmth and energy. Her awareness divided between the box and the passageway, she listened and remembered and analyzed . . .

❧❧❧

A metallic *thump* outside but somewhere nearby startled Pagan. She dashed to the window and peered out. The woman she had seen earlier had just emerged from her car and was carrying a bulging plastic bag in each hand toward the RV--and toward the only entrance and exit. Pagan's sap flowed faster as she moved into the passageway, and stood just inside the doorway to the hygiene room. The door opened, and the woman stepped inside. For a moment she paused, as if sniffing the air, puzzled by an unfamiliar aroma. Then she turned away and made for the kitchenette. In a trice Pagan shot outside, a light breeze trailing in her wake.

Sheltered by the woods again, Pagan caught the sound of voices. They seemed to come from the area where she had descended and spent the night. Moving swiftly from tree to tree she approached the site. Mister Wolfe was gone--and she understood enough now to know that he had not left under his own power--and a yellow plastic vine now delineated an area and connected several of the trees and some plastic sticks that had been plunged into the grass. Just outside the perimeter of this vine stood, if the words on his car were any

210

indication, a county sheriff.

The other voice Pagan had heard was coming from the radio inside the car. Into the hand-held mike the sheriff spoke words that Pagan could not make out, and then placed the mike back inside the car. Suddenly he looked up, and his right hand dropped to the holster on his hip.

Smiling, Pagan stepped carefully on the grass just outside the yellow vine. The sheriff straightened, and seemed to relax. "Hello there," he called. "You live around here?"

He spoke with a flavor to his words that Pagan had not detected on the television programs. She understood him well enough, but had no response for him, other than the smile. She came to a stop about four paces away, and gazed at the dark smudge on the grass where Mister Wolfe had fallen.

The sheriff gestured toward the RV, just visible on the far side of a copse of trees. "You staying with Miz Vartan?" he asked. "Her niece, maybe?"

"Niece?"

"What's your name, Miss?"

"Pagan."

The sheriff--his name, she read on the black rectangle affixed to his shirt just above the pocket, was Mason--looked at her expectantly. Finally he said, "Is that your first name or your last name?"

Pagan nodded to herself. Right, that is what the television meant. The inhabitants had two names here. One that they were called. One that identified their derivation. "Day," she said, with more truth than the sheriff would ever understand. "Pagan Day."

"Do you have any identification, Miz Day? A driver's license?"

"Identification?"

Mason sighed. "All right. Were you around here last night?"

"I stayed among the trees."

"That so? And did you hear anything unusual last night?"

Pagan began to drift along the yellow vine toward Mason. "There are many sounds in the trees."

"Have you been drinking, Miss?"

Now she frowned. Had he seen her take the sap from the tree

211

earlier? She had not been aware of any lurking creature, but then her senses were still attuned to the life forms on Dholin, the world she had just left. He might have seen her . . . but he was asking the question as if the drinking somehow affected her. She thought back to the television programs. Yes, the inhabitants of this world drank liquids that affected them in various ways, not all pleasant. She shook her head, and allowed her smile to return.

"Did you hear anyone fighting?" Mason pressed. "A shot, perhaps?"

"I heard birds and insects talking."

Mason reached into the car and withdrew the mike. After identifying himself, he said, "I might have a witness, but she's . . . well, she's strange. She says her name is Pagan Day. About five-ten, 130 or so, green eyes, hair is . . . hard to say, a sort of greenish grayish blonde. Run it through Records and let me know what you find. And get hold of Doctor Bourlain and ask him to come in. He may need to start a detox, or send her to the East Wing at St. Cat's."

"Doctor Bourlain has gone fishing for the weekend," Pagan heard.

"Just a sec," said Mason. He took the mike away from his mouth. "Where do you live?" he asked Pagan.

"Among the trees," she said simply.

Mason held her gaze for a moment. Then: "Mary, is there a hippie commune around here that I don't know about? Anything like that?"

"I don't think so," Pagan heard. "And that name comes up with no record at all. Do you want to hold her?"

"She's talking, but she's not making any sense. I'll bring her in, maybe we can figure out who she is and what she saw or didn't see. And you'd better alert someone from Juvy, she looks like she's maybe sixteen, seventeen tops. And check the runaways listings. Mason out." After he replaced the mike, he said, "I want you to come with me to the station, and answer some questions. All right?"

"Okay."

Mason unclipped a set of handcuffs from his belt and ordered her to place her hands on the car hood. After she complied, he patted her clothes, then shackled her hands behind her back. "Sorry about this," he told her. "I don't think you're a danger, but it's procedure."

"Procedure?"

"It means it's the way we do things."

"Oh. Okay."

He rolled his eyes--Pagan noted that they were almost as green as her own, but with a hint of gray--and eased her onto the back seat, taking care not to let her head bump the roof of the car. A metal grating separated the back seat from the front seat. Pagan sat back and watched while he operated the instruments and wheel and drove away. There was much she still did not know about this world, she decided. Perhaps if she fostered a relationship with Mason, like on television, she might learn more.

They traveled along the road in the same direction Montclair had driven the night before. Absorbed in the scenery, Pagan was only remotely aware that Mason was talking to her. When she looked his way at last, he was reaching into a small bag on the console. While she watched, he withdrew two roundish objects, one red and one yellow, each emblazoned with a "w," or perhaps it was an "m," and popped them into his mouth. She heard a *crunch*, followed by softer sounds of chewing.

"Will this take thirty six hours, this procedure?" she asked.

Mason paused in his chewing. "What's that?"

"This procedure," repeated Pagan, bemused by his lack of understanding. "First you control your erectile dysfunction, and then you will be ready at any time for the next thirty six hours."

Mason's hand jerked at the wheel, and the car tugged toward the shoulder of the road momentarily before he corrected it. "What . . . what are you talking about?"

"Your erectile dysfunction," Pagan said easily. "Almost all males have it, which is why there are so many advertisements on television. That's why you took those pills just now. That's so you will be ready when the time is right, at any time for the next thirty six---"

"Wait . . . *what?*"

Her voice took on the tone of an advertisement. "And don't forget to seek medical help if you have an erection lasting more than four hours."

213

Mason twisted in the seat to face her, but the car tugged toward the side of the road again, and he was forced to recover. "What . . . what the hell are you talking about? These are *M&Ms*. I took--I mean, I *ate* two M&Ms. I'm trying to stop smoking, that's all."

Pagan nodded. "Smoking can cause erectile dysfunction," she said, somewhat distracted, now that they were coming up on a village. "That's what they said on television, I saw it. And so can diabetes, and heart problems, and oh, if you should experience a sudden drop in blood pressure you should---"

"I don't have ED!"

"ED? Oh, yes, of course, *ED*." Suddenly she pointed toward a group of people that had gathered at the front of a building, snapping the handcuff chain with a *spung!* Fragments of links went flying. "Look, there's Montclair!"

Brakes squealed as Mason halted the car, and Pagan spilled from the back seat into the well behind the front seat. "Jesus *Christ*!" yelled Mason, reaching for his pistol as he twisted again in the seat. "What did you do? How did you do that?"

Pagan struggled back to her seat, and examined her wrists ruefully. The shiny metal circles had bitten into her skin, and were already sticky with sap, but she quickly closed and sealed the wounds. "I am sorry. I didn't mean to break these. Do you have any more of them I could wear? I'll be more careful with them, I promise."

"Just what the hell *are* you, lady?"

"I'm . . . I am . . . I do not know your word."

Mason dragged thick fingers through his hair, then scratched the back of his neck. The gestures were incomprehensible to Pagan, unless he had an infestation. She was about to inquire after this when the mike squawked. After Mason picked it up and identified himself, Pagan heard the voice that had spoken to him earlier.

"There's no record of a Pagan Day anywhere, Sheriff. And I can't find anything that asks us to hold a person of the description you gave me. Are you planning to hold her as a material witness?"

"I don't know, Mary. On the one hand she seems totally harmless, and then she goes and breaks . . . never mind. I'll call you in a few minutes." Mason twisted in the seat to look back at Pagan. "I sure as hell don't know what you are, young woman, but like I told Mary, I don't think you mean anyone any harm. But I need to talk with you, find out if you know something I need to know. Maybe it's best in a less official setting. That all right with you?"

"Is this part of the procedure?" Pagan asked.

"Please don't start that again. They're M&Ms."

Mason eased the car back onto the road, and presently turned toward the sunrise, onto a narrower road flanked by houses of various shapes and ages. Those on the north seemed to act as a barrier for the forest that surrounded the village, as if one were encroaching upon the other, though it was impossible to determine which was winning. Mason wheeled the car onto a very narrow, gravel-covered road that led directly to a small gabled building that seemed to be attached to a larger structure, as if the latter had given birth to the former. He stopped the car within a few paces of the large, square door, got out, and held the passenger door open for Pagan.

Pagan climbed out and slowly straightened, sniffing the air, cautiously at first, then in huge, joyful gulps. Friends she recognized--sensuous maples, sturdy oaks, even a bitter spruce. Others she thought might be related, their scents not as familiar to her.

"Coming?" asked Mason. He jerked a thumb toward the front door in clarification.

Pagan paused in her sampling of the air. "You wish me to enter?"

"We'll be more comfortable, talking inside."

Pagan shrugged. Perhaps he would permit her to assimilate more information by watching television. She followed him along a narrow walkway lined with low plants bearing orange flowers, and waited while he opened the door and held it for her, following her inside.

"There's some lemonade in the fridge," said Mason, and moved off to the right, toward a bright room partially obscured by a wall.

The words meant little to Pagan, whose attention suddenly was focused elsewhere. The smells were different in here, surrounding her with whiffs and memories of death. An inexperienced youngling, she could not fully grasp the significance of the smells, only that something was horribly wrong in this place. She stood very still, all of her senses to the fore, testing. Her sap thinned by fear, it flowed almost like water now as she took in the room, searching for signs of danger.

The room was approximately the size of the RV in which she had received her first briefing regarding the denizens of this world. It contained several objects whose apparent purpose was to support a seated or reclined person. In a front corner on a metal stand rested a television set rather larger than the one in the RV, and beside it shelving of some inert material bearing colorful thin objects aligned vertically. From that direction she sensed no danger, and withdrew her attention from it. The most powerful smells came from her left, and after checking again for active threats elsewhere and finding none, she turned toward the wall there.

The wall, as she had come to understand walls, was incomplete. The upper half of it looked solid enough, divided as it was by a vertical column of rectangular, dark red blocks of heat-hardened clay, the same sort of blocks the Others on Dholin had used to construct their dwellings before the Bad Times came upon them. Below the dividing point--and she could not bear to look at this, not yet--the column seemed to split, to create a deep, squarish opening, and it was this opening and the smell emanating from it which weakened Pagan's knees and sickened her soul. She got down on hands and knees to peer into the opening, sniffing tentatively now, testing to see how bad the wound was. A metal screen barred her way, and she brushed this aside as if it were facial tissue. It clattered against the wall to her left.

From the kitchen Mason called, "What's going on out there?" but Pagan had no ears for him, not now.

Delicately she leaned into the opening. On the floor below her face lay two identical pieces of blackened metal that were situated as though something were intended to be placed across them. The floor of the opening, and especially the area between the two pieces of metal, was thickly laden with coarse gray ash.

The last time Pagan had felt this sort of soul-sickness, she had been about to depart from Dholin.

Not here too.

Tiny globs of liquid beaded in the corners of her eyes, but she ignored them. Carefully she withdrew from the opening. Still on hands and knees, she looked at a rack to the right. The odor of dryness radiated from it, stinging her nostrils. Quartered sections of a skeleton filled the rack, and now she had no doubt as to the source of the ash on the floor.

Who were you? she wondered. *Did you dream?*

Pagan got to her feet. Smears of dust on the knees of her black denims looked like patches, but she took no notice of them, her eyes now fixed to the horizontal stretch of varnished wood that divided the upper and lower wall. The grain and the color were as familiar to her as her own, for this was--had been--a sap-kith, a maple, a denizen of the highest order on Dholin and surely here on this world as well.

A maple, murdered. Killed and wantonly placed on display. Worse, itself used to display trinkets, for there were a few odd pieces of fired clay recumbent upon the varnished slab. A representation of a forest creature, its tongue extended, an insect on the tip of it. A blue shoe. A drinking cup emblazoned with the word "Vermont" and directly under that a multicolored design.

Pagan felt a nudge at her shoulder. Mason said, "Here's your lemonade."

Her lips drew back from her teeth, revealing the canines, now extended. A growl caught in her throat, stilled at the very moment of emission by a ferocious act of will. *Not. Now.* She closed her mouth and licked her lips. By the time she turned around, her countenance had softened, the fury in her concealed behind eyes only slightly moist.

She accepted the glass he proffered, and caressed the varnished wood. Her voice was low and controlled. "Did you do this?"

"That mantel? Hardly. It came with the house. I bought the place about five years ago."

"It seems a large dwelling for one person," said Pagan.

"I wasn't . . . alone at the time," Mason told her. "That came later. How is it?" She looked a question at him, and he added, "The lemonade."

Pagan took a sip. It had a fruity bitterness softened by sugar, reminding her of sap after a heavy rain. She detected traces of nutrients--tacky potassium, the gentle nip of a weak acid. The beverage was a poor substitute for living sap, but it would do for now.

"You pointed out Montclair," said Mason.

Pagan recalled having done so, but she remained distracted by the evil in the opening before her.

"How do you know him?" Mason persisted.

"I only saw him last night," muttered Pagan. Her heart remained a weight in the center of her chest. This world was incompatible with her kind. Her friends might as well be rocks, stones, the mud on river bottoms, for all their worth here. There were but two choices: to move on, or to make at least a portion of this world compatible. Pagan was in no mood or condition to journey onward.

Mason was growing agitated now. "Where? Where did you see him last night? What was he doing?"

"He was with Mister Wolfe," Pagan said. She turned around. In front of a place to sit squatted a low rectangular table. It too had been ripped from a sap-kith. It did not smell quite right, as if the surface were maple, but the interior had come from some other living source. Pagan's nose wrinkled. Yes, bitter. Pine, she thought. Perhaps spruce.

What kind of creatures lived on this world, that they thought to elevate the status of an inferior wood by concealing it within a shell of a sap-kith? As if the exterior were all that mattered. Beauty was in the soul, the very spirit . . .

Mason grabbed her by the shoulder and spun her around. In that moment Pagan snarled. Mason's eyes widened, and she savored the fear in them before seizing him by his collar and crotch and lifting him overhead. His struggles were as nothing, and she had no ears for his cries, not now. With the effort one might brush away an insect, she cast him into the opening under the slab of maple. Bones snapped audibly, and Mason lay limp. Spots of red began to appear on his shoulder, an arm, a leg, and a shaft of pink-white protruded through his trousers and through a widening crimson puddle.

Pagan studied the rack and the quartered sections of wood it contained. On top was a metal container filled with a pungent and somewhat alcoholic liquid. Beside it sat a small, oblong box that smelled faintly of phosphorus. Fire, Pagan thought. This was what they used to ignite the skeletal shards. She would have to be careful.

She emptied the container onto Mason, and then, holding a match as if it were about to explode in her hand, struck it on the side of the box. The orange flame frightened her, she who had journeyed between stars. The smoke from it stung her nostrils. She cast the match onto Mason, turned away, and departed from his house.

Montclair, she thought, standing in the walkway between the rows of orange flowers and sucking in great gulps of air laden with the aromas of her kith. Montclair was the enemy of Mason and Mister Wolfe. Perhaps he would prove to be her friend. She needed *someone*. In time on Dholin she might have taken one of the Others to herself for her need, when none of her own kith were near, but here she also had to find someone who could help her grasp the ways of this new, adopted world. Someone who could help her change that which was so terribly wrong.

Above, the yellow sun had begun its descent toward the far horizon. In the heat of the day Pagan basked in the sunlight and yet shivered. On this world with just the one star to warm it, she could be vulnerable if she failed to absorb enough light to last her till the morning. A cloudy day or a storm might put her at risk. She might bring kith across, but the intensity of such transfers required energy. Finding a friend could put her at ease, at least until she was able to make the necessary living adjustments.

Flying as to another world, Pagan returned to the village and to the gathering she had seen. From the air the building was not difficult to find, but the people in front of it had dispersed. Her movements quick and darting, she avoided detection, and came to ground beside a willow whose leggy stems kissed the creek that flowed behind it and afforded her cover.

At the gathering, Pagan recalled, Montclair had encased his lower body in blue and upper in gray. Her eyes took in the building and the street and the vehicles, and found no one who matched her memory of him. On the far side of the street a vehicle very much like Mason's was parked, with two occupants, one in front, the other in back, the alignment in which she had ridden with Mason. The figure in back resembled what she remembered of Montclair.

More swiftly than the eye could follow, Pagan darted to the back door of the vehicle. The handle of the door broke off in her hands, and at the sound the man inside looked out at her. It *was* Montclair, and Pagan felt a momentary relief.

By this time the driver had emerged, his face taut with anger. He aimed a pistol at Pagan. "Hands on top of the car, and spread 'em," he shouted.

Pagan, not quite certain what he wanted, tried to pass him the door handle. His eyes widened when he spotted the remains of Mason's handcuffs like bracelets on her wrists. Flashes of light emerged from the pistol, accompanied by three sharp but brief thunderclaps, and Pagan felt three tugs at her body. Sap began to leak inside her, and while she repaired that damage she snagged the pistol from the driver and wadded it up in her hands, and cast it aside. Mouth agape, the driver turned and fled.

Montclair was pounding on the door. Pagan dug her fingertips into the seal of the door, and pulled it off the car. Montclair, staring at her, bumped his head against the doorframe as he emerged. Pagan heard shouting, and the sound of a car horn. People were pointing in her direction.

"We have to leave here," Pagan told Montclair.

Instinctively she knew to avoid an open display of her differences by simply flying off with Montclair. Even on Dholin, where the Others were at least friendly despite their inept management of the planet, it was considered prudent not to accentuate the differences between species by overt displays of physical prowess. Seeking cover and concealment, Pagan looked around. The small park behind them offered the possibility of both. She swept Montclair across the grass with her toward the stand of cultivated trees and shrubs in the center of the park, her brisk darting scarcely slowed by the drag of his bulk. His pale eyes were wide with fear and consternation as he struggled in vain against the circle of her arms. Pagan's abrupt changes of direction shook him as if he were nothing more than a stuffed doll and stifled any protests he might have made.

Directly they had reached the cover of the trees Pagan thrust him against a massive oak trunk and held him there at arm's length while she peered around the trunk at the street. People were gesticulating in her direction, but without accuracy. Two men attired as Mason had been were staring at the park, searching for anything that did not belong. Pagan decided against altering her skin color to blend with the foliage. To be fully camouflaged she would have to disrobe, and in any case Montclair would be visible, once spotted.

Montclair was tearing at her hand, pressed against his throat to hold him in place. "Can't breathe," he croaked, unable to budge her.

Pagan lowered her hand to his chest and pressed there, still confining him. His heart pounded against her palm.

"What the hell *are* you?" he managed, coughing.

"You are not like Mason?" Pagan asked him.

"What? The sheriff? No, I'm . . . he's . . . what do you mean?"

"He uses my kith for his own pleasure," said Pagan. "Do you also do this?"

"I don't know what you mean. Who *are* you? Deputy Bradley *shot* you. I *saw* him. How---?"

Pagan ducked back behind the tree. "They will come to look for us. Can you fly?"

"Can I *what?* No, I---"

Pagan scooped him up in her arms, cutting off the rest of his response. Using the thick foliage to cover her flight, she lifted into the air, a great dragonfly flitting hither and yon. Any observers below would only have thought they saw something, but looking again, would see nothing. Over houses and buildings they soared. Montclair was rigid in her arms. Pagan could smell his fear in the thin sap that oozed from his skin. For a short time he had stared down at the village, but now as they began to pass over forests and small farms his eyes were closed. He could not bear to look.

I know that feeling, thought Pagan. The stack of cordwood beside the place of fire still sickened her heart. Cordwood, she cried silently. To these Others my sap-kith are to be burned for their warmth and pleasure.

Monsters!

Montclair cried out in pain. She had squeezed him in her arms.

221

She had not meant to. "Sorry," she whispered, over the rush of air.

"What. *Are.* You?"

Abruptly Pagan changed direction, arcing now over a paved road that she recognized as leading to her place of first descent. Mason had asked her that same question, with the same amount of intense amazement in his voice. She had had no answer for him then, nor had she one now. She knew many words, thousands of words, taken from television and from conversation, and not one of them had referred to her. The closest had been "vampire," but that was merely an indelicate approximation. In a parallel manner she fed and brought forth her own kind, insofar as she understood their methods from an advertisement for *Dark Shadows*, but she had never before regarded Others as inimical or subservient. Metaphorically speaking, Others were useful whenever an itch had to be scratched, but by and large on Dholin they had kept respectfully to themselves. On this world of Earth, it was clear to her now that Others lived in opposition to her. They feared her. She knew that they would try to kill what they feared. She had seen it on television.

She understood Mason's handcuffs now. They were meant to restrain her, confine her. She had broken them as casually as she might have swatted an insect. Montclair was unable to fly, yet she could fly, and dart here and there almost invisibly on the ground, certainly faster than the eyes of the Others could follow. She could lift---

Pagan shifted her grasp of Montclair, and for an instant her arms did not support him, and he fell a couple of inches before she recovered. He cried out. He was afraid she would drop him.

"I will not drop you," she said.

"Tell me what you are," pleaded Montclair. "A witch? I did not believe in witches, yet the evidence of my own eyes tells me---"

"A witch," Pagan repeated. "Yes."

Rather to her surprise Montclair seemed to relax at this. His identification of her had given him solace. Her existence, even if incredible, made sense to him. She raked her mind for references. In the three and a half hours she had watched television, its programs and commercials, she had heard that word and another similar to it in reference to women. A witch cast spells, used magic, and flew astride cleaning implements. But a witch was also someone whose powers were feared and misunderstood. Pagan saw how that might apply to her.

"Yes, a witch," she said again.

"What do you want with me?"

"I *need* you," answered Pagan.

They had reached the edge of the forest where Montclair had killed Mister Wolfe. The yellow streamers were still in place, but she saw no vehicles, not even that which belonged to Miz Vartan, the resident of the Winnebago. She might descend with Montclair unnoticed. She did so.

Montclair stumbled when Pagan released him, and sat down heavily on the grass. For a moment he remained there, looking up at her, eyes wide with astonishment and a bit of curiosity. He no longer smelled afraid, as if he now supposed that because she had brought him safely to this place when she might easily have killed him, he was in no immediate danger.

But Montclair also knew where he was. "You saw me," he said. Dryness made his voice gravelly. "Last night, you saw me here."

Pagan drifted toward saplings. Already she felt the kith-call. Within her sap surged, and stormy seas roared in her ears. A mighty effort suppressed her need; this was not the time, not yet. There were things she had to know. Her fingers trailed along supple branches and curled around a bole. She swung round to face Montclair, who only now had risen to his feet. He stood with hands at his sides, weight on the balls of his feet, poised to flee or to listen.

"These are my kith," said Pagan. Before he could question the word, she added, "My people. Sheriff Mason harmed them. Sheriff Mason wished to harm you because you killed Mister Wolfe. I believe you do not wish to harm my people, and that is why they oppose you. That is why I have brought you here. I wish to know who you are."

Montclair straightened, and relaxed a little. For long seconds he gazed back at her, his expression unfathomable. Again Pagan felt the rush of sap within her, the pounding of seas, but now the lifebeat was uncertain. Had she grasped the conflict accurately? Nothing was ever simple, but surely---

"These trees," said Montclair. "These trees are your people? You live in the forest?"

Pagan's heart soared. Perhaps he did understand. "I am the forest," she told him.

The look on his face slowed her heart. She felt diminished. He did *not* understand.

"Mister Wolfe owned a company that was chopping trees down indiscriminately," said Montclair, addressing her initial question. "We went to court to try to stop him, and our case was denied. We did receive an injunction against further harvesting during the appeals process, but he violated this injunction and we have received no redress."

"I have no idea what you are talking about," said Pagan. She drifted further into the forest, wending between trees and watching him out of the corner of her eye to see whether he would follow. He did, slowly and reluctantly. "Why was Mister Wolfe chopping down trees?" she asked.

Montclair pushed foliage from his path. "He owned a company that wanted to build a mall here. He bought the land, but the people of LeClerc did not want the mall. When he started to clear the land, we tried to stop him. After all, these trees are our livelihood."

"What is livelihood?"

Montclair gave her a funny look. "You're not from around here, are you?"

Pagan leaned back against a sugar maple and folded her arms across her chest. "I came here from Dholin."

"Where is that? New York? New Jersey?"

Once again his words meant nothing to her. Soon enough she would learn, perhaps from him. But was he friend, or was he foe? She had to know.

Montclair came to a stop some five paces from her, clearly unwilling to approach any closer. Pagan caught just a whiff of fear, but it stemmed from uncertainty now, and not of what she was capable of doing to him. Within her, *need* was still awake and hopeful. It would be easier to couple with Montclair, to ease that need, than to bring a kith across. Thus it had been on Dholin, until the Others had destroyed the planet and themselves with it. But here on Earth . . . Montclair seemed unaware that he might ease her need.

The thought of him now incited her, and almost against her will she swung round to face the maple. Legs apart, she pressed herself against the trunk and began a series of brief vertical movements. Her mouth was half open, and she gasped for breath, and stopped. Control, she thought. I *need*. But I need control more.

"What *are* you doing?"

"I *need*," whispered Pagan. "I need you."

Again she moved, and wrapped her right leg around the trunk to increase the pressure against her. Her calf struck something hard and metallic. Puzzled, she peered around the trunk. A container hung there, a semi-circle of metal wire looped over something that resembled the faucet she had seen inside the Winnebago. One end of the faucet had been inserted into the bark. From the other end, open and bent downward, viscous beads formed and oozed into the container.

All air left Pagan, and she dropped to her knees, gulping like a fish out of water. She felt ill. Her insides churned. Thunderstorm emotions blurred her vision momentarily, and she leaned a shoulder against the trunk to steady herself. Finally, with a huge effort, she ripped the faucet from the bark and cast it aside as if it were something loathsome. Her mouth felt tighter--the canines were extending, fed by the power of her rage and outrage.

She stood up and whirled around. Montclair retreated until branches stopped him. "*What is this?*" she snarled. "*What are you doing?*"

Montclair looked bewildered. He glanced around as if seeking an escape route. "That's a tap. We take the sap and boil it and make maple syrup with it, and sell it. That's our livelihood. What did you suppose?"

Pagan felt simultaneously powerful and feeble. The enormity of what these monsters were doing to her kith left her weak with rage, yet it was the rage that lent her strength in this moment. Her eyes became orbs of deepest jade, with a tiny pinpoint of flame in each. To think that she had actually wanted to slake her *need* with this . . . Other, with this *monster*. There could be no compromise, not now, not after what she had learned about them.

Montclair turned and fled, branches whipping at him as he rushed through the foliage. Pagan did not pursue him. Soon enough, when she was ready, she would find him. She would deal with him. With *all* of them.

A series of deep breaths calmed her soul and gave her will and purpose. Canines fully extended now, she sank them into the bark of the sugar maple. Rich sweet sap gushed into her mouth, and she drank, hungrily at first and then deliberately. The trunk felt good against her body, and she wrapped her legs around it to draw it even closer, to join with its spirit. But there was no urgency now. Her need could wait. She swallowed a last dollop of sap, then sank her teeth into her arm. Pain was something remote, pale against the act of creation that was upon her. She thrust the wound of the arm against the wound in the bark that her teeth had made. Sap mixed with sap. The sensation was not ecstasy, but a harbinger of it.

Need need need, she thought.

Soon, she told herself.

She disengaged herself from the tree and stepped back. Dappled by sunlight, the tree shimmered. She drew the clothes from her body and cast them aside. It had been a sacrilege to attire herself as an Other of *this* world. Never again would she compromise with them. But she would make this world safe, for herself and for her kith.

For *all* her kith. Everywhere.

The sound behind her she had never heard before, yet it was as familiar to her as her own sapflow. Bark shifted and parted, to the sound of a coarse hissing. Foliage shifted, and still she did not turn around. Her own sap quickened with her excitement as she felt a mild impact in the earth beneath her feet.

Pagan sensed her creation, and heard a whispered, "*Qui etes-vous?*" Then, uncertainly: "*Et qui suis-je?*"

The words meant nothing to her. Perhaps he---

She sighed. *He.*

226

She turned around. Of her kind he was, with the same gray-green hair and the same green eyes and same pale skin. Like her he was slender and wiry, and of her own age, as had been the tree from which she had freed him. Sugar maple he might be, but right now he was as hard as oak.

Sapflow made her groin sticky.

"*Qui suis-je?*" he asked again, and this time Pagan was able to sense his meaning through their kithness. *Who am I?*

Pagan had many answers for him. He was the first of many that she, the sap-mother, would lead out to destroy those Others who would harm and abuse her and her kind. He would be her consort, her Second. He, too, would create more sapkith like him and like her. Massed, they would secure this world for themselves.

But first . . .

She tapped at the lush grass with her bare foot, and sat down, motioning him to join her there. He did so without hesitation. Already he had fallen under her spell, yielded to her will. Instinct took control of her, yet it was tempered, for now she would explain to him who she was and who he was to her.

She would explain this to him very slowly and very, very thoroughly.

The Martian Women

1: crucible

Fourcade waited behind the defense table while the woman's resolute strides swept her toward the witness stand. A dozen times, in and out of the courtroom, he had protested the convening of the United Nations Court of Special Prosecutions, to no avail. That she was a citizen of the United States afforded her no protection whatsoever. Too many other countries had been adversely affected by what she had done—or so they had howled. To be fair, he thought, too many *international corporations* had been affected, and their screams of anguish had brought about the temporary constitution of the UNCSP. And the loudest scream of all had been emitted by MarsCorp.

Balm had to be applied to the economic gonads she had kicked, the damage contained, if possible. If she could be discredited...if further dissemination of her discovery could be prevented. Fourcade chuckled silently. *If she could be cast into a dungeon for a millennium.* Already the hierarchs had positioned themselves to act, and their corporate power transcended territorial boundaries. Any two countries might disagree with each other's policies, might even be at war with one another, but a corporation might conduct peaceful and profitable trade with both. In the previous century the United States had decried the terrorism of Iran while importing its dates and oil, had accused China of violations of child and slave labor laws while importing goods manufactured as a result of those violations...had even purchased items of Chinese manufacture for American military uniforms. Business as usual.

The woman had disrupted business as usual, the most heinous and grievous of offenses. Over the past several months enough national leaders, including those of her United States, had been "convinced" by the economic powers behind the thrones that her transgression was planetary in scope, and she was convicted and sentenced.

First, however, she had to be tried. What was to be done to her had to be made legal. Accordingly, she was charged with "population endangerment," a legal contrivance as vaguely defined as "crimes against humanity." In no country on Earth was population endangerment a crime. Although "public endangerment" was prohibited, it referred to such acts as discharging a firearm harmlessly inside a public library, or driving one's vehicle along the center island. Population endangerment was an *ex post facto* crime, and referred only and specifically to what she had done, *after* she had done it.

The charge should have been laughed out of court. But, like the offense, the UNCSP was itself an artifice. The case had long been decided, the verdict rendered. She would have her day in court only to maintain the facade of a fair trial. We will have our way with her, said the hierarchs, through the judicial panel, which overruled all substantial defense objections.

The trial was almost over. Her testimony would bring it to a close.

Slowly Fourcade looked over his shoulders, left, then right. Spacious as a cathedral, the courtroom was filled but not full. He recognized few faces. Conigliaro, of course, from MarsCorp, its Chair of Operations. Akres was there, the President's Chief of Staff. An expert witness, he had already testified to the drop of morale among the men on the Orbital Processing Station after she became the first woman asteroidier, and to the subsequent decline in profits. An odd decline, Fourcade had attempted to elicit through testimony, for production had actually *increased* during the period of her employment. But the prosecution had raised objections on the basis of relevancy, and these had been perfunctorily sustained. The message was clear: evidence was irrelevant and immaterial, because the verdict had been reached before the court had convened. Even Conner's powerful testimony in her favor as a character witness had been squelched. Helpless, Fourcade had retreated to the defense table. *She* had warmed him then with a smile that scarcely tickled the corners of her mouth, and had touched his arm, and he had quelled the urge to go out and slay monsters. He had not far to go, he knew; he was surrounded by them.

She reached the witness stand, wearing for the occasion of her testimony not formal attire but the outsuit of a Spaceworker, this one pale emerald, and she looked, he reflected, like Joan of Arc while they had tied her to the stake—she knew what they were going to do to her, but she was somehow beyond it all. She waited in front of the stand while the bailiff affirmed her in, oblivious to his frown of disapproval and disgust when she failed even to acknowledge by a downward glance the Holy Bible which he presented to her left hand. At 180 centimeters she was his equal in height, and her arctic gray eyes gazed steadily into his, as if studying her own reflection there.

Striking in appearance, she was not beautiful, not even pretty, as men regarded these qualities. She had hair the color of fresh cinnamon, which she wore long and loose in defiance of the current trend. She had the delicate freckled complexion of the true redhead, lightly tanned by spatial ultraviolet. She had a straight nose that had been broken on two occasions—once by a fall into one of the internal support struts on an Orbiter, and once by a man who subsequently accepted No for an answer. She had other answers of equal clarity. In response to the bailiff's recited solicitation of Truth, Fourcade heard the words, "I do," but he saw her lips form a different pronoun and verb, in a different sequence. The bailiff stiffened, about to protest, but already she had turned and seated herself behind the stand without invitation.

The presiding judge, garbed in a robe that in Fourcade's opinion was better suited to a Ringmaster than to a Chief Justice, demanded that she state her name, residence, and occupation for the court records, and she complied in a clear contralto that required no amplification to carry to the rear of the courtroom and to the pre-selected members of the media seated in the jury booth along the wall to her left. She stated her full name, adding, "Aboard the *Ennis*. Asteroidier."

Chief Justice Krishnaman demanded clarification of her address. "My 'skip," she said tersely. Inwardly Fourcade winced. She had neglected to add the courtesy tag, "Your Honor," despite his advice, his pleas.

"Surely there are berths available in the Mars Orbiters or in the Outer Processing Stations, *M'selle* Timberlake."

Fourcade relaxed slightly. At least the judge had not called her Traci. Courtroom decorum aside, to have done so would not have elicited a desirable response from her.

The woman's thin lips parted in a bleak smile. "There are rules there."

Someone in the back of the courtroom applauded her response, and Krishnaman issued a general caution against further outbursts. "What, exactly, is the function of an asteroidier?"

Again her response was tight and direct. "I locate, identify, analyze, attach, transport, and deliver asteroid shards that warrant processing for mineral content."

"For a fee."

"Of course."

"And to whom do you deliver these asteroids?"

"MarsCorp."

"Do you understand the charges against you, *M'selle?*"

"I am *aware* of the charges against me."

"Then a reiteration of them would seem in order here."

Fourcade rose. "Your Honor, I believe the testimony of my client will address each of the several charges."

Krishnaman conferred in whispers with his two colleagues. Fourcade, reading faces, predicted the vote two to one, the balance uncertain.

"See that it does, Counsellor. Proceed."

Fourcade remained standing behind the defense table. His task, as he now saw it, was to lead her through her day in court. At this, he felt a twinge of guilt. By encouraging her to play it their way, he granted sanction to their actions. But he knew no other rules. He owed fealty to the law, to procedure. She worshipped a different god, one which, he hoped for her sake, would not manifest itself in the courtroom.

"*M'selle*, on Earthdate 17 March 2102 you embarked upon *Ennis* Mission 113. Would you please describe in your own words—"

The woman shook her head once, side to side, slowly, gravely. "This is *my* testimony," she said, as if that fact had somehow been forgotten.

Krishnaman considered this. "We do not have a lot of time, Counsellor."

"No," said the woman. "You don't."

Fourcade displayed a stack of papers. "I respectfully submit this narrative, as composed by the defendant, be entered into the record. In order to spare the court a lengthy testimony, her oral statement," he glanced at the prosecution bench, "by prior agreement will reflect only the substance of this document."

"So ordered," said Krishnaman. "Proceed."

2: legacy - Traci's story

I had just finished stowing the last two plastic containers of my allotment of fuel water aboard the *Ennis* when the hangar intercom paged me to the UniRes Dispatch Center. I almost didn't go—the front office and I have yet to negotiate a non-aggression pact. But they controlled the fuel water, and they bought the asteroid shards I mined. It is not a symbiotic relationship. More like parasitism. So I played host once again.

The receptionist shifted nervously in her seat when I entered the anteroom. She was a pale young thing from Mars Colony, up here to wait for her husband to complete his tour and/or to get pregnant. In the meantime, the job gave her something to do. Already she had developed a twitch in the corner of her mouth from the anxiety brought about by the occupational hazard of having to deal with men where they outnumbered the women. I gave her a sympathetic nod as I walked past her desk toward the open doorway. Maybe she would survive the ordeal, maybe not.

Conner stood against the rear bulkhead, facing me, hands jammed into the utility pockets of his outsuit. He acknowledged me with a curt nod that dislodged a lock of sepia hair. I sighed just loud enough for him to hear. "What is it now?"

"You're temporarily grounded," he said, without as much relish as I might have expected.

"Last time you tried that, profits diminished eleven percent during the report period. Or is MarsCorp past caring?"

Conner drew himself up to his full height, which was about half a hand below my meter eighty. "It isn't official, Timberlake. The next shuttle is carrying some cargo of yours. It's due to dock in an hour."

At least he'd gotten the name right. I'd weaned him from Traci by walking out of the room in his mid-sentence, the last three times in front of a small audience. Some men are slow learners. But Conner had learned, and he was far from the worst supervisor I'd had on these tours, so I softened. "A cargo of what?"

He sat down at the work table and keyed a few commands into the rolopad. "Personal shipments and cargo generally aren't authorized here because of mass and space limitations. As you know," he added quickly, before I could tell him I already knew as much. "I'd guess it to be in compliance with corporate regulations. You weren't expecting it?"

I shook my head. "What's on the bill of lading?"

He'd called it up to the inlaid desk monitor. "It says it's a steamer trunk. What the *hell* is a steamer trunk?"

"A portable sauna?" At least I knew why Dispatch hadn't simply advised me of the arrival over the station intercom. Someone else, curious, might have asked Conner the same question, and prattled to others of his ignorance. Defaulting himself to me was safe...and mentally I shook my head to clear it of the compliment, resisting the brief temptation to consider weaning him back to Traci. "So I'm cleared after it arrives. I'll be in the cafeteria."

The anteroom had one more occupant when I returned. I didn't recognize him, but he wore a mining-class outsuit, like mine. He stood leaning over the front of the receptionist's desk. I had a fairly good idea of what he was saying, because she was looking everywhere but at him.

"She's married, chum," I said, against my better judgment.

He ignored me as I passed them.

A little voice inside my head cautioned me against perverse forms of satisfaction, and I duly ignored it. "Well, it's not my problem, is it? You'll never tumble *me*, so who cares if you catch it?"

I wondered how many steps I could take toward the corridor. His voice caught me at four. "Hang on, then. What's she got?"

"I don't know for certain," I said, hesitation meant to convey reluctance. "Her husband picked up a solid case of measle-chancres while on Earth furlough. Screams when he pisses, and all that. But from what I understand, it doesn't take long to cure."

The chum faked a smile at her. "Gotta run. Loading to do, and all that. Maybe I'll see you later."

I waited until the door slid shut behind him. "They *may* leave you alone for a while."

Her eyes filled with tears. "How *could* you? Rich will *kill* me if...if..."

"What's your name?"

She told me, and I cringed. But humanity had re-entered one of those sociological *psychles* where men applied cute little diminutives to women as a subtle reminder of which sex was in possession of the other. Traci was hardly more mature, but I had given it to myself.

"Right, Patsy, just before he returns, have the medic give you a checkup and have it certified. Make sure it's the first thing Rich sees. How long have you been married?"

She sniffled, and dried her eyes. "Not even a year."

"And how long has he been away?"

"Almost two months."

"Ah, make it the *second* thing Rich sees. And don't even show him at all, unless he mentions the problem."

"I still wish you hadn't interfered."

I began edging toward the doorway. "Once you yield, it's open season. You know that."

"I guess so. You're the one they call...you're Timberlake, aren't you?"

"I know what they call me. And yes, I am."

"The one who named her spaceskip after her grandmother."

"Great-great-grandmother. Ennis Timberlake."

She flashed an uncertain smile. "Do you really think they'll leave me alone?"

"That's up to you, isn't it? And...you can trust Conner to help you, if you ask him. But if you tell him I said so, I'll start a rumor about you that you'll *never* live down." I waved her a see-you-around, and walked out.

As usual, the cafeteria smelled as if someone had overnuked mildewed styroplast. I took the first table to the left of the entrance, where the air was freshest. In the far corner a group of mining vets hassled one of the new chums, a young man too green to defend himself against the hazing. Someone tripped him, and he fell, sloshing coffee everywhere. While he was down, two vets mopped him back and forth over the spill. It was none of my concern. I keyed the coder on the wall for COFFEE BLACK, and gingerly tugged the hot cup from the chute.

Steamer trunk...what the hell was I going to do with a steamer trunk, whatever it was? All of my very few personal possessions were stored in the cargo hold aboard the *Ennis*. There was nothing else in the Universe that I needed, except, right now, a good cup of coffee. I took a tentative sip, and tasted failure.

The commotion in the corner waned. I stared off into inner space and withdrew from the outside world, mulling over my credit account, my immediate plans, and my future. I saw a little more than 11,000 MarVals, a chunk of iron I had spotted on my previous trip Out, and...a vast, unfathomable darkness. So many things I might do one sol. Volunteer for cryogenic hibernation and a trip to the stars. See what Earth was like. Explore the atmosphere of Titan. Of a certainty I would not spend the remainder of my life hunting and retrieving asteroids.

"Um, hello."

It was the new chum. Curiosity lent a glow to his green eyes, as if he was not quite certain what he was about. Space is a bad place to have that look. He seemed about my age, twenty six, but the coffee stains and the rumpled outsuit could have added a year or two. He had been set up by the vets, of course. Let the Ice Witch shred him. But the chum had not offended me, and I was not feeling especially combative.

"Do us both a favor," I said gently. "There are five other empty tables. Claim one."

"Okay," he agreed, and got back to his feet.

I am impulsive to a fault—it's how I lost my virginity—but I usually activate my brain before enabling my mouth. Not this time. "No, wait. Sit back down. What's your name?"

"Allan."

"And were your parents acquainted?"

So help me, he blushed. "O'Toole."

"I'm Timberlake. What did they tell you to do here?"

Scarlet seemed his favorite color. "They said you were a..."

"Don't mince words with me. It's not as if *you* said it."

He swallowed hard. "A layover."

That was a new term. "And that possibility encouraged you to approach me?"

"Well, no."

"You mean you would turn down an easy tumble?"

"Well, no. I mean, yes." Angry jade eyes glared at me. "You're confusing me."

"You're confusing yourself, I think. Do you prefer easy or difficult access in relationships?"

He shifted in the chair, crossing his legs under the table, and uncrossing them. I guessed he feared their laughter more than what I might push him to. "I don't know what you—"

"Belay all after, O'Toole. Which of them put you onto this?"

"The one called Konradt." I barked a laugh, and he asked, "Do you know him?"

I recalled a thug of that name who had tried to force me in one of the alternate corridors a year earlier. He was stronger, more massive, and persistent. There was nowhere for me to run, no help to call. I knew a few moves. I tried two or three and learned that he had read the same book, or at least looked at the pictures. When he got himself down to the bare essentials, I pointed to it and laughed loudly, and said, with great clarity. "That's *all* you have?" His breath had exploded as if I had hit him in the stomach with a mining hammer. I had walked away, still laughing.

"We've met, briefly. He wasn't up to the task he'd set himself. I guess that makes you his surrogate. You're out of luck, too."

I leaned back and surveyed O'Toole in the harsh artificial light.

Maybe his lashes were too long, his facial bones too delicate—certainly he looked too vulnerable for the profession to which he aspired. With the hazing, they might have broken him in short order. Emptied of fundamental human decency, he would accept their misbegotten notions of masculine behavior. I drummed my fingers on the table top, trying to beat an absurd inspiration into submission.

"Do you have a spaceskip lined up yet, O'Toole?"

"Uh, I'm not sure. Pavlov is supposed to go out in a few days, and Konradt said I *might* be able to hitch on with him."

Don't do this, Traci...

"If you hitch with me, you do exactly *what* I tell you to do, *when* I tell you, and you will probably survive your apprenticeship."

"You're serious?"

Maybe there was something behind those pale eyes that I could not define, some inner strength. Perhaps I was making a fatal error in judgment. O'Toole's inexperience could get him killed, which would be too bad. It could also get me killed, which would grievously annoy me.

But I still owed Konradt. Deliberately I got up, rounded the table, and kissed O'Toole full on the lips. After the initial stiffness of surprise, they yielded, and blossomed briefly before I withdrew. "You're hitched," I said.

The intercom chose that particular moment to page me to the Dispatch Center, drowning out his response.

O'Toole struggled with the trunk until I grabbed a handle and helped him lug it aboard the *Ennis*. Bulky, and large enough for me to fit comfortably inside, it had been constructed of a hard and rough material, which, after a deep dredge of my memory, I tentatively identified as wood, a dark, aged, hard wood. Hinges of ancient iron in back and a very sturdy hasp down the middle of the front secured the lid. The key to the hasp had arrived with the bill of lading and was now safely deposited in an outsuit pouch. Around the seam between the lid and the body of the trunk were simple flat strips of a dull gray metal, possibly zinc. All eight corners of the trunk were protected by round iron bulbs burnished and dented by travel and by time.

A steamer trunk.

It was, as stated on the bill of lading, a family heirloom, as were the unidentified contents. I had known for years that I would inherit something, but because I was the sole surviving heir there was no one left to tell me just what that might entail. The conditions of the bequest stated only that I would be allowed to take possession of my inheritance, *i.e.*, the steamer trunk and its contents, upon reaching the age of twenty five. Tired of waiting for me to make Marsfall, Storage had shipped it up.

After stowing the trunk in the personal cargo hold I attended our departure. O'Toole sealed the main hatch and sat down, uninvited, in the starboard captain's chair. After we had secured our seat straps, I toggled intercom and announced us.

"*Ennis*, you are cleared for departure in forty seconds from my mark. Mark!"

"Counting, Center. And remind Conner that I get Apprentice Credit for this trip, so my cargo counts double. He tends to forget these things."

Conner's baritone came through the transceiver. "Don't clog the freqs, *Ennis*."

"I hear and obey, O Mighty Center. Ten and counting."

The initial burst of one gee cleared us from the off-load dock. Another programmed burst took us to one point three on a trajectory that led to the outer belt.

Retrieval of an asteroid of exploitable size is not as complicated as the men have made it out to be. With MarsCorp Engineering's development of the Retriever Model AX9rM, of which my *Ennis* was a modified example, a single individual can frankbuck an asteroid. Drilling and towing are the fundamental skills required for success. It is necessary to drillsink two braces into any unfractured portion of the surface of the asteroid, linkchain the braces to the motive power, and gently tug the asteroid toward the Orbital Metal Processing Point. A certain amount of finesse is required. Properly, one applies a gradual acceleration of 0.001 meters per second squared until the maximum permissible velocity is reached as calculated by the 'skipcomp, said maximum including in its resolution inertia, momentum, and available braking distance. Manifestly, some retrievals require a Standard month or more to complete, while others take days, even hours. The 'skip and asteroid dock as a unit in the OMPP, the 'skip is detached, and I get paid. Simple.

A knowledge of lithology is helpful in the field. Obviously, it would not do to drillsink braces into faulty rock, nor would it be profitable to retrieve olivine or silicon. Also obviously (to me), none of the requirements of the profession are grounded in gender.

To me...but not to O'Toole. Over styrocups of real steaming coffee properly brewed in my very own galley from real beans actually smuggled from Earth (Sulawesi, if it matters), he asked the ancient question about nice girls and places like these.

"I locate, retrieve, and sell asteroids to MarsCorp, O'Toole. What did you think?"

"You know what I mean."

"Also, I'm not a nice girl."

At that he averted his eyes, pretending to study something in the Visor above the instrumentation console. As the contents consisted of one or two stars and a lot of intense indigo, I wondered what held his attention. Something in his tone suggested that the probe had been amiable, even ingenuous. But I was wandering into unfamiliar territory, unaccustomed to company on the bridge.

"What...am I supposed to call you?" he asked.

"What would you have called Konradt?"

"Skipper."

"Spot on. How old are you, O'Toole?"

"Twenty one."

I swore at the Universae at large. "Mind telling me *how* you managed to soak up three years of UnivTech studies, two years of *in situ* training, and assorted time periods of applications, medical examinations, and other impedimenta, between your eighteenth birthday and now?"

"I entered the University when I was fourteen," he said quietly, not quite ashamed of the revelation.

"You did *what*? Was UMars aware of your age?"

239

"Oh, yes."

"Either you have connections or you have brains, O'Toole. Odds favor the former, but I hope for both our sakes it's the latter."

"Why?"

"Because you can't use your connections out here to get the work done. I don't care if you are Conigliaro's *sole heir*, it won't make any dif—"

"Who?"

"Conigliaro? You *have* heard of him? He only owns MarsCorp."

"Oh, yes. He really owns the corporation?"

I permitted the diversion. "Maybe forty five percent of stock, and he is the largest shareholder. O'Toole, do you understand what I've been telling you? This is not virtual reality out here. It is not a classroom. If you do something stupid and get yourself killed, I'll cluck and tisk and hoist a private drink in your memory. If you get me killed, I'm really going to be annoyed."

He sobered. "I'll try not to annoy you, Skipper."

"We'll reach the zone in fifteen hours. Finish that, then hie yourself to the sleeper. You get five hours before I wake you."

I gave O'Toole half an hour to fall asleep, then went aft to the cargo hold to inventory my inheritance. Kneeling on the deck beside the steamer trunk, I tried to remember her. In her younger days, I supposed, she looked like me. Mom I had called her, though she was not, *could not* have been my mother. She had died almost twelve years ago, on the day I had kind of borrowed Mister Forrest's ATV to show him that a girl could *too* operate it. Unfortunately, I had kind of operated it in the direction of Olympus Mons, and by the time I had returned she was dead. Under the circumstances no one tasked me for what I had done, not even Mister Forrest, who gave me a passing grade in social studies, although I was anything but social. There was a cremation, and a reading of the will at which the audience consisted of myself, but I was not paying a lot of attention at the time, suffering from enormous disillusionment. I had assumed that she, like myself, was immortal and would always be there.

Unfuckingtrue. *Not true...*

Shiny wet spots appeared on the top of the trunk. Angrily I thumbed the tears from my cheeks, savoring the physical pain to ward off the emotional. Presently, hands shaking, I drew the key from my pouch and inserted it into the hasp, and twisted. The hasp snapped out audibly, and I snatched my hand away. I don't know what else I expected—a hiss of air perhaps, or a flight of ghosts. I pushed the lid up before I could change my mind.

Dust particles released from the trunk activated the hold's air filter. It began to whirr like a dynamo, and little orange traces of Mars wafted up toward the grating, accompanied by whiffs of something musty. Peering inside, I caught sight of a yellowish cloth that had been stained here and there with a rich mahogany. It lay on top of several small square containers stacked in the far left corner, and I reached for it, urged on by a vague memory. Mine it had been once, consigned now to time past. I shook it free of dust, teasing the filter, and flicked it around my shoulders—digital memory, the way an amnesiac sews when presented with needle and thread. The cloth was a balm to my loss.

The contents of the trunk seemed to have been placed there in no particular sequence, organized according to categories of things that were alike. Another piece of cloth, blue this one, was just visible under a stack of loose sheets of brittle yellow paper. The fabric fragmented in my hands. There was a number in dark yellow, or part of one, sealed onto the material A six, or perhaps a nine. It vexed me that I had lost the memento before I understood its significance. I wondered whose it had been, and why it had come to be in the trunk. The only person who could tell me was dead.

Someone had written on the papers with a delicate but irregular hand, as if the writer had been educated but in great pain. The upper edge of each sheet was ragged, as if it had been torn from something. The top sheet crackled when I picked it up.

ration box, now certainly empty, on the utility shelf. I looked inside: not one chit remained. He had used it all.

I sat down on one of the stone slabs and cried and cried. Thoughts jumbled. I felt...angry, hurt, confused. Utterly despondent, emptier than the landscape. What was the use? Why bother? Why dream? The baby kicked me back to reality. I rested my hands on my stomach and felt the sharp blows, just below my rib cage. This was the baby Ron had wanted, had insisted on. After all, his buddies were fathers, right? I was obligated to equalize his status at work, right? I felt nauseated ...tasted bitter acid, and caught myself hating the baby...

Which of my ancestors had written the passage? And the others, to judge from the similarity of handwriting. I felt dim, distant. The past was here and now, but not yet a part of me. I poked around gingerly, slipping my hand under a rolled sleeping bag that still looked functional, and prodded something hard. It was a bound sheaf of papers. Cloth binding, cloth cover, still blue but fading. On the cover the words Daily Diary had been embossed in old gold, and below that a name...

...I almost dropped the relic. Heartbeats echoed off the walls of the hold as I clutched the diary. It was too precious to release, sacrilegious to touch. At any moment it might burn my hands, sear my mind. I returned the relic to the trunk. My hands tingled. I had touched it, I had touched *her*. I was now capable of miracles.

Before me, gathered by my ancestors for this particular moment, lay the personal history of the Timberlake women. One item I had already identified. But which of the other items belonged to whom? What else was in there? I noted a large brown envelope stuffed to capacity, and several clear plastic cartons of databalls that the sound heads in the bridge instrumentation console could accommodate, assuming that something had been recorded on them and that the recordings had survived magnetically. I might hark to the words of an ancient goddess. My hands trembled as I picked up the loose papers and began to read...

3: lineage - Korei's Story

...Ron and I had made for ourselves a good place to live. The habitation structure, built inside and into the crater, was sturdy and secure. Someone from the early years had hewn the vermilion

Martian stone by hand and constructed a quarters of four rooms and an outhouse, more than enough for our simple needs. Adjacent to the quarters stood the Parker, large enough for both our Solskips, and beside that was the solarium, where we raised a small crop. The acetex dome, added after the original builder had abandoned the dwelling, covered all three structures. From a distance the compound resembled one of those pueblos in the southwestern United States, except, of course, for the transparent dome. Someone else had blasted a cut through the crater wall, conveniently for us. I envisioned one more major project: expanding the solarium so that we might become self-sufficient in crops.

In practice, Mars already was viable, and had been for some time. I had a want list, but I could obtain locally anything I needed—except plants, which we had to import. I wanted berries, and maybe some dwarf fruit trees, like the ones I had seen in the Sears Diskalog. If I continued to work, we might be able to afford them.

I docked the Solskip in the Parker and slid the Domedoor shut before I went inside the quarters. Now that I was approaching the end of my term, I was less than enthusiastic about housecleaning. The quarters needed a good dusting, but assembling the blower was a major project, given my condition. I toed the dust on the bare floor and decided it could wait one more day. I opened a package of rations, set the nuke time, and waited for Ron to come Dome.

The baby kicked. It hurt, and felt good. Ron had spoken of our having five or six, but one was more than enough for now. It wasn't as if he had to lug them around. He had the easy part, a quirk of evolution. If ever I meet Charles Darwin, I will eviscerate him with a ladle. In the meantime, I closed my eyes and waited for the soccer match in my abdomen to subside.

The front door slid open. Before I had a chance to greet him, he grouched at the Universe. "First that *fucking* valve, then the clean-up," he began, and stepped on a tube of sealant that I had inadvertently dropped on the floor. "Dammit, Korei! Haven't you put the supplies away yet? Do I have to do everything around here?"

I apologized quickly. "I was just finishing up before you came Dome."

He kicked the tube at me, missing. "So finish with this! What's for dinner?"

"Rations." I could not bend over, so I squatted to retrieve the tube, hoping that his abuse had not put a hole in the lining. We needed the sealant to airtight the Domedoor before sandstorms. The five tubes we received every twenty days were sufficient, but the loss of even one could prove devastating, even fatal, if the sand forced open the door. I unfolded back to my feet and placed the tube next to the others on the utility shelf.

"Rations! What about those greens you said you were going to pick?"

"I didn't get Dome in time. I'm sorry, dear. I'll gather some tomorrow."

He jabbed a finger at me. "That job of yours is beginning to get on my nerves, you know that."

"You said I could earn some money to buy plants with."

"That doesn't mean I want to live in the outhouse, Korei." He stalked off toward the sleeper. "Call me when the fucking food is ready."

I knew he must have had a difficult time of it at work. I did not know which valve had aggravated him, but all of them in the Energy Complex were critical to the settlement's operation. Ron was one of only three specialists, at least until the next influx of Newbies. There had been four, but one of the older valves had gone awry somehow and killed its operator. Ron said that management was too cheap to replace the valves. From what I had heard from other sources, even the older equipment is self-maintaining, and all one has to do is keep an eye on things. I did not know much about Ron's work, though. Maybe the valves *were* a problem.

"It's ready," I called, when the nuke *bong*ed.

"I'm not hungry."

I trudged to the sleeper and stared down at him on the doublecot. "You mean I've fixed dinner for nothing?"

"I'm tired. I need to wind down. That ration crap will keep."

"It won't. It's not made for storage once it has been heated."

"That's not my problem," he said harshly. "That's *your* problem.

244

You're supposed to manage this sandtrap, so *manage* it."

"This 'sandtrap,' as you call it, is *our* Dome. *We're* making it a place to live."

Abruptly Ron sat up and glared at me, his face red, even the top of his head under the very short brown hair. I had no idea what I'd done to make him so angry. "You call *this* living? This is *crap*! It's all crap. Your damned solarium and your damned plants are crap. We're just here while I, while *I*, make enough money to get us back to Earth, where we belong."

My voice seemed to have departed just after my sense of hearing. He *couldn't* have meant to say what I thought I had heard. I felt the rush of angry tears, and tried to blink them away. I felt numb, like a hand gone to sleep, but all over. "Ron, you can't mean that. What about all the work I've put into caring and cleaning and gardening? What about all that?"

"We're going back where we belong, as soon as I can arrange it. I've already made a deposit, in fact."

"How? How?" He refused to meet my eyes, and I had a horrible thought. "Oh, no. You didn't use my plant money. Tell me you didn't use my plant money."

"I used *our* plant money, of course I did. You weren't going to get any plants anyway."

I wanted to scream and shout and hit things. I wanted to hit Ron, but I knew I could never do that. Mumbling and sobbing, I staggered from the room and toward the ration box, now certainly empty, on the utility shelf. I looked inside it. Not one single chit remained. He had taken it all.

I sat down on one of the stone slabs and cried and cried. Everything jumbled inside me: anger, pain, confusion, helplessness. What was the use? Why bother? Why dream? Before I could wallow too deeply, the baby kicked me back into reality, sharp blows just below my rib cage. This was the baby Ron had wanted, had insisted upon. After all, his buddies at work were fathers, right? Ten minutes of fun and games, and I could equalize his status at work, right? Suddenly I felt nauseated, like morning sickness haunting me. I swallowed bitter acid, and caught myself hating the baby, *Ron's* baby, and cried some more.

I sat for minutes, hours, before I felt Ron's hand on my shoulder. In no condition to squirm away, I submitted and endured. He said something that eluded me because I was not tracking very well, and I asked him to repeat it.

"I said I was sorry. I didn't mean to upset you."

"Ron, you *stole* my plant money."

"Yeah, well, I can get it back. Let's talk about it in the morning, okay?"

"There's nothing to discuss," I said, as his hand fell away. "You've already made up your mind without me."

"I said I was sorry."

His lips brushed the back of my neck, and I knew what he wanted. My objection came weak and remote, not a part of me. "I'm about to have a baby. Or hadn't you noticed? I'm not in the mood right now."

"But I am. Anyway, there's other ways..."

I wanted to refuse him, but I saw a chance for peace between us. Maybe we *could* resolve our differences rationally in the morning. It was worth a try. Images of our future, our life here, and our family flashed through my mind. I had worked too hard for these; I would not surrender now. We could work this out.

"All right," I agreed, and got slowly to my feet. "Go get on the 'cot. Let me rinse my mouth out first."

"That's my baby."

4: lineage - Korei's story (cont'd)

The commo awoke me in the morning. Ron still snored, so I got up and answered the buzz. Papiorek was still on duty; his voice came in over the speaker, asking me to sit down. I verified his ID and asked him if he knew what time it was.

"I'm sorry to have to be the one to tell you, Korei, but...your great-grandmother passed away last night. I'm really sorry, Korei."

"When...," I began, and could not finish.

"The cremation and reading is set for 1300 hours. I can get it

246

postponed for an hour or two, if you want."

"No, I can make it."

"I can send out an escort, if you wish. I know you weren't planning to come in to the Complex today."

"The solar batteries should have a full charge by now," I said. I had learned that lesson the hard way. "I'll be on time."

"You're sure?"

"Thank you for telling me, Vik."

"One of the duties I don't relish, Korei. I'm just glad I don't have to do it often."

I had been so engrossed in the news that I did not hear Ron approach, or know he was standing behind me until he spoke. "So the old witch finally bought it."

"*Goddammit, Ron!*"

He took a quick step backward as I whirled to confront him. "Okay, sorry. But she never liked me, anyway. What did she ever do for me?"

"Ron, if you can't say something nice..."

"Okay, okay. You seem awfully chummy with that Papiorek. What's going on?"

"He's a friend. We work together sometimes."

"I'll bet you do."

I started trembling. "That's not what I meant, and you know it. That's a *rotten* thing to say to me. I'm your *wife.*"

"And don't you forget it. Fact is, I think maybe you'd better quit that job of yours. There's too many men out there."

"You mean you don't trust me?"

He looked away. "You know what I mean."

"No, I *don't* know what you mean. There are women where you work, aren't there?"

"That's different."

"How, different?"

"It just is."

I felt something along my spine then, something hard and stiff, but now a part of me. Only if I stood up straight would the discomfort wane. So I stood up straight. "I have a memorial service to

247

attend, so if you'll—"

"Are you going to get her stuff?"

The question caught me off-guard. Inheritance was not something I had considered...or sought. The possibility evoked images of scavengers yanking flesh from an animal not yet dead.

"I suppose so. I'm the only living descendant, as far as I know. But she didn't have all that much. Would you mind getting my Solskip out of the Parker while I dress?"

"That means I would have to dress, too," he complained. "It's cold out there right now. And today is my day off."

I squeezed my eyes shut and stood very still. My voice sounded like two Martian rocks rubbing together. "You can at least get out the Solskip for me. It is difficult for me to maneuver inside the Parker."

He did not move. "How long are you going to use your pregnancy as an excuse?"

"Dammit, Ron!"

"Okay, okay, don't have the baby right here. I'll get it out, okay?"

"Thank you so much. When I return, I'll want to discuss that little matter you brought up last night."

He nodded. "Maybe the...your great-grandma left you enough for us to get back."

"Ron, we *aren't* going *back*."

"So you say now. But you'll change your mind, baby. You always do."

I steadied myself with a long breath. The baby objected to the intrusion. "I'll be dressed in a few moments. If you could have the Solskip waiting for me, I would appreciate it, thank you."

I had never visited Kourou Settlement IV but after I reached the Bubble Complex, I headed north on the unmarked road—north the correct direction to travel, and this the only route. It *seemed* right; so maybe I had inherited a direction bump. The road was straight and flat, a rarity on Mars, and required little concentration to maintain control of the Solskip, so I allowed myself to dwell on childhood memories. In them I sat on great-grandma's knee, listening to her tell stories of trips to Earth and of settling on Mars. None of them made sense to me at the time, because I was too young to understand, but my only vision of Earth I saw through her eyes. I saw her in her garden. She had cultivated my interest in plants—and in that moment I understood the importance I attached to the solarium, for it was an extension of her, and of my memory of her. Through me, as long as the solarium endured, she lived.

Other memories stood in queue to filter through my mind. I saw her as the old woman "they" talked about, the recluse. But she had been more than seventy years old when I was born, and she was entitled to behave as she wished. "They" whispered of her in awe sometimes, and I did not know why. The manner in which Ron had spoken about her began to gnaw at me. She had never done anything to harm him in any way. True, she had not approved of our marriage, but her behavior had always been proper. She was more than just source of heirlooms, and Ron would have to understand that...somehow.

"Who am I kidding?" I yelled...a mistake, with my head inside the helmet.

My ears rang. No one responded. Maybe the wind picked up a little.

The Bubble of Kourou Settlement IV came into view just past KM26, and moments later I spotted the cut through the crater wall, a beacon to home in on. I was desperate for beacons.

Papiorek was there to greet me when I arrived. He waited until I had docked and shed the outsuit, then took both of my hands in his, face properly somber for the occasion, voice gentle. "I'm sorry, Korei," he said, once more.

"How old was she, over ninety? It wasn't unexpected, Vik...but then, it always is, isn't it?"

"Ninety three, she was."

"The way I picture her, she was always active, always doing something."

"I never actually met her," said Papiorek, releasing my hands. "She was before my time. I only heard stories about her...she was very special."

"Do you know how she died, or where?"

We headed toward a small structure at the interior surface of the Bubble. "She died in her garden, Korei. There was no official cause of death. She just wound down. It was her turn."

"Maybe that's the best way to say it. Is that the crematorium? I've never seen one before."

"The only one in this sector. It's arranged so the opening where they insert...it's inside the Bubble, but the rest is outside, so the smoke passes into the atmosphere. Which brings me to a delicate question, Korei. What do you want done with the...her ashes?"

"Can you put them in something?"

"Of course."

"Then I'll take them with me. I really can't think right now, Vik. I'll decide later."

"I understand. And...I hate to have to bring this up, but you are also the sole heir. Or heiress, I suppose. There isn't much, just some titled landholds, and the garden, and I believe there is a dwelling somewhere."

"I don't remember where it is, though."

"I'll have it located for you, when you're ready."

"What about her sister? Aunt Pony Lee? Whatever happened to her?"

"She was presumed dead over ten years ago, Korei. Sandstorm, from what I recall. Probably we'll never know for certain, unless someone comes across her." He gazed out into the Marscape. "More than one has gone missing out there...but no one will dispute your inheritance."

I felt a brief anger. When it passed, I said, "You really think I care about that, Vik? Being the only heir?"

"It's my duty to tell you, Korei. I don't like this any more than you do."

Only a few people had gathered in front of the crematorium. "Not many mourners," I said, as we drew near.

"She'd outlived most of the Originals, and they'd've remembered her best. Um, MarsCol is willing to make her garden a memorial, and see that her plants are cared for, if you agree."

"I think she would like that."

"The land around it would remain yours, of course."

"I don't know what I would do with it, Vik. Why not make the entire area a memorial? If five percent of what they say about her is true, she deserves it."

"I'll pass that on. If it's approved, there will be a formal agreement to seal."

"Will I have to make a special trip?"

He shook his head. "On commo—"

"Oh, my God!"

His arm went around my shoulders. "It's all right," he whispered. "It's her outsuit. They have to wrap her in something for the cremation."

"I didn't realize..."

"I'm right here, Korei. Cry if you want to."

I blinked back the tears. "I'll be okay."

But I did not hear his response. I stared at the outsuit, and through it, lost in memory, until the mortician began the final services. I came back slowly, missing the introduction to the eulogy.

"...homage and respects to a woman whose position in the history of the Martian Settlements is among the most significant of all involved, Colonel Nancy Sue Timberlake." He spoke as if from text, from the bottom of a test well for ice rock, the praise perfunctory. I could not meet his face, and stared down at the orange-red surface of Mars while he droned on. "Colonel Timberlake was a member of the international group that founded the first permanent settlement on Mars. She gave birth to the first native citizen of Mars, Adrianne Timberlake. She is credited with having developed strains of corn, beans, and peppers that would grow in treated Martian soil, and she practiced primitive agricultural methods which eventually proved successful. Eccentric and uncomfortably direct in her relationships with the other Originals, she nevertheless commanded their utmost respect. Given the fragile circumstances surrounding the initial settlement, it is difficult to understand in this distant time how she or any of the others could have survived, but survive they did. Now, the inexorable passage of time has finally accomplished what the droughts and sandstorms and bitter cold and inhuman conditions failed to do. May she rest in peace. She has earned it, many times over.

"Colonel Timberlake is survived only by her great-granddaughter, Mrs. Korei Anderson, who is here with us this day. Her daughter Adrianne did not survive the Terran Disruption some thirty years ago, and her granddaughter Jeney was killed during a resupply twelve years ago. Colonel Timberlake's younger sister, Brevet Major Poinsettia Lee Timberlake, was the victim of a sandstorm two years after that resupply." The mortician paused, and gazed down at the makeshift stone bier. "Godspeed, Colonel Timberlake," he said, his voice softer and less formal now. "Return to the ashes from which you came."

At his signal, two men lifted the flight suit and inserted it into the crematorium. I watched through bleary eyes as the mortician closed the metal door and flipped a series of toggles on a side panel. I heard a *puff,* or perhaps I saw one. Presently he opened a door I had not noticed before, under the main opening, and withdrew a metal box not much larger than his two fists. The lid to the box was open. He slid it shut and handed the box to me. I thought I should say something, but my voice had fled with the tears flowing down my cheeks.

While I stood there, numb as a statue, Captain Francois Hunaguchi, the MarsCol representative detailed to attend the ceremony, drew the mortician off to one side, well away from the rest of us. For the better part of a minute they conferred in whispers. I glanced at Papiorek, but he shook his head to indicate ignorance.

Finally the mortician ahemmed for attention. "It is my understanding that others had wished to express themselves at this ceremony. Unfortunately, I have just been advised that a large sandstorm is headed this way, and I must now require a termination, so that security preparations may be made. The DETA is approximately ninety minutes from the northeast. Please, go to your places of responsibility and await further instructions. Thank you all."

Papiorek drew up beside me. "That could cut you off if you try to return now."

"I can make it," I told him, with less certainty than I would have liked. He was an incessant worrier. "I can cut terrain after I reach the Bubble Complex and save time. Sixty minutes at the most, if I leave now."

He accompanied me to the Solskip, objecting. "There could be advance flurries."

"I've maneuvered in those before. But you don't understand, Vik. Ron is Dome. It's his day off. I know him. He'll have the Scannar and Commo disabled, so he won't be disturbed."

"That isn't very smart."

"No, it isn't, but what can I do, except seal the Dome..."

He spun me around, eyes probing to the back of my skull. I hadn't realized until that moment the strength of our friendship. I had done nothing to deserve it, or encourage it. The discovery shook me.

Finally he said, "If you're sure that's what you want to do."

"It's what I *have* to do, Vik. My husband's life is in danger." I drew the outsuit up around me as I climbed into it. "I'll commo when it's over."

"Do that, please."

"Promise," I said, and tucked the metal box into a side pouch on the Solskip.

By the time I reached the intersection, the horizon was orange and angry. The mortician had been right—this was a huge sandstorm, to judge from the arc-minutes of horizon that it covered. I seemed to be headed directly into the middle of it, although I knew it would pass diagonally across my bearing as I veered east. Uncertainty nagged at me, but I had no option but to push on. Without Scannar and Commo, Ron was at the mercy of the sandstorm. At the moment he was not exactly my favorite person, but I did not want his death, even by misadventure or self-negligence, on my conscience. I felt confident that I could cross the next eighteen-plus kilometers despite the high probability now of sand flurries. The Solskip would hold to the road well enough. The seals were in place—no sand could get inside to damage the boards, disks, and moving parts. My outsuit was sturdy and warm—I had already begun to perspire. My hands felt clammy inside the flex gloves as I clutched the guidance wheel. A cross-wind arrived, and the Solskip yielded slightly until I was able to regain equilibrium.

The first flurry hit me as I passed KM6. I left the road momentarily, sand obscuring my vision. The terrain rocked me, and I struggled with the guidance until I felt the road beneath the wheels once more. Sand hissed against the visor and swirled around me. Visibility withdrew to two meters, and I decelerated, hoping to make up the lost time down the road.

When the flurry passed, I had a clear view of the road all the way to the next crater some two kilometers ahead. The orange blemish on the horizon was measurably closer now, and plumes of vermilion burst from the ground nearby to birth another flurry. It coalesced and billowed toward the road, and my heart sank. If I continued, surely it would cross my path at intersection, or surround me if I halted. I maxed the accelerator, hoping without a shred of hope to outrun it. The flurry devoured loose Martian dust to feed itself, now a sandstorm in its own right. I yelled several words I had learned from Ron, and screamed the last of them as the cloud rushed to smother me.

Somehow I managed to keep the Solskip upright and moving, but the guidance trembled and quaked, and I knew I had left the road. Visibility was zero. I saw dark colors—orange black, brown black, and black. Sand buffeted the vehicle. Even inside my outsuit I heard the wind howl and felt the impact of sand clumps. I tightened my grip on the guidance and clamped my legs under the seat. Secure and warm inside my womb, she slept on...*she*. Suddenly I wanted a girl. I wanted my baby to be a girl. And I wanted her to live, even if I did not.

I peered through the visor for any indication of a thin. All four wheels of the Solskip bounced over rocks and small boulders, jarring everything, including my mind. I heard and felt the scrape of metal on stone. Too busy with the controls to be afraid, I shunted fear into a dark nook for later indulgence. Something large and hard and sharp broke through the side of the vehicle and tore into my left sleeve, gashing the fabric, and cold and sand rushed into my outsuit. My heart raced. I had scant minutes left, maybe only seconds. My internal breathing apparatus still functioned, but the cold stiffened my rib cage, and respiration now required deliberate, calculated effort. The Solskip bounced once more, and flipped.

The helmet saved me, but with the impact a bright flower of rockets lit up my brain. A sharp pain stabbed through my abdomen as my left arm began to freeze. The sandstorm roared in my ears as it closed around me.

5: lineage - Korei's story (cont'd)

I could not understand why I regained consciousness. Perhaps the surges of intense pain in my abdomen and groin awoke me. I had the absurd notion that I was being born. My hands reached down and touched something wet and alive, something that was and yet was not a part of me. I screamed as another blast of pain shot from my groin up through my abdomen and into my chest. Inside me something tore, a feeling and a sound, and I screamed without sound. I felt sand in my eyes, in my hair, and under my body. My nails drew blood from my palms. A slippery lump passed out of me and I screamed again, and darkness came for me once more. I welcomed it gratefully.

☙☙☙

The face hovering over me like a lost moon was old, but the eyes had remained young. I recognized it, but could not remember the name that went with it. The old woman smiled faintly, adding pleasant wrinkles, and vanished from view. I was too weak to move. I felt very cold inside. I closed my eyes and waited for something to happen.

"You should breast-feed her," she said softly. "While you still can."

I opened my eyes again. My throat was parched. I tried to speak, and she hushed me, handing me a bundle in a blanket of real wool. I parted the flaps to peer inside it. "My..."

"Your daughter," she announced.

"...daughter."

The woman opened my shirt to expose my left breast, and helped me slide the baby toward my nipple. Her little mouth gulped and

255

searched all around until it found what it needed, and I felt a warm tingle as the milk flowed from me. Her little face felt so warm against me. I began to cry. She was alive, my baby was alive.

"It was a normal birth," said the woman. "She's fine."

I tried to lick my lips, but even my tongue was dry. The woman put a plastic tube to my mouth, and water flowed freely. I was so thirsty. I wanted to drink as much as I could, but she took the tube away. "More," I croaked.

"Later. It is not good for you to drink too much at once."

"Who...are you?"

"You know very well who I am, child."

"...Aunt Pony Lee?"

"Just Pony Lee, please. 'Aunt' adds years to me. How do you feel?"

I examined my body from within. There were sharp and dull pains in my groin. My left arm no longer felt a part of me. And weakness, everywhere, even in my eyelids. Pony Lee sat down on the floor beside me and caressed my forehead, brushing hair from my face, while my daughter, the daughter she had delivered for me, drank her fill to the tune of little squeaky sounds, like a vacuum hose not attached properly. "That feels good," I whispered.

"You've had a rough time of it, my dear."

"It was a difficult birth?"

She shook her head sadly. "Not the childbirth."

I tried to remember what had happened to me. Fragments of memories flew through my mind like subliminal advertisements of events, pausing scarcely long enough for me to identify them. There had been a sandstorm, and now I had a daughter. So *that's* where they come from. "You rescued me?"

She did not seem to mind the obvious question.

"And you delivered my daughter."

She smiled again.

The dream slowly returned. I saw darkness and felt pain again. "Something happened to me," I said.

"There was a hemorrhage. You lost a lot of blood."

"I feel weak."

"Just how strong are you, Korei?"

I peered down at my daughter. She was still noisily engaged in food gathering. "Is something wrong...?"

"She's fine. Hey, would your great-aunt ever lie to you?"

"No..."

"Korei, you've lost a lot of blood, and you are dehydrated. You should be in a coma. I doubt you have a concussion—I've examined your pupils from time to time, and neither is unusually dilated or fails to respond to sudden light."

She paused, not for my reply, but to confirm to herself her next words. A vague apprehension replaced the weakness...but I knew what was coming, now.

"Korei, this is the worst sandstorm I have seen in many years. It may not pass for days. We have no commo, and even if it worked nobody could get out here to transport you to the dispensary. I can give you only so much medical attention. Do you understand what that means?"

I understood Pony Lee all too well. "I might pull through this, or I might not. Odds on the latter."

Again she shook her head sadly. "It isn't quite that simple, my dear. I have no food for your daughter. Only you have that. I cannot predict the effect feeding her will have on your condition."

"Meaning that I have a choice?"

"*Do* you think you have a choice in the matter?"

I did not hesitate. "None at all."

"I've rigged some diapers for her," Pony Lee went on, quickly, no further discussion warranted. "Water for washing them is putting a minor strain on my resources, although I cannot think of a better cause. And...it looks to me as if she has gone to sleep."

Confirming her estimate, I eased my daughter free and passed her to Pony Lee, who disappeared from my view once again. When she returned, I asked, "Was that her first feeding?"

"Fourth. She seems to awaken about every four hours. As soon as the storm ends, we can commo for help. In the meantime, we'll be warm enough—"

"Where exactly are we?"

257

"You're inside a subterranean dwelling that my sister and I dug out years—"

"Oh, God! Pony Lee...Great-grandma died! Oh, God."

"Hush, child. I know." Her hand soothed my forehead, quieting the pains. "I was at the cremation."

"How? I mean, I didn't see you."

"I didn't want to be seen."

"But...then you were caught in the storm, too."

"I was right behind you, child."

"But..how? I mean—"

"Korei, I'm eighty five, not delapidated. As I was saying, we dug it out years ago. It's still a common practice in Australia, I've heard. So I survived here in the sandstorm that was supposed to have killed me. Afterwards, I...decided to remain dead. There was nothing left for me to do with the settlement, and I did not care for the direction society was taking. Too many power plays."

"I don't understand."

"No, you don't. Korei—"

"Oh, God, a lecture."

"No lectures. You claimed a lack of understanding."

"I'm sorry...*ow!*"

Instantly her weathered face wrinkled with fresh worry. "Are you okay?"

"Post-partem pain, I think. Sorry."

"Stop being sorry, dammit!"

"Sor..."

"Just so. In the old days...," she began, and barked a laugh. "I sound just like my father, rest his spirit. Nancy Sue and I rarely apologized, except immediately after we had done something we regretted. Nowadays, women use the word as punctuation. That's one change. But I was thinking in more general terms.

"When we first settled Mars, all of us bound together in common cause. All of us fought for our lives, for our existence. In a survival situation you need the active participation of everyone. But later, after our survival was assured, the viability of the settlements was assured, people began to carve their own niches. A supervisor here, a manager there...and in marriage. We went from equality—Death didn't inquire as to our genders—to specificity. You have your place, and I have mine. I didn't like the place they wanted me to inhabit, so I left. Here I am. Nancy Sue knew, no one else. We survived it all: sandstorms, the cold, food shortages, general assorted hardships, and men." She touched my forehead. "You seem to be running a slight fever. I'll have to watch that."

"I do feel a bit chilly."

She tucked the blanket tightly around me. "Have you selected a name for your daughter?"

"Only if it was a boy." I had an inspiration. "Why don't you choose? After all, you delivered her."

Pony Lee smiled her acceptance, making me incongruously aware that, even at her advanced age, she still retained most of her teeth. "We should each choose. You first."

The name I had picked privately, just in case, came easily. "Teresa,"—

6: legacy - Traci's story

I absolutely could not fucking breathe! One word, in my mind, a moving finger having writ, continuing, over and over, looped forever...in cadence with a heart which kept beating, louder and louder.

Mom?!?!

Korei Anderson was my *mother?*

Pony Lee...*why didn't you* tell *me?*

And I peered back inside the steamer trunk. *Maybe you just did.*

My rib cage was screaming at me, and I took a breath, and another. Water from the canteen moistened my throat. I wanted to say...something ...but there was no one to say it *to.* Dead, all dead now. I was the last.

And I was alone. I had a greenstick apprentice sleeping in the stateroom, who might one day stand on his own two feet. Not a friend, just...not an enemy. And Conner, who...meant well. Not a friend, just...not permitted to get too close.

259

Alone. The last of my kind.

But what kind was that?

Maybe the answers lay in the remaining yellow, brittle pages, now freshly spotted with drops of water...

But don't tell anyone I did this, I whispered, fingering one of the spots.

7: lineage - Korei's story (cont'd)

just in case, came easily. "Teresa," I told her. "Without the aitch."

"A good name," she applauded. "The name of a saint who suffered from the diseases and guilts of a materialistic world dominated by men."

"I didn't know that...what about yours?"

"I think Minerva is appropriate."

I chuckled, once, and my insides protested the disturbance. "Minerva?"

Pony Lee did not smile. "Do you know the origin of the name?"

"It sounds like the name of a...an aunt, or something."

"As in a stereotype. Yes, I see that. In Roman times, back on Earth, Minerva was the Goddess of War." She placed an ominous, hushed emphasis on the final word, and I stared up at her. A *frisson* of foreboding swept through me.

"Teresa Minerva Timberlake," said Pony Lee, savoring the syllables. "A good name, that is."

I objected feebly. "Not Anderson."

"Tell me, dear, what do you know about your maternal ancestors?"

"Not as much as I should, perhaps."

"I will not dispute you. Korei, turn your face to the right. Do you see, over against the wall? Have you any idea of its contents?"

"None at all."

"Korei, there have been Timberlake women on Mars since the first landing. Our memorabilia is in there, except yours and Teresa's, of course. Old records, diaries, TWXs, letters, historical documents and items pertinent to the social, economic, and political development of the settlements. Perhaps Teresa is the one for whom Nancy Sue and I intended this. The timing is right. Approximately every five generations, a new frontier opens up."

She had lost me after the first landing.

"Equality is not a matter of law, Korei. It is a matter of circumstance. Mars does not care about your gender. It is *merciless*. It takes no prisoners, and gives no quarter. It doesn't even allow you time to surrender. It kills men and women indiscriminately. When we arrived, we had to pull together. Now that the danger has lessened, society retrenches. Are you Ron's equal, in the eyes of society?"

"Yes!"

My answer startled her. She sat back on her haunches. Her eyes were impossible to read in the dim light. I saw in them a benevolent pity, sweet yet sad. She held my gaze until I had to look away. Her whisper barely carried to me. "Do you have to put money aside, in a separate place of your own, to buy the things *you* want?"

Once I started to cry, I could not stop.

I had nothing to wipe my eyes and nose on except the ruined sleeve of my outsuit. The harsh, cold fabric abraded the skin. Between sniffles I heard Pony Lee.

"Your great-grandmother had half a mind to string up that whelp you wed by his gonads and teach him some rules of behavior. I might do it myself. Korei...you're supposed to be a team, like Nancy Sue and Sydney. Your byword isn't competition, it is support." She stood up to stretch muscles that had been in one position for too long, and sat down again. "A moment ago you made the most difficult and merciless decision of all. Your daughter, Teresa Minerva Timberlake, will live even at the cost of your life. And I will give you no reason to hope. Much depends on how long the wind and sand continue to howl above us. But you can give her something else, Korei, if you can summon the strength. Teresa must know her ancestors, which includes you. She will see you as role models, the good and the bad. Write to her, Korei. Of your thoughts, your experiences, your feelings, as much as you can. Write of your relationship with Ron; even negative information can be useful. And write of how you came to this place to give birth."

I stretched out on the makeshift cot and pulled the blanket over me. My head and shoulders rested on an air pillow against the inner wall of the underground shelter, and I had just given Teresa her feeding, so I was as comfortable as I was going to get. Pain continued, everywhere, except in my left arm. The feeling had not returned. From the expression on Pony Lee's face, I knew I was going to lose it, even if I survived the rest of the ordeal. Above us the storm continued to laugh. Pony Lee handed me a tablet of blank paper and an everlast pen, in a pointed reminder of her request, then lifted my left hand and let it drop. "Can you feel anything at all there?"

"Above the elbow. Nothing below."

She looked away.

I felt the chill of a terrible anxiety. "Pony Lee, I *have* to know. Am I going to lose it?"

She took a deep breath. "I don't know that I can perform an amputation, Korei. I may have to, able or not. I know something of frostbite, and a little of gangrene. And that storm has not abated. I have no idea how much time we have."

"Pony Lee, I'm going to die anyway, arm or no arm. So leave it. An amputation might accelerate the end. I must live long enough..."

"Hush, child." She put her hand over my mouth. "Hush you, now. I was *right* about you. There is some of Nancy Sue in you. Give that to Teresa."

I looked at the pen. "It's a long story."

"Just write about the past few days. We'll worry about the rest later."

I bent my knees up to brace the tablet and stared at the blank paper. I had not written anything in a long time. Even the pen felt alien. But thoughts gathered, and I began to write.

👁👁👁

I was exhausted, but Teresa was adamant about the vacancy in her stomach, so I floated a loan from my inner reserves and fed her. She was healthy—certainly her squalls were healthy, for they echoed

262

around in the dugout for long minutes after she fell asleep. The upper half of my left arm had swollen, and lumps formed in my armpit. The dizzy spell and aching body bespoke a fever. Pony Lee said nothing. It is impolite to point out to a dying person the imminence of death.

Teresa was an equal-opportunity suckler. Her head wobbled across my chest, seeking another source of nourishment, giving it her full attention, while I asked Pony Lee about one of Adrianne's diary entries.

"Women were permitted to do lab work back then," she answered. "It was an accepted occupation. If you find that unusual, consider that Nancy Sue frequently served as a raw-data scout."

"She went out *alone?*"

"Most of the time. She preferred it that way, after Sydney died. I've done scouting myself. But times change, Korei. We didn't fight the right battles. Nancy Sue and I lived long enough to witness the regression to subservience first-hand, and we understood it in a historical context. But very soon a new frontier will open. Mars Corporation will begin to mine the asteroids. There is talk on Earth of sending out a sub-light manned expedition which may open up an infinite frontier. *If* such a frontier opens, the social, political, and economic equality of women is forever *assured,* because pioneering will become a permanent attitude. There will always be some new place to go, some new danger to face *together,* women and men, side by side, the way it is *supposed* to be. Teresa has a future."

"But...women can't pilot craft in the asteroids."

"Hush, child. Enough nonsense for today. You have more writing ahead."

"I'm tired, Pony Lee. I'm almost up to the sandstorm. Let me sleep."

"Of course, dear."

☯ ☯ ☯

My head lolled. I was too weak to hold it where I wanted it. I slumped onto the blanket, coarsened now by sweat and blood. I stank of old, weak milk. I felt the sandstorm coming back for me now, a banshee that had missed on the first pass, and I cried.

"Tears," said Pony Lee.

"Can I...hold my baby? My Teresa?"

She shook her head. "I had better hold her." She peeled back the softer blanket so that I might see Teresa's face.

My voice had grown so weak that I barely heard my own words, but Pony Lee heard them. Her face had that sweet sad smile I had come to know in the past hours...days. "I'm sorry," I said.

"Why, dear?"

"I won't be able...to finish my story." I closed my eyes, to the after-image of Pony Lee cradling Teresa in her arms.

"She will," whispered Pony Lee. "She will."

8: legacy - Traci's story

O'Toole roused me five hours later. I had found a reasonably comfortable position in the captain's chair and made a pillow of my hands, acquiring a slighty stiff back en route. The pile of old papers rested in my lap, the last one—in Pony Lee's hand, with Korei no longer able to write—on top, the dark ink blurred here and there. I had no idea how long O'Toole had been making little tentative sounds—captains evidently are not supposed to weep—but I finally groused at him to stop. He sat down in the starboard chair, which disturbed me because I was much too accustomed to seeing it empty. He asked why I was frowning.

I keyed for our present coordinates in the Astrogational Positioning System and compared the result on the monitor with the course-set estimate. The *Ennis* was precisely where she was supposed to be, though I'd had no doubt of it. "I always frown."

"If you did, Skipper, you'd have permanent furrows in your brows."

"I tamp in a filler. O'Toole, you have the bridge. That means you touch *nothing* and that you wake me for any event, however slight."

He looked crestfallen. "What about communications?"

"Can you say, 'Just a moment, I'll get her'?"

"I am out here to learn," he protested.

I headed for the sleeper. "Learn to follow instructions, then."

I dreamt, and slept fitfully. Visions in tangerine and vermilion and sienna, and shadows in the dust. Pain, but someone else's. A succession of orange-haired women who were strong in different ways.

Who was I?

I sat up, woke up, blinked, looked around. How had I gotten here? Bulkheads of structural plastic, metal gray and unadorned, gave no clue to the identity of the occupant. An overhead glow-plate—I recalled having installed it, though I could not now remember why. For light to read by? Had I anticipated receiving diaries, letters, ancestral writings? Who was I, and where did I come from, and why was I here? Eternal questions all.

Who cares?

The rejoinder grated against the facade over my self-imposed indifference. Like an undiscovered planet perturbing the orbits of those around her, the faint memory of a woman drew my thoughts back to the steamer trunk and its precious contents, and I went along willingly, asleep or awake. I'd identified my mother, at long last. Whoever else I was, the answer was in that trunk...somewhere.

I swung my feet to the deck and started to rise when something dealt the *Ennis* a massive blow and I went sprawling. Vibrations of the outer hull echoed deafeningly throughout the 'skip, there was pain in my ears and in my elbows and on my shins, and bright light inside my head. "*Mom!*" I cried, once and again, but before I could chastise myself for the fleeting weakness someone let there be dark.

I regained consciousness almost wishing I had not. My head hurt. Upon further reflection and self-examination I concluded that *everything* hurt. The hatch to the sleeping compartment was now ajar. I tried to call out, but managed only an unintelligible hoarse rasp. The bulkhead supported me as I stood up. Nothing oozed or dripped or spurted, which was a pleasant discovery, but there was a lump behind my left ear and a *very* tender area just above the floating ribs on my right side, and neither of them encouraged me to dash to the bridge and find O'Toole. Still, it had to be done, so I did it.

O'Toole was still alive. He was on his hands and knees on the deck behind the port captain's chair. He had pried open a trap hatch and was staring down at the primary power cable leading from the fusion generator to the circuitry interstices that carried juice to all of the 'skips modules and components. Something, it seemed, was wrong down there.

Ahemming got his attention. His frightened green eyes glistened, and for a mad moment I thought he was in tears. "There was a frayed area on the cable, just behind the clamp," he explained. "Fiber came in contact with the clamp, there was heat, a power surge...then everything fused." His tone added, "I guess."

The primary cable lay in the well like a fiber-glass noodle, the end blackened. The clamp and terminals were still plugged into the interstice box port. There was a black oval on one of the horizontal supports; apparently the end of the cable had landed there while it was still juiced. The damage was serious, but not irreparable. I had to excise the end of the cable, separate the leads, fit them back into the port clamp, re-enable the breaker sequence at the generator port, power back up, upboot and initialize each fucking component discretely. Tedious work, but it was better than the alternative.

"The helm is without power, Skipper," advised O'Toole. He did not look at me. "But emergency life-support back-ups are functioning on auxiliary power."

"So I see. Are you all right?"

"Yes, of course."

"Allan?"

At first I thought the use of his first name had softened the edge between us. Then I realized he was in shock. The light in his eyes faded to aqua and went out, and he collapsed. I caught him just in time to ease him onto the deck. Cradling his head, I snagged my seat cushion to pillow him. A quick scan of his flight suit revealed no tears or rips, no stains, no sign of injury, but he had been much closer to the power surge. It occurred to me that I had no idea how long I had been unconscious, or whether O'Toole had been. Principles of emergency aid beckoned. Having determined that he was in no danger of exsanguination, I check for respiration and pulse, and found both to be strong and steady. He had...well, he had fainted.

Proper procedure (to say nothing of prurient interest) called for me to facilitate his respiration by loosening clothing—his, I guessed, as the manual is not specific on this point—so I broke the frontal seal of his outsuit and opened the garment. Though somewhat slender, he looked fit enough, a thin, wiry young man. Underneath the outsuit he was wearing a light white pullover, and under that a body bandage. The bruise on my ribs reminded me that I might avail myself of such a device, and I wondered whether he suffered from a previous injury. I tugged the pullover up around his shoulders and unwound the bandage...and found no sign of injury . . .

I needed to think. I needed to complete repairs on the *Ennis*. The latter demanded priority, so I ignored O'Toole, who had come to and was now watching me from the starboard chair while I fitted another fiber into the port clamp. Muscles protested abuse, so I took a moment to drop back on my haunches. Progress was slow, the position uncomfortable. Unable to disconnect the power cable from the other end without major disassembly, I was forced to lean down into the opening to perform the repairs. Verify the schematic, snip a fiber, finesse fiber into port, sit back, catch breath, steel self against pain in side, do it again. And again.

"I could help."

I growled something incoherent and bent down. Sharp pain scurried up from my ribs to the top of my skull, where it celebrated the New Year, and I straightened immediately. My head struck the back of my chair, and the celebration continued.

"Let me do something."

I climbed to my feet and kicked at a clump of fiber debris, seaweed on an abandoned beach. O'Toole continued to plead with me. "Take a long break and relax, Skipper. This job will get done, but it doesn't *have to* be completed by you this instant. Let me do something, *please*."

"Can you read a schematic?"

"My concentration was circuitry and energy systems."

"All I want is each little fiber in its own little hole," I said. "Can you do that?"

267

"I can do it."

I motioned toward the cargo hold. "I'll, um, just be back there...reading, or something."

For several minutes I was just back there, um, gathering my courage. There was so much for me to think about that I did not want to think at all. I wanted to be lost.

I lost myself inside a diary.

9: legend - the diary of Nancy Sue Timberlake

April 1, 1 AM

What a day to start a year. April Fool's Day. Mars has days a few minutes longer than Earth's, but the year is 687 days long. That translates into 22 months and 22 days, if I adopt the Earth calendar for the sake of this diary's continuity. So I begin the year in April and end it with a 22-day month called February Prime. Poor February—it always gets shorted. Must be a female month.

The choice of year is arbitrary—*my* diary. AM is for Anno Martis, hopefully. My Latin isn't very good. I have five diaries, all smuggled. May have to endisk them after the paper runs out.

April 29, 1 AM

This time Robinson called me "doll." I told him I was Nancy, Nancy Sue, Lieutenant, or even Ms Timberlake, but if he ever called me anything else again he was going to lose a bone or an organ, depending my mood at the time. He's the only American male on the team, and how he passed the psycheval...favor for a friend, maybe. No *real* man would risk annoying me that way.

June 9, 1 AM

First kick today. I'm so excited! I hope it's a girl—the ESA medics and the Harvard people know, but I asked them not to tell me that or the identity of the father. Four months and maybe a week to go. Do they have weeks on Mars? My pregnancy hardly shows yet. I can't imagine a tougher set of circumstances in which to have a baby. The medic is Consolasao Mafra, the ex-volleyball star from Brazil.

She and I can handle the delivery—well, I'll handle it, she'll assist—but after that? Women had the same circumstances in 1790 Australia and 1840 Kansas. I'll manage. The dispensary has artstate facilities. Must remember not to slack off on my exercises. Muscle tone is great, I feel great.

Curiosity: who else is pregnant? Trinka, or Agnetha? My own timed impregnation was kept secret until we had landed. Once again the women are the pawns in the men's power antics. Which country gets the first person born on another planet? I went along with it because a direct representative of the President of the United States made it VERY CLEAR to me that my position on the team depended on my voluntary consent. Even now only Consola and I know. And she told me *she* isn't. Trinka, Agnetha, or both?

July 16, 1 AM

Trinka and Agnetha are pregnant. We compared notes. It looks like America, Uruguay, and Sweden, the last two in a photo finish. The race is on. And Consola has nothing with which to induce labor, so cheating will be kept to a minimum. Wonder if there are bonuses involved?

August 1, 1 AM

We just got the TWX an hour ago. The *Mirage-Kepler*, the Franco-German resupply craft designated to support us this biennium, blew up on the launch pad at Canaveral, God knows why. I wish they had used Kourou rather than Canaveral, because of the far better safety record, and because, since the US opted out of space exploration and confined its activities to orbiting military and surveillance payloads, there has always been this little whisper about DASE, NASA, and the CIA—if the US won't play a significant role in the exploration of the Solar System, neither will anyone else. Would the CIA sabotage the resupply from Canaveral? Certainly, if ordered to do so. Who would order it? The President, absolutely. Since when has a politician shrunk from bloodshed to satisfy personal political aims. Or maybe the CIA acted unilaterally...no, they'd never do that.

Meanwhile, panic and chaos around her. Robinson in tears,

useless as usual. Bordinov seems stable, holding up well. He wants a meeting at 1500. Sorry for the crew and families, it's the risk we all take, and hope it never happens. Fifty years from now no one will remember the names Fahrnkopf, Lamberti, Ortiz, and Lauffer, just as no one now remembers Grissom, White, Chaffee, or the Challenger (except us). I checked the hydroponics, as we'll need food and water. Everything operational, but will it be sufficient? Need to gather up all the spare equipment, pieces of metal, nuts and bolts and screws and bobby pins, and so on, and put them in a holding area for when we have to improvise. Suppose I'll have to see to this chore, since I thought of it. Martinez slashed his wrists, the idiot. Consola is patching him up in the dispensary. Oxygen reserve for the Bubble is okay...we should rig a battery or generator to process oxygen from water...no idea how much good that will do, but you have to try. It beats slashing the wrists.

Martinez didn't make it. Lost too much blood. Consola cried and cried and cried on my shoulder. She hates failure. Doing diary entry on who is left, good point of reference:

Consolasao Mafra - medic and biotech, Brazil

Michael Robinson - geologist and asshole, United States

Viktor Bordinov - Mission Chief and commo, Ukraine

Katrina Schmidt - computer tech and structural engineer, Uruguay

Agnetha Wanhainen - meteorologist and probe tech, Sweden

Sydney Hough - chemist and electrical engineer, Australia

Nancy Sue Timberlake - agriculture (ha!) and hydroponics, good ole Kansas

Vincente Martinez - crew psychologist and astronomer, Angola, deceased

Four women and three men. All of us passed our reciprocal compatibility tests, had to (even Robinson), but that ratio might throw a rod through the engine block. Of course, if Robinson maintains his attitude, the ratio may improve to four to two.

August 2, 1 AM

Situation hopeless. Bordinov was calm, clear, and frank. We have a remote possibility of resupply in eight months, if. *If* they can get the emergency funding. *If* final craft testing is accelerated, and test parameters relaxed. *If* crew training is advanced. *If* we can hold out long enough. If, if, if. We have dried food stores for five months, figuring on a seven-way split. Oxygen is not a problem, yet. Water is severely limited, because we cannot risk overloading the recycling units. But there is no way they'll get a relief craft to us in eight months. Why not send an unmanned craft or drone, to avoid the problems with acceleration? Found out they're going to try to persuade the Americans to postpone one of their precious military payloads and load a capsule that'll fit the new *Mirage*. The Americans won't go for that. Their security might be weakened irreparably, poor babies.

Hough is an English stereotype, stiff upper lip and all that, don't you know? He has the cutest clipped way of speaking. I'm going to have to be careful around him. He's a nice man. He suggested we go on with our mission as best we can, and retain control of the matters within out control. Makes sense, not that there is another choice.

Nobody has said anything, yet, but my baby is now a liability. But I'm not giving her up. Us Kansas babes are tough—have the baby in the morning, and plow the back forty in the afternoon. My private, unvoiced opinion, is that nobody's going to come. It just isn't cost-effective.

NO! NO! NO! *Enough* of this gloom shit. I'm *mad!* My baby WILL survive!

September 21, 1 AM

Corn grows on Mars! Incredible! All the seeds have actually done in the soil—advised word, that, soil (ha!)—is sprout, so I don't want to excite anyone just yet. I have ten plants so far, which I have named after the Seven Dwarfs and Winken, Blinken, and Nod, out of a total of 20 planted. Remaining problems include pollenation and nitrogen—but we can piss on the plants! Well, not *on* them,

271

but...have to get Consola to collect specimens for ostensible tests. Might work, worth a try. I don't know how many I can feed on twenty plants, but there's room for more, next to the beans, so I'll furrow two more rows tomorrow. Have to pilfer the water, unfortunately.

September 30, 1 AM
They're writing us off! Fucking bastards (sorry, Mom) are writing us off! They're going to send the normal replacement team here in 18 months to start over. "Resupply effort canceled. Deepest regrets." Words to that effect. I can think of some other words to that effect. How can you cancel something you never intended to do in the first place? Bordinov just shrugs—inertial bureaucracy isn't a novel concept to him, he knows Kiev. As for me, I think I'll be ornery and survive, so I can get back and have a little unpleasant chat with someone about this! Consola tells me to relax—the baby.

October 24, 1 AM
Adrianne Judith Timberlake was born on this day. On Earth she would weigh exactly 4 kilograms. Her length, unaffected by gravity, is 56 centimeters. Linebacker material. She has a full head of hair and a full set of vocal cords. Boy, is she pissed! She wants food NOW!
Perfect birth. Hurt like hell, but that goes with the territory. Consola assisted, she's a gem. My first, her first, but we got it done. Where's the back forty?
Adrianne, because I like the sound of the name. Judith for my several-great-grandmother, who fought Indians and winters in pre-statehood Nebraska alongside William. I never met her. I heard of her. She lived to be 94. William died when she was 90, and they told her she was too old to run the farm by herself. She ran off some speculators with a shotgun, and made the farm go until she died slopping the hogs. Tough lady. Adrianne will need the namesake. Mars is a little harsher than Nebraska.

October 31, 1 AM
Had an idea about getting us more water. Told Bordinov to shut

272

down the transmitter. We have no reason to send messages—we're dead. We can divert the energy to the recycling and processing units, and increase supplies (hint, hint, for the plants). Robinson and Trinka are a little nervous about the cutoff. Have to keep an eye on Robinson; he may try to switch the power back on without our knowing. I can preempt that by confiscating a circuit board, but which one? Have to ask Sydney, he'll know.

Sydney and Consola and Agnetha show a genuine concern for Adrianne's welfare. Nobody else says much, and I can't tell what they're thinking. I'm trying to recall the fate of Virginia Dare, who was born in colonial United States under analogous circumstances. Wasn't she part of Raleigh's lost Roanoke settlement? But Adrianne and I will not vanish conveniently. I could use some extra rations— I'm still eating for two, but I don't dare push the issue.

November 1, 1 AM
Oh, Jesus. Oh, dear God.

November 2, 1 AM
I can't keep any food down, just thinking about it. Oh, God.

Katrina Schmidt had her baby yesterday. A boy. Stillborn. DOA. Consola delivered him, I assisted somewhat by handing her stuff. About an hour later Consola came into my cube, and grew like a vine to me, and cried. And I cried. And I threw up all over her, and we cried some more.

Hans Joaquin Schmidt was born with three holes in him. One through the left eye into the brain. One through the chest cavity into the right lung, and out the back. One through the left thigh. I don't know what she used...there are no coathangers on Mars. Any piece of wire would suffice, I suppose.

Jesus.

I don't want her anywhere near me.

December 31, 1 AM
We have lasted three months since our official abandonment. I've expanded the capacity of the hydroponics, thanks to the extra

water due to the energy provided from severing communications. I wonder what they think on Earth now. Probably that the lack of commo means we've had it. Oh, is someone in for a surprise! Algae looks like spinach, tastes flat, but has nutritional value. Would taste great on pizza.Situation still hopeless, but we have food. Sydney and I have taken to consumption of rations every other day, hoarding every other day. Bordinov has lost weight...he may be doing the same. I have calcium tablets, and I'm still lactating, which is great. Adrianne is growing, a sign of good health. Twelve more months. I would kill for a Hershey bar and a Coke right now. The next shift is due to launch in June. If we can hang on that long, maybe the hope of their arrival will keep us going long enough.

February 2, 1 AM

It has been six months since the *Mirage-Kepler* blew up, and we are still here, in decent shape except for Robinson. He's emaciated and dehydrated, and he will be the first to go. Consola says nothing wrong physiologically. Thinks he has given up. Mental catatonia—nobody can reach him at this point.

Adrianne crawled maybe five meters in one stretch today. Soon she'll pull herself erect, and walk. She has taken a liking to Sydney, and I must confess so have I. I admire any man these sols who is willing to help with the child care by cleaning up the poo-poo. But it's more than admiration. In his own quiet way Sydney gets things done. Wish I could find an opportunity to hustle him off to bed, but we are all so busy, and with our limited diet we exhaust easily. We are eating fresh beans and corn, even if from a minimal supply. Adrianne eats the bean mush I make, with commentary—apparently the word "tofu" is of onomatopoeic origin. We should have another crop soon. Twelve more months and the relief should be here.

February 12, 1 AM

Lost Robinson this morning. He just died. No reason for it medically. Consola is aggrieved. I didn't like the man, still don't, but I'm sorry he's dead.

Sydney came to see me this afternoon. He sat down next to me on the cot and cried. Just cried. Said not a word. I wanted to put my arms around him, but thought better of it. When he was finished, he just stood up and looked at me and walked away. It's something we all need. My outlet is the diary.

I think I love that man.

August Prime 2, 1 AM

Anniversary assessment: Six of us left—Adrianne, Consola, Agnetha, Per, Sydney, and me. Food situation slightly improved, as Bordinov intended when he committed suicide. He should get a medal, or something in his memory, for his Captain Oates. Sydney agrees, and that it should be something here.

We are gardening like mad. One vat of hydroponics failed, guess the warranty ran out. We'll salvage what we can eat and recycle the water, and maybe divert energy back into communications.

Assessment: We are still here, you fucking bastards.

10: legacy - Traci's story

In the foundation schools on Mars, children learned of discovery and colonization through the benevolent eyes of MarsCorp. The Originals knew what she had done, but they were dead now, and unable to speak up for her. At home I had been taught to revere her.

Now I understood why.

The history promulgated by MarsCorp had to be defective. It held that women could not operate vehicles in space, but I was living proof that this was untrue. I had to wonder what else was a lie.

And then there was O'Toole...

...who was lounging in the starboard captain's chair, either having finished the repairs or taking a respite from the tedious labors. "Are you angry with me?"

I plopped down in the port chair. "Anger is not the emotion that comes to mind, no. I want to feel deceived, but you did not deceive me. You hired on as an apprentice, and you are qualified for that position. There was no pretense about it, no deception."

"I'm sorry, Skipper."

"For failing to follow instructions? You should be. If there were barnacles in space I'd have you on EVA right now, scraping them off with your goddamn fingernails. 'Touch nothing' sounded clear to me. What confused you about that order?"

O'Toole's eyes dropped to the deck between us. "I wanted to impress you..."

"Is the reconnection complete?"

"Each fiber. And Min has performed diagnostics on the discrete functions. All are ready to go back on line."

"Discrete. What about wholistic?"

"I was waiting for you." After a brief pause, O'Toole added, "There is precedent, you know. I'm not the first, nor even the thousandth."

"Precedent."

"Robert Shurtleff, for one. My inspiration. And like myself, he was injured . . . I'm glad this happened, Skipper. It's good to be able to breathe again."

"As long as we're bandying names about, you can tell me which one goes with O'Toole."

"Ellen."

We sat in the galley lunching contraband—fresh citrus fruit, appropriated from a MarsCorp EO's private stock. O'Toole expressed surprise that I would jeopardize my employment in such a manner.

I cleared tart fibrous debris from my lips. "Possibly that Executive Officer is very good at management and organization and all those little things you need a desk to sit behind to do. But he wouldn't know an asteroid from his first dump of the day. Without asteroidiers to collect the raw material for the smelters, there would be no corporate profits, and no salary for him." I shrugged. "It occurred to me that I too deserved an orange now and then."

"In point of fact, these are tangerines."

I stared at her until she looked away. "Robert Shurtleff was really a woman named Deborah Sampson," I said. "She cut her hair and bound her breasts, as you did, and fought in the Revolutionary War. The doctor who treated her for wounds discovered her secret.

What war are you fighting, Ellen?"

"I had not thought of it as a war. This was the only way I could see for me to get into Space. If it is a war, then it is one for equality."

"Mars dust! The institutions are structured so that you *cannot* win."

"So you would destroy the institutions?"

I shook my head, and passed her a small plastic bag of raisins, which we shared heading back to the bridge. "Corporations are not necessarily evil. They just shouldn't be run by men—or by women who behave like men. But as long as there is competition, there will be aggression. And men wrote the book and all the field manuals on that. Anyway, I would not destroy it, even if I could."

She looked bewildered. "Then I truly do not understand you. I thought you, of all people, would understand the struggle for equality. How then do you achieve it?"

"You don't. We don't. As for your war, you wanted Space, and here you are, in Space."

"Thanks to you."

"To impulse..."

O'Toole read my hesitation. "And?"

"Had you presented yourself as a woman, I would not have taken you on. But then, had you so presented yourself, you likely would not have gotten up here without . . . how long have you been carrying on this charade?"

"I applied for apprenticeship three months ago." She laughed, and sat down in the starboard chair. The identity she had been compelled to adopt now evaporated, she looked far more at ease with herself, and with me. "I see. You were wondering whether a sexual relationship might have gotten me up here. I considered that option. This seemed easier...and cleaner . . . what's wrong?"

I waved her silent and vocoed the 'skipcomp. "Min, commo. Center, this is *Ennis*."

There was no reply. Communications systems were functional within specified parameters, and the little orange dot that blinks whenever transmission is active was blinking.

"What's wrong?" whispered O'Toole.

I gave it ten more seconds. "Min, did that transmission go through?"

Min's voice droned, with minimal modulation and inflection. Someday I am going to instill in her a personality. *"Transmission sent, awaiting reply."*

"Has this ever happened before, Skipper?"

Her voice carried just enough quaver to betray the tension she was feeling. Captain's Rule 3, Only tell the crew what they need to know, was in conflict with Rule 5, Maintain crew morale, and with Rule 1, The Captain is omniscient.

"The truth, O'Toole? No, not to me. But there are any number of reasons for the delay, not all bad."

"What happened to 'Ellen'?" I gave her an eyebrow and she added, "Hey, you did kiss me, you know."

I almost choked on a raisin. "Don't remind me."

"Thanks a lot!"

I dragged my eyes away from the commo module on the instrumentation console and took a long look into green irises flecked with dancing gold. Women sought out strength when they were afraid. So did men. And I was the only object aboard the *Ennis* that might qualify as a supportive pillar.

But there was something else, a subtle message conveyed by cavorting golden speckles...mischief, and a bit of wonder, and—

"Go ahead, *Ennis.*"

I jerked my head to the front and spoke quickly, relieved in more than one way. "What the hell kept you, Center? Commo check, please. I have you five-by-five here."

There was no response.

"Saved by the bell," whispered O'Toole.

"You're out of line, O'Toole."

"Sorry, Skipper."

I swore softly, hoping Center would not detect the epithet. Men have strange ideas of what women should say—although most of them had gotten around my occasional lapses of language by regarding me as something else entirely. I turned to her again.

"Ellen, *I'm* sorry. You're frightened . . . and the truth is, so am I,

278

a bit. Something is not right, and I can't get it to hold still so I can look at it."

"Why the excessive response time?"

I nodded, and returned once more to the console. "If Dispatch was in the WC . . . unlikely, and where's the backup, but I could understand. But this is two transmission delays . . . inconsistent with bodily functions."

"How long was the delay?" she asked.

I relayed the request to Min, who answered, without delay, *"113 seconds."*

"And the elapsed time now?"

"106 seconds."

"*Ennis*, this is Center, acknowledge your five-by-five, read you five-by-five, and be advised next time you check commo be ready to transmit. Your delays clog up the freqs. Center *out.*"

"*My* delays?" I yelled. "*My* delays!"

"Skipper," O'Toole said, her voice hushed. "We're ten and a half million miles out."

"There's no other explanation." O'Toole repeated.

We had retired to the stateroom—well, I had retired, and she had followed, defending her assertion.

"Elapsed time divided by two and multiplied by the velocity of light," she said, leaning against the stateroom hatch, now closed, arms folded across her chest, countenance firm. "That's how far we are."

"Not possible, O'Toole."

"Please? Ellen?"

I threw up my hands. "Okay, *Ellen*. Tell me *how!* Given our rate of acceleration, we should be a mere quarter meg from Center. That's a delay of just over a second, scarcely noticeable."

"At some point in the journey we must have exceeded the velocity of light."

"Not possible."

"And yet . . . here we are. You and I."

"Something you did, not meaning to?"

She gave a hesitant nod. "Irresistible force versus immovable

279

object."

"The *Ennis* is fairly movable, Ellen." I sat down on the bed and bade her join me. "What do you believe happened to her?"

"She has a lot of momentum," O'Toole said slowly, thinking her way. She crossed her legs at the ankles and straightened them briefly, eyes on her gripsole-shod feet as if seeking guidance. "But that's nothing more than inertia with a vector. As for the irresistible force, it might have come from the pressure of energy."

"I just gather asteroids."

She chuckled. "Sorry."

"Don't be— Damn!" I shot to my feet and moved away from her.

"Skipper . . . ?"

"I didn't mean . . . "

In speaking with O'Toole I had touched her, a squeeze of her leg meant to reassure, adding punctuation to the statement. Somehow, without advising me, our intercourse had traversed from Skipper-to-Crewmember to person-to-person, and the difference caught me unprepared. My face felt hot, and I had no idea why.

O'Toole's voice reached me, soft as starlight. "Ten million miles, Skipper. That's what, thirty days?"

'Skip's stores, I thought. I'd laid on enough for eight days . . . but we had already far overshot the shard I had marked earlier, if O'Toole's analysis was correct. Optimistically, fuel would be very tight for the return. Half-rations would extend the food supply. But the air and water recike . . .

I raised my voice a little, although the transceiver was keyed to sound pattern, not volume. "Min, head us back to Center. Optimal course, optimal velocity." After a few seconds thrusters received their instructions and kicked in, staggering us. I held O'Toole up and steadied her, and this time my face felt fine.

"We'll make it, O'Too . . . Ellen."

She forced a wan smile. "No, we won't. But we'll try."

We spent the next few hours apart, I in my stateroom reading ancient diaries and sifting through other documents that I had retrieved from the cargo hold, O'Toole on the bridge holding convoluted discussions with Min while monitoring the wholistic diagnostic. Nothing in the Timberlake family history suggested a solution to our predicament. Somehow, *they* had survived. Nancy Sue and Pony Lee. Jenay, until silenced at last in a loading accident. Mom, who lived long enough to give me a chance. Adrianne, until they caught her and shot her for . . . being a disruptive influence, I suppose. The advisory condemning her was unclear.

I slipped the acetate protector from the envelope and scanned the document once more.

COMMOCOPY
MARSDATE 15 NOVEMBERPRIME 38 AM
TO: ALL MARS COLONY SETTLEMENTS
FROM: CHF ADM MARSCORP

1. FUNDING DENIED FOR PERMANENT RESUPPLY AND RELIEF EFFORTS DUE TO REQUISITE FINANCIAL RESOLUTION OF SOCIAL ISSUES AND TO VARIOUS INTERNATIONAL DISAGREEMENTS ON EARTH. MARS COLONY IS EFFECTIVELY AUTONOMOUS UNDER MARSCORP.

2. TO INSURE THE CONTINUED VIABILITY OF THE COLONY AS A WHOLE, THE FOLLOWING MEASURES ARE IMPLEMENTED:

A. ALL EQUIPMENT WILL BE OPERATED ONLY BY TRAINED TECHNICIANS. ANY EQUIPMENT NOT IN USE ON A SOL BASIS IS TO BE CENTRALLY LOCATED AT MARS COLONY ONE FOR FUTURE ISSUE AS NEEDED.

B. CHIEF, RESOURCE MANAGEMENT (CRM) IS DIRECTED TO IMPLEMENT SURPLUS STORAGE PROCEDURES TO INSURE SUFFICIENT FOOD SUPPLIES IN THE EVENT OF HYDROPONIC FAILURE. CRM IS DIRECTED TO ESTABLISH STANDARDS FOR DIETARY MAINTENANCE FOR INDIV FAMILIES, AND TO

CONFISCATE ALL SURPLUS FOOD FOR STORAGE AS APPLICABLE.

C. TO INSURE POPULATION GROWTH THE FOLLOWING MEASURES ARE DIRECTED:

(1) THE USE OF ARTIFICIAL CONTRACEPTIVE MEASURES IS EXPRESSLY FORBIDDEN. POSSESSION OF CONTRACEPTIVE DEVICES IS EXPRESSLY FORBIDDEN. AMNESTY FOR TURN-IN PERIOD OF FIVE SOLS IS AUTHORIZED.

(2) TERRITORIAL AND FINANCIAL GRANTS ARE AUTHORIZED FOR EACH FAMILIAL BIRTH OVER TWO (2). MEASURES TO REDUCE RISK OF PREGNANCY LOSS AND CHILD INJURY ARE AUTHORIZED AT THE DISCRETION OF THE SEVERAL SETTLEMENTS.

(3) MANDATORY SEPARATION OF ALL CHILDLESS PAIRS WITHOUT REGISTERED PREGNANCY DURING A PERIOD OF ONE (1) MARTIAN YEAR WILL BE ENFORCED. ALL WOMEN OF CHILD-BEARING POTENTIAL ARE INSTRUCTED TO SEEK FAMILIAL LIAISON WITHIN THIRTY (30) SOLS OF RECEIPT OF THIS DIRECTIVE. AT THE END OF THIS PERIOD, IT IS DIRECTED THAT THE PENALTY FOR RAPE OF A NON-FAMILIAL WOMAN OF CHILD-BEARING AGE BE REDUCED TO 30 SOLS IN CONFINEMENT.

(4) PREGNANT WOMEN ARE EXPRESSLY FORBIDDEN TO PERFORM ANY AND ALL DUTIES THAT MAY CAUSE THEM TO DEFETALIZE. CHF, MEDICAL (COM) IS DIRECTED TO PROVIDE THIS OFC A COMPLETE LIST OF SUCH DUTIES. CHF, PERSONNEL (COP) IS DIRECTED TO DETERMINE AND CORRECT VIOLATIONS.

D. THE FOLLOWING AREAS ARE DECLARED UNAUTHORIZED ENTRY ZONES: COMMUNICATIONS CENTER/

STORAGE FACILITIES/ ADM RESIDENCE/ MEDICAL DISPENSARIES/CONFINEMENT FACILITIES/ CRAFT DOCKS/ MAINTENANCE FACILITIES/ HYDROPONICS UNITS/ CULTIVATED AREAS (EXCEPT FAMILIAL TRACTS, LIMITED TO THE RESPECTIVE FAMILIES)/ TECHNOLOGICAL LABORATORIES/ ENERGY AND POWER FACILITIES.

E. EXECUTION OF THE FOLLOWING INDIVIDUALS IS MANDATED FOR COUNTER-REPRODUCTIVE ACTIVITIES: PAUL RIKER, ANNETTE O'TOOLE, ADRIANNE TIMBERLAKE, RODGER VESTRY, KILETA BASTIANINI.

F. THIS DIRECTIVE REMAINS IN EFFECT UNTIL SUPERSEDED.

BY THE AUTHORITY OF:

GORDON J. GIBSON
CHIEF ADMINISTRATOR
MARS CORPORATION

The colony had survived, although the specific contribution of those extreme measures to that survival was in my mind questionable. The advisory served, more than anything else, to legislate and harden gender roles. Earlier I had questioned O'Toole about the method she had employed to gain access to a career in space. My own method was not above question. A Timberlake, I could not be denied, merely discouraged. I would have preferred employment based on my own merit...as, I suspected, O'Toole desired, in her heart.

In accordance with Captain's Rule 3, I had neglected to mention to O'Toole that the energy for air and water recike derived from the same source as primary power. I'd given Min the marching orders to determine which rate of return consumed the least fuel water for the most speed. But I knew, as perhaps O'Toole did, that *Ennis's* momentum would have to keep us going after the first fifteen days of the journey. Factor in recike requirements, and we would be on momentum after ten, perhaps eleven days. If we survived, it would be after a journey of forty or more days, not thirty.

O'Toole was right. We were not going to make it.

Knuckles rapped lightly on the hatch, and I bade O'Toole enter. She looked as if she had been crying, but her eyes were dry now, and green as serpentine. I invited her to open a collapsible chair and sit down, but she remained standing.

"Skipper," she said, and stopped.

I looked at her across the diaries and the documents and the notes, across the past century. A tautness in her voice demanded it.

"Min says the base around the starboard navigational sensor has worked loose," she said, gathering momentum now, as if afraid I would interrupt her. "I have to go EVA to realign and tighten it. I thought I should inform you before I went." She turned to leave.

"Stand fast, O'Toole!"

Her voice barely reached me. "Goddammit..."

My heart stuttered, then began a steady *whump-whump* I was certain she could hear. I tried to spin her around by the shoulder, but she was rooted in place. She twisted away, and I dove into her, knocking her against the bulkhead and onto the deck. She writhed, struggling to free herself, but I had her by fifteen pounds and five years of experience. She did not try to hit or kick me, only to liberate herself from my grasp. The lack of directed violence enabled me to pin her there, and finally to hold her still.

"You goddamn fool!" I hissed.

"One person has a better chance!" she cried, her voice breaking. "*You* can make it!"

"You're not going EVA without a suit, O'Toole. *Ennis*'s rules." I rose to my knees and sat back on her thighs, my hands holding her shoulders down. The seal of her outsuit separated, revealing several white undershirts. She had intended to leave with as much mass as she could carry. "And my orders, which you agreed to follow when you accepted this posting."

Her eyes met mine, and I felt fire from them. "I did not agree to get you killed. Besides . . . besides, I wouldn't want to grievously annoy you."

"Then stop splitting infinitives."

"What? *What?*"

I rolled off her and extended a hand. "Get up, O'Toole. If you die on me, I'll pitch your ass into space, and good riddance, but until that time," I swung her onto the bed, and she sat up, rolling her feet to the deck, "if it comes to pass, *we* are in this together. *Ennis*'s rules. *Timberlake* rules." I swept my hand over the memorabilia. "If I take nothing else with me from this, that'll do. One stupid little pronoun. First person plural. It's the way things get done out here, if they get done at all. That much, I've learned. If it's not enough, well . . . kismet happens."

"I didn't think you would try to stop me," she whispered.

"Don't take it personally. There's hardly anyone else to talk to out here."

O'Toole managed a dismal, half-hearted chuckle. Presently she said, "Still going over your legacy. What about *their* voices?"

"Unhelpful in our circumstances."

She reached for a paper. "May I?"

"Mind the age."

It was the MarsCorp advisory from Gibson. I watched her eyes scroll down the document...and widen abruptly when she reached the end. She made a little gagging sound, and for a moment I was afraid she might disgorge all over my inheritance. But she swallowed a lump, and another, and scooted back on the bed until she came to rest against the bulkhead. Her face, always pale, had blanched. She looked about to faint again.

I sat down beside her, uncertain. There's nothing in the Captain's Rules that prevents me from succoring a distressed crewmember, but first I had to determine the appropriate succor. Unfortunately, all I could come up with was, "Hey, Ellen?"

Her mouth worked. I snagged a small canteen that I keep by the berth for, uh, medicinal purposes, and offered it to her. She took a sip, and coughed, and sputtered.

"What *is* this?"

"A fine Irish whiskey. Jameson's. Same source as the oranges."

"...thought it was water." She took another swig, and passed the canteen back to me. "As whiskey, it's not bad. I'm...sorry for that. It took me by surprise, that's all. I mean, I already knew...but of course I did not know who."

I peered into the canteen mouth, and sniffed. "It must be more potent than I thought, to make you ramble."

" . . . you had no way of knowing."

"Tell me."

"Annette O'Toole was my great-grandmother. She and your . . . Adrianne Timberlake were lovers. That's why they were shot."

I shook my head, to clear it and in denial, unconvincingly on both counts. "No, you're wrong. Adrianne and Tom were married . . . well, as married as you can get without the documents. They had Jenay, and Andrew, who died young, and . . ."

"And she met Grandma Netta and they worked out an arrangement, the three of them . . . four of them. Grandma loved Neil, of course, that's how I got here. I traced it back, but I could never find the name, until now. It's not . . . discussed. Annette and Adrianne . . . how wonderful for them, to have had that."

"*Menage a quatre?*" The expression on her face said I had hurt...not her, but some memory of hers. "That was unkind of me," I apologized quickly. "Truly I did not mean it that way."

Her hand went to my knee, accepting. My facial thermostat remained under control.

"There were times Grandma Netta...needed something else in her life. Just for a few hours, a day or two. It eased her...relieved her, I think. Grandma Barbara, her daughter, spoke of it occasionally to me, but she would never say who, and perhaps she did not know." I felt her eyes on me. "You do not appear . . . shocked by this."

Her tone made it a statement of fact, not a question. "The only sex life that concerns me is my own," I said.

"An attitude which would spare so many so much grief."

"Including you?"

" . . . ah, I see what you're asking."

But she fell silent, staring at the bulkhead before her. Of structural plastic tinted dusk gray, it was devoid of posters and other ornamentation, but she seemed to find it quite riveting. Impossible to tell what she was thinking. After shedding her defeminizing sartorial adaptations she had undergone a not-very-subtle metamorphosis. If Allan had been the weak Platonic reflection of The Ellen, then this version herself illuminated. Her apprentice status had faded with the lack of function under our circumstances, aiding in her liberation. I had scant idea who she was now.

"One day I was to meet a man," she said haltingly, still feeling her way. "I would have a career, as would he, but we would join and work together in our respective fields, and raise a family, and...do all the things we should do together. And until that time, I expected to...explore the things I wanted for myself and in relation to others."

"If I gave it any thought at all," I told her, "I might have made a similar response."

"I knew the risks . . ."

I filled in the blank left by her hesitation. "Traci."

"Traci. When I chose Space as a career field. I did not intend my attempt at repairs to maroon us, and it is not a mistake I will repeat. Not that I will have a chance to do so."

"Ellen—"

She dropped to her knees on the deck, and turned to face me, insinuating her torso between my legs until the edge of the bed stopped her. Something irritated her left cheek, and she wiped it on the right leg of my outsuit. "I do not love you. You are authoritarian, overbearingly self-sufficient, reserved to the point of aloofness, and you focus on stars, not galaxies. I could not love you."

"You are disobedient, impetuous, undisciplined, and deceptive. You are too much like me. I trust you, but I always wonder whether I should."

"You left out frightened. I am also frightened. I do not wish to die. Yet I know that I will. I am glad it is you with whom I will meet that end."

"For what it's worth, Ellen, that EVA stunt marks you as the bravest person I have ever known."

". . . you omitted a statement of disavowal, that you could not love me."

"I said all that I meant to say."

She laid her head on my lap. "So . . . history repeats?"

"I have absolutely no intention of allowing anyone to shoot us for this."

"First person plural?"

"I've found that works best in these things."

👁👁👁

" . . . thought you said you couldn't."

"That wasn't love. That was lust."

"You're sure?"

" . . . says so on the label. Apply as directed." Ellen squinted at her mime bottle. "Hmm. No expiration date . . . and a good thing, too, long as it's been on the shelf."

"What do the directions say?"

Her teeth gave me a sharp nip over the floating ribs. "What do you care, you? You never follow them anyway."

"You didn't give me any."

"One."

"'Don't stop!' wasn't a direction. It was a Command From On High, accompanied by thunderbolts."

A bead of sweat rolled down her nose and hung on the tip of it. She wiped it on my breast, a teardrop in a pond. "I seem to recall a few of those, floating around."

" . . . do you have any idea how many laws, regulations, and statutes we've fractured in the past couple hours?"

Ellen sighed. "Yeah..."

"Wanna pulverize them altogether?"

"Well . . . it does say to repeat applications as needed."

"They're needed."

👁👁👁

Eventually, as batteries do, ours ran down and had to be recharged. From time to time I emerged from dozing to find us still vined, and I brushed hair from her eyes, or inspected a crescent scar on her shoulder, or dwelt on the curve of her breast where it molded with mine, or basked in anticipation with her hand spread over my abdomen, fluttering the tiny muscles there, before I climbed aboard the driftwood once again to float onward, gathering strength. I think Ellen did the same—she was never in the same position I'd left her—

288

and I wondered what she was thinking. The odd coincidence of it all? The surprises of us? Pre-conceived notions are all very well and good, but there are always stanchions in the gangways from Here to There, and collisions are inevitable if you fail to look where you are going. Ellen and I had caromed off into a corner, just we two, and pulled the shadows in around us like a quilt until we could puzzle out what was happening. Lust, she had called it. Well, yeah, an intimate relationship unspiced by lust is as dry as the Martian deserts... and as destructive of the spirit. The same face, year after year, might well dull the emotional responses, absent the capacity for excitement, for novelty, and solitary orgasms, however engineered, were of fleeting relief and a poor substitute for the real thing. Had Adrianne felt the need to expand her horizons? And found a kindred spirit in Ellen's Annette?

"Hey, you're awake, too."

Her voice sounded husky, the way I hoped mine would one day, when I awoke beside...who? Conner? Not impossible, given his development into a decent human being. No other names occurred. Well, one other, but she who answered to it was already here.

"And pensive," she added.

"Post-coital lassitude."

She nuzzled my shoulder. "Isn't conservation of energy recommended in survival situations?"

"If we're not going to survive, why conserve?"

"Mmm, a million years from now they'll find us still here, mummies, like pretzels. You on top, or me...whose turn is it, anyway?"

"Yours, I think. But I'd rather they found us side by side. Misunderstandings could arise. Of course, once they play back Min for the log, they'll know the pecking order . . . so to speak."

Her voice lost an octave. "Min keeps a *continuous* log?"

"Min monitors and records everything aboard the *Ennis* . . . and I am going to have to delete some of today's files." Abruptly Ellen sat up, eyes huge. "Ellen, I thought you knew this."

"Then Min must have monitored what happened when I tried to make the repairs," she said, animation kindling her tone. "Perhaps I can find a way to reverse it!"

11: crucible

The justices conferred, the microphones muted electronically and by hand. Finally Krishnaman centered himself, his nut-brown face lined like hardened glass about to shatter. "If I understand your testimony correctly, *M'selle* Timberlake, the inventor of the faster-than-light system called Track is not yourself, but rather one Ellen O'Toole. Your testimony has made her an accomplice in the unauthorized release and dissemination of information that is the sole property of MarsCorp, yourselves being at the time corporate employees. This Court demands to know where she is."

"She is not here," said the woman.

"Do you possess her power-of-attorney? Are you empowered to speak for her?"

"I speak only for myself."

"You *must* divulge her whereabouts. You are so ordered."

The woman gazed directly at Krishnaman, who seemed to flinch slightly. Her voice had the softness of a fresh rose bloom. "You know I will never surrender her to you."

"How did O'Toole develop Track?" asked Fourcade, breaking in. Krishnaman glared back at him, but allowed the testimony to proceed.

The woman drew a square plastic envelope from her pocket, opened it, and displayed the limp latex fingerskin. A breath of air partially inflated it.

"That is a prophylactic," said Krishnaman. "Those are illegal."

"A rubber," said Timberlake, and held it up for all to see. "But now an illustrative device. The air is mostly in this end. If I squeeze this end—and Track 'squeezes' by a uniformly-applied instantaneous pressure of energy over the mass to be affected—the air moves into that end, as you have just observed. That is how Track works. The object is instantaneously 'displaced,' as you see. Instantaneous may be taken to mean in this context as 'without lapse of time.' Direction is controlled by the alignment of flux patterns and determined by the Galactic Positioning System, and distance is controlled by the quantity

290

of external energy applied, in excess of the minimum external energy necessary to effect 'displacement.'" She paused, and added, "The mathematics of the process are of course considerably more complex. Labyrinthine, even. I do not understand them, nor does O'Toole, fully. What matters—to you, to me and mine, to all of humanity—is that the system *works*. The question remaining is, does *your* system work? And you do not have a lot of time left, Judge Krishnaman."

The Chief Justice bolted upright, his dark eyes eruptive, his face a demon mask of hatred, the monstrousness amplified by contrast with his supposed impartiality as he rose from behind the bench. For a moment he forgot that the trial was being holographed. "Are you *threatening* this Court?"

"Absofukkinlutely."

12: legacy - Traci's story

"What if it doesn't work? What if I'm wrong?"

"I have faith in you, Ellen."

"We could put this off, until . . . until there is no other hope for us."

"You just want to go back into the stateroom and make love again."

"And again, and again, and again . . . Traci?"

"Yes, Ellen?"

"I have faith in you, too. And . . . this is the command sequence."

She handed me a keypad, and I memorized the brief contents. *Min, set course for Center, initiate Track on my mark. Mark.* "This sounds like it came out of a bad science fiction entertainment 'gram."

"Nobody has ever done this before." She drifted to the starboard chair and flopped into it. "I drew on the only experience I had. Aren't you going to sit down? The *Ennis* took quite a bang last time."

"Ellen . . . "

"Yes, Traci?"

"You know what they'll do to us if this works. They'll kill us for certain, after they learn what we know. Our relationship will be insignificant by comparison, although perhaps the excuse for what

291

they do."

"Well, there's only one way to resolve that."

"My thought, exactly."

She issued a series of commo commands to be activated upon proximity to Center, to continue until terminated by her order or mine, or destroyed. Finished, she got back to her feet, and looked at me. Her eyes were green as serpentine again, but softer now, pale brows arched in a question.

I gestured her aft, toward the stateroom, and held the hatch for her as she climbed through. "And if this *doesn't* work, instead of in chairs, I'd rather pass our final instant . . . hmm."

"Entwined?"

"Yeh, I can live with that word."

"As our men will have to."

13: first person plural

"You will explain yourself to this Court, *Mademoiselle* Timberlake."

Fourcade began edging away from the defense table and toward the witness stand. Timberlake had provoked the Chief Justice, his signal. How much time, how much room? Because it was almost over now.

"Even as I speak," said Timberlake, "hundreds, perhaps thousands of people are out there, all over the planet, purchasing small spaceworthy craft and modifying their power sources according to the instructions we broadcast during our return to Center. The Track system, for all its complexity, is quite simple to install, and the directions easy to follow for anyone who can comprehend the written word. The secret is out, Judge Krishnaman, and this particular genie will never be bunged back into the bottle. Now *everyone* knows how to travel among the stars...although how they employ the information is their choice. The corporations you represent will not profit by controlling the information. Space travel belongs to humanity.

"And this," she swept her arm around the vast chamber, at the distant echelons of corporate observers seated in neat rows on the old wooden benches, "this is the reward you would bestow upon Ellen O'Toole and myself. Condemnation for our actions, contumely for our relationship. If you can make of us criminals and pariahs, perhaps our data and discovery are untrustworthy, and you may regain a measure of control . . . you may yet profit, while your vultures gnaw at us in our prison, as they did Prometheus in punishment for his gift of fire. Unlike Prometheus, however, *we will not be chained.* Ellen? You're on."

An immense buffet of air blew out windows of stained glass and bowled people over. The prosecutor, who had been standing, about to object. The justices behind the bench, livid now as they staggered, their dark robes askew. A bailiff, tumbling. Even Fourcade, who had been expecting *something*, grabbed the witness stand and held on, Timberlake's hands around his forearms for additional support. Wood splintered, and shards flew—the defense table had disintegrated.

In the space between the witness stand and the front row of observers now poised an indigo spaceskip, its support pods atop chair fragments and other debris. The port hatch opened, a ramp was extruded, and Ellen O'Toole, attired in camouflage military fatigues and armed with an automatic rifle, descended into the courtroom. Behind her came Conner, similarly garbed and armed, somewhat bewildered by it all, but steadfast nonetheless as he and O'Toole prepared for covering fire.

"You have your gift from us," said Timberlake, stepping down. "That is all we are willing to give you. We are leaving you to whatever destiny you choose."

Fourcade started. She was looking directly at him now. He felt the Universe contract to include only himself and the woman and the *Ennis* and her passengers.

"Coming?" said Timberlake.

He glanced at Ellen O'Toole."I thought you and she . . ."

"You thought correctly. Hey, we'll work something out. A time-share arrangement, maybe."

Fourcade hesitated. Whichever way he decided, it would be irrevocable. The Earth, or The Stars? To look down, or to look up?

The woman clucked impatiently. "There are rules *here*, Colin.

Not," she pointed up, "Out There. Or do I have to use the L-word to entice you?"

A memory of her testimony wormed its way to the fore. "You mean lust?" he asked, a smile at last tugging at the corners of his mouth.

"We can start there," she said, "and see what happens."

He followed her aboard the *Ennis*.

www.ingramcontent.com/pod-product-compliance
Lightning Source LLC
Chambersburg PA
CBHW071850220626
47052CB00002B/47